The Study of Contemporary Western Ethical Dilemmas
— Taking the Novels of Ian McEwan as an Example

西方当代伦理困境研究
——以麦克尤恩小说为例

张 洁 著

天 津

图书在版编目(CIP)数据

西方当代伦理困境研究：以麦克尤恩小说为例：英文 / 张洁著. -- 天津：南开大学出版社，2025.9.
ISBN 978-7-310-06660-5

Ⅰ.B82

中国国家版本馆CIP数据核字第2025QQ4911号

版权所有　侵权必究

西方当代伦理困境研究——以麦克尤恩小说为例
XIFANG DANGDAI LUNLI KUNJING YANJIU
——YI MAIKEYOUEN XIAOSHUO WEI LI

南开大学出版社出版发行
出版人：王　康
地址：天津市南开区卫津路94号　　邮政编码：300071
营销部电话：(022)23508339　　营销部传真：(022)23508542
https://nkup.nankai.edu.cn

天津泰宇印务有限公司印刷　全国各地新华书店经销
2025年9月第1版　2025年9月第1次印刷
240×170毫米　16开本　16.5印张　2插页　247千字
定价：88.00元

如遇图书印装质量问题，请与本社营销部联系调换，电话：(022)23508339

Contents

Chapter One Ian McEwan and His Literary Creation ························ 1
    Section One Early Career: Short Stories and "Ian Macabre" Phase ······· 5
    Section Two Mid-career: Focus on Political and Family Issues ·········· 11
    Section Three Later Career: In-depth and Thought-provoking Style ··· 17
Chapter Two Ethical Literary Criticism ································· 28
Chapter Three The Ethical Dilemma in The Cement Garden ················ 47
    Section One The Morbid Family Ethics ································ 50
    Section Two Ethical Flaws in Social Relationships ····················· 61
Chapter Four The Temporal Paradox in *The Child in Time* ················ 73
    Section One Paradox in Individual Ethics: Child vs. Adult ············· 76
    Section Two Alienation of Time in a Certain Space ···················· 94
Chapter Five The Class Ethics in *Atonement* ··························· 107
    Section One Roots of the Sin ··· 110
    Section Two Atonement for the Sin ·································· 129
Chapter Six The Rational Ethics in *Saturday* ··························· 141
    Section One Collision between Literature and Science ················ 144
    Section Two The Collision between Rationality and Sensibility ······ 163
    Section Three The Collision between Civilization and Barbarism ···· 171
    Section Four The Urban Cultural Dilemma ··························· 177
Chapter Seven The Ethical Failure in *Solar* ···························· 185
    Section One Beard's Narcissism ····································· 190
    Section Two Beard's Phallocentrism ································· 203
Chapter Eight The Ethical Imbalance in *Sweet Tooth* ···················· 219
    Section One Power Imbalance in the Parent-Child Relationship ······ 223
    Section Two Unequal Position in the Relationship between Serena
                 and Tony ·· 228
    Section Three Discriminated Relationship between Serena and Max ·· 232

Section Four　Untrustworthy Relationship between Serena and Tom … 236
Conclusion … 242
Reference … 248

Chapter One   Ian McEwan and His Literary Creation

Born in Aldershot, England, on June 21, 1948, Ian McEwan moved around throughout the Far East, Germany, and North Africa in his childhood, following his father, who worked as an officer in the army. He was educated at a boarding school and later obtained an undergraduate degree from the University of Sussex in 1970. After graduation, he attended the MA Creative Writing course by Malcolm Bradbury and Angus Wilson at the University of East Anglia, which immersed him in an ocean of postwar American canon. McEwan's writing business started from short fiction, greatly influenced by his coursework submitted to Bradbury. "The ambition, the social range, the expressive freedom of American writing made English fiction seem poky and grey," McEwan explained. "To find bold and violent colors became my imperative."[1]

McEwan described his father as "quite terrifying," a "great stickler for all the spit and polish of traditional army life." McEwan's mother, Rose, was the reverse. She was a "timorous" woman who could not bear her husband's disapproval and was ashamed of her working-class accent. His parents' marriage was quietly dysfunctional. David had a drinking problem, and McEwan once mentioned domestic abuse. Even if their relationship was in trouble, he was the favorite child in his parents' eyes.

Rose was in a marriage when she met David during World War II. They had an affair, and Rose became pregnant with McEwan's brother. The child was adopted soon after his birth. When McEwan was at the age of eleven, he was sent away to a British boarding school, and his parents were still staying abroad. Since McEwan knew about the existence of his brother, David Sharp, he believes that his parents' lives were traumatized by their first accidental pregnancy and that they distanced themselves from their other children to hide from the painful reality of their actions. Following graduation from Anglia, McEwan left Europe to spend a year in Afghanistan. Upon his return, he married a young and liberated girl named Penny Allen. McEwan and Allen had two sons, but their marriage didn't last long. As McEwan's fame grew in Britain's literary world, Allen became frustrated, and the two were divorced shortly after that. Later, McEwan married Guardian editor Annalena McAfee, and they two continued to raise McEwan's sons.

Since he began publishing, McEwan has been the focus of considerable attention from critics and reviewers alike, and their responses to his work have increased with his fame. Renowned for his audacious ingenuity in storytelling, a substantial portion of his fiction delves into peculiar expressions of sexuality and jolting acts of violence. Ryan Roberts (2010) explained that McEwan "has dealt with a wide range of human experiences, including the effects of losing a child, religious fervor, psychological obsession, the intricacies of relationships, euthanasia, and happiness in a modern world bent on conflict and destruction."[2] Some critics did not like his early writing style and criticized his dark themes. McEwan was then known as "Ian Macabre." McEwan was also named by some critics as a "pornographer." Although the critics have highly commented on his short story collections, *First Love, Last Rites,* and *In Between the Sheets*, these studies are still limited to the sexuality and the rebelliousness of his works. However, all these cannot change the fact that he is a serious and objective novelist.

Ian McEwan is a highly acclaimed author whose works have garnered critical acclaim worldwide. Since 1970, McEwan has written numerous novels, plays, essays, and children's works, becoming one of the most sought-after writers in the UK. McEwan began his literary career with short stories, first submitting *Conversation with a Cupboardman*, a morbid tale about a man who lived in a closet, to *Bradbury*. This was followed by his debut collection of short stories, *First Love, Last Rites*, which earned him the prestigious Somerset Maugham Award. Another short story collection, *In Between the Sheets*, soon solidified his reputation as a writer of deeply unsettling, macabre themes.

In 1978, McEwan published his first novel, *The Cement Garden*, which drew significant critical attention. During this period, his works often focused on dark and disturbing subjects such as death, murder, incest, and sex, earning him the nickname "Ian Macabre." These early works reflect a pervasive pessimism about life and reveal McEwan's fascination with exploring humanity's most unsettling aspects. As McEwan himself remarked in an interview with journalist Phil Daoust in *The Guardian*: "I had been invisible to myself in my teens. A lot of my terror of things was in those stories—my terror of not making full or rich emotional relationships."

Despite the macabre themes of his early career, McEwan's writing has consistently revolved around the exploration of human relationships. He explores the most intimate connections between individuals, using these as a lens to examine broader social dynamics. This thematic focus has continued throughout his career, as seen in novels such as *The Comfort of Strangers*, *The Child in Time*, *The Innocent*, and *Black Dogs*. Through these works, McEwan has demonstrated a remarkable ability to capture the complexities of interpersonal relationships while maintaining a keen awareness of their societal implications.

These works continue the gloomy style of McEwan's earlier works, so literary histories often mention his focus on depicting the darkness of human nature and ethical taboos. While some find the themes of his works too obscene and offensive, many believe that they are a true reflection of modern society. McEwan's sharp and poetic writing, as well as his forthright depictions of contemporary society, have earned him unanimous acclaim among critics. In 1998, his novel *Amsterdam* won the British Booker Prize, cementing his status in the British literary world. Since then, he has published three more works with a serious tone: *Atonement*, *Saturday*, and *On Chesil Beach*. In these novels, McEwan's sense of responsibility to explore the confusion and helplessness in ordinary people's lives is evident. However, he no longer blindly pursues the sensational stories of his early works; instead, he focuses on the "accidental events" that occur in the lives of ordinary people. Through vivid descriptions of characters and twisting storylines, McEwan shows us the universal inner workings of individuals at different stages of life, portraying their emotional states of loneliness, confusion, and the contradictions of modern life. McEwan's novels expose the bestiality that lurks beneath the surface of contemporary civilization, the deformity and perversion that hide behind the facade of a decent gentleman. While providing entertainment for readers, his works also sound the alarm for society. McEwan's concern for the psychological growth of individuals has become an important feature that sets him apart from other writers. In a sense, he is writing cautionary tales for a world that has gone mad.

Apart from his prose fiction, Ian McEwan has written screenplays for television and film, such as the Ploughman's Lunch (1985) and Sour Sweet (1988), to name a few. Film adaptations of his novels include *First Love, Last Rites* (1997), *The Cement Garden* (1993), *The Comfort of Strangers* (1991), *The Innocent* (1993), and *Atonement* (2007). He also wrote the libretto to Michael Berkeley's music for the oratorio *Or Shall We Die?*. Besides, he is the author of a children's book, *The Daydreamer* (1994).

McEwan is widely regarded as one of the greatest writers of contemporary British literature. His works have earned him numerous prestigious awards, reflecting both his critical acclaim and his popularity among readers. McEwan's career began with remarkable recognition when he won the Somerset Maugham Award in 1976 for his first collection of short stories, *First Love, Last Rites*. Over the years, he continued to garner major accolades, including the Whitbread Novel Award in 1987 and the Prix Fémina Étranger in 1993 for *The Child in Time*. In 1999, he was awarded Germany's Shakespeare Prize by the Alfred Toepfer Foundation, further cementing his international reputation.

McEwan achieved a milestone in his career when he won the Man Booker Prize for Fiction in 1998 for his novel *Amsterdam*. His 2001 masterpiece, *Atonement*, is one of his most celebrated works, earning multiple awards such as the WH Smith Literary Award (2002), the National Book Critics' Circle Fiction Award (2003), the Los Angeles Times Prize for Fiction (2003), and the Santiago Prize for the European Novel (2004). The novel's adaptation into an Oscar-winning film further amplified its legacy. Other notable achievements include the James Tait Black Memorial Prize for *Saturday* in 2006 and the Galaxy Book of the Year award for *On Chesil Beach* at the 2008 British Book Awards, where McEwan was also named Reader's Digest Author of the Year.

McEwan's subsequent works continued to receive acclaim. His novel *Solar* won the Bollinger Everyman Wodehouse Prize for Comic Fiction in 2010, while *Sweet Tooth* was awarded the Paddy Power Political Fiction Book of the Year in 2012. Beyond individual works, McEwan's contributions to literature have been widely recognized. He was appointed a Commander of the Order of the British Empire (CBE) in 2000 and received the Bodleian Medal in 2014. Additionally, he is a Fellow of the Royal Society of Literature, the Royal Society of Arts, and the American Academy of Arts and Sciences.

Critics have consistently praised McEwan's literary mastery and cultural impact. A veteran reviewer at *The Washington Post* once asserted, "No one writes novels in English today like McEwan." He has been shortlisted for the Booker Prize five times, a testament to his enduring excellence, and his works, including *Atonement*, are celebrated as cultural landmarks. *Atonement* itself was listed on the British List of "Most Important in Life," reflecting its profound influence. McEwan's novels are as ubiquitous in British culture as commuter tickets on the London Underground, symbolizing their resonance with a wide readership. Through his prolific output and relentless pursuit of literary excellence, McEwan has firmly established himself as one of the most renowned authors of our time. Ian McEwan's books are available in numerous translations across the globe, including Brazilian, Dutch, French, German, Italian, Japanese, Chinese, Portuguese, and so on. The most widely translated books are about political and family issues, published after 1980.

Section One　Early Career: Short Stories and "Ian Macabre" Phase

The political, economic, cultural, and social conditions in Britain during the 1970s contributed to a general sense of despair and anxiety in society. A group of writers, including McEwan, used an experimental style to reflect the fall of England and the prevailing sense of despair and anxiety. McEwan's use of themes such as dirty sex, violence, death, and perverted behavior, which were non-mainstream at the time, was influenced by the popular Gothic literature of the era as well as by his own personality tendencies. McEwan's childhood loneliness, experience of boarding school, and exposure to countercultural influences at university contributed to his development of a melancholic personality. For those with a melancholic mindset, fringe topics and dark styles are ideal literary elements. The inspiration is closely related to his environment and experiences as he grew up. Dominique points out that McEwan writes not only about the chaos of modern society but also about himself through his works and that the characters are parallel to the author, which is an essential stylistic style of McEwan's work[3].

McEwan's early works are deliberately offensive and uncomfortable and can be called a kind of "literature of shock," full of incest, brutality, perverted sexual acts, and murders, depicting a gloomy and terrifying picture of modern society and a soul struggling in it tormented and distorted by various desires. McEwan's gothic features are mainly reflected in his gloomy writing style. McEwan published two collections of short stories, *First Love, Last Rites,* and *In Between the Sheets*, in 1975 and 1978, and then published *The Cement Garden* and *The Comfort of Strangers.* These four works are all about the sexual perversion of the civilian class. His creation background is the decline of Britain's imperial power which is reflected in economic, political, and cultural crises in the 1970s. The onset of the recession of the economy led to further decline: "growing conflict and terrorism in Northern Ireland, a miners' strike, and then a serious balance-of-payments deficit, weakened successive governments, and all culminated in the Winter of Discontent of 1978, which opened the way to Mrs. Thatcher and Thatcherism."[4] Beginning with his second collection of short stories, *In Between the Sheets*, published in 1978, his work gradually showed his social consciousness. He began to dissect more deeply how the chaos and turmoil of modern society hindered the development of normal relations between people and thus destroyed the individuals. McEwan intertwines these events into a dark gothic depiction involving murder, incest, and immorality. Influenced by his wife's Transcendentalism and Freudian psychology, McEwan is good at depicting the dark side of human nature, ethical taboos, and other subjects with mild and concise language. All these dark and gothic descriptions labeled him "Ian Macabre" or a "literary psychopath." He is regarded as a "bad boy" in the literary world who challenges the established order and ethics. The first four works sparked considerable controversy due to their exploration of extreme subject matter, addressing themes such as pedophilia, murder, incest, and violence. This controversy was further intensified by their unsettling narrative framework, challenging conventional moral perspectives, and often luring the reader into an uncomfortably intimate engagement with the characters. McEwan's "perpetrator-narrators" draw us into complicity with their crimes, whilst his victims seem strangely collusive in their exploitation and destruction.

Ma Ling said: "McEwan's horror, instead of the psychological horror caused by ghosts of the night, or the sensory horror aroused by astonishing screaming, is the kind of uncovering a stone and finding a worm wriggling alive under it; it is the terror of life itself that cannot be transformed from the physical to the metaphysical."[5] "McEwan's novels are like sharp blades, and the process of reading them is like touching the blade with nerves and emotions, and then finding permanent wounds on his nerves and emotions. This is the sequela of reading McEwan."[6]

McEwan's narrative seems always to be on the edge of hope and disappointment, horror and comfort, cold and warmth, absurdity and realism, violence and weakness, intellect and emotion, and so on. Most of the protagonists in McEwan's stories are marginal or lonely, unsociable people or even weirdos. By depicting their loneliness and ignorance of society, McEwan spies on and reveals the most secretive and darkest corners of human nature. Because the subject matter of the early works was too narrow and the theme was too limited, it was even thought that McEwan would only write "shock literature." He felt that he was "writing himself into a corner that was too crowded" and had trapped himself. Through the new novel genre of the Anglophobic archival style coupled with the unique "youth perspective" literary genre, in the context of the recent failure of the countercultural movement, young people urgently needed to find their voice, and McEwan became popular in this environment and initially established his unique literary theme.

McEwan's gloomy writing style is reflected in his use of calm tones to tell appalling stories. The tone of the novels of this period is sometimes restrained, and thus highlighting the alienation of McEwan's novels from the readers. At the same time, the protagonists in McEwan's early novels often have no names. McEwan's characters are those who have been deprived of social relations and isolated by society. It is difficult for them to define their position in society, and more often, they present a state of ignorance and difficulty in integrating into society. In a sense, this mirrors McEwan's own situation, as his experiences and environment have constrained his writing style. Therefore, the characters' dazed ignorance reflects McEwan's overall feelings about British society, which is why his works display a strong sense of uncertainty.

Instead, McEwan's novel in this period also focuses on the most authentic portrayal of human nature. The so-called moral bottom line is only the rules that apply to human society, and it is difficult to expect how much power such laws can exert on human nature. McEwan's novels from this period show us how morality falls apart in a small environment free from the constraints of the outside world, such as *The Cement Garden*. The advantage of this approach is that the reader can become immersed in the novel and see themselves as the protagonist, which highlights the horror and darkness of the novel.

First Love, Last Rites, which won the Somerset Maugham Award in 1976, instead recounts episodes of child sexual abuse: an adolescent boy's rape of his younger sister, a man's molestation and murder of his neighbor's nine-year-old daughter, and a schoolboy's submission to his aunt's transvestite fantasies. *First Love, Last Rites* brought him instant recognition as one of the most influential voices writing in England today. The book is described as "taut, brooding, and densely atmospheric; these stories show us how murder can arise out of boredom, perversity can result from adolescent curiosity, and sheer evil might be the solution to unbearable loneliness."[7] "As frightening as anything written by Clive Barker or Stephen King, these tales are more crafted with a lyricism and intensity that compel us to face our secret kinship with the horrifying."[8]

Seven stories in the collection *In Between the Sheets* (1978) are derived from transcripts of dreams. They engage readers in the terrifying ways that they can imagine. In "Reflections of a Kept Ape," a female bestselling author who has writer's block tries to get inspiration from having a sexual relationship with her pet chimpanzee. "Dead as They Come" is about a man in love with a mannequin. "With three other fragmentary pieces that don't achieve much impact, this slim collection is hardly McEwan at his best (he remains a writer of tremendous style who seems limited by his obsessions), but at the very least, it reinforces his position as the Roald Dahl for the sexually eruptive 1970s."[9]

The Cement Garden is Ian McEwan's 1978 novel that explores complex themes of maturing, family, and dealing with loss. Although classified as psychological fiction, *The Cement Garden* contains elements of horror and domestic fiction as well. Drawing heavily on Gothic settings and Victorian motifs, it tells the story of Jack's family with the elements of incest and trauma. The plot follows four siblings as they navigate the trauma of their parents' death and struggle with their deviant desires. However, due to their incompetence and wrong ethical awareness, serious misdoings occur not long after.

After their father died of a heart attack and their mom of illness, the protagonist Jack and Jack's siblings bury her body with cement in their cellar in order to keep it a secret since they don't want to be separated by the authorities. Jack and Julie, the oldest two, act as "mom" and "dad" in the family. The youngest brother, Tom, retreats to a baby, and Sue is obsessed with her diary. Later, Julie has a boyfriend named Derek, who gets suspicious about the cellar because of the smell. They tell him that they buried the dog down there. Finally, Derek knows the truth from Tom, and he enters Julie's room only to find her having sex with her brother Jack. Derek is furious and smashes the cement in the cellar. He reports the police, and the story ends.

One of the significant themes featured in this novel is the theme of abnormal love, incestuous love. In a family where the father is extremely strict and the mother is boundlessly tolerant, the children cannot be brought up with regular and healthy ethical norms. Jack, his brother Tom, and even their father have the Oedipus Complex. That's partly why the six-year-old Tom regresses into babyhood after his mother's death. Even the love relationship between Julie and Derek isn't normal because there is no love at all. All of these contribute to the abnormal ethics in the family.

In the final work of this period, the exquisite short novel *The Comfort of*

Strangers is also a very stunning story that is worth the fame of Macabre. A twisted relationship develops among these four characters, Colin and Mary, who are spending their holiday in a city very much like Venice. They meet Robert and his wife. A shocking story plot never fails the readers. *The Comfort of Strangers* creates a classic tale of suspense and erotic menace with psychological precision and a mesmerizing tone of inevitability.[10] The novel is more about psychological states than relationships between, for example, individuals and their societies. These things are not entirely within one's control, and he does not think they should be.[11] *The Comfort of Strangers* was inspired by McEwan's trip with his wife to Venice in 1978. He asserts that "something of our visit found its way into the book."[12] After having been to Venice, McEwan made some notes about it, which were lost and then found one and a half years later. "It seemed to me that I had already been describing two characters who were not quite like either myself or Penny, and already it seemed to be describing the city in terms of the state of mind and vice versa. The novel took off from the notes. Those notes contain the phrase 'self-fulfilling accusation,' as well as the first sentence, so I must have been thinking about a novel even then."[13]

The Comfort of Strangers is the story of Mary and Colin, a middle-aged English couple married for seven years. Their relationship has lost all excitement. In Venice, they are finding a place to get something to eat when they meet Robert. Robert, a hypocritical man, drags them to a bar for a drink. The next day, they meet Robert again, who invites them to go to his house for rest and entertainment. In the place, they find Robert's disabled wife, Caroline. Later, Mary and Colin pass their house, and out of nowhere, they accept their invitation and enter their home. Robert and Caroline deal with the couple respectively to implement their horrible plan. Robert takes Colin to the bar. Caroline tells Mary about her injury. Robert forces Colin to choose between obeying Robert's orders unconditionally and saving Mary's life or watching Mary die. Tragedy ends up with Colin's death when Mary wakes.

As overwrought as the story is, emotionally and structurally, it is pretty simple. The tragic narration proceeds in a linear style, occasionally intersperses some flashbacks, and ends with a resounding death. The novel has drawn divergent critics, as some think it is repulsive because of the sexual scenes, while others appreciate it as a wonderful story better than his first works. It is a character study into the most primal and often disgusting parts of human nature that make for an agonizing but alluring read.

Section Two   Mid-career: Focus on Political and Family Issues

Since the limited themes in his early creation, McEwan reluctantly began experimenting with the creation of television, film scripts and stage plays to expand his creative ideas. With the development of the feminist and peace movements, starting with the oratorio "Or We Die," his creation began to "step into the world" and began to pay attention to society and politics. After six years of deviating from fiction writing, McEwan published *The Child in Time* (1987), officially restarting his career as a novelist. The 1980s were a productive decade for McEwan. In the 1980s, McEwan's work also became increasingly diverse in subject matter, extending to gender relations, history, politics, the environment, science, and religion, which attracted substantial attention from critics. As McEwan started a family, his novels transitioned away from being insular and sensationalistic, focusing more on family dynamics and political intrigue. He began paying greater attention to significant issues, both social and political. This period marked a notable change in his writing style. McEwan's mid-career works are his most well-known, widely adapted, and studied. These include *Amsterdam* (1998), *Enduring Love* (1997), and *Atonement* (2001), etc.

This period witnessed McEwan's first great transformation in his writing career. This change is radical from the perspective of the genre, writing style, and focus. Zadie Smith (2005) says that McEwan's prose is "controlled, careful, and powerfully concise; he is eloquent on the subjects of sex and sexuality."[14] McEwan writes about his extreme care with language in the "Mother Tongue" and how he spends long hours framing a sentence in his mind, and only when he is totally sure that everything is "secure and complete" does he write it down. After that he asks himself, "Did it really say what I mean? Did it contain an error or an ambiguity that I could not see?"[15] With the gradual maturity of McEwan's writing skills, the arrangement of storylines has complexity and depth. His consistent and sharp attitudes to social issues and delicate psychological depictions continue to draw the focus of the critics. Head concluded that "as a reflection of a complex, paradoxical world whose multiplicity constantly perplexes and confounds us, McEwan's fiction too is confusing and ambiguous. This uncertainty reflects the troubled state of the world at the beginning of the twenty-first century—but McEwan's work will continue to explore... what days are these."[16] Slay defines his works as "more socially conscious literature."[17]

Class conflict is one of McEwan's prevailing topics in his novels. The reason that he is concerned about class conflict is rooted in his family background. In his article "Mother Tongue" (2001), he indicates that his mother was always uneasy and aware of her accent, particularly when she encountered people of higher social rank[18]. Similarly, in an interview with Zadie Smith (2005), McEwan comments on "his mother's awareness of her accent and language, of belonging to a working-class family, and how his mother's 'hesitancy in language was a crucial element of [his] English class position'".[19] In this period, McEwan's creation was no longer confined to the small people at the bottom of society but began to pay attention to the elite groups of society and the conflicts between classes. McEwan shows his great interest in people's relationships, particularly incompatible relationships in his stories. Since then, he has gradually stepped out of the great influence of the Counterculture Movement on him. With the improvement of his social status, McEwan began to have opportunities to reach out to the British upper class. McEwan soon discovered the existential problems in this class. In the novels, what the elites do reflects the problems in the society, which shows McEwan's concerns about the social life and problems in contemporary Britain.

The Child in Time has been hailed as McEwan's "transformational work" because it deals with political and social issues such as government policies and child abductions, marking the expansion of his literary work from the early claustrophobic and cramped inner corners of the individual to the vast and complex social, political and historical space. Since then, much of his work has been placed in social, historical, and political contexts, focusing on politics, the promotion of vested interests, male violence, gender relations, science and reason, nature and ecology, love and innocence, and the search for ethical universal perspectives with a strong political and social consciousness.[20]

Often considered one of McEwan's best works, *The Child in Time* is about a children's author and his wife as they survive after the kidnapping of their 3-year-old daughter Kate. The story comes from McEwan's nightmarish and torturous experience he had gone through after his son was kidnapped by his wife. In 1999, McEwan argued over the custody of his son with his wife, Allen, from whom he separated, and then Allen took their son to France. McEwan and his friend, Timothy Garton Ash, followed them to France. The incident inspired him to write the story of *The Child in Time*, in which a little girl was kidnapped in a supermarket. Time in the novel has become exceptional; time stops for Stephen because Kate is always a toddler to her parents. Their memory about her forever stops at the last time when they see her. In the novel, in Stephen's apartment, time there never changes. To Stephen's parents, time seems to fly. Strange things happen when Stephen comes to visit his wife. It seems that he has seen his parents at a young age. It is not a horror novel. The greatest achievement of this novel is perhaps that it makes its reader feel the same longing for Kate to be found as her parents do, and feel the same helplessness and hopelessness with every passing year. Kate is both absent and present, both alive and dead, and McEwan deals with this devastating situation with great skill.

Stephen is a successful writer of children's books. In order to give his wife, Julie, more time to sleep, he takes his three-year-old daughter, Kate, to the market where Kate is kidnapped at the counter. Since then, he has devoted all his time to looking for Kate. Julie is overwhelmed by the loss of her daughter, and she falls into a devastating situation. She eventually cleans out Kate's room and moves out. Stephen's only friend, Charles, a former publisher who issued Stephen's first book, now works as a cabinet minister. His wife, Thelma, a quantum physicist, indulges and supports Charles' decision to quit his job and live in seclusion as a child. Stephen, persuaded by Thelma, visits his wife Julie in her house far from London. During the journey, Stephen meets with his young parents in a pub named Bell. There he sees his mother who is thinking of aborting the baby. His mother gives up this idea because she seems to have found him outside the window. Charles has a good time in the woods, enjoying his lost childhood, but the current Prime Minister asks him to come out of his seclusion. However, it caused Charles to kill himself in the woods. At the end of the story, Julie gives birth to their second baby.

  The novel portrays love and progress as Stephen tries to cope with his guilt about losing their daughter. It shows that the disappearance of children brings about the loss and return of the adult world. These themes about children and time connect the different episodes while highlighting the delicate relationship between childhood and adulthood.

  Enduring Love was published in 1997. The novel is a postmodernist novel with elements of paratext, intertextuality, and metafiction. The novel was made into a 2004 film starring Daniel Craig and Samantha Morton. The novel remains a classic and disturbing tale of unrequited love and obsession. "There's a deceptive coolness about the fiction of Ian McEwan. His prose is severely chiseled, and his strong interest in science lends a clinical air to his narratives, but this must not distract the reader from the deep vein of feeling that runs through them. Certainly, it has never been more powerful than in *Enduring Love*, a novel that is at once an ingenious and formidably intelligent study of one form of mental illness and a wrenching evocation of the risks to which love can be put."[21] (Jonathan, The Washington Post)

  The novel starts off in a field where the protagonist, Joe Rose, is picnicking with his wife, Clarissa Mellon. They hear the shouts of a child, Harry Gadd, in the basket of a hot-air balloon. His grandfather, James Gadd, is attempting to save the child from the basket to the ground. Joe and the other men are racing the balloon in order to help. John Logan, a local doctor, holds the rope, but the burst of wind blows the balloon into the air, and unfortunately, he falls from the high air to the ground and gets killed. Jed Parry, a stranger in the crowd, has a mental illness, de Clérambault's syndrome or erotomania. He misunderstands Joe's eye contact as a declaration of love. He begins a disturbingly obsessive relationship with Joe by writing to Joe and stalking him. Clarissa believes Parry is harmless and asks Joe to treat him gently. Joe finds that there is more rift in his relationship with Clarissa. One afternoon at a birthday luncheon for Clarissa, Clarissa's godfather, an elderly scientist and professor, is shot in the shoulder. Before they can shoot him a second time, Joe recognizes Jed to prevent the shooting. Jed has sent the men into the restaurant to kill Joe, but they shoot the wrong person.

Joe buys a gun from his old drug dealer to safeguard himself. On his way home, he receives a call from Jed, who tells Joe that he is now with Clarissa. When Joe arrives home, he finds them sitting on the sofa, and Joe shoots Jed in the arm to prevent him from his apparent suicide attempt. In the end, Joe and Clarissa overcome their rift and adopt a child.

"What's striking about McEwan's later work and his new novel *Enduring Love* is its intimacy with evasion and failure, combined with an alert intelligence about these things which itself looks like grounds for hope... opens with a moral puzzle so beautifully posed that you wonder if the book is ever going to escape from the parable into the larger, looser fiction... As the story unfolds, it is evident that dependence and interdependence are the ideas McEwan wants us to think through, although nothing prepares us, or Joe, for what happens next or the turn these ideas take. This is where the parable opens brilliantly into a novel."[22] (Michael, the London Review of Books)

Saturday caused a certain amount of controversy when first published. Some said that, frankly, it wasn't up to his usual standard. Others felt that he was cashing in on the anti-Blair, anti-Iraq War thing. The New York Times Book Review gives its comments that "the distinctive achievement of McEwan's work has been to marry literary seriousness and ambition with a pace and momentum more commonly associated with genre fiction. He is the master clockmaker of novelists, piecing together cogs and wheels of his plots with unerring meticulousness."[23]

Saturday is a masterful novel set within a single day. The story takes place on a single day, February 15, 2003, in London. The novel's protagonist is a neurosurgeon named Henry Perowne, who is forty-eight years old. He loves his wife and cares about his two children, Daisy, a gifted writer in her twenties, and Theo, a musician. On Saturdays, his usual routine includes playing squash with his friend and colleague and having a family dinner in the evening. In the morning, when he is on his way to the racquet club, he meets with the protesters. There he has a little accident with Baxter, a small-time thug. In order to escape from the accident quickly, Perowne uses his professional knowledge to get away. Afterward, Perowne drives to the nursing home to visit his mother who suffers from dementia. At the end of the day, he returns home to prepare dinner for his family. However, Baxter, who is meant to avenge the humiliation in the day, breaks into his house. In the process, Baxter breaks the nose of Perowne's father-in-law. Baxter threatens Daisy to get undressed. When Baxter finds that Daisy is pregnant, he asks Daisy to read one of her poems. The poem moves Baxter. Theo pushes Baxter downstairs when he is off guard, and he hurts his head seriously. At the end of the story, Perowne does the operation for Baxter himself to save him.

McEwan's novels never fail to impress us with his description and concern for humanity. His narrative style and storytelling greatly attract our interest. In *Saturday,* he created a story that provides a full understanding of human nature and the facets of contemporary society. What happens unexpectedly in a day can really destroy happiness and peace.

On Chesil Beach is one of those stories that dive so deeply into its protagonists' heads that they almost step out of the pages. The story takes place in July 1962, when Edward and Florence just get married. The newlyweds spend their honeymoon in a hotel at Chesil Beach. The couple attempt to have sex but fail. Their misalliance is caused not only by their different social classes but also by sexual anxiety and ignorance. Edward comes from a normal family whose father is a primary school principal, while Florence's family belongs to the upper-middle class. They all grow up in sexually repressed circumstances. All of these conditions have a deep influence on their sexual perception, which in turn causes them to be separated even though they are in love with each other. Later, Edward has several relationships with other women and Florence becomes a successful violinist. They two continue to think of each other, but the fact is that Florence will never walk into his life again.

Amsterdam, written in 1998, is a satirical, darkly funny tale about contemporary morality. The novel opens with the sudden death of Molly Lane, who is a restaurant critic. Her old lovers come to pay their last respects at her funeral, among them Clive Linley, the most successful modern composer; Vernon Halliday, a news editor of the quality broadsheet, *The Judge*; and Julian Garmony, the British foreign secretary. At the funeral, Molly's quick physical decline reminds Clive of his unexpected future. He asks his friend Vernon to euthanize him if he has a terminal disease. Vernon agrees on the condition that Clive will do the same to him. Later, George, Moll's husband, discovers some pictures of Julian in women's clothing when the two have affairs. George realizes he has an opportunity to take revenge and make a profit, because Julian has the chance of taking over the party, and these pictures may cause him great trouble andeven end his political career. George offers the pictures to Vernon, who is working hard to change the dwindling readership. Vernon talks with Clive about the matter. Clive strongly disapproves of the publishing of the pictures because he thinks it will be immoral to hurt Julian and Molly.

Before the publication of the picture, George's wife reveals some pictures and stands by him. This forces Vernon to resign from the newspaper. Vernon is going to use their euthanasia pact with Clive to take revenge. Clive witnesses a murder on his trip and chooses not to report it to the police. When Vernon knows about it, he exposes this to the police and Clive is very angry. He starts to plan his revenge too. They two travel to Amsterdam, where each one hires a Dutch doctor and arranges to have the other killed. The novel is readable, even entertaining, but lacks the moral menace and disconcerting mood of the previous tales. Its flavor is a sort of "McEwan-Lite," and it is the integration of a radical presence into the comfortable contemporary mainstream.

Section Three   Later Career: In-depth and Thought-provoking Style

McEwan's literary success continued in the 1990s. During this period, troubles came after his divorce from his wife, Penny Allen, in 1995. It had been a hard time because they fought for the custody of their son. In 1997, McEwan married journalist Annalena McAfee, whom he first met during her interview with McEwan. His second wife greatly inspired him in his creation. "In the new millennium, McEwan continues to enjoy numerous accolades and an expanding catalog of works."[24] Additional novels *Solar* (2010), *Sweet Tooth* (2012), *The Children Act* (2014), *Nutshell* (2016), and *Machine like Me* (2019) were published, as well as another collaboration with Michael Berkeley for the libretto "For You" (2008).

In a broader historical, social, and political context, these novels delve into the power of individual emotions as a driving force, propelling the exploration of inner personal experiences and interpersonal relationships. They reflect the psychological traumas, ethical dilemmas, social injustices, and other social and moral phenomena that individuals encounter within their cultural milieu. Moreover, they shed light on the decay of social morality, the distortion and darkness of human nature, and the existential crisis faced by humanity in the modern era. In this sense, McEwan's novels are in fact pursuing the "great tradition"[25] of English literature which focuses on the social and moral sense of literature. From the above background, we can see that contemporary social problems continue to emerge, the traditional value system collapses, beliefs and morals are lost, and cultural concepts are confused. In terms of "emotional structure," the whole of British society is in a state of anxiety and melancholy. Writers are bound to pay attention to it from a literary point of view, reflect this social mood in their works, and struggle to find ways to overcome it. Following his transformation, McEwan ceased being perceived solely as the representative of the "angry youth" and gradually emerged as a spokesperson for social melancholy rooted in concerns about social and political issues. His melancholic stance signifies an active engagement with the crises confronting humanity, embodying a spiritual expression of his artistic mission.

The greatest feature of this period is his in-depth writing style——that is, the transformation of his writing style and the story structure. McEwan's novels in this period began to pay more attention to the problem of human nature. Central to this view of McEwan's evolution is the belief in the concomitant refinement of his ethical sensibility. David Malcolm, in his study, states with confidence, "Overall, McEwan's career shows a trajectory from quite extreme moral relativism toward a clear moral focus."[26] McEwan's focus is also on issues like climate change, science, and human nature. In an interview, McEwan explains why his themes are always interwoven with "loss, deprivation, and absence." In the story *The Last Day of Summer,* he describes a drowning scene in which a boy accidentally causes the death of his mother and a tiny baby. He believes that the story was written under the influence of his unconsciousness because when he was in his thirties, he suddenly realized that the story was the reflection of his own thoughts about the death of his mother and his childhood. "The woman in the boat is clearly my mother, the baby in the boat clearly myself, as is the boy."[27] His life experiences have a great impact on his literary creation. Wars and politics are also involved in his creation in this period. Kate Kellaway (2005) explains that McEwan's life was affected by the twists and turns of war and the "detritus of war was always around him" in his childhood, and even "his babysitters were corporals"[28].

"Since his ethical turn in the 1980s, McEwan's fiction has been most acute in its examination of elemental ethics in its depictions of literal face-to-face encounters, moments when he pits individual characters against one another at crucial points of the decision during which they must choose between self-gratification, or even self-preservation, and genuine benevolent action."[29] McEwan adopted a more peaceful, warm, and complex narrative method to show his power and stability of language and his experimentation with different kinds of narrative voices.

"With their emphasis on dramatic interactions between characters, McEwan's mid-career and recent novels highlight the role that fiction can play in soliciting our imaginative understanding of others and in enacting for our consideration the vicarious challenge of behaving towards them with genuine compassion."[30] McEwan remains confident that his fiction can produce, through the creation of believable characters and compellingly readable narratives in the tradition of the great English novelists, the imaginative conditions for entering into the minds of others and achieving greater moral awareness.

Atonement is a 2001 bildungsroman novel by McEwan, which is set in 1935 but the whole story spans the whole life of the protagonist, including World War II and the present day throughout. *Atonement* is a challenging and ambitious work. Hugely acclaimed, this is writing on a new scale, recognizably McEwan in the well-wrought prose and fine articulation of character, the cool precision of moral nuance, the adept and surprising effects of plot, but also a revelation in the new and powerful sense of history, of the pattern of individual lives and actions within the sweep of great events—in this case, the 1939-1945 War.[31]

The novel describes a complex narrative that encompasses multiple themes and elements. It revolves around love, guilt, shame, forgiveness, war, social class, identity, and the loss of innocence. At its core, the story focuses on Briony Tallis, a self-important individual with a passion for literature. Briony's prejudiced perception of Robbie, the son of her father's housemaids, leads to the loss of happiness for both Robbie and her own sister, Cecilia.

Briony Tallis, a 13-year-old, lives in an English country estate in 1935. They entertain her cousins, 15-year-old Lola Quincey, and 9-year-old twins Jackson and Pierrot Quincey, because their parents are in a divorce. Briony's older sister Cecilia is in love with Robbie who is studying with Cecilia at Cambridge and plans to become a doctor with the Tallises' financial support. Briony mistakenly believes that Robbie is a threat to her sister. Later, her cousin Lola is raped, and Briony convinces Lola it is Robbie who commits the crime. After many hours, Robbie returns to the house with the twins but he is put into prison because of Briony's testimony. Cecilia leaves the family and starts a career as a nurse. Robbie is enlisted in the army. Briony works as a nurse during the war and becomes mature as she sees the harsh conditions. Later, Briony attends the wedding of Paul and Lola and gets to know the truth that Paul is the one who raped Lola. Briony has realized there is nothing she can do to correct her mistakes and she has to make an atonement for her sins the hard way.

In the novel, Briony searches for her way to fulfill an atonement, for she feels responsible. However, even though Briony's bias certainly causes the furthest-reaching consequences, in the novel, McEwan wants to show us that no character is capable of seeing the world in a truly objective, balanced way. Relying heavily on shared narratives and perspectives, Ian McEwan's *Atonement* will leave his reader questioning the ability to overcome guilt as well as the power of storytelling and the literary tradition.

Solar was published in 2010, which means that it was published after the end of the two terms of American President George W. Bush (2000-2008), as well as after the term of British Prime Minister Tony Blair (1997-2007), and the Iraq War that these two men prosecuted following the September 11th, 2001 terrorist attacks on the United States. In the novel, these historical events have been mentioned a few times.

Solar tackles the topical issues of climate change and environmental stewardship using an allegorical framework reminiscent of *Saturday*. The narrative is divided into three different parts, corresponding with the years 2000, 2005, and 2009 in the life of the largely unlikeable protagonist, the Nobel Prize-winning physicist Michael Beard, who has no achievements after he won the Nobel Prize many years before. He marries five wives and cheats on all of them, so his marriages all end up with divorce. His fifth wife, Patrice, takes revenge on him by having affairs with Tarpin, their builder. Once, he confronts Tarpin since Tarpin hits Patrice, only to find himself no match for Tarpin. He is now a fat older man who eats whatever he wants and drinks a lot. In his career, he hasn't had any achievements and is obsessed with giving lectures to earn money. He leads government-backed programs on global warming halfheartedly. A young postgraduate physicist, Aldous, from the program, talks about his recent idea on solar energy in which Beard has no interest.

Beard is invited on a trip to the Arctic Circle along with some prominent men and women from different fields. Their purpose is to observe global warming and the melting of icebergs. On the trip, he is disappointed about human nature. When he gets home, he finds Aldous sitting on the sofa in his bathrobe. In the argument, Aldous falls off himself and hits his head on the coffee table, and gets killed. Beard calmly makes the scene into a crime spot by planting it on Tarpin. After Aldous's death, he plagiarizes Aldous's research on solar energy and starts the project with the government's support. He has two mistresses and has a daughter with one of them. When he thinks he finds his purpose in life again and his program is going to be tested, he is testified to plagiarizing Aldous' research by staff in the government. At the end of the novel, he is confronted by Tarpin and the two mistresses.

Solar is reviewed as "a book so good—so ingeniously designed, irreproachably high-minded and skillfully brought off—that it's actually quite bad... This may be Beard's story, but it's McEwan's vehicle, constructed to let him pull all the showy turns of the major contemporary novelist and ambitious public intellectual: personalizing the political, politicizing the personal and poeticizing everything else. The tip-off is Beard, who's endowed by his creator with precisely the vices—apathy, slothfulness, gluttony, and hypocrisy—that afflict the society the book condemns, threatening to cook the human race in the heat—trapping gases released by its own arrogance. Because a fictional character can exhibit only so much awareness of his own thematic utility, Beard doesn't notice any of this, merely regarding himself as a colorful eccentric. But readers will see him for what he is: a figure so stuffed with philosophical straw that he can barely simulate lifelike movement."[32] (Water Kirn, The New York Times Sunday Book Reviews)

Ian McEwan's 15th book of fiction is *Sweet Tooth*. In *the Washington Post*, Jonathan Yardley calls it a "delicious new novel [that] provides all the pleasures one has come to expect of [McEwan]: pervasive intelligence, broad and deep knowledge, elegant prose, subtle wit and, by no means least, a singularly agreeable element of surprise."[33] The novel is set in the 1970s, and takes its title from a fictional clandestine mission by Britain's MI5 intelligence service to sponsor writers espousing the Cold Warrior cause.

The protagonist in *Sweet Tooth*, Serena, is the narrator. She is a pretty woman who is recruited by the MI5. Serena Frome was brought up in a bishop's family in a small English city. Her mother encourages her to study mathematics at Cambridge University even though Serena is keen on studying literature. In college, her boyfriend introduces her to his tutor, Tony Canning, an older historian. Serena and Tony then begin a long, secret affair. Tony teaches her about politics and trains her to prepare for the interview with the British intelligence organization MI5. Then Tony breaks up with Serena. Serena meets Max Greatorex in MI5, who is her superior. Serena has been attracted by Max, but Max is engaged to a woman whose family is much better than Serena's. Later, she is assigned to carry out Sweet Tooth due to her love of literature. Her target is a young writer named Thomas Haley. She falls in love with Haley. At work, Serena defends Haley's work and she worries about her job at the same time. Max tells Haley about everything, which causes them to have a big argument. Haley forgives Serena in the end and asks Serena to marry him.

The novel provides McEwan with a creative space that mediates between self and other, writer and reader, private and public. In *Sweet Tooth*, he deftly uses all the tricks of the novelist's trade to craft a delicious, multilayered literary treat that reads by turns like a spy thriller and romantic tale, a metafictional puzzle and sweeping historical novel, and last but not least, "a muted and distorted autobiography."[34]

The publication of *Sweet Tooth* in 2012 confirmed McEwan's interest in the Cold War themes. "The assured return to Cold War history in *Sweet Tooth* draws on these precedents, bringing the material up to date and closer to home. The novel uses the 1970s setting as a vehicle for the creation of one of McEwan's most complex and convincing women characters to date, for the exploration of conflicts between personal and public relationships, and as an opportunity for an unprecedented level of authorial self-reflection on his own work and on the relationship between readers and writers as it persists in the unnervingly transformed twenty-first-century cultural world."[35] It is a remarkable achievement, not only in the context of the contemporary British literary scene but also within the body of its author's work.

McEwan's creation shifts to global politics, combining the individual experience. The themes cover the 1970s politics of the cultural sphere to the second decade of the new millennium. *Sweet Tooth* provides an intriguing exploration of McEwan's favorite themes but also contains a notable dimension of intertextual and metafictional playfulness, which in this case is highly self-reflective as he makes direct references to his fiction, namely to his short stories from the collection *In Between the Sheets* (1978). Therefore, in terms of its thematic and narrative framework, *Sweet Tooth* can be especially linked with two of his earlier novels, *The Innocent* (1990) and *Atonement* (2001).[36]

Nutshell is a retelling of Shakespeare's Hamlet set in modern London. The most interesting part of *Nutshell* is that it is narrated entirely by an eight-month-old fetus. Trudy's unborn baby hears about his mother and his uncle Claude's plan to kill his father, John Cairncross. He is frightened by the plan. He knows that they are going to poison John and set it up a suicide scene. Judy is overwhelmed by the guilt of killing John, and she breaks down. After the police investigation, the two decide to escape the country. The baby decides to be born. Claude hesitates for a while, decides to stay, and helps Trudy with the baby. The police arrive and arrest Claude and Trudy.

This novel is one of the best funny novels by McEwan. *Nutshell*, involves a character whom the narrator calls "the owl poet." "Over a long and distinguished career, Ian McEwan has proven himself to be among the least narrowly confined artists imaginable—a kind of anti-owl poet. In just the years since his novel *Atonement* made him as famous here in the U.S. as he'd already been for decades in his native Britain, McEwan has written about a neurosurgeon, a newly married couple on a disastrous honeymoon, a Nobel Prize-winning physicist, an MI5 intelligence agent, and a family court judge.[37] Nevertheless, *Nutshell* manages to make such an idea plausible, and critics respond well to this adaptation of Hamlet.

The Children Act was so named after the Children Act of 1989 in the UK Parliament which sought to mandate the interests of children and their wellbeing. The novel was published in 2014 and made into a film that hit cinemas in 2017, starring Emma Thompson and Stanley Tucci.

Although some critics argue that McEwan fell short in portraying Fiona's character and her husband's implausible motivations for seeking an affair, the intricate moral dilemma presented in *The Children Act* remains compelling, especially due to its involvement of a minor. The novel features Fiona Maye, a highly esteemed High Court Judge, juggling the demands of a high-pressure career and a deteriorating marriage. As her personal struggles intertwine with her professional responsibilities, Fiona finds herself embroiled in a complex case involving a young Jehovah's Witness diagnosed with leukemia, whose life depends on a blood transfusion. The story portrays the intricacies and challenges of making decisions in the best interest of individuals, even when their own beliefs are at odds with those decisions.

In the novel, the protagonist, Fiona, a middle-aged High Court judge, is having troubles in her marriage. Her husband, Jack, is attracted to his colleague, who wants to have an affair with her. Fiona is busy with a case where a seventeen-year-old Adam, suffering from leukemia, refuses a blood transfusion as a member of Jehovah's Witnesses. The hospital sues the parents in order to save the boy. She decides to meet with Adam whether he is capable of denying treatment or not. She finds they have a natural bond. Adam plays a tune on his violin while Fiona joins his playing with a song. Returning to court, she decides that the hospital be allowed to give him the blood transfusion. When Fiona arrives home at the end of the day, Jack is sitting in front of their door, admitting that he is foolish to pursue the idea of an affair. Fiona later receives letters from Adam, who sees the hypocrisy of his parents and has some special feelings about Fiona. Adam eventually confesses that he wants to live with Fiona. Fiona refuses Adam. Fiona ignores letters from Adam, and her relationship with her husband gradually changes. On the night of the concert, she is informed that Adam dies after his leukemia returns, and he refuses treatment. Fiona feels his death is her fault because she refuses to let him live with her. This brings her and Jack closer, and they experience a renewed commitment to one another.

Machines like Me was published in 2019. He takes a dystopian turn, taking the reader back to the 1980s in an alternative version of history. In the novel's timeline, the United Kingdom lost the Falklands War, and modern technologies like social media and the internet exist. The mathematician Alan Turing is still alive and has created artificial intelligence in this parallel universe. Machines have already begun to rule beyond what they were programmed to do. Everyday people can purchase robots, so-named Adams and Eves, and the protagonist of this novel, Charlie, does just this. It's a thought-provoking warning against artificial intelligence and its dangers, one that feels uncomfortably close to home.

In *Machines like Me*, Charlie Friend uses his dead mother's money to buy the newest model of the artificial human, Adam. Miranda Black, his upstairs neighbor whom he is in love with, helps him with programming Adam. Charlie feels Adam is lifelike yet distinctly nonhuman. Adam tells Charlie not to trust her because she is a liar. With their relationship growing, Charlie believes Miranda is hiding something from him. After a quarrel, Miranda invites Adam upstairs to charge in her apartment. Charlie is furious when he hears that they two have sex. Miranda argues that sleeping with Adam does not count as cheating because he is a machine. Charlie later asks Miranda whether Gorringe actually rapes her; she tells the truth and says that Gorringe will kill her.

Adam suggests they all pay him a visit to Gorringe to tell him why he goes to prison. During the visit, Adam records Miranda's confession. Adam takes over buying and selling stocks for Charlie, and they secure a large sum of money. Adam reports the police about the case and, simultaneously, gives all their money away. Charlie smashes Adam over the head and sends the body to its inventor. Miranda is put into prison for six months. After her release, they successfully adopt a boy.

"There are some decisions, even moral ones, that are formed in regions below conscious thought," McEwan writes at one intense turning point. *Machines like Me* explores some of those decisions. It also manages to flesh out—literally and grippingly—questions about what constitutes a person and the troubling future of humans if the smart machines we create can overtake us.[38]

The Cockroach, published in 2019, is a novella that follows the transformative journey of its protagonist, Jim Sams. Initially an unremarkable individual, Jim undergoes a profound metamorphosis when he wakes up one day to discover that he has become the Prime Minister of Britain. This metamorphosis has brought about a profound change in Jim. In his previous existence, he was either ignored or despised, but in his new form, he has become the most influential figure in all of Britain. Tasked with fulfilling the desires of the people, Jim is determined to overcome any obstacles, regardless of who or what stands in his path. His sole purpose is to execute the will of the people, and nothing and no one must hinder him: not the opposition, nor the dissidents within his own party, not even the established principles of parliamentary democracy. With his characteristic intelligence, insight, and biting humor, McEwan pays homage to Franz Kafka's renowned work, using it as a framework to explore a world turned completely upside down.

Lessons is the latest novel by McEwan. *Lessons* skillfully disrupts conventional notions of "good guys" and "bad guys," challenges clear-cut motivations, and subverts expectations of tidy closure by offering fresh perspectives on familiar themes. Amidst a world still grappling with the aftermath of the Second World War and the closure of the Iron Curtain, the life of eleven-year-old Roland Baines is turned completely upside down. Stranded at an unconventional boarding school, separated by two thousand miles from his mother's protective love, Roland's vulnerability captivates his piano teacher, Miss Miriam Cornell. Their connection leaves lasting scars and a timeless memory of love.

Years later, Roland's existence takes a tumultuous turn when his wife mysteriously disappears, leaving him to care for their young son. As the radioactive fallout from the Chernobyl disaster spreads across Europe, he embarks on a search for answers that delves deep into his family's history and spans a lifetime. Against the backdrop of events such as the Suez Crisis, the Cuban Missile Crisis, the fall of the Berlin Wall, and the current challenges of the pandemic and climate change, Roland often finds himself swept along by the tides of history. Yet, he also grapples against them, haunted by missed opportunities and seeking solace through various avenues—music, literature, friendships, love affairs, political pursuits—only to encounter tragedy and, ultimately, redemption.

Despite the plot's clever structure, including strategically placed clues and coincidences that suggest a gratifying conclusion, the novel deftly explores historical upheavals through the lens of the character. In this epic, mesmerizing, and profoundly humane tale, *Lessons* serves as a chronicle for our times—a powerful contemplation on history and humanity, viewed through the prism of one man's lifetime.

Chapter Two   Ethical Literary Criticism

From an etymological point of view, in the West, the word "ethic" is derived from the Greek "ethos," which was used in Homer's epic to denote the common residence and domicile of a group of people (haunts or habitats) and was later extended to the character and habits of a group of people, which is the prototype of ancient human thinking about ethics. The term "ethic" was first used by the ancient Greek philosopher Aristotle. In the 4th century BC, Aristotle constructed the adjective "ethicos" from the noun "ethos" and clarified the meaning of its virtues, and then derived the new noun "ethika," which is what we call "ethics" today, represented in English by "ethics." Aristotle opened up the meaning of the special temperament of character (temperament, disposition) and talked about moral virtue (i.e., character or special temperament-related virtues).

The word "morality" is derived from the Greek word mores, which originally denoted fashions or customs and gradually acquired the meaning of character and morality. By the 4th century, moralitas was derived from Latin, and its meaning was gradually clarified as the modern concept of morality. It can be seen that from the etymological perspective of Spanish, there is no essential difference between "ethics" and "morality," and they can be used interchangeably. The Cambridge Philosophical Dictionary[39] states that the word "ethic" is "often used interchangeably with 'morality' and is sometimes used narrowly to refer to the moral principles of a particular tradition, group, or individual."

"Ethics" is often used to refer to a set of standards set up by a group about right and wrong, and is imposed on group members to regulate and restrict their behavior. The branches of philosophical value theory include the branches of ethics and aesthetics, and each branch is related to value. Ethics was originally part of early Greek philosophy. The development of philosophy is helpful to the development of ethics, and finally makes ethics an independent subject. As

Stephen R. Sterling[40] states, "ethics is not a specialist study of marginal relevance to the real world, nor is it narrowly moralizing and didactic; instead, it is (or should be) a fundamentally relevant integral dimension of human conduct which links practical action with concepts of ultimate ends and, indeed, spiritual goals." In concrete literary works, the core content of ethics is the ethical relationship between people, the ethical relationship between man and society, man and nature, and the moral order formed based on these relationships (Nie, 2014:13)[41]. Ethics attempts to solve the human moral problems by defining the concepts of good and evil, right and wrong, and justice and crime. As a field of intellectual research, moral philosophy is also closely related to moral psychology, descriptive ethics, and value theory.

The development of ethics is influenced by specific socio-historical and cultural conditions. Different social, historical, and cultural backgrounds will produce correspondingly different ethics. The ethics of each era are marked with the distinct imprint of this era, carrying its unique connotation and essential characteristics. Plato was arguably the first philosopher to grasp the entire realm of existence and its inherent goodness by exploring a transcendental purpose. His ethics, known as the ethics of goodness, posits that in the realm of truth, the concept of goodness represents the highest ideal and manifests the existence of truth.

As ethics progressed, the ethics of virtue emerged, placing the cultivation of one's own virtues at its core. This perspective is also referred to as perfectionist ethics or self-actualization. Confucianism similarly emphasizes the process through which an individual attains virtue as the process of becoming truly human. According to Confucian thought, although one is born as a natural being, this does not automatically make one a complete person. To become such a person, moral perfection and ethical development are necessary. One needs to perfect oneself morally and become an ethical person. The evolution of ethics is determined by the evolution of the essential connotation of the concept of "man".

According to Liu Jianjun's exposition, human self-understanding has evolved through three distinct stages: the "natural man," the "social man," and the "cultural man." Correspondingly, the essential connotation of "man" has undergone transformations aligned with these three phases. The stage of the "natural man" refers to human existence in ancient or primitive tribal societies, where relationships were primarily governed by blood ties. In this phase, human actions were dictated largely by instinct and nature, with the fulfillment of natural desires regarded as the highest moral principle. The defining characteristic of this stage is that individuals act in accordance with their inherent instincts, prioritizing their natural needs above all else.

With the emergence of class society, humanity transitioned into the stage of the "social man," a concept akin to Aristotle's notion of man as a "social animal." Unlike the "natural man," whose behavior was driven by instinctual satisfaction, the "social man" operates within the framework of collective norms and regulations that shape various aspects of social life. At this stage, the highest moral standard is no longer the fulfillment of personal desires but rather adherence to societal norms and expectations. During the Renaissance and the Enlightenment, the values and evaluative criteria guiding the "social man" underwent significant transformations. However, despite these shifts, the core of shared social values remained intact, continuing to regulate human behavior.

The transition to the "cultural man" stage marks a further evolution in human society, particularly from the twentieth century onward, with a notable acceleration in the mid-twentieth century. The one-dimensional description of "creatures of nature" and "social animals" is no longer suitable for people who find themselves in a network of elements woven by "mythology, language, art, religion, history, science," and so on. "Here we have no obligation to prove the unity of the entity of man. Man is no longer seen as a mere entity that exists freely and can be known by oneself."[42] "Here we do not have any obligation to prove the unity of the human entity. Man is no longer seen as a simple entity that exists freely and can be known by oneself."[43] Scholars abandon the previous one-dimensional excavation and research of man, and begin to reveal the connotation of people from the complex network dimension of culture.

Ethics takes the real moral phenomena in human society as the research object, serves the moral relations in reality, and is applied as literary ethics criticism in the field of literature. Although it borrows and absorbs ethical methods in the process of formation, in the final analysis, the object of its research is still a moral phenomenon in literary works, serving the purpose of studying literature. Since ethics reflects the relationship and order naturally formed between people or things, defining and analyzing ethics with reference to the development of the connotation of "man" has become the primary task of literary ethics criticism.

"Literary ethics criticism focuses on literature in the historical sense, while ethics focuses on society in the sense of reality."[44] Therefore, the content of literary ethics criticism as a method of literary criticism should include the study of literary works themselves from the perspective of ethics and morality, the relationship between writers and literary works, the relationship between the writer's moral concept and the tradition, the influence of the writer's moral concept on other writers, and the relationship between the literary works and the moral education of society.

Literature is an artistic reflection and poetic inquiry into man's actual existence. Ethical attributes, as fundamental aspects of this existence, naturally become a central focus of literary exploration. Drawing from the rationality and idealism of ethical norms, literature reflects complex socio-political and cultural issues. People's ethical concepts and structures are shaped by socio-political, economic, and cultural factors, which also influence human relationships. The changes in these relationships, in turn, reflect broader social dynamics. In the context of literary works, the ethical relations among characters reflect the creative subject's exploration and contemplation on the rationality of the elements that constitute the prevailing state of social ethics. People's ethical concepts and frameworks are indeed shaped by socio-political, economic, and cultural factors.

The study of literary ethics is a crucial aspect of both understanding and applying literary principles. In contemporary ethics, the scope of ethical relations has been extended from the relationship between individuals and individuals with people as the subject, the relationship between individuals and social groups, and the relationship between social groups to the relationship between man and nature and even man and self. Therefore, in the theoretical construction of literary ethics, the definition of ethical relations follows this extended category, including the relationship between man and nature and man and self. Li Dingqing once defined the four dimensions of literary ethics criticism as the relationship between man and nature, the relationship between man and others, the relationship between man and society, and the relationship between man and self.[45] Nie Zhenzhao further clarified it in his paper as "in specific literary works, the core content of ethics is the accepted and recognized ethical order formed between man and man, man and society, and between man and nature, as well as the moral concepts formed on the basis of this order and the various norms for maintaining this order."[46]

Ethical Literary Criticism was initiated by Nie Zhenzhao in 2004. Ethics has always played a crucial role in literary research. Since literature inherently revolves around human nature and social phenomena, ethical choices and considerations hold significant relevance to human social life. Thus, interpreting literary works from an ethical perspective allows readers to gain a deeper understanding of the ethical implications within the works and to build an ethical framework for literary criticism, but also prompts profound reflection and vigilance from an ethical standpoint. This approach enhances the educational significance of literary works. Studying literary ethics entails interpreting, analyzing, and understanding works from an ethical perspective. It involves uncovering the ethical implications embedded in literary works, analyzing their ethical propositions, and offering literary avenues to foster healthier ethical cognition and ethical systems.

As a method of literary criticism, Ethical Literary Criticism emphasizes the social responsibility and teaching function of literature. As far as Ethical Literary Criticism is concerned, its object of criticism is literature. It studies the moral phenomena in the art world of imagination created by the author, as well as the moral relationship between authors and literature and society. It highlights the importance of adopting an ethical perspective aligned with the historical context when interpreting literary works. By doing so, the ethical elements that shape social practices and impact the destinies of the characters in the works can be analyzed. From an ethical standpoint, the methods, processes, and outcomes of the ethical choices made by different characters can be elucidated and assessed. At the same time, valuable civilizing functions of Ethical Literary Criticism are stressed. In "Ethical Literary Criticism: Its Fundaments and Terms," Nie further explains: "Ethical Literary Criticism is a method of literary criticism, which is mainly used to interpret and analyze literary works, to study literary authors and literary problems from the standpoint of ethics."[47]

It is relatively recent that literary ethics research has been theoretically proposed and applied practically as a method of literary research. In 1997, Min Ze and Dang Shengyuan's "Theory of Literary Value" took Marxist values and its basic principles as the theoretical basis, explored the aesthetic relationship between man and reality from the value relationship, and strengthened the study of literary characteristics and literary value[48]. In the same year, Gao Nan launched the first monograph in China to study ancient Chinese art from the perspective of culture, which was an early cultural interpretation of ancient literature and was also a representative work of ancient Chinese cultural poetics that still has pioneering significance.[49] Since then, Gao Nan's research on literary ethics has continued to advance. The National Symposium on "Chinese English and American Literature Studies: Review and Prospects" held at Jiangxi Normal University in June 2004 has a special significance for the development of literary ethics criticism. In his keynote speech at the conference, Nie systematically proposed the concept and theoretical framework of literary ethics criticism in his keynote speech, "Literary Ethics Criticism: A New Exploration of Literary Criticism Methods." "What we call ethical literary criticism, which can also be referred to as literary ethics criticism or literary ethics, is not a new academic discipline. It's actually just a research method that studies literary works, as well as the relationship between literature and writers, literature and readers, and literature and society, from an ethical and moral perspective."[50]

"In the past fifteen years, from the initial introduction and the construction of its theoretical structure to the promotion, enrichment, and application of its critical approaches, the expansion and consolidation of its theoretic principles, as well as the systematization of its critical practice, Ethical Literary Criticism has gone through a long journey of development before reaching its full maturity and broad recognition today."[51] The development of Ethical Literary Criticism can be divided into three stages:

First stage: the Ethical Literary Criticism is put forward. In this period, Nie made the most outstanding contribution to the construction of the theory of Ethical Literary Criticism. He pointed out the necessity of Ethical Literary Criticism and demonstrated the core argument of the theory and its literary origin[52]. On this basis, he also made a detailed discussion and practical guidance on significant fundaments and terms concerned in the theory, and further improved the framework of the theory. After Nie, Wang Ning, Liu Jianjun, Qiao Guoqiang, Zou Jianjun, Li Dingqing, Xiu Shuxin, Knut, and others have contributed to the further improvement of the theoretical system from different aspects. For instance, Liu Jianjun (2005) mentions that the essence of Ethical Literary Criticism is to realize the harmony between different individuals, communities, and cultures in the essay "The Current Nature of Ethical Literary Criticism."[53] While Qiao Guoqiang (2005) declares his idea from another aspect. He suggests when we apply Ethical Literary Criticism, we should not only concern about the relationship between people, but also explore the relationship between people and society, people and nature, as well as people and themselves. In terms of time, we can expand it to the past (history, tradition), the present (reality, fashion), and the future (human existence, possibility). What's more, the ecological ethical problems should also be included in terms of discussion on human existence morality[54]. Exploration of the relationship between people and ecology is a focal point in Wang Ning's essay "The Environmental Ethics of Literature: The Significance of Ecological Criticism." This essay approves of the significance of Ethical Literary Criticism and brings about the possibility of putting forward a new theoretical construction on the level of ecological criticism by fully exploring the rich resources of ancient Chinese ecological criticism (2005).[55]

Second stage: the theory is promoted and applied to practice. In this period, it is manifested more in the practical application of the theory. Researchers apply this theory to various literary forms, such as novels, poems, and plays to verify its effectiveness and persuasiveness. Alternatively, based on this theory, they examine a writer's works created at different times to analyze the evolution of the writer's ethical and moral concepts. For instance, based on Nie's theory, Li Dingqing interprets the human spirits of Western literature from four perspectives, thus expanding the scope of application of Ethical Literary Criticism with his distinctive understandings and explanations.[56] In this stage, Ethical Literary Criticism also fits in studies of Milton's poetry, Watanabe's works, Toni Morrison's novels, Jelinek's works, etc. For example, Ethical Literary Criticism can be used to examine the themes of marriage and relationships in Toni Morrison's novel *Purple*; ethical default in *Desire under the Elms*; Dimmesdale's self-realization in *The Scarlet Letter*; the alienation of human nature caused by industrialization and the loss of marriage ethics reflected in *The Shadow in the Rose Garden*; marriage ethics in *Emma*; disillusionment with the "American dream" in *The Great Gatsby*. Ethical Literary Criticism, regarded as a fresh contribution to Chinese literary criticism, has received increasing attention during this period.

Third stage: the theory of Ethical Literary Criticism is refined and evaluated. Since 2013, Nie Zhenzhao has continued to publish a series of papers, expounding the basic theory of Ethical Literary Criticism and demonstrating the practice of criticism. With the increasing influence of literary ethical criticism, many scholars have written relevant comments and research articles. In particular, Yang Jincai's[57] "Realms of Ethical Literary Criticism in China: A Review of Nie Zhenzhao's Scholarship" and Shang Biwu's[58] "The Rise of a Critical Theory: Reading Introduction to Ethical Literary Criticism" are written in English, aiming to provide foreign scholars some information to understand Ethical Literary Criticism (Su, 2019)[59]. Currently, professors and researchers continue to refine the theory. However, some scholars have identified certain issues in both the theory and its practical application. These include the confusion between ethical and moral concepts, a lack of clarity regarding key terms in literary ethics criticism, and the overlap between literary ethics criticism and moral criticism. In 2020, Nie Zhenzhao released his latest book titled *A Study on the Theory of Ethical Literary Criticism*. Diverging from previous singular research paradigms, this work takes an interdisciplinary approach and utilizes comparative literature research methods to expand the horizons of ethical literary criticism. It further explores fundamental positions, concepts, and methodologies within the field. The aim of this book is to construct a comprehensive research paradigm that integrates ethics, aesthetics, psychology, linguistics, history, culture, anthropology, ecology, politics, and narratology.

While Ethical Literary Criticism has garnered considerable academic influence both domestically and internationally as a creative critical method within literary studies, previous research has primarily focused on the realm of literature alone. However, this work pioneers interdisciplinary and multilevel research approaches, offering valuable insights for future investigations within the realm of Ethical Literary Criticism.

Therefore, while they keep trying to study literary works based on the theory, Chinese scholars have additionally published some relevant academic papers to discuss how to perfect the theory. In Che Fengcheng's[60] article, different groups of ethical relationships are distinguished to improve the researchers' understanding of these ethical relationships. Also, many other professors and scholars have made extensive and in-depth discussions on the related theories and methods of Ethical Literary Criticism.

In the West, the application of ethical criticism in the field of literature has a long history, and the earliest can be traced back to the emphasis and application of Plato and Aristotle in the ancient Greek period on the teaching role of moral literary works. Ancient Greek literary criticism takes "good and evil" as the standard for evaluating the literary works.

However, in modern times, the rise of new critical approaches, such as formalist criticism, structuralist criticism, and psychoanalysis, has, in fact, contributed to the marginalization of ethical and moral considerations in literary analysis. It was not until the 1980s, when gender, race and other elements attracted the attention of many scholars in the field of literary criticism, that ethical criticism, which was closely related to it, showed a return boom. A number of representatives and masterpieces of ethical criticism began to emerge. The representative figure of modern and contemporary Western ethical criticism is the American ethical critic Wayne C. Booth. In his book, *The Rhetoric of*

Fiction (1961), Booth[61] took ethics as the main line and expounded the history of the development and evolution of the European novel. American scholar Laurence S. Lockridge's[62] *The Ethics of Romanticism* (1989) is a resurrection of ethical criticism in the literary field. These papers by famous artists explore the moral function of literary works and the relationship between aesthetics, art, and ethics. It is precisely based on the gradual revival of ethical criticism in the West that many experts and scholars have written articles to express their views on ethical criticism from various angles. Since the 1980s, ethical criticism has gained more and more attention in the West.

Recent research on ethical criticism in the literature field has explored various aspects. Some have focused on the theory of ethical literary criticism, which adopts an interdisciplinary perspective and expands its boundaries by integrating ethics, aesthetics, psychology, linguistics, history, culture, anthropology, ecology, politics, and narratology. This study aims to construct a research paradigm that combines multiple disciplines and provides insights for future research in ethical literary criticism.

A critical literature review on ethical dilemmas in qualitative research is also prevailing. It is to analyze and synthesize ethical dilemmas encountered during the progress of qualitative investigations and propose strategies to address them. This research highlights the need for ethical considerations in qualitative research and provides recommendations for addressing ethical dilemmas.

Overall, recent research on ethical criticism in the literature field has delved into the theory of Ethical Literary Criticism and examined ethical dilemmas in qualitative research. These studies contribute to expanding our understanding of ethical issues in literature and provide insights for conducting ethical research in the future.

When scholars engage in literary ethics criticism, they frequently draw upon the concepts of interpretation, literary theory, and literary terms to analyze and understand literary works. Interpretation involves the process of making meaning from a text and involves various theoretical frameworks or schemas, such as psychoanalysis, Marxism, feminism, and more, to understand the world depicted in the literature. Literary theory provides the underlying principles and tools used to comprehend and interpret literature, exploring relationships between authors and their works, the significance of race, class, and gender, historical context, and linguistic elements within the text. Additionally, scholars rely on literary terms to identify and analyze elements within a work, such as characterization, dialogue, genre, imagery, plot, point of view, style, symbol, and theme, which help facilitate interpretation, argumentation, and analysis. By employing these concepts, scholars explore the ethical dimensions of literature, including its portrayal of ecological ethics, family ethics, social ethics, and other moral concerns.

Ecological Ethics. Ecological ethics, also known as environmental ethics, is a field of study that examines the moral concepts of right and wrong behavior in relation to humans' interaction with the natural world. It explores the ethical responsibilities and values that individuals and societies should uphold in their relationship with the biosphere. Ecological ethics addresses the moral implications of human actions on the environment, including issues such as climate change, pollution, biodiversity loss, resource scarcity, and genetic manipulation. The original human beings, like other life, originated from nature, but since human beings took the first steps towards human civilization, they have also begun a journey away from nature. Although the separation of man from nature means the progress of mankind in the history of its development, it is also the beginning of man's enslavement and destruction of nature. Ecological ethics requires human beings not only to extend their concern to non-human natural existence, but also to establish a moral relationship between man and nature from an ethical perspective.

Traditionally, ethical thought about the environment has focused on the adverse effects of environmental conditions on human interests, adopting an anthropocentric perspective. As Buell (1995:7) put forward, "the nonhuman environment is present not merely as a framing device but as a presence that begins to suggest that human history is implicated in natural history." Man's exploitation and utilization of nature have brought all kinds of irreversible harm to nature, and this harm accompanies the process of human civilization and increasingly reacts to human beings themselves. It is necessary and urgent for human beings to have a better understanding of the relationship between man and nature.

In today's society, although human civilization has developed to an unprecedented level, the destruction of nature by human beings has also reached an incomparable point. Ecological ethics, which examines the relationship between humans and nature, has garnered increasing attention. This discussion and attention are expressed in the field of literature as a newly emerging ecological ethics criticism.

The traditional approach views nature and other living beings as means to fulfill human needs and wants. However, modern ecological ethicists advocate for a transformation of moral principles and obligations, acknowledging the interconnectedness and relatedness of all living beings and the holistic nature of ecosystems. This viewpoint broadens the scope of moral consideration beyond humans and recognizes the inherent worth and ethical rights of individual organisms, species, and ecosystems. The ethical discourse in ecological ethics encompasses discussions on sentient creatures, safeguarding biodiversity, and maintaining the integrity of ecosystems.

With the development of environmental ethics, the theoretical viewpoints of ecological ethics became diversified. The influential and representative theoretical viewpoints mainly include ecocentrism, anthropocentrism, biocentrism, ecological coordination theory, ecological anthropology, and human cybernetics. Ecological ethics seeks to provide a framework for ethical decision-making and responsible practices in ecological and conservation management, considering the complexities and moral dilemmas that arise in the field of ecology.

All in all, Western ecological ethics research tends to pay more attention to excavating the value of nature and the internal restriction of natural laws on human behavior. Consequently, the commitment to establishing a sustainable relationship between humans and the natural world has become an area of growing focus. Li Dingqing[63] pointed out in the article: "the current Ecological Ethical Criticism, which focuses on the different relationships between humans and nature in literature, can be said to align with Literary Ethical Criticism in terms of perspective and can be regarded as an organic part of Ethical Literary Criticism."

Family Ethics. Family ethics is concerned with the ethical values and principles that guide behavior within the context of family relationships. It refers to the relationships and structures formed between members in the family environment and background, mainly including the relationship between parents and children (which can be refined into several levels of father and son, mother and son, father and daughter, and mother and daughter), brothers and sisters (which can be refined into brothers and sisters or between brothers and sisters, sisters, etc.), and the many forms of relationships that exist between grandchildren. This field explores the moral obligations, responsibilities, and decision-making processes that operate within families. It encompasses a wide range of topics, including the prioritization of obligations, the role of family members, the definition of family, and the resolution of ethical dilemmas that arise within family units. Family ethics has now become an important and established part of moral and political philosophy. The increased attention may in part reflect actual changes in the family as a social institution over the last decades.

Family ethics explores broader issues such as the prioritization of obligations to children versus other family members, the moral claims of blood relatives versus those acquired through marriage, and the influence of different family structures on moral considerations. While still ideologically dominant, the traditional nuclear family has been joined by a variety of different family forms in many countries, to varying degrees. The attention may also be due to advances in reproductive technology, which put pressure on the question of what it is to be a parent, and which threaten, or promise, to raise even more difficult ethical questions in the coming decades.

In order for an individual to survive in society, they must have various relationships with other individuals under some norms that are either conventional or imposed externally, and these norms are what we call ethics. The original intention of the relationship between individuals and other individuals lies in the demands of social people for the realization of individual value. The family is the basic unit that constitutes society, and if society is regarded as an organism, then the family is the cell that constitutes this organism. The core personal values of traditional Chinese Confucianism are to help the world and be human. In traditional Western social culture, the construction of the family follows a patriarchal ethic. "In the construction of the family under the care of the patriarchal ethical law, the father is often the core of the family field, the subjective existence of power in the family, and the representative of a law or norm." The mother and child in the family field are the objects of the father's subjective power. The family is of particular importance and is seen as the place where everyone's character is formed, as well as the basis of social morality; the understanding of the relationship and structure within the family is of great significance for the perspective of the reality of the society in which it is located. Various approaches to family ethics exist, including metaphysical, biological, economic, political, psychological, and narrative perspectives, each emphasizing different moral theories and dimensions of family life.

Understanding family ethics is essential for fostering positive family dynamics and guiding ethical decision-making within the family context. Family ethics encompass the principles and values that govern interactions among family members, emphasizing open and supportive communication, active participation in decision-making processes, and the consideration of the well-being and interests of all members. At its core, family ethics serves as a fundamental guideline for how family members interact and coexist. The family ethics of a particular society often reflect that society's mainstream values, playing a crucial role in promoting social stability. On an individual level, family ethics shape the way individuals navigate their relationships within the family. However, the formation of these individual ethical guidelines does not occur in isolation; they are deeply influenced by the collective ethical value system of the family and the broader social values that surround it. Therefore, the disorder of family moral norms is a precursor to the disorder of the existing social order. By navigating ethical dilemmas together and upholding moral values, families can maintain strong bonds and create an environment that fosters the flourishing of its members.

Social Ethics. Social ethics refers to the relationship between people and people, people and society. The fundamental attribute of human beings lies in their social nature; that is, individuals occupy specific roles in the processes of production, distribution, exchange, and consumption of material goods, assuming corresponding responsibilities. Social ethics involves a methodical analysis of the moral aspects of social structures, systems, issues, and communities. It entails evaluating the ethical implications of social problems and utilizing ethical reasoning to find solutions. As a branch of applied ethics, social ethics encompasses a wide range of topics, including the equitable distribution of economic resources, ethical considerations in human subject research, animal welfare, euthanasia, abortion, discrimination, affirmative action, pornography, crime and punishment, and war and peace.

Society holds the responsibility of providing individuals with the material and spiritual conditions necessary for their development, while individuals, in turn, must fulfill obligations that contribute to the development of society according to their roles in social production. If society is likened to a machine, individuals are its components, with the normal functioning of the machine relying on the coordination of all parts. Similarly, the role of each part can only be realized within the larger framework of the machine.

As humanity develops and society progresses, the relationship between individuals and society continues to evolve. In the Victorian era, when George Eliot was writing, society was undergoing a significant transition from an agrarian to an industrial structure. This transformation was accompanied by a shift in social ethics, moving the focus from collective values to individual ones. People began paying more attention to the realization of human values and the pursuit of personal interests, reflecting a broader change in societal priorities.

Ethics, including social ethics, is a branch of philosophy concerned with determining what is morally good, bad, right, or wrong. Social ethics refers specifically to the code of conduct followed collectively by members of society to maintain harmony and stability. It seeks to address inequalities, discrimination, and injustices that arise due to differences in social status. By promoting equality, calling for the responsible use of power and privilege, and considering the influence of social contexts on moral decision-making, social ethics becomes a tool for creating a more just society.

All ethics, in essence, are shaped by the social context in which they arise. Within a society, people belong to different classes, and these classes often adhere to distinct ethical and moral standards. Ethical norms fall under the category of ideology, which is part of the superstructure determined by the economic base. A particular mode of production gives rise to specific ethical relationships and corresponding moral expectations. Consequently, differences in people's social and economic positions lead to variations in moral consciousness and practice. People in different economic positions often follow different ethical norms, and the prominence of these norms within society is shaped by their economic foundation.

The interplay between individual moral decisions and the social context is crucial. Individual actions can influence the broader social framework, just as the social context shapes individual moral values. Social ethics, therefore, operates at the intersection of individual agency and societal structures.

Social ethics consists of three key tasks. First, social ethicists examine social conditions to identify those that conflict with ethical principles of benefit, justice, or fairness. Second, they analyze possible actions to address these problematic conditions. Third, based on their analysis, they propose solutions to these ethical challenges. These tasks reflect the role of social ethics as a means of addressing social problems, promoting justice, and guiding decision-making at the societal level.

In summary, social ethics is the branch of ethics that focuses on the moral dimensions of social structures, systems, and communities. It involves evaluating social conditions, analyzing potential actions, and providing ethical solutions. Ethical norms, as the collective code of conduct, represent the shared interests of a group and serve to protect and promote those interests. By addressing social inequalities, promoting justice, and guiding ethical behavior, social ethics plays a vital role in fostering a fair and harmonious society.

Individual Ethics. Individual ethics refers to the moral principles, values, and standards that guide the behavior and decision-making of an individual. It involves examining one's own beliefs, values, and principles and applying them to various aspects of life, including personal interactions, professional conduct, and moral dilemmas. Personal ethics shape how individuals perceive right and wrong, make choices, and navigate ethical challenges they encounter. Regarding the definition of the concept of individual ethics, from the current research situation, Qiang Changwen[64] (2006) believes that "the individual as an ethical and moral concept refers to a person with an individual independent personality as a moral subject, who has certain rights and bears corresponding responsibilities and obligations."

The exercise of the right and the assumption of responsibility constitute the basic connotation of the individual as a moral person. The individual manifests their independent existence not only through their own personality, but also manifests themselves as a member of an ethical community through their association with others, the collective, and society. Zhu Hejin[65] (2014) discussed issues related to individual ethics when defining the concept of individual ethics: "Individual ethics reflects the relationship between the individual and the external world. The construction of the relationship between the individual and the external world is influenced by the individual's ethics. The concept of individual ethics is a reflection of individual ethics, and is the criterion that individuals follow when dealing with the relationship between individuals, between individuals and collectives, between individuals and society, and between individuals and nature, which is the basis for individuals to settle down and live. Individual ethics embodies the individual's attitude towards self, others, and life. The concept of individual ethics is an ethical appeal to individuals when they pursue an ideal state of life."

The core position of individual ethics lies in the relationship between the individual and society, and the important influencing factor for the establishment of this relationship lies in the establishment of individual ethical concepts, so when the novel text discusses the practical problems between man and society, it will inevitably face the writing of this individual ethics. In order to deal with the relationship between the individual and the members within a class, the individual must be subject to the collective ethics of the class. In the traditional social value system, the personal attachment of individuals to the class is closely related. The control and influence of a class on the individual is extremely large, and it is difficult for the individual to have space to develop individual ethics outside the class.

The traditional understanding of the relationship between individuals and society, which is mainly handled by individual ethics, is based on a macro perspective of society. The process of entering the ethical understanding of individual life is also entered through the perspective of society. Creators pay attention to the lives of individuals with the help of different social ideologies, and in essence, the relationship between society and individuals is presented in the text. However, the individual ethics problem defined here is completely based on the individual's self-life. This is an ethical construction process that examines the relationship between the individual and society from an individual perspective. This approach largely separates ideological discourse from society, focusing instead on the expression of individual ethics within the self-life. In the novels, most characters transition to social life after developing their individual ethics. The concept of individual ethics explored here emphasizes the interplay between the individual and society. Shaped by the individual's self-life experiences, it primarily influences their understanding of existence. Following this ethical development, the individual applies this self-knowledge to the construction of social life. Rather than being a total catharsis of the self or a judgment imposed by society, it represents a natural part of life and a response to the modern individual's lack of life experience.

A personal code of ethics is a set of principles that an individual creates to establish a moral framework for their actions and define their values. It reflects an individual's value system, moral standards, and professional background. Individuals can create their personal code of ethics by reflecting on their beliefs, experiences, and core values. An effective personal code of ethics should be relevant, use personal pronouns to express accountability, provide specific examples, and include reasons for beliefs. By having a personal code of ethics, individuals can have a clear set of principles to guide their behavior, make ethical decisions, and enhance their overall motivation. Examples of personal ethics may include honesty, loyalty, integrity, respect, selflessness, and responsibility. These ethics shape how individuals interact with others, make decisions, and conduct themselves in both personal and professional settings.

Individual ethics are essential because they affect personal integrity, character development, and relationships with others. Personal ethics serve as a guide for making ethical decisions, promoting trust and credibility, and maintaining consistent moral standards. They contribute to shaping an individual's identity and reputation in personal and professional settings. Adhering to personal ethics allows individuals to live in accordance with their values and encourages ethical behavior within society. It is important to note that personal ethics are intertwined with broader ethical frameworks and principles. Ethical theories and systems provide a foundation for understanding the nature of ethics and offer different perspectives on what constitutes morally right or wrong actions.

In summary, individual ethics refer to the moral principles and values that guide an individual's behavior, decision-making, and interactions with others. Personal ethics are shaped by an individual's beliefs, experiences, and values, and they play a crucial role in maintaining personal integrity, making ethical choices, and building meaningful relationships.

Chapter Three The Ethical Dilemma in The Cement Garden

Among McEwan's early works, one Gothic horror novel, *The Cement Garden*, has darkly romantic plots with the exploration of complex minds, unconscious desires, and internal conflicts, which earned the young author the nickname "Ian Macabre." In this novel, McEwan depicted the interpersonal relationships in an enclosed environment, "with shocking, morbid and full of repellent imagery." "It could be considered a treatment at greater length of familiar McEwan territory, including sibling rivalry, taboo sex, and the simmering threat of violence."[66]

The Cement Garden is a psychosexual tale of four British children who, fearful of being taken into foster care, hide their mother's death from the outside world by encasing her corpse in cement in the cellar. The story begins with Father, Mother, and their four children, Julie, Jack, Sue, and little Tom living together. When Father dies, Mother and the children are left alone. Mother grows increasingly sick day by day and soon dies. Jack and Julie decide to bury Mother in the basement and fill it with cement so that no one will ever know. Jack and Julie must now take care of the family and prevent the authorities from splitting them up.

The Cement Garden is a short novel, under 200 pages in most editions. A synopsis of *The Cement Garden* reveals all the necessary themes and plot events to analyze McEwan's literary take on domestic life in a postwar world.

Jack, an unsociable and isolated 14-year-old boy from a family of six, narrates McEwan's macabre story. Jack has three siblings: Julie, age 17; Sue, age 13; and Tom, age 6. The novel begins with Jack reflecting on how a large cement delivery led to his father's death. The father dies unexpectedly of a heart attack. After the father's death, the family stores the rest of the cement in the basement. Jack likes to play perverse games with Julie, Sue, and himself. Jack confesses his desire to see his older sister, Julie, naked. Julie is a popular athlete. Even though Julie has impressive achievements in sports, her father neglects her. Shortly after, Jack's mother becomes ill. Her worsening sickness brings the family more chaos.

Jack begins to masturbate more and more frequently. He destroys the garden with a sledgehammer. Julie and Jack assume the roles of mother and father because of their mother's bad condition. On her deathbed, Jack's mother makes Jack and Julie promise to hide her death for fear that the authorities may take over the family and split them up in foster care. When Jack's mother dies, Jack, Julie, and Sue bury their mother's corpse in the basement using the cement delivered earlier.

Jack's youngest sibling, Tom, reverts to acting like a baby because he wants to attract Julie's attention. Since Jack is jealous, he acts oddly without taking baths, which makes him increasingly emotionally isolated from the family. Sue takes journals every day and reads a lot. Julie has a boyfriend named Derek, who later finds out all the secrets in the family.

The house begins to fill with the smell of death from the decaying body in the basement. Derek grows increasingly suspicious of the children. Derek enters Julie's room and discovers the incest between Julie and Jack. At the end of the story, Derek reports to the police. As the only rational character, Derek ventures into the depths of a house that has become the children's prison of trauma.

The ending of *The Cement Garden* has prevalent Victorian motifs that place McEwan's debut novel in a Neo-Gothic tradition. The Gothic imagery and repression of sexual desire manifested McEwan's Victorian inspiration.

The comments on this debut novel are thought-provoking. Amy Taylor (1978) published her review in *The New York Times*: "This brief novel is really a kind of extended dream, although there's nothing dreamy about the precision and clarity of the writing ... *The Cement Garden* describes the process that steadily isolates these four children, until they're so absolutely alone and so at odds with the rest of the world that there is no way of returning to normal life ... what makes the book difficult is that these children are not—we trust—real people at all. They are so consistently unpleasant, unlikeable and bitter that we can't believe in them (even hardened criminals, after all, have some good points) and we certainly can't identify with them. Jack's eyes, through which we're viewing this story, have an uncanny ability to settle upon the one distasteful detail in every scene, to dwell on it, and to allow only that detail to pierce the cotton wool that insulates him… It seems weak-stomached to criticize a novel on these grounds, but if what we read makes us avert our gaze entirely, isn't the purpose defeated? Jack, we're being told, has been so damaged and crippled that there's no hope for him. But if it's a foregone conclusion that there's no hope whatsoever, we tend to lose hope in the book as well." Amy's views on the characters are the points to be discussed in this part.

Through exploring the horror and depravity in his novels, McEwan uses the absurd narrative technique to expose the distortion of human nature and ethical flaws. The "incestuous, violent, and twisted and psychopathic characters" are just like the "embodiments of our neighbors, our acquaintances, ourselves"[67]. An ethical relationship beyond the normal limits may evoke the readers' emotions on human relationships in an abnormal situation. McEwan chooses the first-person narration to reproduce the indifferent narrative voice of the character Jack. Living in the urban concrete jungle, Jack, who cut himself off from the outside world, is confronted with the imbalance of human nature and twisted family norms. He recounts the events that occurred to him and his family, especially his siblings after the death of his parents. His older sister Julie and younger siblings Sue and Tom are exposed to their own desires with no parents' custody. They are struggling to find the ethical relationship out of the unnatural world. Through the description of the horror stories of underage children, McEwan's humanistic awareness can be touched by the undisguised ethical truth.

The dark subject of *The Cement Garden* causes the reader to pander to the most depraved human desires. On the surface, Jack's family is a normal, urban family. However, beneath the visual facade of the family lies a dark mental state of distorted ethics. It truly reflects the state of modern individual psychology. It is of great significance for exploring the spiritual dilemma and family crisis of a common family. In McEwan's novels, the family is usually the core place where the plots are designed. The family relationship in the novel often deviates from the value standards of traditional family ethics. McEwan's early works focus on the distorted family ethical order in the individual crisis, the loss of the character's psychology and the confusion of self-consciousness caused by the split spirit, the choices made by the individual according to instinct or self-judgment that greatly damage the family ethics, and the loss of normal ethical order between family members. Family members often have a wrong understanding of their individual ethical identity, especially their responsibilities as parents. They become desolate and indifferent, and they close their emotions to outsiders. The novel shows a series of violations of ethical rules made by adolescents, shows their problems in ethical choices, their judgments of good and evil, and their individual identification, and reflects the importance of ethical awareness in the process of adolescent growth.[68] Therefore, the binding power which can restrict wrongdoings from happening gradually loses its function, and distorted ethical behaviors turn up. Ethical dislocation may take place. In short, the crisis within individual ethics is the most crucial cause of the disorder of family ethics.

Section One   The Morbid Family Ethics

At the beginning of the novel, the family is living "the humdrum life of the English lower-middle class,"[69] with conventional gender roles. The father, who dominates the family, was cementing the garden when he suddenly died of a heart attack. The mother, passively accepting her family role, dies of illness soon after. The children decide to seal the body in the basement with the cement mix left over from their father's unfinished garden project, so that they will not be separated by the authorities. After their parents' death, Julie and Jack take over the role of mother and father to their younger brother and sister. Eventually they find themselves sexually attracted to each other. Sue, the younger sister, is withdrawn and given to writing in her diary, and Tom, the younger brother, "regresses into his infantile world and likes to be mothered."[70]

Taruna Choudhary Dhall[71] believes that a child's earliest education is received in their family, and their physical, mental, and emotional potentialities reflect the characteristics of their forebears. Parents play an irreplaceable role in children's growth, and meanwhile, in the formation of children's social norms and values. "Values especially of a traditional or conservative kind which are held to promote the sound functioning of the family and to strengthen the fabric of society" (Webster definition).[72] There is always a natural and inseparable connection between parents and children, and giving love and guidance to children is an important part of parental ethical responsibility; children learn their conventional values and code of conduct by observing their parents' behaviors. In this process, children will gradually trust their parents and then form a benign parent-child relationship. If parents neglect their own ethical responsibilities due to emotional indifference and selfishness, the child will become the most innocent victim. The failure of parents as the model of the children or the absence of the parents can both cause ethical dislocation in a family.

Failure to establish a satisfactory relationship with the objects in the outer world, the child will turn to their internalized world to reactivate a safe set of contacts in their psyche with their incorporated objects[73]. In *The Cement Garden*, the redefinition of the concept of traditional family and the reconstruction of family ethics can be glanced at. This pair of father and mother possess different roles in the family. The father acts as a dominator who wants to control everything, whereas the mother is a subordinate who accepts all in silence. When in contact with children, their opposite personalities and status in the family lead to distinct relations between family members: the alienation from the father and excessive attachment but disrespect for the mother cause ethical issues in the family. The father-son relationship and mother-son relationship in *The Cement Garden* deeply reflect McEwan's profound concern for family ethics.

I. Father-Son Relationship

Jack describes his father as a "frail, irascible, obsessive man."[74] Since ancient times, power dynamics have existed within the family, with men and elders often exerting dominance over women and children. However, as society has developed, traditional power structures have increasingly manifested in the hegemonic control of men or elders over other family members. This form of alienated power erodes the physical and psychological well-being of other family members, disregarding their rights and interests, which ultimately disrupts the balance of familial power relations. In the novel, the father, as an authoritarian figure, exercises his will arbitrarily, commanding his wife and children, and strictly controlling the children's behavior.

The father exerts autocratic control over the entire family, a form of authority that creates distance between him and the other family members. His strict and rigid demeanor towards the mother and children fosters an atmosphere of familial disharmony. An abnormal relationship between the father and mother often leads to a rift and estrangement between parents and children. Moreover, this hegemonic mindset further erodes familial harmony and distorts the natural ethical order within the family.

Indulging in his course, the father does not care about family members' states of mind or advice, and he treats them in a stiff way. Because of fear, children have to alienate themselves from Father, so that the distant relations between Father and sons turn up. In *The Cement Garden*, Jack thinks his father's death "seemed insignificant."[75]

Jack's abnormal behavior is caused by his parents and the inharmonious atmosphere in the family. Parents will directly affect the formation of children's healthy psychology and personality. He is emotionally underdeveloped just because of his father. In Klein's view, the role of a father in the child's life and their adult relationships is understood as "the very important part which the father plays in the child's emotional life which also influences all later love relations, and all other human associations."[76] Through establishing family discipline, and forcing other family members to accept various pressures, restrictions or obligations, the father constantly disciplines the children's actions, wills and words. The father infiltrates his power into every part of the daily life of other family members so as to maintain his absolute authority.

This arrogant husband does not respect his wife and only cares about his own so-called course—to build a cement garden. He makes an arbitrary decision to buy a lorry of cement without informing his wife. Considering the family's economy, the mother advises him to send these bags back but only receives his brief refusal: "out of the question." The children talk of their parents' relationship, saying that "secretly they had hated each other and that Mother was relieved when Father died," and they don't think "Mum ever really liked Dad."[77] The father's patriarchy is also perceived from his stern attitude towards children. Jack complains that his father is strict with Tom, "always going on at a needling sort of way." He uses the mother against Tom to fight for Tom's love for the mother. Besides, he is keen on playing some jokes to laugh at the children. Jack's sister Julie held the local under-eighteen records for the 100- and 220-yard sprints. "She could run faster than anyone I knew. Father never took her seriously." "He refused to come with us to the sports meeting" and said it was "daft in a girl, running fast" (25).

Since the father never considers the feelings of the children, quarrels with the mother in front of the children, and does not allow the children to bring any friends to the house, the father is portrayed in *The Cement Garden* as a harsh and ruthless defender of established regulations. His infringement on family members forces their emotions and compassion to disappear, causing the family members to hurt each other, insult each other, and later making the ethical dislocation an inevitable consequence. Jack's psychological inversion and indifference largely result from lacking the love and caring from the father.

When Jack is asked to give a hand to his father, he only does a small fraction of the work while the father is doing this work without stopping. When carrying the sacks in the face of his father, he thinks that his father is delaying and considers, "If I was to do more, then I waited him to acknowledge it out loud." He is always pondering how to release his work even though he knows his father's bad physical condition. "Because of his heart attack my father was forbidden this sort of work, but I made sure he took as much weight as I did" (18). He calmly sees his father lean with one hand against the wall, "breathing heavily" and "coughing loudly" on his way up the stairs due to running out of strength. During the work, they prefer to stay silent rather than talk with each other. "I was pleased that we knew so exactly what we were doing and what the other was thinking that we did not need to speak" (22). Silence makes Jack feel at ease. Even after the father's death, Jack feels calm and peaceful. He has nothing on his mind, but picks up the plank and erases the impression of his father from the soft and fresh concrete calmly.

II. Mother-Son Relationship

Traditionally, women have been defined by the roles of "good wife and mother," characterized by dependence and subordination within the family, often expected to make sacrifices for other family members. They are required to be nurturing, empathetic, and, at times, obedient. In contrast, men are portrayed as strong, independent, and assertive, occupying dominant roles. This traditional family and social ethic can, in some cases, give rise to distorted or harmful phenomena.

In contrast to the father's dominant position within the family, the mother appears submissive. Faced with the father's anger, she remains silent, accepting his bad temper without protest. The portrayal of the weary mother in the novel, who endlessly dedicates herself to family matters, highlights the helpless situation of women within the family structure. Traditionally seen as the symbol of warmth, the mother in the novel, under the father's oppression, is too exhausted to provide the nurturing love and affection expected of her, which leads to a strained and distorted relationship between her and the children. Moreover, the father competes for the mother's attention, often "using her against Tom" to gain her favor, yet "she took all this in silence" (199). This unequal relationship between the parents, along with the father's dismissive attitude toward the mother, inevitably shapes the children's perceptions and attitudes toward her. The couple's dysfunctional marriage and absurd behavior contribute to the breakdown of familial ethics, ultimately leading to a disruption of the natural family order and, as a consequence, incest.

Due to the contradictory images of a strict father and a soft mother, the boys in the family generate Oedipal love towards the mother. When Jack is 8 years old, he pretends to be ill and rushs home from school to enjoy his mother's love. "She knows that I have come home to monopolize her when my father and two sisters are away." Later, after his mother's death, Jack transfers his Oedipus complex to Julie. This suggests that the son is unable to experience the love of his mother in a typical manner, resulting in an abnormal relationship between them. Although the mother is aware that her son's behavior should be corrected, she remains passive and does nothing. The mother's recognition of the dysfunctional relationship within the family contributes to her son's distorted attitudes toward ethical norms, which further influences his aberrant behavior.

Jack's physical growth indulges him in masturbation all day, which brings his mother extreme anxiety about his health. The insufficient communication between the mother and son makes this situation even more awkward. The mother undertakes a talk with Jack in order to persuade Jack to control "doing that." Jack describes his feeling that "my heart was beating very fast, I stared past her head at the ceiling" (34). The conversation, in which the gentle and passive mother attempts to offer care and guidance to her son, ultimately reveals her lack of authority in educating him. That he dodges the eye contact with the mother makes her continuously use "you" as the beginning of her speech in order to ask for his son's attention to his own health condition. However, due to insufficient daily communication between the mother and Jack, both of them do not know how to clearly express themselves and fully understand each other. Each time, she expresses her intentions implicitly, rather than making them explicit. Her hesitation confuses Jack. Crucially, Mother has inculcated some incorrect concepts to Jack that "every time ... You do that (masturbation), it takes two pints of blood to replace it" (35), and ends her talk in a hurry by saying that "One day, when you're twenty-one, you'll turn round and thank me for telling you what I've been telling you" (35). The mother does not give any further explanation on that point, but escapes from the kid's doubt and puts the answer to the time when Jack is twenty-one. Her equivocation makes the relationship between mother and son more embarrassing. "I avoided being alone with my mother in case she spoke to me again" (38).

Not a long time after Father's death, Mother is badly sick and bedridden due to an unknown disease. When the mother mentions that she has to go away soon, Jack asks a few questions: "Where?", "How long for?" and "When do you go in?". He earnestly wishes that his mother would go earlier, and "a sense of freedom was tugging at my concern" (8), rather than care for her health. The absence of the father's guidance and love, coupled with the silent and passive nature of the mother, shapes Jack's narcissistic personality, which ultimately leads him to derive masochistic satisfaction. He enjoys the sense of freedom and control within the family. Rather than expressing concern about his mother's illness, Jack is more focused on having his authority in the family acknowledged by Julie, seeking validation of his position.

    The contrasting personalities of the parents undoubtedly shape their children's outlook on life and values. Jack's indifference to his mother's illness highlights a flaw in his ethical upbringing. The mother's natural timidity and the father's tyranny give rise to two polarities. A stern father brings kids infinite fear and lack of security, whereas a kind but cowardly mother makes the kids compete for her concern. Excessive love for children, in essence, can cause an unhealthy attitude towards relationships, which will drive people into choosing to ignore the rules in society at their own will. The absence of the father's guidance and the mother's excess love finally cultivate Jack's selfishness and ignorance. Many of his actions have ignored reason, rules and consequences. Jack shows indifference and estrangement in the face of their autocratic father, and presents ignorance of their tender mother's care. In the end, the death of the father is "insignificant." When the mother dies, Jack feels that he is free from the restriction: "beneath my strongest feelings was a sense of adventure and freedom which I hardly dared admit to myself and which was derived from the memory of that day five years ago" (73). The insufficient concern and love from his family cause the ethical flaw, which in turn leads to the distortion and absence of people's natural emotions. The youngest son, Tom, also experiences distorted and perverted emotions. He exhibits a clear Oedipal complex towards his mother, consistently seeking comfort from her, as though the world around him is inherently insecure and hostile. Children in the family of authoritarian parents are usually required to be in complete obedience; their freedom is restricted by the parents. And the children in a family with permissive parents usually have complete freedom, but they are inclined to depend on their parents.[78] In *The Cement Garden*, the father is authoritative, who frequently forces the children to do everything according to his willingness and is always trying to establish his authority by all means that are unreasonable, but meanwhile, the mother is permissive and indulges the children a lot. They neglect the necessity of establishing correct relationships with family members and with the outside world, which hinders children's ability to form social connections.

In the novel, McEwan emphasizes the significance of parental care and correct guidance because without them, children can go astray easily. Children's misconceptions about proper relationships, especially about sexuality and love, finally result in the dislocation of ethical identities and the failure in ethical selection. These make Jack unable to establish good interpersonal relationships with his own siblings, let alone with other people.

III. Brothers-Sisters Relationship

The misalignment and distortion of gender ethics represent the most disturbing aspect of the novel. The siblings' progression from innocent sexual exploration to shocking incest is deeply unsettling, and even Tom, who is only five or six years old, becomes gender-confused under the influence of this abnormal ethical environment. Jack's descriptions about his siblings show the defects in his character and cognition. His values and judgments are underdeveloped due to his age and family education respectively. "A person who suffers from an inferiority complex is always looking for the easiest way out, and sometimes finds this by excluding most aspects of life and exaggerating sexuality."[79] This statement is exactly the portrayal of Jack. He is ignored not only by his classmates, but also coolly by his siblings. Even though he tries hard to get mingled with his siblings, his odd behavior keeps him away from his family and the outside world.

Siblings are supposed to care and support each other, but in *The Cement Garden*, indifference is a common response to each other in the family. Jack states, "I had some status at school as Julie's brother but she never spoke to me or acknowledged my presence." In order to attract their attention, Jack goes to the kitchen with an apple picked out in a bowl; he "slouched in the doorway," keeps tossing the apple in his hand, and "catching it with crisp smacks against the palm." After receiving his sister's refusal, he "slammed the front door hard and crossed the road."[80] This description clearly shows that he is disliked by his siblings, and alienation has been a common scene in the family. In Jack's cognition, "Father never took her (Julie) seriously" and "He'd (Tom in dress) look bloody idiotic" (55).

Compared with Jack's narrative of his parents, he becomes even more indifferent in describing his time with his siblings. From Jack's account, he makes various efforts to fit into and get along with his brother and sisters, seeking his identity and belonging among his sisters in a pandering and flattering way. "I felt easier with Sue. She was two years younger than I, and if she had secrets I was not intimidated by them" (30). The hostile relationship between the family members has been revealed implicitly by Jack's usage of "intimidate." Julie and Sue have been consciously or unconsciously rejecting Jack, causing Jack to disguise himself in front of his sisters to get their love. This sibling love evolves into a power struggle between Jack and Julie. During her mother's illness, Julie uses the power her mother gives her to control Jack. After his mother's death, Jack was very hostile to Julie's "power," and they quarreled several times over the issue of pocket money. He is overwhelmed by his failure and totally at a loss when "she unwound the ribbon from her finger and draped it round my neck"; he didn't take it off because he would become "a spectator again." When Julie and Sue are crying over their mother's death, Jack appears so restless. "I watched my sisters crying; I sensed it would seem hostile to look elsewhere. I felt excluded but I did not wish to appear so" (62). In order to win Julie and Sue's attention, Jack "simply gave up all routines of personal hygiene," arguing that "[i]f people really liked me, they would take me as I was" (26). It turns out that Julie and Sue make excuses not to go to school with him, and avoid being seen with him.

In narrating his relationship with his younger brother Tom, Jack shows his carelessness and indifference, too. When his younger brother Tom is bullied at school, he describes his brother's tragic experience from a bystander point of view: "Once he was cleaned up, he did not look so badly hurt, and the sense of drama ebbed away." (54) There is a disapproval of the brotherhood flowing between the lines. Jack, like the father he describes, competing with Tom for the love of his mother and later of "Julie," treats Tom with no love nor patience. Jack once comes home from school to monopolize his mother's lover while other family members are out of the house. He even mistakes a woman on the street for his mother and Julie, which implies his fantasy about his mother and sister. After the mother's death, Tom "went to Julie most often when he wanted attention" (66), and he "had made up his mind that Julie was to take care of him now" (66). Inwardly, Jack considers, "Tom, of course, wanted Julie all to himself" (123). As a little boy of six, Tom can't understand the true meaning of losing both parents. He has to find a "surrogate mother" to obtain warmth and emotional support. Therefore, Tom and Jack have to transfer their Oedipus complex from Mother to Julie, which in turn causes an abnormal sibling relationship. Julie changes since their mother died, and she becomes gentle and soft, just like her dead mother. Julie takes Tom in her arms, "[resting] one hand on the small of his back" (119). Tom "sat swaying slightly as Julie unbuttoned his dress" (119), as if Tom is showing off his victory in monopolizing "mother's love." On this occasion, Jack is ignored by Tom and Julie. Tom "did not seem to notice that I had come in and went on making small sucking noises with his thumb." Jack "could not resist watching them together." Julie seems to enjoy her new role of being a mother, especially when she sees Tom and Jack fight for her love; she "seemed to enjoy an audience, and she made jokes about it." She laughs, "What am I going to do with the two of you?" (123). Julie and Tom's adaptation to their new identities as mother and son, and Jack's jealousy of their close relationship are the embodiments of their deviant sibling relationship.

  Kinship is always regarded as the most intimate relationship among family members. In a family, it has to be the most caring and relaxing environment; however, Jack's situation makes it hard to please his sisters. It shows that the ethical relationship between brothers and sisters in the novel is distorted and pathological. Moreover, this psychological crisis of self-isolation eventually triggered the degradation of Jack's lifestyle: his body became dirtier—"yellow teeth, smelly feet, dirty fingernails and long, greasy hair." In addition to that, he feels life is so meaningless and even loses interest in masturbation. "As far as I was concerned, there was not much point in getting up. There was nothing particularly interesting to eat, and I was the only one with nothing to do." (93) "I stopped masturbating. I did not feel like it anyway." (121). This degradation makes Jack even more lonely. Apparently, he had forgotten his mother's instructions to him before her death—"The house must be run properly, Jack, and Tom has to be looked after" (59). The indifference and disregard for family members greatly hinder the mutual affection among them and prevent solid and lasting healthy emotional relationships. Their remote relationship totally differs from that in normal families, which demonstrates the ethical deviation of sisters and brothers' relationships.

As for Tom, in order to avoid being bullied by others, he wants to protect himself under the cover of a dress. On this matter, Julie has "a theoretical discussion" with Jack. During the discussion, Julie believes that "[i]t would be for Tom, to look like a girl." On the contrary, Jack holds that Tom would be idiotic and stupid. "It's humiliating to look like a girl, because you think it's humiliating to be a girl." (55) They argue a lot on the point of what Tom would be like—beautiful or not, humiliating or not. Two sisters, Julie and Sue, denote their inclination to help Tom satisfy his aspiration. However, Jack's objection to Tom's transvestitism is simply out of the reason that it will make him "look stupid" (55), not because it will cause harm to Tom's future personality development, or physical and mental health. In the face of this issue, family members ought to have given Tom proper guidance, and helped him to establish correct gender identity consciousness. The misguidance exhibited by the sibling in relation to the younger brother's cognitive development underscores a significant ethical dilemma within their familial relationship. Due to being regarded as a bothersome adolescent and even despised by his family members, Jack experiences profound alienation from his sisters. He, in turn, perceives them and his brother as inconsequential strangers. He regards Julie as an object of sexual fantasy and a competitor of the householder rather than a sister. Without their parents' proper instruction on Jack's sex education, he forms his own understanding of sex and sexual ethics. At the moment of his father's death, Jack masturbates for the first time and has an ejaculation, which indicates the growth of the young generation to substitute the old. This portrayal, introduced from the outset, subtly suggests a deeply troubling ethical framework. To a significant extent, it serves as the foundation for the impending ethical chasm—embodied in the incestuous act that Jack and Julie are about to perpetrate. The distorted family ethics will lead directly to the ethical dislocation of sex. The children in the "cement garden" do not have any normal ethical concepts, and they are indulged in absurd games that abandon all normal ethical concerns. At the beginning of the novel, when the parents are fighting and quarreling, the children cannot give any sympathy and comfort to the disadvantaged mother. "Julie, Sue and I slipped away upstairs to Julie's bedroom and closed the door ... We rapidly stripped Sue of her clothes and when we were pulling down her pants our hands touched" (15). In the game, Jack can explore his sister's private parts unscrupulously, and meanwhile, he is thinking of Julie. When their father dies, the game ceases. One day when Jack tickles Julie, "as I moved forward to be in a better position to hold her down, I felt hot liquid spreading over my knee" (37). Though there is no actual sexual intercourse happening, this event turns into reality at the end of the novel. In addition to Jack's incestuous behavior with Julie, there is also a perverted sexual relationship between him and his sister Sue. When the children opened their mother's door after their mother's death, "I thought of Sue and myself as a married couple about to be shown into a sinister hotel room."

When his parents are alive, Jack's sexual fantasies about Julie are repressed because of their parents' constraints. Shortly after his mother's death, his deeply buried Oedipus complex is transferred to Julie without guilt, which finally leads to the incest he and Julie commit while Tom and Derek are present. Jack and Julie successfully transform into a host and hostess in the family. Describing the motivation for his narrative, McEwan said, "I had an idea that in the nuclear family the kind of forces that are being suppressed—the oedipal, incestuous forces—are also paradoxically the very forces which keep the family together."[81] In the morbid, absurd and deteriorated ethical relationships, the kinship becomes inextricably intertwined with the pathological manifestation of the Oedipus complex and incest.

Section Two   Ethical Flaws in Social Relationships

The environment in which the children are nurtured exerts a significant influence on the development of their personalities. A harmonious neighborhood, in some way, can facilitate the children's healthy development. Modern society tends to view industrialization as a force that advances civilization, as a positive development in human history. It has undoubtedly improved living conditions and catered to materialistic desires. However, as one of the fundamental social units within this process, the family is gradually eroded by materialism, which fosters emotional detachment and indifference among its members. "The novel remains a work of art, a creation, but in Britain it never ceases (as it often does in France) to be closely linked to the real. It serves as an opportunity to question the society which we have formed, its mechanisms and its blockages."[82] The blockade of human nature creates indifference and hostility between people. The metaphor of the hard cement covering the lawn in the garden implies that human nature is concealed and even destroyed. People lose basic trust and mutual assistance. Influenced by this ethical thinking, children who are not instructed to learn the basic principles and protocols of sociality properly may hold a hostile attitude to the world. In *The Cement Garden*, instead of receiving love and advice from their parents, the children are left to figure out how to survive by themselves. The "cement garden" is like a deserted island standing alone on a moral wasteland. Usually, the garden, which is assumed to be a relaxing place where people can get close to nature, has to live with grass and flowers. However, here, applying the "cement" before the garden is counterproductive to people's original intention. Men's original enthusiasm and warmth have been covered by hard cement. While Jack is quite excited because spreading the mixed cement over the leveled garden was a "fascinating violation." In his deep sense, his carelessness and indifference to nature can be seen from his expression about the destruction of nature. The cement is cold and lifeless, enclosing people in their own zone and cutting their connection with the outside world. In this environment, these four children seem to be immune to all the elements of civilization. McEwan depicts the children's abnormal development in the enclosed area with sympathy.

In a modern city, people are not far from each other. "The city becomes a tangible entity, encroaching upon and interfering with individual lives and relationships."[83] However, the family in this novel lives in a house that stands alone in the ruins of the block, away from other households. It is excluded from civilized society. A family of six creates a more closed and isolated family environment, which highlights the psychological crisis of family members: being away from the external environment. From the perspective of the family's internal environment, the home's garden is surrounded and covered with cement, uninterrupted by the outside world. "Individual psychology accepts the viewpoint of the complete unity and self-consistency of the individual whom it regards and examines as socially embedded. We refuse to recognize and examine an isolated human being."[84]

While cutting themselves off from society, in what way can the children form healthy social ethics?

McEwen further excavated the distortion of interpersonal relationships by the closed psychology of the self, especially in the family, where it is difficult for individuals not to empathize with other family members. In this psychological crisis, the individual not only rejects the care of others for himself, but also ignores the needs of others due to excessive emphasis on his own feelings and central position, and the intimate relationship of the family is gradually disintegrated. Among them, especially the eldest son, Jack, is represented.

I. Indifference and Untrustworthiness of Human Nature

From the description at the beginning of the story, it can be inferred that Jack's family lives in an urban area. "Our house had once stood in a street full of houses. Now it stood on empty land where stinging nettles grew round torn corrugated tin." (27) With the development of modern science and industrialization, the surroundings are torn out for urban construction. "The other houses were knocked down for a motorway they never built." (27-28) These "never-built" motorways deprive the neighborhood of its liveliness and vitality and make it into a wasteland. Jack and his family are living in a wasteland, isolated from the outside world. His living situation deprives Jack of the chance to get along with others. The four children without parents' supervision live in such an extreme isolation and alienation area in which no one cares.

"No one ever came to visit us. Neither my mother nor my father when he was alive had any real friends outside the family. They were both only children, and all my grandparents were dead. My mother had distant relatives in Ireland whom she had not seen since she was a child. Tom had a couple of friends he sometimes played with in the street, but we never let him bring them in the house. There was not even a milkman in our road now. As far as I could remember, the last people to visit the house had been the ambulance men who took my father away"(28). The process of industrialization and urbanization accelerates the alienated and remote relationship between individuals. This issue of the modern world revealed in *The Cement Garden* by McEwan is shocking and terrifying.

In essence, the "cement garden" itself is the epitome of the postmodern urban ethical ecology. People are greatly affected by materialism, which leads to differences and untrustworthiness. Let alone the four children living in the isolated house with no parents' guardian. Dehumanization is a consequence of this inundating modern metropolis with ruthlessly cold cement buildings. The children in the "cement garden" are completely distorted by the cold world, and the distorted emotional and ethical orientations put these children in panic-inducing chaos. The chaos in the family finally generates serious unethical behaviors.

When Jack's father decides to cover the lawn completely with cement, "to surround the house, front and back, with an even plane of concrete" (21), he is destroying nature, replacing it with hard and cold concrete. It seems that he is depriving the garden of vitality, but metaphorically, he is depriving the family of its natural function and harmony. In the process of expelling the flowers and plants from the garden, Father deprives the last purity and innocence of the children, making them cold as concrete. For the long-ill mother, the children have never had the slightest worry and concern. The most direct reaction to the mother's imminent death is not the worry about the mother's illness and the pain of the mother's death, but the hope that the mother will never come back, so they can enjoy the so-called freedom from the mother's absence. When it is confirmed that the mother is dead, the children's first concern is who will take charge of the keys of the house. The intergenerational relationship between mother and child presents a cold emotional void. After the death of the parents, without proper guidance, the children have no access to social ethics and moral principles. The children's indifference and recklessness force them to give up the social norms. In this chaos, they have created a new standard of their own that is totally unacceptable to outsiders and commit serious mistakes.

Human beings are social animals who grow up and develop along with social interaction with others. However, in *The Cement Garden*, Jack's family is alienated from the outside world and isolated from society. They lose contact with other people. Jack's father and mother once attended a relative's funeral. Instead of taking the chance to educate the children about the proper manners when someone is passing away, they don't mention anything about the funeral. While the children are very excited about the transient freedom they can get when their parents are away. They have had a pillow fight. Who died "meant very little to his parent" and "meant nothing" to the children. Their unhealthy family ethics has left the children with a wrong understanding of the mutual communication between people. Therefore, there are no visitors ever coming to their home. The mother lets her life wither in loneliness in the indifferent "cement garden." She does not trust anyone. Even in the period of the mother's serious illness, nobody else outside his family comes to visit. When she is alive, the mother and Jack go to the pharmacy for her prescription. His mother said, "Oh, they're all talking rubbish. I've done with the lot of them" (41). Other than educating their children to get along with others, the mother gives their children wrong perceptions about the world. They rely on themselves and decline to establish any contact with the outsiders. When the mother told the older children about the issue of family responsibilities before her death, once again, she expressed her distrust of the society and her concerns about strangers breaking into the house. She stressed that the children must keep the family clean. Otherwise, "the house would stand empty, the word would get around and it wouldn't be long before people would be breaking in, taking things, smashing everything up" (59). The mother believes that the people outside are all barbaric and greedy, treating the weak mercilessly. As a result of the education they have received, children never think of seeking help for their mother's illness and death. "Because there were no visitors, there was no one to ask what was wrong with her, and so I did not really put the question clearly to myself" (228). The indifference and hostility between people in society are vividly displayed, which will oblige the children to be hostile to the world. After the death of the mother, the children believe that "people will break in, there'll be nothing left" (66). "Those kids will come in and smash everything up" (67). The children have no choice but to bury their mother inside the cement in the cellar. "Trust is one of the most important comprehensive forces in society. Without general trust among people, society itself becomes a mess, and almost no universal trust is based solely on an exact understanding of others. If trust can't be as strong as rational evidence or personal experience, almost all relationships can't last."[85] During their most desperate times, the government and social institutions, meant to provide assistance, often fail to materialize, leaving individuals to fend for themselves. Paradoxically, it is during these moments of distress that the police, representing the state apparatus, tend to intervene, assuming control over the situation.

Because of the long-time alienated life from the outside world, the children in the family have distorted social norms in their understanding about normal social interactions. When Jack notices that Julie has received a pair of leather boots as a gift, he has many questions. "Where did you get these?" "In a shop," Julie said without turning round. "How much?" "Not much." "They cost thirty-eight pounds." When Jack hears the price, his instinct response is that "If you didn't buy them," I said, "then you must have nicked them." "Can't you think of another way?" I shook my head. "There isn't another way, unless you made them yourself." Julie laughed. "Hasn't anyone ever given you a present?" (89) From Jack's perception, an item can only be obtained by buying, stealing or making it by hand, and he has never thought that it can also be given as a gift. Because of her father's aversion to noise and chaos, Sue's eight-year-old birthday party is the last party for the family. Sue recalls that "No one came to our house" (21) and "I didn't have any close friends at school" (19).This causes Jack to rarely accept gifts and not to have a deep understanding of the concept of giving gifts.

Jack's poor knowledge of social communication causes another failed social activity. Derek, Julie's boyfriend, takes Jack out to play snooker with his friends in a bar. Playing snooker is something Derek knows well, so he can manage it with ease. Compared to Derek's rich activities, Jack only does one thing—observation. Jack's lack of communicative ability to have a natural conversation with other people is presented to the reader. For him, everything surrounding him is unfamiliar. He almost keeps in dead silence except to give answers to Derek's inquiry about his family. "I felt sick. I leaned back against a pillar and looked up at the ceiling." "I felt like leaving" (116). He is very uncomfortable being with strangers and can hardly have a normal connection with them. When Derek, on a whim, wants his friends to make fun of Jack, he feels sore and would like to cry. "Water was collecting in one eye, and though I snatched at the tear as soon as it rolled out" (117). Jack fully exposes his uneasiness by feeling "hot and sick" and "something heavy and dark was pressing down on me" (117). The long-time seclusion from the outside world disables Jack of normal communication skills, and even Julie, the most normal person in the family, has been affected by the habitual seclusion and distrust of the outsiders. Once Derek talked about moving into the house, but Julie was repulsed and said, "He's getting on my nerves" (319). The family's deliberate seclusion from the outside world profoundly impacts the psychological and social development of the children, rendering them isolated, emotionally stunted, and unable to navigate normal social interactions. This insular environment deprives them of opportunities to engage with diverse perspectives and form meaningful connections beyond the confines of their family, fostering an insularity that warps their understanding of ethical and social relationships.

At its core, this seclusion cultivates a distorted moral compass. Shielded from the norms, values, and mutual obligations of broader society, the children are left to internalize a skewed sense of right and wrong shaped solely by their isolated familial dynamics. This detachment not only inhibits their ability to participate in the social fabric but also creates a breeding ground for mistrust, alienation, and ultimately, a breakdown in ethical relationality. Such an environment reflects how the lack of exposure to a shared moral framework can lead to the disintegration of both individual morality and the broader ethical relationships that bind society together.

The estrangement of society strengthens the disorder of normal interpersonal communication and causes a crisis of faith. Indifference and violence have taken place in every part of society. One day Jack leaves the house and wanders in the street. At the footbridge, he mistakes the woman in red for his mother first and his sister Julie later. He runs under the bridge and frightens the woman by saying, "I ain't got any money, so don't you come near me." (84) She takes Jack as a robber. Mistaking one for another is normal in society and saying sorry will resolve the awkwardness. In the novel, the incident uncovers a profound societal issue: within this neighborhood, the traditional bonds of community have eroded. Neighbors, once a source of mutual care and support, have become estranged, treating one another with indifference or even hostility. This breakdown of trust at the community level reflects a deeper psychological and moral crisis.

Individuals who fail to develop a foundational sense of trust during childhood struggle to cultivate a well-rounded character, often approaching others with suspicion rather than openness. In a society marked by emotional coldness and social detachment, individuals are no longer compelled to adhere to established norms to sustain interpersonal relationships. When the moral fabric of a community weakens and social norms lose their regulatory power, ethical boundaries become fragile. This erosion of communal and individual responsibility creates fertile ground for ethical transgressions, as individuals prioritize self-interest over collective well-being. The absence of trust and moral accountability not only alienates people from one another but also threatens the ethical cohesion necessary for a functioning and humane society.

II. Ecological Disorder Reflected from *The Cemented Garden*

In *The Cement Garden*, the image "cement and garden" is the premise and foundation of the entire emotional system. Literally, cement and garden, an ecological paradox, are a pair of contradictory things. The former represents industrial civilization, while the latter represents natural civilization. The combination of the two heralds the trampling of industrial civilization on natural civilization. Industrial civilization means arbitrariness, barbarism, indifference, stubbornness, isolation, and natural civilization, representing freedom, innocence, enthusiasm, and kindness, is ruthlessly snuffed out by industrial civilization. Therefore, when the cement itself, which represents modern architecture and modern lifestyle, replaces the garden, it means that modern people's way of living has been greatly influenced by modern industrialization and civilization. The city is a large modern garden made of cement, the speed of urban construction is amazing, and the development of modern civilization is also commendable. The city's original harmonious and beautiful part is under the destruction of scientific and technological civilization, and the city's own rich cultural heritage has been seriously weakened, including neighborhood culture. Because of the hard and cold nature of cement, it is difficult for people who seem to enjoy the fruits of modern civilization happily on the surface to give each other a sense of truth. Cement destroys the city's organic and harmonious construction, turning healthy people into atomized machines in an individualized society. They are driven by the fast speed of modern life and have long lost their pursuit of a pastoral life. In order to accelerate the process of civilization, people make nature into a construction site without considering the effects on nature. All the characters in the novel have been more or less eroded by industrial civilization, forming a resistance to natural civilization. The houses in the neighborhood are knocked down for the "four twenty-story tower blocks." Whatever the reason is, the construction stops and the land is wasted. In the family, the father uses cement to cover the garden, and due to his sudden death, the project is also wasted. Cement has special implications and symbolism whose meaning has been used to contradict nature. Cement causes the sudden death of the father, causing the mother's life to slowly wither in the midst of cement, causing Tom transvestite, and finally causing Jack and his sister Julie to commit incest.

The cement garden itself is a microcosm of the postmodern urban ethical ecology. The image of a "cement garden" symbolizes the strangulation of life, humanity and emotion by industrial civilization. Except for the ecological problems outside Jack's house in the pursuit of industrialization and civilization, his father is going to use cement to change nature. "When my father bought 15 bags of cement to fix the garden, his aim was to cover the lawn completely and build a cement platform around the house from front to back." "Mixing concrete and spreading it over a leveled garden was a fascinating violation." (21)

Cement will not only deprive various plants of free growth, but also deprive people of the space for the development of nature and human emotions. In the family, the father uses his autocracy to suppress children from their nature, just like he uses "cement" to cover the free growth of the grass. The father is "so convinced of the sanity of his ideas" that his persistent interference with nature makes him fall into the ethical abyss, which significantly affects his attitude towards his children. He defined children's natural happy behavior as "chaos." He prefers strict order with no feelings. From his viewpoint, the children's vigorous vitality is just like wildflowers and plants which need to be inhibited. In his family, he sets up the rules of the game, and the children have to line up neatly and wait quietly for their chance to play. They can't laugh and run and jump at their will, and this natural behavior will be severely stopped by the father. He suppresses the free spirit of children. He harbors hatred for natural, true emotional catharsis. Just like the garden where children can relax and play, now it is going to become a patch of land covered with hard cement. The father is going to "construct[ed] rather than cultivate[d] his garden according to plans" (19). To him, the garden is not the place serving for fun. Therefore, as a parent, he constructed the order he admired in the home and suppressed the nature of the children.

In addition to making rules for children at home, he does the same with their social life. He does not allow children to participate in any activities at school, nor does he allow the children to invite their friends to come over to their house. He doesn't come to the sports meeting to congratulate his daughter for winning the running race. On the contrary, he thinks it is stupid for a girl to run fast. He responds with ruthlessness and indifference to any achievements and joys made by the children because such a thing has nothing to do with his norms. He constructs a spiritual "cement garden" with cold "cement" in the children's minds, only allowing children to live according to the rules he established, never allowing anything outside the norm to happen. He is even more adamantly opposed to the children's act of making friends, and he stipulates that no one is allowed to bring their friends home. He strangles the children's nature with a cold order and the vitality of the children with precise norms, just as he strangles flowers and plants with cement.

The father uses cement to deprive happiness of the whole family. His obstinacy forces the family to suffer from the cold concrete. He successfully transformed his wife's beloved garden into a cement one without consulting her opinion in advance. He resolutely controls his wife's life and thoughts, and makes her a shadow of his. And the shadow is essentially what the father wants to achieve. He never expresses his emotional concern for his wife, and even when she is sick, he is still cold to her and fights with her. He rules his family as hard as the concrete with no emotion nor love at all. Compared with the cold father, the mother is like a weak plant, struggling to survive under the cement. She treats her children with love and tenderness—she carefully prepares birthday gifts for them and protects their natural character. She disputes with the father about the construction of a "cement garden" several times. Unfortunately, she is powerless in the face of hard and cold cement. The mother's attitude towards "cement" before her death is worth thinking about. After the death of the father, the children hate the "cement garden" built by their father, so they find a hammer to smash it. Her mother is desperate to stop it, saying that smashing the cement would give her a headache. She has now accepted the cement garden. The father succeeds in changing his wife with powerful cement "rules" and builds a "cement garden" in the mother's spiritual world.

The "cement garden" is built because of the father's panic about the thriving wildflowers and weeds. "Wildflowers and weeds" can be regarded as the representatives of exuberant nature. The completion of the "cement garden" is a metaphor for the success of the construction of modern industrialization and civilization. Nature is submitted to human construction. It is impossible for contemporary people living in "cement gardens" not to be affected by cement, so it is not uncommon to see modern people become cold and indifferent in such an environment. The father "had intended to build a high wall around his special world" (19). It is a reflection of modern people. People with distrust tend to enclose themselves in their own world, and cut themselves off from the outside world. As a result, people living in their "cement gardens" have lost their natural emotional pursuits and ethical orientations. The desertification of the individual spirit becomes an inevitable result.

The pace of construction of contemporary cities drives people to go crazy. In the end, their emotional well-being is no longer a consideration. People are accustomed to a sense of order and success in a well-ordered world. People gradually give up their pursuit of personal satisfaction and the pleasure of the soul. The well-ordered urban culture is so much like a garden covered in cement. The dislocation of ethics has generated a perverted sexual orientation, and utterly distorted family affection, which makes people unable to live a normal life. The cement-built city "took people completely out of nature, which led to depravity and ruins." In such a "cement" world, the ethics of the human world are plagued by cold feelings. The indifference and loneliness deprive people of sympathy and pity. "*The Cement Garden* is a book about the fears and yearnings of childhood and adolescence, and it, therefore, brings to mind many other novels concerned with children isolated from adults, most notably William Golding's *The Lord of the Flies*. However, whereas Golding's children run wild, fighting each other, McEwan's grow closer together, such that the reader is reminded how the adult world provides checks not on their natural aggression but on their natural sexuality."[86]

The grim portrayal of ethical dislocation in *The Cement Garden* serves as a powerful critique of the profound moral decay and ethical erosion prevalent in contemporary Western urban life. Through its dark and unsettling narrative, the novel exposes how the fragmentation of traditional values and the disintegration of communal bonds have led to a vacuum of moral accountability. In this ethically chaotic environment, the foundation of value orientation is not merely destabilized but entirely subverted, leaving individuals adrift in a world devoid of shared principles or purpose. This moral collapse extends beyond personal failings, representing a larger existential crisis where human dignity—the cornerstone of ethical existence—is mercilessly stripped away.

Chapter Four   The Temporal Paradox in *The Child in Time*

In McEwan's literary career, *The Child in Time*, written in 1987, is undoubtedly his transformational work. From "Ian Macabre" to an introspective writer, McEwan himself has said, "The turning point for me was *The Child in Time*, when political, moral, social, comic, and other possibilities moved in. Actually, it liberated me to try to capture a flow of thought. It was moving inwards in one sense."[87] "With none of his previous delight in things macabre, McEwan sets a story of domestic horror against a disorienting exploration in time, and ends up with a work of remarkable intellectual and political sophistication—his most expansive and passionate fiction to date."[88] Controversial intellectual Christopher Hitchens called *The Child in Time* Ian McEwan's literary masterpiece.

His change of theme and style is marked by his description of the youth after *The Cement Garden*. "McEwan's characters are adolescents; they bristle with the sudden violent consciousness of selfhood like a hatching pupa. Or they are children, prematurely burdened with egos that give them the wizened gravity of infants in Renaissance paintings. Or they are men whose bodies have grown but whose minds have never broken free of the appalling second womb of puberty. Cruelty comes easily to them: they can wound or kill with the offhand grace of animals for whom the self is the only reality. They are profoundly disturbed by their own capacity to love another, which creeps up on them from behind like a pad-footed intruder on their barred and bolted rooms."[89] Childs comments on ten of McEwan's novels, and his opinion on *The Child in Time* is captured in the chapter title "True Maturity."[90] Malcolm also describes *The Child in Time* as a novel that, "with its positive, adult ending, does mark a point of change in McEwan's fiction."[91]

Stephen and Julie's daughter Kate was kidnapped two years ago when

Stephen took her to the supermarket, and ever since then, the couple has fallen into a deep depression. Stephen becomes an empty shell who enjoys a title as a member of a child welfare committee but drinks scotch on the sofa and watches television to kill time all day long. Julie, on the other hand, moves out to a cottage, living in the extremity of her seclusion, and rarely contacts Stephen. Hence, the publisher Charles Darke becomes his only source of companionship. Having published his first novel, Charles is now a cabinet minister favored by the Prime Minister, and his wife, Thelma, is a quantum physicist who constructs her theories of time and space that time is flowing and amorphous. Anomalously, Charles resigns at some point and they move to the countryside. It is years later for Stephen to learn that Charles has ended his own life. At a pub named The Bell, Stephen experiences a bizarre hallucination that his own parents magically turn into a young couple, heavily implying that Stephen has actually traveled back to the moment he is in his mother's womb. The ending of the novel suggests a promising reconciliation between Stephen and his wife Julie, who makes a phone call to Stephen informing him that she is going to give birth to their baby.

McEwan conveys his understanding of time through the quantum physicist Thelma. He asserts that time is a relative concept, so the protagonist is able to realize time travel by appearing as both parent and child at varying stages. Besides, grief is the central theme in the novel. As in Stephen's case, he shows great rejection of grief before he accepts the fact that Kate has gone. The issue of Stephen and Julie's marriage disintegration after the kidnapping is also widely and deeply analyzed. There is an interesting study in human nature and our tendency to attribute blame to someone else for every event that occurs. It is noteworthy that in many real-life cases of child abduction or murder, many parents of snatched children end up in divorce because, even if not verbalized or expressed, blame is nonetheless felt—a powerful undercurrent that can upset the calmest of marital waters.

The novel begins in search of the child who disappears as the main line and ends with the birth of the child, and the "child" occupies a central place in the construction and theme of the structure. The theme of childhood is not only very prominent in *The Child in Time*, but also has considerable significance throughout McEwan's creative career. Most commentators point out from the difference between children and adults that the loss of the child symbolizes the loss of adult innocence. Everyone has a child in their heart that we should seek, recognize, and cherish, so adults should maintain the child's natural instincts and inner creativity against the depravity and alienation of modern human beings. In fact, instead of opposing children to adults, we should see childhood as a continuation of innocence and the state of nature. It is better to see it as a metaphor for the author to shift his gaze from the child and the inner world to reality and adult society. It is true that the childhood in McEwan's novels often expresses the author's nostalgia for escaping from time, but it is also self-knowledge and growth. The "child" eventually needs to take a step out of childhood to grow into adulthood.

The concept of individual ethics is the criterion that individuals follow when dealing with the relationship between individuals, between individuals and collectives, between individuals and society, and between individuals and nature, which is the basis for individuals to settle down and live for. The essence of individual ethics has some common features of binary opposition. In reality, people may have different kinds of binaries, like hard and soft, kind and evil. The characters in the literary works may have binary opposition features which will make the characters rich and round. The contrast will highlight the realistic features of the characters. A person may have two opposite aspects of individual ethics, while the binary opposition is very useful in the profound analysis of a person's character.

Binary opposition is a concept that originated in structuralism, a critical theory that can be applied to a variety of disciplines like sociology and anthropology. In the preface of the book *Cromwell*, Hugo put forward the principle of binary opposition. He pointed out that if art is to express real life, it can't avoid the binary phenomena in real life. Thus, he introduced beauty and ugliness that belong to a unified category in art creation[92].

In structuralism, the binary opposition is the practice of placing two ideas or concepts in opposing categories in order to study how they interact with and function in relation to one another. It is common for people to create binary opposition in real life, which can lead to societal problems of exclusion and oppression. A classic example of binary opposition is the presence-absence dichotomy; in other words, it involves viewing things as polar opposites and contrasting presence and absence, good and evil, the present and the past. This mode of thinking forms a fundamental element of thought in many cultures. Literature, the connection between art and reality, is created to present artistic images to the readers. Therefore, this concept can also be applied to literature. In literary works, the binary oppositions can be shown in the characters: groups of characters with two distinctive binary oppositions. The writers may use these features to reflect certain social problems or some ethical wrongdoings. This provides the authors' deep understanding of the world for the readers to "explore the motivations behind this kind of categorization and sometimes to deconstruct the potential harm that binary opposition can pose."

"All McEwan's works are suffused with a genuine sense of human sadness and suffering informed by a more consistent sense of responsibility, a deeper and more coherent political awareness."[93] Ryan believed this new novel embodied the new experiences of McEwan, and it was the longest and most ambitious work, illustrating the perfect collision between the experience of masculinity embodied in religious dramas and scripts of the past and the disillusioned realism.[94] McEwan connects the state with the family, the society with the individual, and consciousness with unconsciousness in the novel, in which his concerns about the world and his understanding of human nature are manifested.

Section One   Paradox in Individual Ethics: Child vs. Adult

Individual ethics reflects the relationship between the individual and the external world. The construction of the relationship between the individual and the external world is in turn influenced by the individual's ethics. Smoodin Roberta asserted that "the book is really about the nature of childhood, positing that many adults have much stronger ties to the children they used to be than one would suspect, particularly adult men."[95] The child in the adult's heart is one way to manifest the protagonists' concern or dissatisfaction with the society, which is reflected in the characters' inner struggle or escape from the reality.

The novel begins with the loss of the Stephens' daughter Kate, and the couple's grief is narrated. 3-year-old Kate suddenly disappeared while she was shopping with Stephen in the supermarket. His wife, Julie, is very depressed. Stephen blames himself his whole life. In order to escape the pain of losing her daughter, Julie goes to live alone in a cottage in the countryside, and Stephen lives in the city to continue to search for his daughter's whereabouts.

The background of the novel is London in the mid-1990s, which ironically reflects Britain's social conditions in the 1980s when Margaret Thatcher was in power. The time of the novel is an era not so unlike our own; the licensed beggars working the London streets are a product of post-Thatcher extremism—a period of even further privatization and more brutal self-interest. With the malfunction of the city service, the Government as the authority enforces problematic policies to control the individuals, "advocating self-reliance for the poor and incentives for the rich."[96] The stringent political setting is presented as the background of the novel. The authority in society, which is usually presented in the forms of the government, media, police, etc., is the force that imposes on individuals and can lead them to morbid development. The external world exerts greatly influences on the individual's ethical recognition, and all of these can be presented in the form of literature.

At the beginning of each chapter, a maxim from the Authorized Childcare Handbook (hereinafter referred to as the "Handbook") is inserted at the beginning of each chapter. These aphorisms provide a normative explanation of how parents educate their children. Through the Handbook, the projection of social ideals on children's education is manifested to the readers. Ostensibly, the Handbook is the result of a joint discussion between the experts from the official parenting council, was in fact under the control of Minister Darke, and the supervision of the Prime Minister, whose central idea is to set up the discipline for the child which is exercised by adults. In essence, society at that time symbolizes that pattern.

"Perhaps," Morley said, "Downing Street needed to carry a few

Ministers along for political reassons."

...

"They couldn't have it both ways," Morley said. "Even though they tried.

They couldn't leave it to the great and good, experts and celebrities gathered for public consumption, to come up with exactly the right book.

The grown-ups know best." Morley was probing his cut with his fingertips.

He winced. "Anyway, this is how seriously they take it. You've heard it all, I'm sure, how the nation is to be regenerated by reformed childcare practice." (150-151)

The appropriation of aphorisms from the Handbook is nothing more than an implication of the manipulation of children's education by government officials, indicating that children and adults are in a relationship of controlling and being controlled. Parents should not hesitate to establish authority at the expense of separation, which is an inevitable part of the growth of all children. In the eyes of politicians, the relationship between the government and the public is the same as the relationship between adults and children, and the government should manage the public.

It had been shown that there was deep concern among parents and educators about falling standards of behaviour and lack of civic responsibility among many elements of society, particularly the young. Upbringing clearly played an important part in this, and there was no doubt that parents in the past had been led astray by foolish and fashionable theories about childcare. There was a call for a return to common sense, and the Government was being asked to take a lead. This it was doing, and would continue to do, undeterred by the pathetic slurs, the irresponsible calumnies of its political opponents. (16)

The authors of the Handbook seem to have forgotten the childhood they had spent, rejecting or denigrating the childhood factors in their hearts, and falling into the vortex of adult-centrism. In the author's view, it is another word for the centralization system of the British government. The way they are going to discipline and regulate children is their way to do the same to the people. This is the binary contradiction between authority and people, the opposing and conflicting relationship between those in positions of power or authority and the general population or individuals. It signifies the tension and opposition that arise when there is a disparity in power, control, or decision-making between those who hold authority and those who are subject to it. The authors of the Handbook seem to have neglected or disregarded their own childhood experiences and adopted an adult-centric perspective; the binary contradiction between authority and people manifests as a clash between the authors' views and the needs or perspectives of the children they are trying to discipline or regulate.

Children and adults are always thought of as two opposite groups. Children are characterized as being naive, pure, and irresponsible, while their counterpart is mature, complex and responsible. Therefore, the nature of children in the Handbook is defined as selfish, and that "altruistic" ideas are anachronistic. In the Handbook, it instructs parents to be firm, dignified, strict, and calm, especially fathers, who should be prepared to "separate" from their children. Adult-centrism is a tendency of adults to look at children and their problems with prejudice. Parents represent authority and have a full voice in children's education. Therefore, it is necessary for adults to carry out "educating the children." The child is reduced to an absent "other" before them, becoming an object in relation to the adult. This idea creates a potential conflict between the child and the adult. This indicates the binary contradiction between authority and people, where authority figures or governing systems may employ similar methods of discipline, regulation, or control to maintain their dominance over the general population. The authority's actions and policies may be perceived as attempts to impose their will on the people, disregarding their needs, desires, or individual agency.

However, childhood is not the opposite of maturity or a morbid thing, as described in the Handbook. Compared with adults, children can bring creativity, imagination, and a sense of naive reality, and they are a valuable asset. Though they are young, they have their own personal standards that govern their way of interacting with other people. The Handbook in the novel to some extent ignores the fact and disregards that children have their individual ethics, which are formed under the correct guidance from the parents. However, if the parents follow the instructions from the Handbook, their adult-centrism will finally distort the children's values. After dissolving adult-centrism, McEwan advocated the return of "children" and established symbiosis between childhood and adulthood.

I. Stephen—Mental Escape from Reality

In the novel, there are two adults hoping to escape from the adult world into childhood. Stephen's mental escape from reality into daydreams, and Charles' mental and physical escape from adulthood into childhood. Due to different reasons, they are both escaping from their adult world, trying to get away from a world full of despair, frustration, and hypocrisy.

The protagonist, Stephen, a writer of children's books, decides to escape from the trauma of losing his daughter. He lost his daughter two years ago mysteriously when they were lining up at the checkout in a supermarket. The loss has a devastating influence on Stephen's life and marriage. He hopes to find her eventually. He keeps up a frantic search for Kate for two years, but the reality disappoints him. What's worse, he and his wife, Julie, have become estranged from each other.

At the beginning of the novel, after Kate's abduction, "Stephen and Julie had clung to one another, sharing dazed rhetorical questions, awake in bed all night, theorizing hopefully one moment, despairing the next. But that was before time, the heartless accumulation of days, had clarified the absolute, bitter truth" (23). They still have hope. They keep Kate's stuff in her room in its original state. Her clothes and toys still lie about the room, and her bed is still unmade. As time goes by, the hope of getting Kate back is gradually disappearing. The sweet and peaceful life changes. Their former intimacy and the assumption that they both agree on collapse. "Now there was no mutual consolation, no touching, no love. Their old intimacy, their habitual assumption that they were on the same side, was dead. They remained huddled over their separate losses, and unspoken resentments began to grow" (150-151). They carefully get along in a dangerous emotional situation. They are faced with two possibilities that are on par with each other and balance on the millstone pillars. As long as you tend to lean on one side and the other side that has always existed, either side will irretrievably disappear without a trace.

One afternoon, when Stephen comes back home, he finds that the clutter is gone. The bed is stripped and there are three bulging plastic sacks by the door in her bedroom. Julie gradually accepts the truth, so she cleans Kate's room and prepares to move on. However, Stephen is very upset with Julie's behavior; he is still searching around in the city. He is angry with "destructiveness, a willful defeatism" (19, 23). This fastens the discrepancy in their marriage.

In some sense, Stephen retreats into his childhood after his daughter's abduction.[97] He is clearly aware that he has to face the fact in a sensible, rational manner, but it is not the time. He will still do nothing but search. "He visited child minders. He walked up and down the shopping streets with his photographs displayed. He loitered by the supermarket, and by the entrance to the chemist's next door."[98] He has tried every single effort to find her back, refusing to admit the truth that Kate may never be found.

Searching and thinking about Kate becomes his habitual way of living. "Jigging and weaving to overtake, Stephen remained, as always, though barely consciously, on the watch for children, for a five-year-old girl. It was more than a habit, for a habit could be broken. This was a deep disposition; the outline experience had stenciled on character" (8).

In the process of finding his daughter, the actual time Stephen experiences has stopped. He tries to ease his pain by searching for Kate desperately. He is obsessed with his recalls to the past and his endless daydreams. His mind is filled with his wife and missing daughter, and his plan for what he is going to do with himself. Stephen daydreams a lot about "what was and what might have been." "Sometimes he delivered his compulsive imaginary speeches, bitter or sad indictments whose every draft was meticulously revised" (11).

Besides his journey to Whitehall, he has nothing obligated. Therefore, most of the time, he often spends his time in front of the TV, clad only in his underwear. He moodily sips neat Scotch, reads magazines, or watches the Olympic Games. After the disappearance of Kate, Stephen loses his life aims, totally at a loss. Though two years have passed, he still hasn't made himself ready for the fact. He pleads for time to stop to rectify his mistake.

> At nights the drinking increased. He ate in a local restaurant, alone.
>
> He made no attempt to contact friends. He never returned the calls monitored on his answering machine. Mostly he was indifferent to the squalor of his flat, the meaty black flies and their leisurely patrols. When he was out he dreaded returning to the deadly alignments of familiar possessions, the way the empty armchairs squatted, the smeared plates and old newspapers at their feet. It was the stubborn conspiracy of objects—lavatory seat, bed sheets, floor dirt—to remain exactly as they had been left.
>
> At home too he was never far from his subjects, his daughter, his wife, what to do. But here he lacked the concentration for sustained thought. He daydreamed in fragments, without control, almost without consciousness. (12)

Bitterness fills him. What Stephen wants to do is to escape from reality. As has been discussed earlier, the adult world is often known for its rationality, norms, civilization, order, etc., but that of children is full of sensibility, innocence, and disorder. The description of Stephen's living condition, "squalor of his flat, the meaty black flies," "the empty armchairs squatted, the smeared plates and old newspapers at their feet," and "lavatory seat, bed sheets, floor dirt in the real world" (12), doesn't look like a civilized world, a world with order and norms. He cuts off his connection with his friends and doesn't answer his phone calls, which shows his escape from reality and his responsibility. To Julie, it is "typically masculine evasion, an attempt to mask feelings behind displays of competence and organization and physical effort" (23). The description gives the reader the impression that the time around him has stopped. Things around him remain the same day after day. However, his miss for Kate has never stopped.

Chapter Four　The Temporal Paradox in The Child in Time

Kate is growing in his mind. His frantic search for Kate is his dream for the orderly life of the past. He is so eager to return to a stable state that no longer exists that he refuses to accept reality.

> There was a biological clock, dispassionate in its unstoppability, which let his daughter go on growing, extended and complicated her simple vocabulary, made her stronger, her movements surer. The clock, sinewy like a heart, kept faith with an unceasing conditional; she would be drawing, she would be starting to read, she would be losing a milktooth. She would be familiar, taken for granted. (8)

The strong feelings towards Kate motivated him to watch unconsciously the girls at her age. He feels Kate in them. He can't let any detail go; in shops, past playgrounds, at the houses of friends, he will search for Kate among other children. "Her phantom growth, the product of an obsessive sorrow, was not only inevitable."[99] He couldn't stop the fantasy. Without it, time will stop. In his own mind, he is the father of an invisible child. The domination of emotion and his sensibility make him behave like a moody child. He stubbornly keeps the images and his emotion of the day when Kate was missing in his mind, which prevents him from facing the present and keeping his life moving. His sadness and depression grow deeper and deeper inside him, but he still refuses to confront it bravely. If there is anything related to Kate, he will let it completely control his mind.

> Solitude had encouraged in him small superstitions, a tendency to magical thought. The superstitions had attached themselves to daily rituals, and in the constant silence of his own company his adherence had become rigorous. He always shaved the left side of his face first, he never began brushing his teeth until he had replaced the top of the toothpaste tube, he flushed the lavatory with his left hand although it was inconvenient, and these days he was scrupulous in placing both feet at once on the floor when he got out of bed. (117)

The heartbroken trauma of losing his daughter, the indifference to his wife and the boredom at work all contribute to his withdrawal from the adult world. His escape is an indulgence in the negative and passive response to the reality. Before Kate's sixth birthday, he uses all the superstitious beliefs to "[rationalize] a trip to the toy shop," because "it would be an act of faith in his daughter's continued existence" (117). He intends to buy only one birthday gift for Kate, but in the end, he can't help buying many presents for her. This is like a child who can't resist his demand for gifts, ending up with a lot at home. He even naively believes that Kate's missing is one of Julie's excuses to get away from the marriage.

> This was a short distance from another well-prepared channel, the argument from malice. Julie had been waiting for an excuse to leave the marriage, being too great a moral coward to do so on the basis of her own grievances. She had used Kate's disappearance to effect her own. Or, more elaborately, she had wanted him out of her way, Kate was living with her in secret, the abduction in the supermarket had been carefully and cynically planned, probably with the help of some old lover. Or a new one. (125)

He even laughs at himself for thinking in this way, but this gives him a feeling of self-destructive and childish pleasure.

His childish behaviors have become even more ridiculous in his search for Kate. On his way to have lunch with the Prime Minister, he impulsively runs out of the car when he misrecognizes a girl as Kate. In the process of tracking the fake Kate, it seems that Stephen has returned to his childhood: he walks into a classroom where he is taking an art class on the role of a student; the teacher asks the children to draw a medieval village, and he immediately completes the task conscientiously and obediently. Stephen's actions clearly reveal his lingering childishness. As an adult, his eagerness to impress his teachers might seem unusual, but it reflects a deeper longing for validation that ties back to his formative years. The adult world, with its instability, complexity, and uncertainty, can be overwhelming. For Stephen, briefly escaping into the simplicity and comfort of childhood memories offers a temporary reprieve from his pain.

There are other instances that indicate his withdrawal from the adult world, but this does not alleviate Stephen's pain and confusion. His ethics about the world collapse with the missing of Kate. As an adult, before the accident, he is a healthy and responsible father, who likes to play with his daughter and takes good care of his wife and their daughter. The unfortunate incident destroys him and his beliefs. This destruction, in turn, causes his individual ethics to change and forces him to withdraw from the adult world. Individual ethics play a crucial role in shaping a person's values, beliefs, and behavior. In the novel, Stephen's individual ethics undergo a profound transformation as a result of the tragic incident involving his daughter, Kate. Prior to the accident, his ethics were aligned with the societal norms and responsibilities associated with adulthood. However, the loss of his daughter shatters Stephen's world and profoundly impacts his individual ethics. The pain and confusion he experiences lead to a collapse of his ethical framework. The tragedy challenges his previously held beliefs about the world and raises questions about its fairness and purpose. Stephen's grief and the profound loss he endures cause him to question the meaning and value of his previous ethical commitments.

As a result of this traumatic event, Stephen's individual ethics undergo a significant shift. The devastating loss forces him to reevaluate his beliefs, priorities, and sense of purpose. The weight of the tragedy may lead Stephen to question the efficacy of his previous ethical framework and the values associated with the adult world. His withdrawal from the adult world can be seen as a response to the inner turmoil he experiences and a reconfiguration of his ethical perspective. His withdrawal may stem from a sense of disillusionment and an inability to reconcile his previous ethical commitments with the tragedy he has endured. The loss of his daughter may have eroded his trust in the world and caused him to question the inherent fairness and meaning of life. This reevaluation of his individual ethics compels him to withdraw from the adult world, as he struggles to find meaning, purpose, and a new ethical framework that can accommodate his pain and confusion.

Since his childhood, Stephen has shown great interest in railways. When he goes to find Julie, he is at the station, enjoying the view of the station. "He remained on the footbridge, taking childish—or boyish—pleasure in the polished rails pointing away in both directions into the silence" (48). He continues to recall the pleasure he has had with his father at the station. The knowledge he gets from his father becomes a sweet memory. Actually, in the process of searching for Kate, Stephen goes to his mother's house many times to seek inner peace. His parents give him great support. On his way to Julie's secluded house, Stephen meets his parents when they were young. Through the glass window of the Bell pub, Stephen hallucinates his parents dating here when they are young. He sees his parents talking about something serious. His mother is thinking of abortion, but the stare at Stephen out of the window changes her mind. "A cold, infant despondency sank through him, a bitter sense of exclusion and longing. Perhaps he was crying as he backed away from the window; perhaps he was wailing like a baby waking in the night" (57). He feels like he is being abandoned and this feeling greatly hurts him, just like Kate's missing. He is so helpless, like a baby, that there is nothing he can do to save the mistake.

There is a plot that echoes the beginning at the end of the novel. The episode in which Stephen encounters a car accident on the road whose driver is crushed under the truck and Stephen saves the driver on the brink of death plays the anaphoric function. This scene is like delivering a baby. When Julie is in the pot, Stephen acts as a midwife and delivers the newborn. It also shows Stephen's return from a lost adult world, which symbolizes the rebirth of the family and the rebirth of Stephen. This parallel between saving a life and the birth of a child further emphasizes the theme of rebirth. It signifies not only the physical rescue of the driver but also Stephen's own personal transformation and return from a lost adult world.

In the context of adult vs. child, this scene highlights the contrast between the responsibilities and roles associated with adulthood and the vulnerability and dependence of childhood. Stephen, as an adult, takes on the role of a midwife, symbolizing his ability to provide support, protection, and guidance to those in need. In contrast, the driver who is in a life-threatening situation represents vulnerability and the need for assistance, reflecting the childlike qualities of helplessness and reliance on others. Stephen's act of saving the driver bridges the gap between the adult world and the child's world, blurring the boundaries and highlighting the interconnectedness of these roles.

Furthermore, this scene also signifies the rebirth of the family and Stephen himself. By metaphorically delivering the driver, Stephen not only saves a life but also experiences a renewal of purpose and a reconnection with the values associated with family and compassion. It represents his return from a lost adult world, where he was emotionally disconnected and withdrawn, and his rediscovery of the importance of human connection and responsibility. It symbolizes the rebirth of the family and Stephen himself, highlighting and emphasizing Stephen's transformation from a lost adult to someone who reconnects with compassion and the importance of human connection and his regaining of healthy individual ethics.

II. Charles—Mental and Physical Escape into Childhood

Charles Darke, different from Stephen who is searching for his missing daughter, is pursuing the ideal and invisible child in his heart. When Stephen struggles in still time, searching for his missing daughter, Charles is torn between a fantasy childhood and a secular adult world. His mental and physical escape into the childhood that he has never experienced is his longing for the childhood he has been deprived of by his parents. As one of the key members of the government, Charles is in two worlds: one of public life and the other of his childhood. "Charles Darke epitomizes the fatality of a masculinity fractured by the division between a repressed, aggressive public self and the fantasies of childhood that possess it in private."[100] His contradictory binaries are between the social self that is the adult Charles and his true self that is the boy Charles. In public, he presents himself as a mature and eloquent politician. He deliberately dressed up in appearance, bluffed in words, and deliberately posed as a politician in behavior, leaving a complete image of a hypocrite to the readers. Charles is the kind of person who is favored by God. He is a successful businessman, and later he moves to the government and makes himself a brilliant politician, maybe the Prime Minister one day. Just as his career is moving into top gear, Charles suddenly quits his job and moves to the countryside to enjoy his missing childhood life. As the author of the Handbook, he tries to escape the chaos and political pressure of the adult world by entering the quiet and safe world of childhood, and to escape from this harsh world to the innocent world of children, which was undoubtedly extreme irony. "Darke's return to childhood means an escape, a freedom from political pressure."[101]

Charles's mother died when he was 12, and his father, who is authoritarian under the patriarchal world, deprives Charles of his childhood. He has to behave like an adult at his young age. "It shows him standing next to his father who was fairly important in the city, a dull man I remember, but tyrannical. In the photograph, Charles looks like a scaled-down version of his father—the same suit and tie, the same self-important posture and grown-up expression. So perhaps he was denied a childhood."[102] Due to his lack of maternal love, he married Thelma, who is 12 years older than him, out of his desire for motherly love. It is Thelma's mother-like warmth that is what Charles yearns for.

> He was also unfashionably successful in his choice of a wife twelve years his senior. Thelma was a lecturer in physics at Birkbeck with a respected thesis recently completed on—as far as any gossip columnist could tell—the nature of time. She was not the obvious wife for a young millionaire in the kitsch music business, a man young enough, some said cruelly, to be her son. (30)

Charles' sensitive little boy inside him needs to be carefully taken care of. Thelma is an intelligent female physicist. Her mature behavior and rational thinking as a scientist greatly comfort Charles. This is one episode in the novel. Stephen is going to be picked up by Thelma and taken to their house. He is thinking about whether Kate is back, but there is nobody in it. Therefore, he asks Thelma to leave a message on the door. "Rather than argue that Kate could not read and was never coming back, Thelma returned upstairs and pinned her address and phone number to his front door" (40). This is her charm and competence in the face of anything emergent. She is gentle, warm and mother-like, which Charles totally needs. To her, science is Thelma's child and Charles

Chapter Four The Temporal Paradox in The Child in Time

is another. "Charles was her difficult child, and she had enlisted Stephen's help many times" (38). While Stephen visits him, Charles stands behind his wife with one hand resting on her shoulder and the other holding a glass of milk the entire time. Then, Charles obediently goes to bed as asked by Thelma at barely half past eight. Thelma even goes upstairs to make sure Charles is in bed as commanded. A minister in public, he is like a little boy at home facing his mother-like wife. "Stephen watched his friend closely, marveling at how much smaller he appeared, how slight in build. Had high office really made him larger?" (39).

Under her tolerance and even connivance, Charles quits the ministerial position. They have made some well-considered decisions. Charles is giving up his career, and Thelma also resigns from her job. They move into a cottage in the countryside after selling their house. They are leaving their luxurious life behind in the city.

> The big house in Eaton Square was solidly established. The then almost valuable oil paintings of sea battles and hunting scenes were already in place. So too were the thick clean towels in the guest bedroom, the cleaning lady who came four hours every day and spoke no English. While Stephen and his friends were in Goa and Kabul with their frisbees and their hashish pipes, Charles and Thelma had a man who parked their car, a telephone answering service, dinner parties, hardback books. (30)

There are clues out there in the novel for Charles's weird decision. When Stephen first meets Charles in his office, the decoration in the office catches his attention.

> On the walls, instead of framed black and white photographs of the early twentieth-century giants who had made great the name of Gott, was a portrait not of Evelyn Waugh, surely, but a frog in a three-piece suit leaning on a cane by the balustrade of a country house. Elsewhere, tacked to the few feet of wall space, there were pictures of teddy bears, half a dozen of them at least, attempting to jump-start a fire engine, a mouse in a bikini holding

a gun to its head, and a grim-faced crow with a stethoscope round its neck taking the pulse of a pale young boy who appeared to have fallen out of a tree. (66)

The decorations are not fit for Charles' identity as a famous publisher who is six years older than Stephen. The little boy inside him becomes apparent, along with the reason he insists that Stephen's novel be designed for children. "The greatest so-called children's books were precisely those that spoke to both children and adults, to the incipient adult within the child, to the forgotten child within the adult" (29).

When Charles first moves to the countryside, he plays in the woods all day and comes home to eat and sleep. When Stephen goes to visit him, he meets a boy when he is thirty feet away from a tree. The boy steps out from behind the tree and the two stare at each other. Stephen is so surprised to see a boy, whose "face was pale and fringed with sandy hair" and whose "look was far too confident, cocky in that familiar way" (100). The face turns out to be Charles'. His life now is full of fun, giving him great satisfaction. He busies himself every day playing in the woods. He finds amusement in nature, always excited and ready for the challenge in the open land. He even builds a treehouse in the deep woods. "It's really good ... been building it all summer ... by myself ... my place" (100). To Charles, it is a great pleasure to enjoy what he has missed in his childhood. He is now living a life that he may have dreamed of for long. His treehouse is filled up with child items. "There was a ball-bearing, a toy compass, a piece of rope and two empty cartridge cases, a fish hook embedded in a cork, a feather, two oval pebbles" (105). He enjoys nature and the brilliant view from the tree-house, learns the names of plants and animals, and shoots birds with stones, all of which provide him a chance to return to a cheerful childhood. He is now not a mature middle-aged man, and instead, he is an actual boy.

Stephen had time to notice that his friend had not, as he had first thought, actually shrunk. He was slighter and suppler in his movements. He had grown his hair forwards into a fringe, and cut it short behind the ears. It was his wide open manner, the rapid speech and intent look, his unfettered, impulsive lurching, the way his feet and elbows flew out as they swung round a corner to take a second, even narrower path, the abandonment of the ritual and formality of adult greetings which suggested the ten-year-old. (101)

To get away from mundane life, from his duties, and from the endless pressure, Charles finally finds what he has missed in his childhood. He always wants a childhood which is away from money, decisions, plans or demands. He cherishes the freedom of childhood, the powerlessness, and the obedience.

However, Charles has not really gotten rid of the shackles and the bother from reality. Charles is very satisfied with his present childhood life, but it doesn't ensure a carefree life for him forever. Charles is a smart and cunning politician. In Charles' employment in the government, he chooses the right camp not because he supports it, but because "it was in power and likely to remain so" (36), from which we can see he has to suffocate his true self in order to get a higher position. This discrepancy between what he thinks and what he wants gradually causes him to have mad lows. He wants to be famous and to be the Prime Minister one day in the future; however, at the same time he wants to be the little boy living in a carefree world, with no responsibility and no knowledge of the world outside. Finally, this leads to something fatal for a politician. "He wore his short trousers and had his bottom smacked by a prostitute pretending to be a governess." (185) Not only that, but in the face of the prime minister's favor (especially sexual favor) and the temptation of the official position, he tries his best to cater to it. "I stood for this programme. A majority elected me because of it. It doesn't matter what I think" (37).

After experiencing a joyful childhood in the woods, he one day receives a letter from the Prime Minister, awakening his dormant adult ambitions. From that moment, he feels as though everything begins to go awry.

Then the weather turned, rather suddenly as it happened, and Charles began to fret about what was happening in London. He wanted us to take newspapers, and I refused. He tried to mend an old radio and got in a fury when he failed. Then he started on about how we were going to run out of money unless he went back to work, which was nonsense. Worst of all, he was getting letters from the Prime Minister inviting him to Downing Street, hinting that a place could be found for him in the Lords, a peerage that is, and a job in Government with even better jobs to come. (187)

This makes him suddenly aware of his duties as an adult and a husband. Thus, he tries to stop escaping reality and decides to cope with it. However, Charles ultimately fails to return to reality and ends his life in tragedy through suicide. "Through Charles's regression into childhood, McEwan suggests that although it is important, even crucial, for the adult to accept the child that resides within themselves, it is dangerous, even suicidal, to become wholly that child-self or to surrender entirely to that desire. Acceptance and acknowledgment of the child-self can lead to a greater joy of life; submersion in that child can lead to a breakdown of the adult spirit."[103] He is trapped in his own conflicting values. On one hand, Charles deeply desires to remain in an innocent and carefree childhood forever; on the other, he is burdened by concerns about his adult responsibilities. Despite this, returning to London would not offer him solace, as he has grown too attached to the idealized version of his childhood. Back in his old life, he would once again face his unfulfilled desires, inner struggles, and lingering worries.

If he went back to London, to the old life, he knew from experience that the old longings, the compulsions, would start to drag him down and he would be craving the simple and secure life he had made for himself here. And if he stayed here he would be agonising forever about his growing irrelevance in what he was beginning to call the real world. (187)

Thelma knows well what the future will be for Charles. This is a vicious circle that he will never be able to jump out of. She is clear about the fate of Charles. "He had survived out there for years, and if he was going to be unhappy, it would be no more than the unhappiness of the child who could not have everything" (187). His contradictory ideas inside break him down and then lead to a fatal result.

This internal struggle consumes him, creating a profound disconnect between his outward success and his inner turmoil. Beneath Charles's successful exterior lies an untold complex—to be a real child. On the surface, he performed a vigorous performance of life, but the soul has long been at odds with things that are not in harmony with nature. Charles felt the absurdity of the adult world and pinned his hopes on the primordial state of humanity—children. He suffers from a split personality and he wants an innocent, carefree childhood as well as a successful career in politics. Charles's inner conflict and tragedy as an adult are deeply intertwined with his individual ethics and his struggle to reconcile opposing desires. His desire for a successful career in politics represents the responsibilities and expectations of adulthood, while his longing for an innocent and carefree childhood reflects a yearning for authenticity and harmony with nature.

However, he could never bring those childlike qualities into public life in any way. Charles's tragedy as an adult lies in his inability to resolve the conflict between these two desires, in his inability to find the right balance between the responsibilities of adulthood and the need for innocence. Charles's untold complexity stems from his recognition of the absurdity and disharmony he perceives in the adult world. He sees children as embodying a primordial state of humanity, untouched by the artificiality and complexities of adult life. He believes that by embracing childlike qualities, he can regain a sense of innocence and escape the dissonance he feels. However, Charles faces a profound dilemma. He desires both the success and power associated with adulthood and the simplicity and purity of childhood. This conflict creates a split personality within him, as he tries to reconcile these opposing desires. His tragedy lies in his profound struggle to bridge the chasm between the burdens of adulthood and his relentless yearning for the purity of childhood innocence.

The clash between Charles's individual ethics and societal expectations becomes a central theme. He finally understands that it is impossible to continue one's childhood forever, and sooner or later, it will end. Ultimately, Charles uses his life to complete an inquiry into the living conditions of mundane people. Charles realizes the impossibility of perpetuating childhood indefinitely and the need to face the realities and responsibilities of adulthood. However, his tragic path unfolds as he attempts to reject the adult world in an extreme and evasive manner, which ultimately leads to his downfall.

His failure proves that rejecting adult responsibility in a retrogressive and evasive way would not work. Charles cannot intelligently integrate the fantasy of innocence into adult life, but chooses an extreme way to reject the adult world, which is doomed to its tragic end. In Ian McEwan's interview with Michael, McEwan mentions that suicide is an option in his utopia: "I think that the only way out would be suicide ... and has to be therefore something that people only do in extremes."[104]

In examining Charles's individual ethics, we see his desire for authenticity, harmony, and a rejection of the artificiality of the adult world. However, his inability to intelligently integrate the fantasy of innocence into adult life hinders his ability to find a sustainable and fulfilling path. His extreme rejection of adult responsibility reflects a flawed approach, which ultimately leads to his tragic end. Charles's tragedy as an adult is closely tied to his individual ethics and the conflict between his desires for success and innocence. His inability to find a balance between these desires and his misguided attempt to reject the adult world in an extreme manner contribute to his downfall.

Section Two   Alienation of Time in a Certain Space

Time and space play crucial roles in the study of literary works, and their indivisibility is emphasized in Bakhtin's theory of the chronotope. In *The Child in Time*, the interplay of time and space not only establishes the backdrop for the story's development but also carries significant symbolic and functional expressions of various elements of characters. McEwan masterfully creates a sense of malleable time, where it can be prolonged or shortened at will. This manipulation of time adds to the intricate complexity of the narrative. It allows for the exploration of the theme of "child" and its various manifestations throughout the story. This dynamic portrayal of time reflects the complexities of human experiences and the ever-changing nature of life.

In conjunction with time, the notion of space is also significant. The settings and physical environments in literature usually provide contextual richness and contribute to the overall atmosphere of the story. Different spaces, such as the family home or the wider political arena, serve as backdrops that influence the characters' experiences, interactions, and development. In the novel, there are four significant places that show their special connection with time. Through the exploration of time and space, McEwan crafts a multi-dimensional narrative that delves into the complexities of human existence and the theme of childhood. The interplay of time—its malleability and its capacity to both shape and be shaped by the characters' experiences—and the depiction of spaces heighten the richness of the story, enabling a deeper exploration of the characters' emotions, relationships, and personal journeys.

The manipulation of time with spaces contributes to the depth and richness of the narrative, enhancing the reader's engagement with the story. Time and space not only construct the background of the development of the story, but also carry the functional expression of various elements such as characters and plots that run through it. In this novel, "McEwan creates a sense of time that is malleable, wondrous, and infinitely complex. Time is a vandal: it is the essence that can make one forget the inner child, that innocent and youthful joy of life. Simultaneously, time is also vandalized: characters experience periods that stall in slow motion, that pass in a blur of quickness, and that are even altered, with the past coming round to the present."[105]

Time, as a force that distances individuals from their inner child, reveals the characters' ethical perspectives and their evolving relationship with innocence and maturity. The ways in which characters perceive and engage with time shape their individual ethics. For instance, some characters may prioritize living in the present moment, cherishing the fleeting nature of time, and embracing the joys of life. Others may become consumed by regrets or dwell on past traumas, which can hinder their ability to reconnect with their inner childlike innocence.

Similarly, the portrayal of space and its profound impact on the characters' experiences underscores the intricate interplay between environment and individual ethics. Each space, whether the intimate confines of the family home or the charged atmosphere of the political arena, is imbued with its own values, norms, and ethical dilemmas, shaping and reflecting the moral choices and internal conflicts of those who inhabit them. Characters navigate these spaces and make choices that align with their personal ethics or challenge societal expectations. The interplay between space and individual ethics can lead to conflicts, transformations, or realizations within the narrative. The malleability of time and the blurred boundaries between past and present highlight the characters' capacity for reflection, growth, and the potential to reconcile with their past actions or experiences. This reflection and reconciliation process aligns with ethical considerations of self-awareness, accountability, and personal growth. Time and space in the novel are closely tied to the characters' individual ethics and their experiences within these dimensions. The depiction of different spaces provides opportunities for characters to exercise their ethical agency. They may confront ethical dilemmas, navigate power dynamics, or challenge societal norms within these spaces. Their actions and choices within the given spatial contexts reveal their individual ethics and moral compass.

The passage of time, its fluid manipulation, and the characters' engagement with its flow reveal their evolving ethical perspectives and their struggle to reconcile adulthood with the remnants of their inner childlike innocence. Likewise, the depiction of diverse spaces, along with the characters' interactions within these environments, underscores the ethical frameworks, dilemmas, and transformative experiences that shape their moral compass. Together, the interplay of time, space, and individual ethics weaves a layered and intricate narrative, illuminating the characters' profound moral struggles, self-reflection, and the broader commentary on human existence.

Stephen's flat

The story takes place in London. Stephen's flat is located in "the Edwardian apartment block, the tarred roofs of its back additions with their lop-sided, crusty cisterns, the mess of South London, the hazy curvature of the earth."[106] Ever since Kate's abduction, Stephen and Julie's consciousness of space-time has been stopped in that exact moment. McEwan uses the abstract metaphor of "time stagnation," which begins with the disappearance of his daughter and ends with the arrival of another child, to indicate the growth of Stephen. McEwan believes that time is the best imprint of consciousness itself. What is recalled may become a reality, but it may also be distorted by personal will. The disappearance of his daughter takes away Stephen's concept of time. Without illusions of her continued existence, he is lost. Time ceases during the disappearance of his daughter. To Stephen, time is "empty and meaningless" and "stagnant and blank." His life now is filled with various melancholy emotions, like panic, sadness, anger, anxiety, and even self-loathing and desperation. All the memories related to Kate remain in the flat in London. In this place, Stephen rather stops his time to keep the memory of Kate or even to reverse the time to mend his mistakes. "Kate's clothes and toys still lay about the flat, her bed was still unmade" (23). The memory of the past lives on in Stephen's mind. The flat prevents him from seeing his present life, and thus keeps the time stagnant.

To Julie, time has stopped also. When Stephen goes to search for Kate, Julie will keep the same position in the flat. "When he left in the morning she was sitting in the armchair in the bedroom, facing the cold fireplace. That was where he found her when he came back at night and turned on the lights" (23).

The incident is a nightmare that interrupts his peaceful life abruptly. In essence, Stephen's process of searching for Kate repetitively is like being played in reverse mode, never moving forward. This action forces Stephen to stop his time, and lies in the memory of the past. The memory flashes consistently in his mind. "The bitter, anti-cyclonic day was to serve an obsessive memory well with a light of brilliant explicitness, a cynical eye for detail" (15).

Because of Kate's abduction, the intimacy between Stephen and Julie gradually changes into unspoken resentment. Julie is tired of "a typically masculine evasion, an attempt to mask feelings behind displays of competence and organization and physical effort" (3). Julie decides to leave the place with sorrowful memories, a place witnessing the missing of Kate, the breakup of the couple, and the frustration of the search. When Stephen one day finds that Kate's room has been cleared, he knows that their relationship is facing a crisis. "Suddenly their sorrows were separate, insular, incommunicable. They went their different ways" (23). When Julie leaves him and leaves the flat, Stephen finally feels what Julie feels.

> Finally he arrived back at Julie's chair, loitered by it a moment, his hand resting lightly on its back as if calculating the odds of some dangerous act. At last he stirred himself, took two paces round the chair and sat down. He stared into the dark grate where spent matches lay at odd angles by a piece of tin foil; minutes went by, time in which to feel the chair's bunched material yield Julie's contours for his own, empty minutes like all the others. Then he slumped, he was still for the first time in weeks. (25)

He remained that way for hours, all through the night, sometimes dozing briefly. Time has lost its meaning, and what is left is pain and grief. He has to chew the bitter himself. He begins to realize "in the small hours to the first full flood of understanding of the true nature of his loss" (25). He begins to cry, and it is from this moment in the semi-dark flat that he is left alone to swallow his bitterness and to date his time of mourning. "Time itself had a closed-down, forbidden quality; he was experiencing the pleasurable transgression" (132). He remains immobile in the chair, unaware of the passage of time. "The mystic's experience of timelessness, the chaotic unfolding of time in dreams, the Christian moment of fulfillment and redemption, the annihilated time of deep sleep, the elaborate time schemes of novelists, poets, daydreamers, the infinite, unchanging time of childhood" (111).

In the following three years, Stephen feels only aimless and chaotic. If these three years are condensed into the flat in London, the place is where the memories lie and the missing keeps. The lavatory seat, bed sheets, and floor dirt are all kept just as they were left.

At home, at this flat, "he was never far from his subjects, his daughter, his wife, what to do" (12). Now, there is no family at this flat. It is only a place that serves as a shelter from the wind and rain. Time has no value in this flat because it is only used to keep the depressing and heartbroken memories of the past. Stephen and Julie sell the flat. Stephen carries two boxes of belongings to live a simple life in a cramped rental house to continue to heal his trauma. The small space of Stephen's rental house not only takes him away from the home that carries the grief of the past, but also allows him to soothe the wounds of his heart in the new space. Compared to previous residences, this one-bedroom and living room rental house is very small. However, this cramped rental house can bring comfort to Stephen, because the space with healing functions does not need to be too large. In the new space, the memory of the old flat will gradually vanish, and Stephen will finally get healed.

In this novel, its structure comes from the feeling of time, or rather the feeling of known time, that is, the time in memory.[107] For Stephen, his time stops with the disappearance of his daughter Katie, and real time is stagnant under the influence of melancholy emotions. Caught in those past memories, he can't feel, sense or act in the present. Stimulated by this melancholy emotion, all his actions are in vain. He is never able to find his daughter, save Charles—who is trapped in childhood fantasies—or implement the concept of a parenting manual. During these two years, in Stephen's eyes, the world around him is an existing wasteland, full of frustration, loneliness, and isolation. He is an emotional and spiritual waste. He is eager to resume the linear process of development that has been interrupted by the disappearance of Kate, and is reluctant to readjust himself. His stubbornness and persistence make self-healing difficult and time-consuming. After three years of confusion and depression, Stephen finally gets rid of his inherent obsession with the past.

Julie's new house

Julie also goes berserk after the disappearance of Kate, spending hours in an armchair without anything to eat. However, there is a reality to face. After many hopeless searches, Julie accepts the harsh reality. She cleans Kate's room and finds herself a retreat in the Chilterns. After a long period of reflection, Julie leaves home one day in February for a retreat in the Chilterns Hills to meditate on the changes in her life, where she is going to adjust herself to start the next stage of her life. "Such faith in endless mutability, in re-making yourself as you came to understand more, or changed your version,"[108] but in Stephen's view, it is an aspect of her femininity.

This isolated house provides the distractions of time and space from the outside world and becomes Julie's new home. In the isolated place, Julie can forget the trauma of losing Kate. She can recover soon and welcome the new life in the future. In here, she picks up her violin that she has dropped for long. In this place, a new life is breeding. It is a place full of hope, with a future in it. Stephen has been there twice. The first time he goes to visit Julie, they both feel restrained since there is still a distance between them.

> There should have been something affectionate to say which would be neither flippant nor expose him further. But all there remained was small talk. He could think only of taking her hand, and yet he didn't. They had used up the possibilities, the tension of touch, they had been to the limits. For now everything was neutralised. Had they been together still, they could have fallen back on other resources, ignored each other for a while, or undertaken some task, or faced the loss somehow. (62)

They are used to the separation; even small talk between them is not easy. They feel upset because Kate is still between them, which is the most vulnerable thing that they avoid touching.

"The old, careful politeness was re-establishing itself, and they were helpless before it" (62). They are careful enough to change the atmosphere between them. Stephen even prepares him for the divorce. "He could learn not to love her, just so long as he could see her from time to time and be reminded that she was mortal, a woman in her late thirties, intent on solitude, on making sense of her own troubled life" (63). However, it never occurs to him that within such a small house—like one a child might draw, with a box-shaped front door at its dead center, four small windows near each corner, and made of the same red bricks as The Bell—a new life is waiting for him. Stephen's second visit to this small house ushered in the birth of a new life. The birth of the second child not only calms the grief of losing their daughter, but also continues the desire for their lives. The birth of a newborn endows their life with its full meaning. Stephen and Julie struggle to break free from the suffocation and numbness of losing their daughter, and the creation of new lives gives them the opportunity to love and hope again, and also allows them to regain each other. Three years later, they can finally cry together for the lost and irreplaceable Kate, and rejoice in the new child who has just arrived. They pledged to perpetuate their love for Kate to the new child. Newborns let time flow, and time can heal the pain and reshape the face of life.

Charles' treehouse

Charles's retreat to the woods and his construction of a treehouse symbolize a profound psychological and emotional journey, marked by nostalgia, escapism, and ultimate tragedy. By abandoning his position as a minister—a role of significant power and societal responsibility—he rejects the present and the future, retreating into the simplicity and innocence of a childhood dream.

> Anyway, we dropped everything and came here ... I was mother to a little boy who played in the woods all day and came home to eat and sleep. I've never known him so happy, so simple in his needs. He discovered he liked solitude. He learned the names of plants, though I never saw him with books. When he was back here he was quite simply merry, and affectionate. At nights he slept ten hours straight through. Before, he used to make do on four or five. (186)

However, this act of withdrawal is not merely an embrace of nostalgia but a deep denial of reality, culminating in his tragic demise.

The treehouse that Charles builds high in the branches of a large tree, resembling a bird's nest, is a physical manifestation of his desire to escape. Perched above the ground, it offers him a panoramic view of the village below and the distant town across the fields. This elevated perspective symbolizes his detachment from the societal structures and relationships that once defined his life. For Charles, the treehouse is not just a dwelling but a sanctuary where he can sever ties with the external world and immerse himself in a self-imposed isolation.

Filled with toys and objects reminiscent of his childhood, the treehouse becomes a private, whimsical realm where Charles reverts to a simpler, purer existence. He spends his days climbing the spiral staircase, playing with his collection, and engaging in trivial activities that bring him joy. This secluded life allows him to evade the burdens of adulthood—the responsibilities, expectations, and disillusionments that have weighed on him. The natural surroundings of the deep woods, untouched by the chaos of modernity, reinforce his escape into an idyllic past.

Yet, the treehouse is also a prison. Its small, confined space symbolizes the limitations of Charles's self-imposed exile. While he finds solace in his nostalgic retreat, the treehouse prevents him from confronting the complexities of the world below. His escape into nature and isolation is not a return to innocence but a withdrawal from the challenges and opportunities for growth that life offers.

Charles's retreat into the woods is marked by a deliberate abandonment of power and hegemonic masculinity. As a minister, he occupied a position of authority, embodying strength, control, and societal influence. His life in the city was one of ambition, responsibility, and achievement. By choosing the treehouse over his previous life, Charles relinquishes these markers of adult success and societal validation.

This rejection is further highlighted by his interactions with Stephen, a visitor to the treehouse. Stephen's confusion and discomfort with Charles's new lifestyle reflect the stark contrast between societal expectations of adulthood and Charles's childlike retreat. When Stephen asks, "Are you happy, Charles?" the response—"Look! It's fantastic. You don't understand it, it's fantastic!"—reveals both Charles' fervent belief in his newfound happiness and his desperation to justify his choices. His insistence on the treehouse's fantastical nature underscores the fragile foundation of his escape. While Charles perceives his retreat as liberating, it is also isolating, preventing him from engaging with those around him and deepening the divide between his internal world and external reality.

In the treehouse, Charles' perception of time becomes distorted. He halts his timeline, retreating into a state of perpetual childhood where responsibilities and the passage of years hold no sway. This regression is evident in his daily routine, which revolves around simple pleasures and solitary pursuits. By learning the names of plants and spending hours in nature, he constructs a life that feels timeless and unburdened by the expectations of adulthood.

Charles' deep sleep and improved demeanor, described by those who observe him, suggest that he finds temporary peace in this lifestyle. Yet, this peace is an illusion, rooted in denial rather than acceptance. His regression to a childlike state—marked by simplicity and detachment—comes at the expense of growth, connection, and reconciliation with his adult self. The idyllic nature of the treehouse, while appealing, is ultimately unsustainable. The small space, both physically and metaphorically, confines Charles to a narrow existence. By choosing to live in the past, he sacrifices the potential for future experiences and relationships. His obsession with recreating a childhood environment blinds him to the richness of life beyond the woods.

The panoramic view from the treehouse's platform—offering sights of the distant town and the setting sun—further emphasizes the poignancy of Charles' retreat.

> The whole wood was spread below them, and beyond it, five miles away across the fields, the town where he had stopped. To the west the sun was setting magnificently, the swirl of colour prettified by the dust of the Thames Valley seventy miles away. Charles was sprawled on a kitchen chair, watching proudly as Stephen took in the view. (104)

While the view symbolizes the vastness and beauty of the world, it also highlights the distance between Charles and the life he has left behind. His choice to remain in the treehouse, disconnected from the world below, underscores his inability to reconcile his longing for the past with the demands of the present.

The treehouse, initially a symbol of freedom and innocence, becomes the setting for Charles's ultimate tragedy. His suicide marks the culmination of his retreat into the past, as he becomes entirely consumed by his own nostalgia and isolation. The act of taking his own life within the treehouse underscores its dual nature as both a sanctuary and a prison. What begins as a space for liberation becomes a site of confinement, reflecting the dangers of living entirely in the past.

Charles's retreat to the treehouse is a deeply layered act, driven by both a yearning for lost innocence and a rejection of the complexities of adult life. His obsession with the treehouse represents a profound inner conflict—a desire to escape coupled with an awareness of the limitations of such an escape. His interactions with others, particularly Stephen, reveal the tension between his internal world and the external realities he seeks to avoid. While the treehouse offers Charles a temporary reprieve from his struggles, it also isolates him from the connections and responsibilities that define a fulfilling life. His decision to withdraw into the woods, though rooted in a longing for simplicity and joy, ultimately leads to stagnation and despair.

The Bell

The Bell pub is a time-traveled place. In here, Stephen's journey through time is the central link of the novel, which enables the protagonist to intervene in his own past and save his own future. This, in some way, is to give Stephen a chance to save himself, and to set him free from his past mistake. The adventure at the pub wakes him from a foggy dream, subtly disrupting Stephen's ingrained sense of time. The Bell incident occurs on the way to meet Julie after they have separated due to Kate's disappearance. This Chrono Cross event creates chances for Stephen and Julie to give birth to a new life, heralding the end of suffering and the rebirth of life and love.

> Through the window of the pub, Stephen is shocked when he sees two familiar faces.
>
> Quite suddenly, with the transforming rapidity of a catastrophe, everything was changed. His legs weakened, a chill spread downwards through his stomach. He was looking into the eyes of the woman, and he knew who she was. She had glanced up in his direction. The man was talking, making an insistent point, while the woman continued to stare. Her

face showed no curiosity or shock; she simply returned Stephen's gaze as she listened to her partner. She nodded vaguely, glanced away to reply, and then looked again towards Stephen. (56)

Stephen hallucinates the dating of his parents when they were young. He sees the look in his mother's eyes at that time, and his mother sees the face of a little baby. "He has slipped through a rift in the fabric of time itself, and for one awesome, mind-snapping moment he gazes through the window of The Bell into the eyes of his own mother, carrying his foetal self within her womb."[109] During the scene, Stephen has noticed that his parents have been arguing about something serious. His mother is thinking about abortion before, and when she sees Stephen's face on the window, she suddenly decides to keep him. His mother later confirms his hallucination and its significance.

> The baby, her baby, was suddenly flesh. It was holding her in its gaze, claiming her. It had acquired an independence of anything that might pass between this man and herself. For the first time she contemplated the idea of a separate individual, of a life which she must defend with her own.. (162)

She can't destroy a child simply because she has some trouble with her fiancé. She feels the baby inside her. Now a complete self is in front of the window, begging her for its existence, and it was inside her, living on the pulse of her own blood.

The Bell incident unfolds during Stephen's journey to reunite with Julie, after their painful separation brought on by Kate's disappearance. This unexpected event serves as a turning point, offering Stephen and Julie an opportunity to rebuild their bond and start anew. It marks not only the conclusion of their past torment but also the dawning of a fresh chapter—one filled with the promise of rebirth, healing, and the rekindling of love. As the echoes of the Bell reverberate, they symbolize a moment of transformation, where the weight of past struggles gives way to the potential for a renewed and deeper connection between them, a chance to embrace life and love once more, free from the shadows of their former pain.

The construction of chronotope is inseparable from the author's creative intentions, and it becomes a metaphor for the discourse of the times in the context of the Political and Economic Reforms of Britain in the 1980s. The static Whitehall space hints at Stephen's rejection of British political red tape, and the juxtaposition of heterogeneous spaces highlights the brevity of childhood and the irreversibility of time. The healing nature of time enables adults to face the cruelty of reality and step out of the shackles of inner space.[110] The novel's exploration of time and space intersects with the characters' individual ethics, revealing their unique ethical perspectives. The manipulation of time and the characters' interactions with it reveal the underlying ethical dilemmas and decisions that shape their journey. Through the depiction of various spaces and the actions taken within them, we gain insight into the characters' moral evolution. These spaces serve as both physical and metaphorical environments where the characters confront their values and navigate their ethical struggles. The dynamic relationship between time, place, and individual morality adds layers of complexity to the narrative, allowing for a nuanced exploration of the characters' ethical growth and internal transformations.

Chapter Five   The Class Ethics in *Atonement*

Though this book is of only average length, *Atonement* has the feel of a big family saga, so completely does McEwan delve into the consciousness of his main characters as they attempt to cope with the long-term repercussions of a "crime" committed by Briony Tallis, a naive 13-year-old with a "controlling demon." Briony's "wish for a harmonious, organized world denie[s] her the reckless possibilities of wrongdoing," so it is doubly ironic that her attempt to "fix" what she sees as wrongdoing involving her sister and Robbie Turner, a childhood friend, becomes, in itself, a wrongdoing, one she feels compelled to deny and for which she will eventually attempt to atone. (Mary Whipple, 2003)

Atonement revolves around the Tallis family living in an English country estate. The story begins in the summer holiday of 1935, when Lola Quincey and twins Jackson and Pierrot Quincey come and stay with the Tallies due to their parents' divorce scandal. Briony Tallis, the youngest and only child in the Tallis family, is a gifted writer with full self-consciousness. Cecilia Tallis, Briony's older sister, has a crush on Robbie Turner who is also holding a resolved romantic feeling for Cecilia but is repressed by his identity as the son of the Tallis gardener. The Tallis family provides funding to support Robbie's education. In turn, Robbie lives up to their expectation, completing his studies with excellent results, getting a scholarship from Cambridge and planning to be a doctor. One afternoon by accident, Briony witnesses the two of them entangling in an obscure scene from the room window. They seem to break an heirloom vase in front of a fountain in the garden, and then Cecilia takes off her clothes, diving into the fountain to retrieve the shards. Briony thinks that Cecilia's strange behaviors are under Robbie's threat and command. Later, Robbie intends to send a letter of apology to Cecilia via Briony, but mistakenly hands her a vulgar note instead, convincing Briony of the idea that Robbie is a rogue. In addition, witnessing a passionate lovemaking between the two with her shallow understanding, Briony cements a sense of resentment and suspicion of Robbie.

Leon Tallis, the oldest brother of Briony, comes home bringing a friend with him, Paul Marshall, a chocolate millionaire. A dinner is prepared to commemorate their visit, but the twins get lost that night, running away from the Tallis house out of strong yearnings towards their parents. Everyone in the Tallis house sets out to scout around for the lost boys. While searching alone, Briony sees someone stirring in the thick grass and finds that the 15-year-old Lola has been raped. The perpetrator flees in a hurry before he is recognized by Briony, but in Briony's mind, the answer to the question of who the suspect is has been determined. Briony firmly believes it is Robbie who commits the crime, and gives testimony to the policeman. Hours later, though Robbie successfully finds the missing twins and brings them back to the Tallis house safely, he is still taken into police custody under an unwarranted charge.

During the three and a half years in prison, Robbie has been in correspondence with Cecilia, while Cecilia cuts off from her family and moves out to London, living alone. The outbreak of World War II provides an opportunity for the early termination of Robbie's sentence. Robbie enlists in the army and goes to fight on the front line. With a painful shrapnel wound, he and his comrades experience disturbing carnage and finally arrive at the coast to evacuate with the British forces.

As Briony grows up, she gradually realizes her fault and begins to atone for her crime by dropping out to work as a nurse during the war. Briony becomes more mature when she suffers from the pain of others, an influx of injured men with harrowing war experiences. Learned that Paul and Lola are going to get married, Briony attends their wedding ceremony, and at that moment, she understands the truth of Lola's assault. Afterward, she pays a visit to Cecilia and pledges to take a necessary step for her atonement by informing relevant legal authorities of her change in testimony.

The book's epilogue confesses a regrettable truth of atonement from the narrator, 77-year-old Briony's first perspective. As a matter of fact, the atonement process is actually the writing of the novel itself, rather than exposing Paul and Lola's evil deeds by publishing her memoir while they are alive, because they are bigwigs and socialites with power and fortune. The atonement is not achieved before Robbie and Cecilia's death, both of whom actually perish in the war. It is impossible for Briony to fulfill her promise in reality, so she takes another way to atone—writing a novel that allows Robbie and Cecilia to live happily.

From the reviews made by James Wood (from *The New Republic*), he believes it is "certainly his finest and most complex novel. [...] *Atonement* is both a criticism of fiction and a defense of fiction, a criticism of its shaping and exclusive torque, and a defense of its ideal democratic generosity to all. A criticism of fiction's misuse; and a defense of an ideal." "The writing is conspicuously good [...] it works an authentic spell." (John Updike, *The New Yorker*) "It is rare for a critic to feel justified in using the word 'masterpiece,' but Ian McEwan's new book really deserves to be called one. [...] *Atonement* [...] is a work of astonishing depth and humanity."[111]

Atonement, a tragic tale of love, suffering, and loss, centers around young Briony's mistake, which serves as the pivotal turning point in the development of the plot. The perjury which Briony committed implicates the complexity of sin. It can be defined as a sheer mistake due to children's innocence and ignorance, or an undoubted crime caused by a human's malicious conjecture. To a certain extent, the boundary between good and evil is not explicit but blurred, so the sin is not executed in an instant but gradually formed in a series of wrong ethical choices and ethical judgments. The disaster of Briony's misconduct ultimately wreaks irreparable harm and a spiritual shackle, tormenting each character round the clock. Though Briony is the exact person responsible for this guilt, factors contributing to the tragedy have something to do with the dark sides of human nature and the limitations of social background in the 1930s.

The novel explores the murky divide between good and evil, highlighting the complexity and ambiguity of sin. Briony's perjury, which becomes a pivotal moment in the story, exemplifies the complexity of sin. It can be seen as a simple mistake resulting from the innocence and ignorance of children, or as a deliberate crime fueled by malicious intent. This ambiguity reflects the nuanced ethical choices and judgments made by the characters.

The social background of the 1930s, along with the darker aspects of human nature, significantly contributes to the tragedy in the novel. The rigid societal norms and class structures, compounded by the inherent flaws of human nature, play a crucial role in shaping the characters' actions and decisions. Social class, in particular, creates ethical dilemmas that influence the characters' judgments, often leading them to make choices that reflect their limited understanding of morality within the confines of their social position. These constraints, shaped by both societal expectations and class divisions, contribute to the tragic outcomes and the characters' struggle for redemption or atonement. The novel underscores how social class can shape ethical conflicts, and the tension between personal morals and societal demands complicates the characters' attempts to reconcile their actions with their sense of right and wrong. Briony's misconduct acts as a catalyst for irreparable harm and spiritual torment affecting all the characters. While Briony bears direct responsibility for her guilt, the tragedy extends beyond her, implicating the entire web of relationships and individuals involved. The consequences of her actions highlight the far-reaching impact of ethical choices and the lasting effects of sin on the lives of those involved. The tragedy that unfolds in the novel demonstrates the profound impact of ethical decisions on individuals and the lasting consequences they face.

Section One Roots of the Sin

I. The Unbridgeable Division between Classes

Class differences are a feature of British society and history. In the history of more than one thousand years, in terms of class attributes, Britain has successively emerged as a primitive tribal military aristocracy, a feudal aristocracy, a capitalist land aristocracy, an industrial and commercial bourgeois aristocracy and middle class "Labour aristocracy," and the main aristocratic rank system and name changes have been gone through five times. And the nature of the nobility also changes with the development of time and history. From the 17th century onwards, the British feudal aristocracy began to evolve into a capitalist land aristocracy. With the constitutional monarchy and the Industrial Revolution, the British secular aristocracy underwent a change in social class attributes. They actively and universally adopted capitalist business methods, safeguarded the interests of capitalist industrialists and businessmen, and gradually became bourgeois. The door of the House of Lords was also opened to the industrial and commercial bourgeoisie, and 1880 was a turning point for the British industrial and commercial capitalists to enter the House of Lords at a faster pace, and capitalists such as miners, manufacturers, financiers, and shareholders of the railway industry entered one after another and became the new bourgeois aristocracy. In the 19th century, the British aristocracy and the middle class reached a certain level of integration. The emerging middle class, often regarded as upstarts, rose during the wave of the Industrial Revolution. Through their efforts and economic success, they climbed the ladder of wealth and gradually merged, to some extent, with the aristocracy. As a result, the upper class and the merchant class became increasingly interconnected, fostering a mutual integration that reshaped the social hierarchy of the time.

  Scholars have found that long-term social mobility is remarkably limited. Whether it involves moving from the lower class to the middle class or from the upper class to the middle class, such transitions typically take as long as ten generations. Class divisions have persisted for thousands of years, and social inequality remains a significant and pressing issue. Class ethics, as a system of moral values and principles shaped by class divisions, plays a pivotal role in defining interpersonal relationships and societal norms. These ethics often reflect the interests of specific social strata, creating moral codes that perpetuate existing inequalities. In *Atonement*, the tragedy at the heart of the narrative is deeply intertwined with class ethics. The inherent biases and prejudices stemming from the incompatibility of classes, the rigid morality of the upper class, and their tendency to manipulate and shield their interests contribute significantly to the unfolding of events.

  The British upper class, historically a group with political privileges and economic dominance, maintained a hierarchical structure that created an insurmountable divide between themselves and the working class or servants. This gap, rooted in centuries of social and economic inequality, is a central theme in the novel. Historically, the term "upper class" emerged in the early 19th century, initially referring to the British landed aristocracy. Over time, with the rise of industrialization, the industrial and commercial bourgeoisie gradually merged with the traditional landowning elite, ultimately becoming the dominant force within the upper class.

By the modern era, the traditional land aristocracy had integrated with capitalists in industry, commerce, and finance, forming a unified upper class. This group, now synonymous with the big bourgeoisie, occupies most of the means of production and personal wealth in Britain, wielding substantial influence over the nation's political, economic, cultural, and social spheres. In *Atonement*, these class dynamics and their associated ethics underpin the conflicts and decisions that drive the story, highlighting the devastating consequences of systemic inequality and the moral compromises it necessitates. In the novel, the Cecilia family, who are the owners of the manor, made a fortune when her grandfather invented patents. Although the ancestors of the Tallis family were sunk in a bog of farm labor, the efforts of the descendants changed the fate of the entire family. Today the Tallis family is undoubtedly a member of the upper class; grand houses, spacious estates, and interactions with celebrities from all walks of life prove this. While Robbie's mother is just a cleaning lady of the Tallis family, and even Robbie is doing some weeding chores at the Tallis's house. When Cecilia Tallis half-runs with her flowers along the path by the river, Robbie Turner kneels nearby, weeding along a rugosa hedge. An insurmountable class divide separates Robbie and Cecilia.

This conception of a hierarchy of servants and masters has existed in British society for many years. From the late Middle Ages onwards, domestic servants became one of the nobility's symbols. Their status underwent a series of changes during the long Middle Ages: from originally being slaves, they developed into free people who relied on selling their labor for wages and accommodation. Although the domestic servants of England were an indispensable and important factor in the good functioning of the aristocratic family, there was still an insurmountable class relationship between the servant and the master. The difference in the ranks of master and servant in British aristocratic families in the late Middle Ages is still evident even in the 20th century. There are also hierarchical differences between master and servant, and the master and servant are two parallel societies, one on the other, observing the principles in their respective societies. In terms of legal relations, the master and servant are the relationships between the employer and the employee, but in real life, the master and the servant are a mixture of multiple relationships such as service, hierarchy, opposition, dependence, and intimacy.

According to the authority relationship, the Cecilia family is the owner of the manor, while the Robbie family is just an ordinary family belonging to the working people at the bottom. According to their professional status, Cecilia's parents and Robbie's parents belong to the master-servant relationship. The two are the upper class on one side and the bottom class on the other, and the wealth, prestige, and power are far apart. Although Robbie receives a higher education than what is typically afforded to his class, even attending the same university as Cecilia, his access to these educational resources is rooted in his status as the son of a loyal and competent cleaning maid employed by Cecilia's family. This favor granted by the family does not alter the underlying class disparity or the substantial difference in social status between them. As for the combination of the two, from the Norman period onwards, the English aristocratic family was maintained by blood and marriage, and in medieval England, the marriage of the children of the nobles was related to the family status and had always received special attention. When planning the marriage between the far-sighted upper class and his relatives, in addition to taking into account the basic conditions such as money and family lineage, the far-sighted upper class must also consider factors such as political prospects and interpersonal relations. Therefore, the combination of Robbie and Cecilia also has a chasm that is difficult to cross. The gap between Robbie and Cecilia can be seen in their daily life and living environment. The Tallis family's house is readily available, tall and gorgeous in appearance: "The falling light magnified the dusky expanse of the park, and the soft yellow glow at the windows on the far side of the lake made the house seem almost grand and beautiful."[112] While Robbie's living environment is very narrow and the activity area is also very small: "All day long his small bedroom, his bathroom and the cubicle wedged between them he called his study had baked under the southern slope of the bungalow's roof" (69). The difference between the two reflects the deep-rooted concept of hierarchy inherited from British history, and this hierarchy has also deeply affected people's thoughts and behavior.

II. The Irretrievable Sin Rooted in Class

As Roman Catholic theology puts it, the seven deadly sins include lust, gluttony, greed, sloth, wrath, envy, and pride. All these latent desires are common motivations which trigger an individual's conduct. However, some behaviors appear the same on the surface but stem from different intentions, be they good or evil. When the truth is deliberately concealed or permanently buried, the moral court turns into a discourse arena.

Characters in *Atonement* are profoundly shaped by the rigid hierarchical structures and class consciousness of 1930s Britain, a period when both family and societal order were tightly regulated by class distinctions. These invisible yet powerful barriers dictated not only behavior but also perception, shaping how individuals viewed themselves and others. This stratification becomes a critical framework within which the novel's central conflicts and moral dilemmas unfold.

The rigid family order reflects the microcosm of class hierarchy. Within the Tallis household, roles and expectations are dictated by an unspoken but deeply ingrained understanding of social rank. Robbie, despite his intellectual capabilities and higher education, is fundamentally constrained by his origins as the son of the family's cleaning maid. His close relationship with Cecilia breaches this invisible boundary, challenging the established social norms that are fiercely upheld by the upper class. This challenge is not simply a personal affront but is perceived as a violation of the broader societal order, underscoring the deeply rooted prejudice that exists between classes.

The broader class order extends this rigidity into society, where individuals are often defined by their social position rather than their personal virtues or achievements. For example, Briony's misinterpretation of Robbie's actions is not merely a personal error but is influenced by her internalized notions of class superiority. She views Robbie not as an equal but as someone inherently suspect due to his lower-class background. Her false accusation of him is, in part, a manifestation of this class-based bias, illustrating how notions of sin and guilt are entangled with class consciousness.

Ethical selection and ethical choice, as terms in Literary Ethical Criticism, refer to the moral option in broad and narrow sense, respectively. The first concept, ethical selection, refers to the civilizational stage through which hominids, after acquiring human form, strive to attain human essence. Analogous to natural selection, it represents the continuous process by which humans become truly human through moral development. On the level of individual life, a person's entire lifespan—from birth to death—can be seen as an ethical selection process. The second concept, ethical choice, denotes the specific moral decisions individuals make within that broader process. While ethical selection represents humanity's grand moral journey, culminating in the gradual maturity of rationality, ethical choice concerns the concrete acts of choosing between moral alternatives. Through repeated choices—between the rational human and the irrational beast—individuals shape their moral character and contribute to the ethical progress of humankind[113]. In short, ethical selection is the long-term moral evolution of humanity, whereas ethical choice refers to particular moral decisions that differ in process, result, and ethical value.

In this novel, class is the main influencing factor on ethical choice. The tragedy is not caused by one person, and everyone is affected by class. Paul Marshall and Robbie Turner both shared the sin of lust, while Lola Quincey and Cecilia Tallis both inherited the pride of aristocracy. (Fifteen-year-old Lola and her nine-year-old young twin brothers are distant cousins of the Tallis family. Their parents are involved in a marital crisis so that family life is in ruins and they have to stay at Tallis's house for the summer holiday.) As for Briony, there is a strong class attribute in her, although she isn't aware of it. Ethical choices of characters pave the way for Robbie's poor fate as a scapegoat.

Sin, as depicted in the novel, is thus deeply embedded in the characters' perceptions of class and their inability to transcend these divisions. The injustice inflicted on Robbie is a direct result of the classist attitudes that permeate the Tallis family and their social milieu. These attitudes allow for the dehumanization of those perceived as socially inferior, enabling actions that ultimately lead to tragedy. The novel suggests that this sin is systemic, rooted not in individual morality but in the broader societal framework that prioritizes class distinctions over human connection.

Furthermore, the class barriers in *Atonement* create a moral blindness that obstructs empathy and fosters misjudgment. Characters are unable to see beyond the constructs of class, which distorts their moral compass and leads to devastating consequences. The tragedy of Robbie and Cecilia's doomed love serves as a powerful critique of the destructive nature of such rigid hierarchies, highlighting how deeply entrenched class notions can dictate the course of individuals' lives.

In this way, *Atonement* portrays sin not as an isolated act of wrongdoing but as a systemic issue rooted in the social fabric of the time. The strict hierarchical concept of the 1930s functions as both a cause and a justification for the characters' moral failings, making it an inescapable force that shapes their actions and the tragedies that ensue. Through this lens, the novel critiques the social structures that perpetuate inequality and highlights the devastating impact of these structures on personal ethics and human relationships.

Lola and Marshall

Paul Marshall is a chocolate millionaire. "There'll be one of these inside the kit bag of every soldier in the land. Standard issue." (68) They make their fortune through war. He visits the Tallis family as a friend of Leon Tallis, an honored guest, and a potential fiancé of Cecilia. However, since he is a hypocrite, the act of using chocolate as bait to deceive ignorant Lola and acquire children's admiration and trust is the first step of Paul's perfect crime plan. When Lola's "tongue turns green as it curled around the edges of the candy casing" (69), the action stimulates Paul's sexual desire, so he unconsciously sits back in the armchair, watching Lola closely. With the expansion of eager lust, he crosses and uncrosses his legs with thrills and then takes a deep breath, giving Lola a tip to make a more seductive gesture with full sexual innuendo: "You've got to bite it" (69). Lola's pride and greed make her an accomplice of Paul Marshall. Lola knows at a young age that she has to plan for her future, and since she is young and has no access to celebrities, the wealthy Marshall is undoubtedly the best choice for her.

The institution of marriage within the English upper class has historically been a complex and strategic arrangement, often manipulated by political, economic, and social interests. Rather than a purely personal union, marriage was frequently seen as a calculated opportunity to consolidate property, extend political power, and enhance social influence. These considerations tied upper-class marriages to the broader fortunes of the entire family, making them a critical aspect of aristocratic life. Within this context, Lola's role in *Atonement* embodies the intersection of ambition, power dynamics, and the pursuit of social advancement. As a sister and, in the absence of their parents, a surrogate authority figure, Lola wields significant influence over her younger brothers, Pierrot and Jackson. During the rehearsal of The Trials of Arabella, her authority becomes evident as she manipulates the twins, using her favorite phrase, "Remember what The Parents said?" (22), as a tool to assert control. This demonstrates her knack for leveraging familial power structures to her advantage. Lola's character is marked by a relentless desire for power, esteem, and social status, traits that define her interactions and decisions. Her ambition surfaces clearly during the rehearsal when she aspires to play the lead role of Arabella in Briony's drama. Although she outwardly feigns indifference, even acting as though she might withdraw, she subtly orchestrates the twins to advocate for her behind the scenes (22). This calculated behavior highlights her skill in manipulation and her ability to mask ambition under a veneer of nonchalance.

Her pursuit of social advancement reaches its peak in her relationship with Paul Marshall. Lola's greed for wealth, influence, and the attention that comes with marrying into prosperity drives her to extremes. She willingly sacrifices her body and aligns herself with Marshall, ultimately securing marriage to him. In doing so, she demonstrates an unyielding determination to achieve her goals, regardless of the moral cost. Lola's narrative arc is a reflection of her ambitions and self-centered nature, as she becomes the architect of her own story. As Briony later observes, "It was her story, the one that was writing itself around her" (165). This statement underscores how Lola consciously shapes her destiny, using the tools of manipulation, charm, and ambition to craft a life that fulfills her desires for status and security.

In Briony's view, Lola is the victim of statutory rape, because "she heard the helplessness in Lola's voice, and in an instant, Briony understood completely" (164). As a matter of fact, Lola knows all about the perpetrator, as the novel writes, "she may have been about to embark upon a long confession in which she would find her feelings as she spoke them and lead herself out of her numbness toward something that resembled both terror and joy" (165), but she doesn't. At first, Lola denies it vaguely: "I'm sorry, I didn't, I'm sorry...", and then she chooses to remain silent when Briony asks, "Who was it?" Until Briony constantly confirms her suspicion that "It was Robbie," Lola at last turns slowly to face Briony and accepts with "You saw him," fabricating a charge against Robbie to exempt Paul Marshall from punishment.

Robbie and Cecilia

Dealing with lust and pride, Robbie Turner and Cecilia Tallis also undergo a series of ethical selections. In the beginning, Robbie controls his lust while Cecilia retains her pride. However, things change subsequently that Robbie's lust bursts and Cecilia loses her pride. Only then do the lovers break through the class distinction and realize their pure love. The ambiguous relationship between Robbie and Cecilia becomes a blind spot for Briony, indirectly causing Briony's false accusation.

Before Cecilia frees herself from the fetters of hierarchy, she also deems herself a noble daughter of the manor master. It is shameful and absurd for her to talk with Robbie or invite Robbie to eat at the same table. Even though Robbie is highly educated, he still obeys the principle of hierarchy by suppressing his humble love. Cecilia knows that the relationship between her and Robbie is hard to accept, and equal marriage has always been an important way for aristocrats to maintain their dignity. Family interests have always occupied an important position in the life of British aristocrats, which is vividly reflected in the marriage life of aristocrats. For the aristocracy, marriage is not a private affair. It is related to the rise of the family's social status, the establishment of political alliances, and the accumulation of family property. Therefore, property and power are the decisive conditions for leading aristocratic marriage, and the ultimate goal is to ensure that the whole family can obtain the maximum benefit in the marriage.

Robbie soberly restrains his love for Cecilia because of class differences, distancing himself from the Tallis family. Similarly, out of a sort of pride, Cecilia "hardly speaks to him in three years" (58) during the days in Cambridge and they have fallen out of touch. Robbie has been subsidized by Cecilia's father through school and university and gets a scholarship to Cambridge. Though he is a well-bred and excellent youth who makes remarkable achievements in his studies, Robbie clearly regards himself as the son of a cleaning lady. When coming to Tallis' house, Robbie intentionally removes his clean boots, takes his socks off and tiptoes across the wet floor with comic exaggeration as if he himself would stain the house with dust. Before he has the boldness of ambition to propose to Celia, Robbie decides to spend another six years studying medicine to be a doctor. While they are arguing about studying medicine, Robbie inadvertently snaps Cecilia's antique vase. Their relationship reaches an impasse, as Cecilia thinks, "If he wanted distance, then let him have it" (136). None of them openly and honestly recognizes their true feelings for each other. A turning point lies in the letter of apology, a revelation of Robbie's enthusiastic love for Cecilia. Robbie writes an elegant letter to ask for Cecilia's forgiveness, but Cecilia receives another note by mistake, on which Robbie scribbles his sexual desire for Cecilia. After being aware of both parties' feelings, Robbie and Cecilia, childhood friends and university acquaintances, whose friendship has become vague and even constrained in recent years, in a state of expansive, tranquil joy, confronted the momentous change they have achieved (138), verifying their love by making love against the library shelves.

This intricate interplay of lust, pride, and class distinctions underscores the ethical dimensions of Robbie and Cecilia's relationship. Their love is shaped not only by personal emotions but also by the moral and social frameworks that define their world. Robbie's initial restraint and Cecilia's pride reveal their internal struggles to navigate the hierarchical structures of their society. The ethical choices they face—whether to suppress or pursue their love—reflect the tension between personal desires and societal expectations.

The turning point, marked by Robbie's unintended explicit letter and their subsequent physical union in the library, signifies a moment of ethical liberation. It is a decisive act of defiance against the class boundaries and moral conventions that have constrained them. By choosing to embrace their love despite the societal repercussions, Robbie and Cecilia challenge the rigid ethical codes of their time, asserting the primacy of genuine human connection over artificial hierarchies.

However, this ethical triumph is short-lived, as their relationship becomes entangled in Briony's misunderstanding and false accusation, leading to tragic consequences. The moral fabric of the narrative is further complicated by the way societal norms and class prejudices amplify the gravity of Robbie's misfortune. The blood of the inferior predestines Robbie's fate that everyone in the Tallis house despises and stigmatizes him and no one tries to believe he is innocent or stand up to speak for him. His lower-class status not only renders him vulnerable to false judgment but also exposes the deep ethical flaws within a society that prioritizes class and reputation over truth and justice.

Briony

Briony advocates order and neatness. Growing up in the upper class, she naturally acquiesces to the incompatibility between different classes, which is the order and rules rooted in her subconscious. She enjoys writing stories and plays and directing and acting in them, which are upper-class hobbies. The factors affecting human behavior include internal subjective factors, such as perception, value, attitude, temperament, ability, and external environmental factors, such as organizational structure, social culture, politics and law. As for the culprit, Briony's distinctive psychological characteristics, as well as her social and family environment, dominated the underlying logic of her behavior, which completely determined her decision-making.

Briony is a child with a creative writer's unique qualities, who is the master of her own imaginary world. Her personality could be summarized in four key words, that is, curiosity, rampant imagination, rationalism/order orientation, and self-consciousness. Each element exerts considerable influence on the process of ethical judgment.

Curiosity is the fundamental driving force for the development of human cognition. Briony's ambition to become an excellent writer impels her to investigate an unknown world, especially the adult world beyond the reach of this precocious girl, because she knows that "vital knowingness about the ways of the world would compel a reader's respect" (15). Peeping is the main method for Briony to enter an arena of adult emotion, from which her writing is bound to benefit (116). The first peek happens through the nursery's wide-open windows when she sees Cecilia out of her blouse and then letting her skirt drop to the ground in front of Robbie. Such barefaced scenes have gone beyond the cognitive world of a 13-year-old child, as she raises two hands to her face and steps back a little way from the window. However, it is impossible for her to shut her eyes and be blind to her sister's shame (46). On the contrary, it is a temptation for her to be magical and dramatic, and a great chance to enter the real adult world rather than a fairy tale. This kind of peeping that Briony violates her ethical conscience to satisfy inner curiosity happens more than once. Briony knows exactly that it is wrong to open people's letters and read them without permission, but a savage and thoughtless curiosity prompts her to rip Robbie's letter from the envelope. Meanwhile, Briony exempts herself from guilt and uneasiness on the pretext that it is right and essential for her to know everything. Thus, curiosity, along with a simultaneous excitement, induces Briony to immorally absorb mystical information. However, her curiosity foreshadows her sin of wrongly testifying against Robbie.

Imagination is another psychological capability to associate memory fragments and create new anticipation so as to comprehend all sorts of things profoundly. Briony's capability of imagining leads her to sink deep into the mire of fantasy. Briony, who has inherent sensitivity and extremely rich imagination, is constantly constructing her own wishful perception of the world and presenting crazy daydreams in the form of literary creations in her inner world. At the age of eleven, she writes her first story and the seven-page play *The Trials of Arabella* at thirteen, and then the self-narrative *Atonement* in her old age. It is typical for Briony to subjectively mix imaginary elements with facts: "what she saw must have been shaped in part by what she already knew, or believed she knew" (125).

Due to the child's limited horizon and ignorance of the adult world, Briony inevitably exaggerates her imagination of good and bad, heroes and villains. All her knowledge is confined to such a pattern she has written before, in which a humble woodcutter saves a princess from drowning and ends by marrying her. Taking the tale as the prototype of Robbie's entanglement with Cecilia, Briony accepts her assumptions for granted that the humble cleaning lady's son Robbie has the boldness of ambition to marry Cecilia, and thinks that this logic makes perfect sense. Setting the rapacious images for Robbie, Briony has no way to understand words on the apology note as attraction and affinity between the opposite sex, but only interprets it as something elemental, brutal, perhaps even evil stemming from obscene men. Correspondingly, she does not doubt that her sister is in some way threatened and will need her help. Therefore, with rampant imagination coupled with groundless background knowledge, Briony envisions a sinful plot that deviates from reality in her mind.

What further promotes Briony's crime is her paranoia about an order, the way in which people or things are tidily arranged, either in relation to one another or according to a particular characteristic, maintaining the condition within a logical and controllable range, so is the broader sense of order: the social order. Ethical judgment underpinned by rationalism has a significant impact on her interpretation, which leads to her twisted identification of Robbie, so compliance with rationalism and order is a prelude to the decisive accusation. Briony herself is the governor of a certain order in the self-constructed world. Immersed in the fictional literary world all day long, Briony finds that her zest for writing is a manifestation of her love for order. Writing stories not only involves secrecy, it also gives her all the pleasures of miniaturization, to build a micro-world where a crisis in a heroine's life could be made to coincide with hailstones, gales and thunder, whereas nuptials were generally blessed with good light and soft breezes (17). Since mayhem and destruction were too chaotic for her tastes, her play *The Trials of Arabella,* the gist of which is "love which did not build a foundation on good sense was doomed" (13), entirely inherited the tradition of rationalism and advocated reason to restrain emotion. Briony's sense of obligation, as well as her instinct for order, is powerful, and this love of order shapes the principles of justice. "Her wish for a harmonious, organized world denied her the reckless possibilities of wrongdoing" (15), so Briony is unable to tolerate wrong behavior and always feels a great compulsion to push things into a reasonable way, to let scoundrels get the punishment they deserve. For Briony, exposing Robbie's offense against Lola is one of the things that must be done. When Briony discovered the scene of sexual assault, "she was nauseous with disgust and fear" (167). A sense of justice and a power of order precipitated her into the thought that if her poor cousin Lola is not able to command the truth, then she would do it for her. (168) Ultimately, the obsession with order is realized in the interrogation and ends up putting Robbie in prison.

As for the love between her sister and Robbie, she subconsciously thinks it is impossible, that love or even marriage between two completely unequal classes is impossible. People of different classes should go to different schools and engage in different industries. She has a distinct and profound class character, and although it is not shown externally, it is reflected in many details. In her play, *The Trials of Arabella*, the heroine meets and eventually marries a poor doctor, but it turns out that the doctor is a prince who covers his real identity to help people. In her mind, the aristocrat will eventually stay with the aristocrat. And aristocrats also have good morals. How can such a hierarchical perspective see the whole picture? Briony's class nature affects her perspective of things at all times, thus influencing her ethical judgment. The established hierarchy concept in her mind has already led her to believe that Robbie harbors malicious intentions. Therefore, her accusation becomes a just act to maintain class order.

Last but not least, it is self-consciousness that makes Briony's sin reach a point of no return. Accustomed to establishing and maintaining order freely in writing, Briony has been indulging in a state of self-mythology with a self-centered characteristic. She is the initiator of Self Theory, an arrogant, willful bigot who insists on her point of view without vacillation. Though Briony seems to be gentle and quiet in daily life, the moment things confront her principles, she will undoubtedly impose her own will on others. Briony is encouraged to read her original stories aloud in the library for her parents and older sister, all of whom are unexpectedly shocked by their quiet girl's bold performance. It is unapologetic for Briony to demand her family's total attention as she casts her narrative spell. In another case, Briony's excitement of performing the play before adult audiences fails to evoke other children's sympathy. Pierrot and Jackson express a feeling of impatience by grumbling that "I hate plays, dressing up and all that sort of thing." Immediately, Briony hits back and angrily rebukes, "How can you hate plays?" Subsequently comes a conceited and bumptious idea that she knows they can never understand her ambition (21). This defect of personality appears in another form of selfishness, leaving no room for effective remedies to the sin. From time to time, Briony is conscious of illogical mistakes she has made and she is driven back to the understanding that "her eyes could not simply tell her the truth and it was too dark for that" (168). Even when she realizes that what she knows is not literally true, or not based on the visible, and that she might have been too arbitrary and misunderstand Robbie, she still insists on her public remarks. She trapped herself and marched into the labyrinth of her own construction (170), being too opinionated to insist on her wrong way.

III. The Unbreachable Gap of the Class

Briony's personality is not the only thing to blame. The external environment also contributes to the development of her personality, values and emotional experience, which further expedites the tragedy. Both ostensibly harmonious family relations and the ingrained prejudice against class indirectly deepened Briony's misreading of Robbie.

Family as the closest growth environment for children subtly influences their character. Not only the status of a family member but also the connection bonds with each other will unconsciously shape children's behavioral patterns, for the reason that love and care from family are vital to internal psychological health, generating senses of security, achievement, intimacy, etc. Supposing that children grow up with the absence of family love and the lack of emotional communication, they will be inclined to isolate themselves from the real world and immerse themselves in a self-seclusion state with extreme loneliness, secretly nurturing a desire for attention from others.

The apathetic atmosphere of the Tallis family, to a great extent, breeds Briony's solitary childhood experience. The Tallis house is a quaint old manor which is located in the desolate wilderness and shrouded in gloom. "Her effective status as an only child, as well as the relative isolation of the Tallis house, kept her from girlish intrigues with friends" (175). No one knows about her secrets about the squirrel's skull she collects beneath her bed. Worse still, no one even wants to know. Mr. Tallis has frequently been away from home, while Mrs. Tallis, who will generously give Briony's appreciation and evaluation of her writing, is often out of spirits in her bedroom. Sometimes when Briony sees her from afar, she knows Mrs. Tallis' mouth is in a downward curve, easily mistaken for the sign of reproach (161). Brother Leon is a selfish playboy, while Sister Cecilia shoulders the burden of the whole family, who actually wants to flee the family and live alone. Thus, Briony lives in a world surrounded by adults without peers and friends. The Tallis family maintains a superficial relationship. It seems that everyone in the family revolves around Briony. In fact, they estrange from each other psychologically, and no one understands her innermost needs and ideas, so Briony can only live in her self-constructed inner world (14).

Out of mental solitude, Briony wallows in self-pity and thirsts for full attention from others. When she feels lonely, she constantly imagines the care of her family as spiritual support. There are moments in the summer dusk after her light is out, when she makes her heart thud with luminous, yearning fantasies. In one fantasy, Arabella is the incarnation of Briony herself. When Arabella sinks in loneliness and despair, Leon's big, good-natured face buckles in grief. In another imagination, Leon boasts to a group of friends that "my younger sister, Briony Tallis, the writer, you must surely have heard of her." It was true that Briony's play "was not for her cousins, it was for her brother, to celebrate his return, provoke his admiration." Incredibly, Briony even has imagined her mother's funeral to realize the emotional reunion of the Tallis family, a funeral at which Briony's dignified reticence will hint at the vastness of her sorrow, and at the churchyard, she and Leon and Cecilia would stand in an interminable embrace in the long grass by the new headstone (161). All in all, what Briony has done is entirely for attention and recognition. However, if she fails to draw others' attention, she will be overcome by her subjective and extreme prejudice. For example, when Mrs. Tallis gives Briony a positive response and comments on her writing, Briony feels indebted and thinks her mother is endlessly kind and sweet and good. When she sees her mother smiling at Lola for the dress making its perfect, clinging fit around her cousin Lola, Briony considers her mother partial and the smile becomes heartless in Briony's eyes.

Likewise, this logic is well applied to Robbie's case. Young Briony has a crush on handsome Robbie in her childhood, although Robbie only takes her as a child in need of care. When she was ten, Briony deliberately jumped into the river in front of Robbie, at the risk of her life, to test whether Robbie would risk his life to save her or simply let her drown, to verify Robbie's concern, care and attention for her. When Robbie tries his best to save Briony and scolds her for being reckless, Briony thinks it is the evidence proving that Robbie takes her seriously. However, Robbie and Cecilia's love disillusions Briony's love fantasy, which turns Briony's secret love into hatred. Failing to attain Robbie's love and attention, she has already buried the seeds of jealousy in her heart when she catches sight of Cecilia and Robbie's erotic interaction, and ultimately develops a prejudice against Robbie, leading her to slander and falsely accuse Robbie in the rape case.

Besides the family ethics going wrong in Briony's family, the class order is definitely the core reason for all the sins. Characters in *Atonement* are deeply influenced by the strict hierarchical concept in the 1930s. Both family order and class order have become invisible barriers to constrain people's thoughts. Before Cecilia frees herself from the fetters of hierarchy, she also deems herself a noble daughter of the manor master. It is shameful and absurd for her to talk with Robbie or invite Robbie to eat at the same table. Even though Robbie is highly educated, he also obeys the principle of hierarchy by suppressing his humble love. The blood of the inferior predestines Robbie's fate that everyone in the Tallis house despises and stigmatizes him and no one tries to believe he is innocent or stand up to speak for him.

The most obvious concept of order is embodied in Briony's father, Mr. Tallis, which has seriously affected Briony. In the Tallis family, Mr. Tallis is the head of the family, the authority of the family, and the master of the adult world Briony lives in, who represents the order and rule of the adult world. When her father is home, the household settles around a fixed point. Though he spends most of his time sitting in the library, organizes nothing and rarely tells anyone what to do, his presence imposes order and allows freedom (124). The father's existence and responsibility for children are reflected in a series of rules, whose authority is invisible but powerful. He has notions as self-evident to him as natural justice. For example, he has precise ideas about where and when a woman should be seen smoking (53).

Briony is the successor of Mr. Tallis' concept of order, for this is the way she is brought up by her father. When Mr. Tallis is confused, he takes Briony into the library to help him find it. If her father is home, Briony can follow her father's instructions and enter the library without appearing cautious when it is time to "go through" the library. But if Mr. Tallis is absent, it is stressful for Briony to cross the hallway at her discretion. It is these thoughts of her father or a symbol of order that make her another discreet order executor. In her world, everything must be in order tidily. People of different classes should go to different schools and engage in various industries. The boundaries are clear and could never be crossed. The affair between Robbie and Cecilia, in Briony's eyes, is no different from the plot that a humble woodcutter saves a princess from drowning and ends by marrying her. The established hierarchy concept in her mind has already led her to believe that Robbie harbors malicious intentions. Therefore, her accusation becomes a just act to maintain class order.

A sense of guilt is a relatively subjective feeling of regret or guilt for one's actions, arising when a person perceives incompatibility between their own behavior and conscience after the event. Irreversible consequences incurred by his conduct will reinforce the gravity of his guilty conscience. Though Briony turns the wicked illusion into a conclusive testimony, in young Briony's mind, the firm accusation is an imperative measure of defending justice rather than a fault. The outbreak of the Second World War brought about earth-shaking changes in the world, and to a certain extent, briefly broke through the barriers between different classes in Britain. Ladies of the noble family also work as nurses in field hospitals, and everyone, regardless of class status, probably lives in the same room. War is like a giant blender; no matter who you are, or which group or class you belong to, people get to know and see so many kinds of people and live a life beyond classes. Briony finally realizes what kind of sin she has committed, causing irreparable harm. It is not until Briony develops mature moral judgment that the sin is formally embedded in her cognition as an intangible shackle. Old Briony admits her fault with a pervasive sense of guilt through a sort of narration like "within the half hour Briony would commit her crime" (156). Thus, what makes this crime a crime is the painful price characters pay for it. When Briony is fully aware that Robbie and Cecilia's promising future life and faithful love are both ruined by her ignorance, the sin generated in her mind shadows her whole life.

Her muddled testimony ruins others' heyday of life, love, and unfulfilled dreams. Robbie and Cecilia's love falls into the abyss of suffering, undergoing long-distance separation and death, and their due happiness cannot be realized and compensated. The innocent and helpless Robbie is unjustly imprisoned and sentenced to three years. Later, he is exiled to serve as a soldier in World War II. Robbie, such a handsome and intelligent man, would become a doctor and marry Cecilia in a brilliant near future, but he is actually expelled due to Briony's arrogance, ignorance and irrational imagination. Though the Tallis' family and the house and park mean the most important thing to Cecilia, she is filled with indignation at the result that no one believes Robbie is innocent, and therefore resolutely cuts off connections with her family to live alone from then on. The action of leaving proves her deep love for Robbie, to the degree that "she was destroying a part of herself for his sake" (204). She is heartbroken and bearing the pain of missing and losing her lover day and night. The love between them enables each other to live tenaciously during the cruel war years and gives each other the courage to survive with a beautiful vision and hope for reuniting and living a happy life after the war. The relentless fire of war finally swallows up this pair of lovers who are not married and do not even meet each other before they die. Robbie dies of sepsis in Dunkirk and Celia is killed in the explosion of Clapham Common tube station during the German air raid. The more determined and loyal their love is, the deeper Briony's sin can be. The cruel and pitiful reality aggravates the deep sense of guilt of Briony and the seriousness of Briony's unforgivable sin.

Section Two   Atonement for the Sin

The sin of class prejudice has been committed, and redemption becomes an inevitable moral demand. In *Atonement*, redemption operates on two levels, each intricately tied to the class ethics underpinning the narrative. On the first level, Briony, as a character within the novel—a participant in the events and the perpetrator of a series of "sins"—seeks to make amends for her personal mistakes. On the second level, Briony, as the author of the novel, attempts a broader act of redemption by reconstructing and reimagining the lives of those affected by her actions. Both levels are deeply enmeshed with the rigid class hierarchies of 1930s England, making her path to atonement not only a personal journey but also a commentary on the oppressive social structures of the time.

On the first level, young Briony's sin is fundamentally shaped by the ethical and social codes of the class system. Her false accusation of Robbie Turner is not merely the result of a misunderstanding or youthful imagination but is also fueled by an ingrained sense of class superiority. Robbie, despite his education and talents, is reduced in Briony's eyes to his status as the son of a cleaning maid. This inherent class bias makes it easier for Briony—and the wider Tallis family—to accept his guilt without question. Her eventual attempts at redemption, such as becoming a war nurse and later confronting her sister Cecilia, reflect her growing awareness of the damage caused by her actions. However, these efforts are constrained by the same class ethics that shaped her initial sin. Her choice of nursing as a form of penance, while outwardly noble, symbolizes her internalization of the class system, as she continues to view her suffering as a sufficient substitute for addressing the systemic injustice she has perpetuated.

On the second level, Briony as an author seeks to rewrite the narrative of her life and the lives of others, creating a form of imaginative atonement. Her decision to give Robbie and Cecilia a fictional happy ending in her novel can be seen as an attempt to redress the harm caused by her earlier actions. However, this act of redemption is also deeply tied to class ethics. By taking control of their story, Briony once again exerts a form of authority over Robbie and Cecilia—an authority rooted in her privileged position as a member of the upper class. Her novel becomes a space where she can rewrite history according to her terms, but it also highlights the limitations of individual redemption in the face of entrenched class structures. The systemic injustice that condemned Robbie as guilty and deprived him of a fair chance cannot be undone by Briony's fictional narrative, no matter how heartfelt her intentions.

In both levels of redemption, Briony's journey underscores the pervasive influence of class prejudice and the moral challenges it poses. Her attempts to atone for her sins reveal the complexities of navigating personal morality within a framework of societal inequality. The class dynamics that facilitated her initial act of injustice also shape her understanding of redemption, demonstrating how deeply class ethics are woven into the fabric of individual and collective actions. Ultimately, *Atonement* presents redemption not as a clear resolution but as a process fraught with ethical ambiguities, reflecting the inescapable legacy of class divisions in shaping human relationships and moral choices.

I. Briony's Atonement as a Character

The Briony discussed in this part is the protagonist of the novel written by the elderly Briony. Here, the identity of Briony is dual. On the one hand, she is the real young Briony, and on the other hand, she is the fictional character made by the old Briony in the novel. Briony here is the combination of truth and fiction. As the protagonist of the event and the culprit of the tragedy, she also bears part of the hopeful vision of old Briony. Her atonement is the most straightforward atonement of the first level.

Her making up for the sin

Everyone should be responsible for their own life, and first of all, they have to reap what they sow. As a consequence, everyone has to improve their human nature, conscience and soul. After Briony realizes how much damage she has done, she embarks on a path of atonement to make amends for her mistakes.

At Lola's wedding, Briony shows up without permission, and at the wedding, memories of years ago emerge. "Now was her chance to proclaim in public all the private anguish and purge herself of all that she had done wrong.

Before the altar of this most rational of churches" (311). Briony weighs the pros and cons and gives up the opportunity to tell the truth in public. She excuses her cowardice: there is no point in telling the truth in the church. But her reaction in the church is not like that: "She remained in her seat with her accelerating heart and sweating palms, and humbly inclined her head" (312). Her cowardice is the reason why she does not complete her confession in the church, which is supposed to be the first concrete measure she makes to atone for her sins, but ends in failure.

During Briony's one-day atonement process, the misfit of her shoe is mentioned several times: "... and her heel was throbbing and had glued itself to the back of her shoe"; "She wedged lavatory paper into the heel of her shoe. It would see her another mile or two" (316). It can be seen that she is in the midst of physical pain during the day of atonement, but she does not make any remedy for this pain, as if she is going to accept this physical pain to alleviate the spiritual pain. After attending the wedding, Briony visits Cecilia. On her way to her sister's house, in part of her inner world, she still wants to escape: "She left the cafe, and as she walked along the Common, she felt the distance widen between her and another self, no less real, who was walking back toward the hospital" (316). However, this time she doesn't run away; she plucks up the courage to continue what she has to do. It is the first real apology, so long after she has admitted her mistake. Unsurprisingly, her sister's attitude is cold and indifferent, but Briony accepts it.

When they talk about how to help Robbie, their conversations are as follows:

"I'll go to Surrey and speak to Emily and the Old Man. I'll tell them everything."

"Yes, you said that in your letter. What's stopping you? You've had five years. Why haven't you been?"

"I wanted to see you first." (324)

Through the dialogue between Briony and Cecilia, it can be learned that

Briony has been escaping from reality all these years. She has long realized how unforgivable her sin is, ruining the lives of more than one person, but she does not begin her substantive remedy at the moment of realizing her sin. In essence, she is still a little girl living in her own fantasy. Her thoughts and fantasies are her safe haven. Every time she has to go through the condemnation of conscience, she hides in her own world of fantasy, so that she can avoid what is happening in the real world and doesn't have to think about what others are suffering. Her life choice of giving up her opportunity to go to school in Cambridge and, instead, becoming a war nurse is an example of this, which will not bring any change to Robbie's life. However, she still enjoys it, and even fantasizes about one day taking care of the injured Robbie as a way to get forgiveness. The atonement and remedy she has made so far have a great element of self-consolation. At the end of the story, she finally overcomes her cowardice, dares to face reality, and is determined to do her best to help Robbie wash away his grievances. At this time, she has grown up and finally strips away the part of herself that always escapes the facts and hides in fantasies.

Briony's journey of atonement is deeply intertwined with the rigid class ethics that permeate the society of *Atonement*. Her initial sin—her false accusation of Robbie—is not merely the product of childish misunderstanding but is also rooted in the hierarchical class prejudices of the time. Robbie, as the son of a cleaning maid, is perceived as unworthy of the Tallis family's favor, despite his education and character. This inherent bias reinforces Briony's erroneous judgment, as her perception of morality and guilt is filtered through the lens of class divisions. Her accusation reflects not only personal immaturity but also the ethical framework imposed by societal hierarchies, where the lower classes are often stigmatized and deemed guilty by default.

Even in her attempts at atonement, Briony's actions are shaped by these same class ethics. Her decision to forego her education at Cambridge to become a war nurse may appear noble on the surface, but it also illustrates her inability to confront the systemic injustices tied to class. Instead of directly challenging the prejudice and injustice she has perpetuated, she retreats into self-imposed penance, believing that personal suffering can substitute for meaningful change.

This is emblematic of a larger societal pattern in which those complicit in class-based oppression often seek self-redemption without addressing the structural inequities that perpetuate such harm.

Briony's eventual confrontation with Cecilia and her admission of guilt signify a crucial turning point, not just in her personal ethical development but also in her acknowledgment of the broader implications of her actions. By choosing to help Robbie clear his name, she begins to challenge the class prejudices that have dictated so much of her life and decisions. However, her realization comes too late to undo the harm caused by the rigid class structures that have already destroyed Robbie and Cecilia's lives.

Her Self-redemption

Briony's remedies for her sin are futile and unhelpful, and the wrongs she has done cannot be undone, and she can never be forgiven. So, rather than a concrete remedy for things, what Briony has done is more of a self-redemption. In order to atone for her sins, she gives up the opportunity to study in Cambridge and chooses to go to the hospital to receive nursing training and become a war nurse in World War II. That she chooses a difficult profession that is completely inconsistent with her ideals is all for self-redemption. In there, she suffers from both mental and physical torture. From the other perspective, she confronts the disasters caused by human beings themselves and does small remedial work under the grand narrative context, which is a seeking for human salvation.

Going to Cambridge is what Briony has longed for since she was a child, and it is her ideal life, but she chooses to give up her ideal life and comes to the field hospital to do the hardest and most difficult work. Nurses not only have to face physical disasters in wartime; the terrible disabilities of the wounded soldiers were sensory and spiritual torture for them. And Briony has to do dirtier, lower works: "She emptied and sluiced the bedpans, swept and polished floors, made cocoa and Bovril, fetched and carried—and was delivered from introspection" (366). She takes these tortures as punishment for herself, and finds peace of mind by keeping herself busy. The more tired her body becomes, the less guilt she feels. No one is asking her to give up the life she wants, and such an approach will not give back Robbie's life, so it is a kind of redemption of her own soul. She probably hopes to find Robbie himself among the wounded and to help him survive, thus omnipotently "repairing" the person whom she has destroyed. She transfers her guilt for Robbie to every wounded soldier she meets. However, the truth is no matter how much despicable work she does, no matter how much she willingly gives up what she craves, she will never make up for the damage she has done. She is unforgivable.

Briony's self-redeeming career choices make her detached from her class attributes. Here, Briony's individual identity is stripped away. No one cares who she is; no one cares what her name is, and the identity of the individual is erased. When she finds out that her name brand is wrong and goes to the head nurse to explain her situation, the head nurse calmly replies, "You are, and will remain, as you have been designated. Your Christian name is of no interest to me" (265). She is just one of many interns, and a new person will be added in a few months. To those around her, she is nothing more than the randomly arranged letters on her badge, stripped of her identity as a girl from a wealthy family. Within the grand narrative of war, individual existence is obliterated, reducing people to mere cogs in the machinery of destruction. The brutality and moral corruption of war are endured by every ordinary person, yet the inner world of the individual— both spiritual and physical—remains obscured. In the chaotic tide of war, personal fate becomes a reflection of the collective sins of humanity, revealing the profound ethical failures embedded in the course of history. Briony is not just herself here; she is countless individuals who have dedicated and compensated for the war, and she can be anyone. In war, life loses its original value, and the number of deaths, casualties, and survivors has become a string of cold numbers. In this particular violent and bloody environment, people's cognitive thinking has changed, no matter which social class they are in. They even take pleasure in killing in war, get excited to see others physically tortured, and even the kind Robbie may have the desire to be violent. The people represented by Briony in the hospital are making redemption for the sins of all mankind, and they cherish life, spare no effort to rescue every injured person, and restore the glory of humanity in saving a life. Here, Briony's personal traumatic memory and atonement are a kind of human reflection and atonement for the sins they have caused.

Briony's role in the hospital transcends her individual identity; she becomes a symbol of countless individuals who have sacrificed and atoned for the horrors of war. In the face of relentless violence, human life is stripped of its intrinsic value, reduced to impersonal statistics of the dead, wounded, and survivors. War erodes moral consciousness, blurring distinctions of class and social status, as even the most virtuous individuals, like Robbie, may find themselves drawn toward brutality. Yet, amid this moral collapse, Briony and those like her strive to reclaim the dignity of humanity by preserving life, healing the wounded, and resisting the dehumanization of war.

Her journey of atonement, then, is not merely personal but deeply entangled with the ethics of class and social hierarchy. The war dissolves the rigid barriers of class, forcing the privileged and the impoverished alike into a shared reality of suffering and sacrifice. Briony's redemption lies in her willingness to renounce the privilege that once shielded her from responsibility, immersing herself in the suffering of others. In doing so, she enacts a broader moral reckoning—one that acknowledges not only her individual guilt but also the complicity of an entire social order in perpetuating injustice. Through her atonement, the novel gestures toward the possibility of ethical redemption, where true reconciliation requires both personal transformation and a fundamental reexamination of the structures of power and privilege that sustain human suffering.

II. Briony's Atonement as the Writer

The Briony discussed in this part is the author of *Atonement*, the elderly Briony, and the archetypal character of Briony in the novel. The elderly Briony said that she wrote this novel as much as she could to restore history, to treat it as an account of history. As the creator of the fictional world, she has the power to construct facts. However, as for the extent to which the facts are restored, only she herself knows. Briony uses her authorship and ability to manipulate words to clarify Robbie's innocence, to some extent restore the truth of the facts, to give Robbie and Cecilia a happy ending, and thus fulfill her atonement. At the same time, it also records the tragic situation of the war. Therefore, on another level, it plays a role in awakening the world. Briony's behavior in writing the novel is both an act of evasion and an act of atonement, which is one way of redemption in the narrative of this original sin, so it can only be repaid by narrative.

Constructing a Novel to Atone for Sin

The true course of events is tragic—Briony never gets the chance to apologize or seek genuine atonement for her actions. In response, the elderly Briony crafts a novel as a means of redemption, rewriting the past in a way that offers the reconciliation she was denied in reality. The painful truth remains: "Robbie Turner died of septicemia at Bray Dunes on 1 June 1940, or that Cecilia was killed in September of the same year by the bomb that destroyed Balham Underground station" (354). This devastating outcome is, in many ways, the direct consequence of Briony's actions, her false accusation having irreversibly altered the fates of both Robbie and Cecilia. If she had not sent Robbie to prison, Robbie, such a handsome and brilliant man, would have had a brighter future ahead. He may become a doctor, and he may get married to Cecilia. The war has exacerbated Briony's sins. Without the war, she might have had a chance to atone for her sin, but before she could make any amends, the lovers, Cecilia and Robbie, both died. So, as a novelist, Briony sees writing fiction as a way of atonement, and in the novel, she gives Robbie and Cecilia a happy ending and endless possibilities for life. At the end of the story, Robbie and Cecilia watch Briony leave, and when Briony turns back, they are gone. No one knows what would happen next and how their lives would continue, but the ending is hopeful and everything is on track. The original ending of the story is desperate, but Briony constructs a hopeful ending in the world of fiction. However, the fictional art world is always only the sustenance of the spiritual world, unable to bring someone's life back or change the facts, so in doing so is more of a self-salvation.

In the novel, Briony seems to have gained some sort of silent forgiveness. When the landlord speaks to her in a bad tone, it is her sister who protects her and stands up for her. When she is about to take the subway back to the hospital, "Robbie and Cecilia walked behind her, hand in hand" (334). Her sister and Robbie insist on seeing her off, and it seems that their happy life has diluted their resentment of Briony to some extent. After arriving at the station, "[t]hey stared at her, waiting for her to leave" (335). They speak to Briony in a tone even similar to that which an older sister and brother-in-law would use with their younger sister: "Robbie reminded her to have money with her when she saw the commissioner for oaths. Cecilia told her she did not forget to take the addresses with her to Surrey" (335). When she apologizes solemnly, Robbie says softly, "Just do all the things we've asked" (335). There are no more accusations; the sentence and the tone of the speech are more like a relieved conciliation. The construction of such a false ending is Briony's self-consolation, and it is also a result of the mental torture and self-condemnation she has suffered over the years.

Using Fiction to Restore Historical Truth

While constructing the novel to make atonement, Briony also uses her novel to restore the truth of facts and history. When describing the events that cause the misunderstanding, Briony switches perspectives and presents the truth. The novel constructs the original appearance of things through the patchwork of multiple perspectives, so that readers can access the complete facts. The novel not only shows the inadequacies of a single perspective through multiple perspectives, acknowledges the limits of human cognition, but also advocates that people should try their best to overcome their own limitations to consider the whole picture of things.

As the author of the novel, Briony not only uncovers the original truth of the main storyline in the novel, but also devotes a lot of texts to describe the war, as well as the fate of individuals in the war. She uses her writing to expose how class affects people's perspectives and cognition and convict an innocent young man who should have had a great future and expel him from the sphere of justice. It also criticizes how the terrible and bloody violent environment of war changes people's cognition, how easy the war is to destroy people's minds and bodies, and the lives of normal individuals. It also reveals how the abominable rich merchants who made their fortunes from the war used their wealth to manipulate their reputations and disguise themselves as philanthropists and live in peace.

It is not easy for the elderly Briony to use fiction to write her true self, and it is also hard to face her true self and the disasters and harm she has caused. She finally breaks through the pressure to restore the truth, faces what she had done directly, and shows everything to the reader, all of which shows that she has made a difficult exploration of herself. She pursues and promotes the good side of human nature, and she writes the novel to repent her sins. She is not to shape human nature according to some kind of blueprint, but to show the light and darkness, greatness and smallness of human nature, and to guide human nature to good.

Through her novel, Briony not only reconstructs the past as an act of atonement but also critiques the rigid class structure that shaped the tragic course of events. Her writing reveals how class prejudice, deeply ingrained in social consciousness, dictated perceptions of guilt and innocence, ultimately leading to Robbie's downfall. By exposing the mechanisms through which class biases distort justice, she highlights the ethical failures of the upper class, who wield power to maintain their own interests at the expense of those beneath them.

Briony's novel serves as both confession and critique, as she recognizes the devastating consequences of privilege and hierarchy—how the innocent can be condemned, and the guilty can manipulate their way to respectability. Her journey of self-exploration is not merely personal but speaks to a broader moral reckoning, challenging the reader to confront the ethical implications of class divisions. In the end, her act of writing is not just about individual redemption but about acknowledging the deep-seated inequalities that shaped the tragedy, urging society to reflect on its own complicity in perpetuating such injustices.

The third level of atonement is the atonement of McEwan, the real author of the work. Repentance and atonement are the responsibilities that McEwan wants to assume as a writer, and it is also a way for him to intervene in society and thus criticize and transform it. McEwan is the creator of Briony, the creator of the whole novel, the creator of the whole event, and the one who really has the power to create the world of text. He constructs a fictional event in which Briony resurrects the dead, and subverts the boundaries between the possible world and the impossible world, allows the novel to present a beautiful vision while providing the truth, and gives the reader the courage and hope to move forward after experiencing the tearing pain of tragedy.

In *Atonement*, Ian McEwan delves into the realm of social ethics to depict the repercussions of prejudice and misunderstandings rooted in class distinctions. McEwan uses his power as a writer to show the public how prejudice and misunderstanding of class ethics can lead to tragedy, and some harm is irreversible and irreparable. Everyone has the possibility to become Briony. McEwan's redemption is beyond the individual, and it is the redemption of the entire class. He hopes to let the reader feel such tragedies and thus call on everyone to prevent this class ethical prejudice from continuing to cause harm to people, which is an effort for British society to abandon the old class ethic and establish a new ethical relationship that is healthy and equal. McEwan tries to wake up the world in his own way, a writer's way, to achieve the transcendence of the individual soul, thus fulfilling the responsibility of the writer.

McEwan's exploration of class dynamics within the novel further underscores the importance of social ethics. The love affair between Cecilia Tallis, a member of the privileged class, and Robbie Turner, a lower-class individual, becomes a focal point for tensions arising from societal expectations and prejudices. McEwan challenges the notion that social status determines one's moral or intellectual worth. Through his narrative, he exposes the flaws in class-based judgments and demonstrates how these prejudices perpetuate harm.

By showcasing the character of Briony as a pivotal figure, McEwan highlights the universal capacity for individuals to fall victim to misguided perceptions and ethical judgments. Briony's actions serve as a cautionary tale, demonstrating how the convergence of prejudice and misunderstanding can have far-reaching consequences. This portrayal underlines the significance of social ethics and their impact on both individual lives and the collective.

McEwan's approach as a writer serves as a powerful tool for instigating change. In pursuing the transcendence of the individual soul, McEwan fulfills the responsibility of a writer. He harnesses the power of his craft to shed light on the consequences of social ethics, striving to evoke empathy, understanding, and a call to action. The author's intention extends beyond the redemption of individual characters; he seeks the redemption of the entire class. By exposing the tragedies born out of prejudice and misunderstanding, he endeavors to ignite a transformative awakening within British society, fostering a more equitable and inclusive ethical landscape. By illuminating the tragic outcomes resulting from class-based prejudice, McEwan prompts readers to awaken society to the harm caused by entrenched class ethical prejudices, urging individuals to work collectively to prevent further harm and dismantle the old class ethic.

Chapter Six   The Rational Ethics in *Saturday*

Saturday is Ian McEwan's ninth novel. From this novel, he discards the previous depressing themes and shifts to social, political and humane issues. His focus on "expertise and professional accomplishment has led reviewers to puzzle over *Saturday*'s bourgeois ethos."[114] In *Saturday*, the novel makes a nuanced depiction of the lives, thoughts and emotions of contemporary urban successful neurosurgeon Henry Perowne, and fully and convincingly shows the infiltration and alienation of contemporary urban culture on human life. *Saturday* is regarded as a realistic novel for its symbolic description of Britain's current situation. McEwan's writing skill can be said to have sublimated to a new height with the publication of *Saturday*. In the novel, McEwan sets the story in contemporary cities, and focuses on excavating the complex human nature of contemporary cities and the living conditions of contemporary urban people. He mapped "the working of the private life and the personal imagination, and the wilder concerns of the nation and the world, and Ian McEwan is the foremost cartographer of our time."[115]

The story of the novel takes place in London with the background of a protest against the invasion of Iraq. The protest, which took place in February of 2003, was the largest in London's history at the time. Set on 15 February 2003, McEwan's ninth novel is a day-in-the-life narrative that follows one character from the early hours of Saturday morning to the dawn of Sunday. It is an introspective, contemplative book in which there is little incident in comparison with most contemporary novels. Throughout this novel, we are exposed to a description of the modern urban life of an upper-middle-class protagonist, with one of the themes being that the future appears unpredictable for anyone. In the novel, the protagonist, Perowne, belongs to the successful elites who, in some ways, have got it all: happiness and success. However, "Perowne is a model of a comfortable, contemporary man who lives in a present-day age of uncertainty.

This uncertainty of the future causes even content men such as Perowne to be thrown off into a world of chaotic events and brings out their strengths and weaknesses."[116] The large-scale demonstration happening on this particular Saturday is the focus of much of Perowne's thoughts and dialogue. McEwan's portrayal of Perowne and his thoughts and actions leave the reader in deep thought. Moreover, through the conflicts with Baxter, Perowne sees something in Baxter's character that he himself has not got, something he can't appreciate from the beginning, so the conflict between science and literature is resolved at the end of the novel, when Daisy's poetry recital makes Perowne realize and appreciate the power of literature.

Saturday is a novel that features a protagonist named Henry Perowne, an experienced 48-year-old neurosurgeon in London. In the early morning, Perowne wakes up reflecting on his work and family life. The first thought flashes through his mind concerning the technically perfect accomplishment of the surgeries he has conducted in the last week, followed by his brilliant family members, his wife Rosalind, a lawyer; his daughter Daisy, a prize-winning poet; and his son Theo, a guitarist. Soon afterward, Perowne gets up, stretching his body, and through the bedroom window he happens to see a burning plane falling towards Heathrow Airport, but it is hard to tell whether the plane crash is an act of terrorism or an unfortunate distress.

On the way to his weekly squash match with his colleague, Perowne's car crashes with Baxter's. The broken wing mirror causes a dispute between the two, but after Perowne dismisses a pecuniary compensation to Baxter and his two malevolent confederates, the argument becomes more violent. During the confrontation, Perowne diagnoses Baxter's character as the early stages of Huntington's disease and successfully escapes the fight by diverting Baxter's attention with this information.

Before the family dinner that evening, which is prepared to entertain his father-in-law, John Grammaticus, a poet, Perowne visits his widowed mother, Lily, who is suffering from vascular dementia, and his son, Theo, who is rehearsing before returning home. Daisy comes home from a trip to Paris and back from attending the protest earlier this Saturday, arguing with Perowne about the impending war. John, Theo and Rosalind arrive in succession, but things take a worse turn. Rosalind is threatened with a knife pointed at her by Baxter and his companion. John's nose is severely broken by Baxter's swipe and Daisy is ordered to remove her clothing. It is at this moment that the family shockingly realizes Daisy is pregnant. Knowing Daisy is a poet, Baxter commands her to recite a poem. Out of surprise, the poem "Dover Beach" by Matthew Arnold touches Baxter emotionally while Perowne and Theo are trying to prevent Baxter from further violence. Baxter falls down the stairs and is in a comatose state. Coincidentally, Perowne is the exact surgeon who heads a surgical operation on Baxter's emergent case. It is Sunday morning when Perowne returns from the hospital. After a full 24 hours, the story ends.

As his literary vision expands, the focus of his works gradually shifts from the intimate horrors of private spaces to broader explorations of social structures and the human condition. This transition reflects a deepening concern with the cultural ecology and logic that shape contemporary urban life. The novel delicately and profoundly portrays the diverse spiritual pursuits of modern urbanites, who, despite being surrounded by material abundance, struggle with existential emptiness. However, with the rapid advancement of technology, individuals experience an increasing sense of emotional deprivation and alienation. The very tools designed to enhance human life instead contribute to the erosion of genuine human connection, ultimately leading to the moral and psychological degeneration of contemporary urban society. "For some in the group the constellation of extraordinary incidents was just too improbable, even for a neurosurgeon supposedly at the top of his game, and their juxtaposition with situational details of little obvious relevance (e.g., the cleaning of the prawns, the preparation of the monkfish) compromised the book's credibility as a depiction of disease and professional duty. However, despite these difficulties, for some the domestic and surgical dilemmas were simply a vehicle for McEwan to explore the tensions between the arts and the sciences, with verse and music the double healing-fix around which was spun the medicine, with the climax interpreted as the final showdown of poem against protein, trochee against trinucleotide repeat, pyrrhic against nucleic substitution."[117]

Section One   Collision between Literature and Science

I. The Development of Technopoly

In Neil Postman's book *Technopoly*, he mentions that José Ortega y Gasset wrote of three stages in the development of technology: the age of technology of chance, the age of technology of the artisan, and the age of technology of the technician. According to this idea, he later divided culture into three types: tool-using cultures, technocracies, and technopolies. The main feature of the tool-using cultures is "that their tools were largely invented to do two things: to solve specific and urgent problems of physical life, such as in the use of waterpower, windmills, and the heavy-wheeled plow; or to serve the symbolic world of art, politics, myth, ritual, and religion, as in the construction of castles and cathedrals and the development of the mechanical clock."[118] The "tool-using culture" is an ideology that connects tools with its culture. They are in some way serving the function of keeping the "dignity and integrity of the culture."[119]

The second stage is technocracy. The idea that Johannes Kepler took a significant step toward the conception of technocracy primarily originates from Postman's discussion in his book *Technopoly*. Postman argues that Kepler, in his Astronomia Nova, advocated for separating theological authority from philosophical (i.e., scientific) reasoning, which marked an early step toward technocracy. Specifically, Kepler stated, "Now as regards the opinions of the saints about these matters of nature, I answer in one word, that in theology the weight of authority, but in philosophy (science) the weight of Reason alone is valid." Postman sees this distinction between moral and intellectual values as one of the foundations of technocracy.

Neil Postman's discussion of Johannes Kepler's role in the early conceptualization of technocracy provides a historical foundation for understanding how technological advancements shape human society. Technocracy, in essence, refers to a system in which technology dictates the cultural and social order. As Postman suggests, Kepler's shift toward prioritizing scientific reasoning over theological authority set the stage for a world increasingly governed by technological rationality rather than traditional belief systems. This transformation has since accelerated, fundamentally altering various aspects of human life.

One significant impact of technocracy is the way it has transformed communication. As Postman puts it, "Technocracy transformed the face of material civilization." A clear example of this is the decline of letter-writing with the rise of the telephone. Before telephones became widespread, writing letters was a crucial part of daily life. People who lived in different places regularly corresponded through letters, often several pages long, in which they detailed their recent experiences, struggles, and personal reflections. These letters provided an opportunity for deep, thoughtful expression. However, as telephones became common, written correspondence quickly declined. The shift in medium led to a shift in the nature of communication itself—telephone conversations, though immediate, often became brief and task-oriented. Unlike letters, which allowed for extended reflection and emotional depth, phone calls tend to prioritize efficiency and directness. This change reflects a broader trend in which new technologies reshape not only how people communicate but also what they communicate.

The evolution of communication continued with the rise of social media platforms such as QQ and WeChat, which introduced yet another transformation. The content of interactions shifted from voice calls to text messages, emojis, and even GIFs, further altering the way emotions and ideas are conveyed. Unlike traditional letters, which required effort and contemplation, instant messaging encourages rapid, often fragmented exchanges. This shift aligns with the broader influence of technocracy—efficiency and immediacy take precedence over depth and reflection.

The impact of technology extends far beyond communication. With the widespread use of computers, people have become increasingly reliant on digital systems for both work and daily life. The efficiency and accuracy of computational technology have led to a world in which human decision-making is often subordinated to algorithms and automated processes. In many ways, this reflects the ultimate realization of technocracy: a society where technology is no longer just a tool for human progress but a dominant force that dictates the rhythm of life itself.

> In a technocracy, tools play a central role in the thought-world of the culture. Everything must give way, in some degree, to their development. The social and symbolic worlds become increasingly subject to the requirements of that development. Tools are not integrated into the culture; they attack the culture. They bid to become the culture. As a consequence, tradition, social mores, myth, politics, ritual, and religion have to fight for their lives. (28)

In this stage, because industrialist fanaticism has just emerged, it is impossible to affect people's inner lives, and expel the memories and social structures that have remained, so there is no destruction of the tool-using cultural worldview. After the rise of technological monopoly, in other words, technology, the traditional worldview disappeared. The new arising concept redefined the meaning of religion, art, family, politics, etc., and became the technological domination of totalitarianism. The new effect of technology is that people around the world are increasingly dependent on it. For example, two young Japanese people relied so much on the GPS that they drove the car into the sea. A farmer blindly trusted the weather forecast. He believed that there would be a heavy storm the next day, and even though it was sunny outside, he still insisted that all his workers take defensive measures against the storm. In the end, it didn't rain for a day. The more we rely on technology, the more technology, in turn, monopolizes our lives. Is rationalism bad? Postman did not give us a certain answer. He believes that the development of rationalism, especially the outbreak of Western science and technology in the 19th century, brought about scientism and scientific and technological determinism, causing people to swing from the extreme of believing in religion to the extreme of believing in science and technology. People think that as long as they master science, they are omnipotent. This kind of thinking gradually spread from the material world to the spiritual world, and people began to treat culture and society with the thinking of scientific and technological determinism, which made Postman have deep concerns.

> ... the first explicit and formal outline of the assumptions of the thought-world of Technopoly. These include the beliefs that the primary, if not the only, goal of human labor and thought is efficiency; that technical calculation is in all respects superior to human judgment; that in fact human judgment cannot be trusted, because it is plagued by laxity, ambiguity, and unnecessary complexity; that subjectivity is an obstacle to clear thinking; that what cannot be measured either does not exist or is of no value; and that the affairs of citizens are best guided and conducted by experts. In his system, which included "time and motion studies," the judgment of individual workers was replaced by laws, rules, and principles of the "science" of their job. This did mean, of course, that workers would have to abandon any traditional rules of thumb they were accustomed to using; in fact, workers were relieved of any responsibility to think at all. The system would do their thinking for them. That is crucial, because it led to the idea that technique of any kind can do our thinking for us, which is among the basic principles of Technopoly. (52)

Neil Postman, in his critique of Technopoly, provides a formal and explicit outline of the assumptions that define a technological society dominated by instrumental rationality. These assumptions include the belief that efficiency is the ultimate goal of human labor and thought, that technical calculation is superior to human judgment, and that subjectivity is an obstacle to clear thinking. In such a system, anything that cannot be measured is either considered nonexistent or deemed irrelevant. Furthermore, the affairs of individuals are best managed by experts, leading to a culture where human discretion is gradually eroded. Postman illustrates this transformation by discussing "time and motion studies," a method used to replace individual workers' judgment with standardized laws, rules, and principles. This approach effectively eliminates the need for workers to think independently, as the system itself dictates their actions. More broadly, this idea extends to the belief that techniques and systems can entirely substitute for human cognition—a core principle of Technopoly.

Auguste Comte's philosophy laid the intellectual groundwork for this shift. His argument that anything that could not be seen and measured was unreal provided a foundation for viewing human beings as objects within a mechanized system. In a culture dominated by Technopoly, this mindset translates into the devaluation of human judgment, intuition, and individuality. Workers are no longer seen as thinking individuals but as components in a vast technical apparatus, where their role is to execute predefined tasks rather than engage in critical reflection. The culture of Technopoly extends beyond the workplace into all aspects of society, fostering an environment where questioning authority or expressing individual concerns is regarded as inefficiency or resistance. When a subordinate asks a superior a question, it may be dismissed as an "excuse" rather than a legitimate inquiry. In this framework, human care, dignity, and personal reflection are seen as obsolete—"worthless" elements that disrupt the seamless operation of the system.

Postman's critique of Technopoly is not merely an attack on technological progress but a warning against the unchecked dominance of technical rationality over human values. He argues that when efficiency and quantification become the sole criteria for truth and decision-making, society risks losing its sense of humanity. The challenge, then, is to restore balance—to reintegrate human judgment, ethical considerations, and personal engagement into a world increasingly governed by impersonal systems. Postman ultimately calls for a reevaluation of the role of technology in shaping human interactions, emphasizing the need to achieve harmony between technological advancement and the preservation of human dignity.

With the emergence and development of modern technology, culture and tradition have given way to it. People began to blindly worship technology, believing that technology is a divine force that satisfies all the needs of the self, just like the protagonist Perowne in *Saturday*. In the computerized age, Postman believes that computers and networks mark the entry of technology into the monopoly era. People are overwhelmed by the massive amount of information brought by science and technology, so they are dependent on it in a superstitious way. People no longer rely on traditional culture, humanistic values and ethics, but instead, use technology and its values as the moral authority. Take Douyin as an example: people are so obsessed with it that, from old to young, it is a popular way of entertaining and information-obtaining. People gradually lose the ability to think independently and even naively believe every piece of information from it. Thus, they lose the ability to discover the truth actively and independently. Postman critiques technology in order to stop mythologizing technology and to try to restore its appropriate and constructive role.

Technopoly is a thought-world characterized by the dominance of technology and its impact on society. It is a system where technology and its associated values shape and control human behavior, often at the expense of individual ethics. Individual ethics refer to the principles and values that guide an individual's moral decision-making and conduct. In Technopoly, the emphasis on efficiency and technical calculation tends to overshadow individual ethics. The relentless pursuit of efficiency as the primary goal of human labor and thought can lead to a devaluation of ethical considerations. The focus on quantifiable measures and objective data may neglect subjective and moral aspects of decision-making. This can result in a disregard for ethical dilemmas, complexity, and the well-being of individuals in favor of achieving predetermined technical outcomes.

Moreover, the belief that human judgment is inherently flawed and that subjective thinking is an obstacle to clear thought can further erode individual ethics. When individuals are encouraged to rely solely on technical expertise and the system's predefined rules, they may become disconnected from their personal values and moral compass. The responsibility to critically evaluate actions and consider ethical implications is diminished, as the system assumes the role of guiding and conducting affairs.

Meanwhile, blind trust in science and technology can lead to distortions in social ethics. As technological advancements shape societal values, tensions arise between the principles underlying scientific and technological activities and the traditional ethical value system. This conflict emerges because technology often prioritizes efficiency, precision, and functionality, while traditional ethics emphasize human dignity, morality, and individual well-being. As a result, ethical considerations are frequently subordinated to technological imperatives, leading to an erosion of human-centered values.

One of the most significant ways technology influences social ethics is by reducing individuals to mere components of a larger system. In modern society, technological revolutions have made the division of labor increasingly complex, amplifying the impact of individual actions while simultaneously narrowing their scope. In a technopoly culture, this process intensifies: labor is fragmented into hyper-specialized tasks, and workers are valued primarily for their ability to function as efficient, replaceable units. The emphasis on technical efficiency dictates that those who can seamlessly fit into predefined roles—performing tasks as dictated by market demands—are immediately employable.

Originally, tools were created to serve human needs. However, under Technopoly, this dynamic is reversed: people are molded to serve the system, functioning as tools themselves. Like a cog in a vast machine, each worker performs their designated task with mechanical precision. Their thoughts, emotions, and personal aspirations are disregarded because the system only values their ability to sustain operational efficiency. No one asks whether a "screw" in the machine is exhausted or fulfilled—its sole purpose is to keep the mechanism running. Once the system no longer requires a particular function, those who have been trained for it are discarded without hesitation. This process, driven by the relentless pursuit of efficiency, reduces human beings to instruments of productivity rather than autonomous individuals with intrinsic worth.

By exposing these dehumanizing tendencies, Postman critically examines the dangers of unchecked technological rationality. He calls for a reevaluation of the role of technology in society, urging the restoration of balance between technical efficiency and ethical considerations. Without such a balance, the very essence of human dignity is at risk of being subsumed by the demands of a mechanized world. Industrialization has made modern society a highly technological and organized world that is difficult for people to control. Is it technology that serves people, or have people become its slaves? This is one of the greatest confusions of modern people. In addition, the standardized mode of thinking of production in modern industrialized society has penetrated all aspects of people's material and even spiritual life, and people's personality is in danger of being swallowed up by this structured, systematic and uniform form. People's obedience to scientific and technological tools is also the observance of the laws of nature, and the tool system embodies the laws of nature in the form of artificial devices. It is inevitable that tool technology has a certain degree of control and suppression of people, so the unilateral development of science and technology cannot make people necessarily happy and satisfied. The control and repression of people by technology tools will finally lead to various ethical dislocations.

Individuals must recognize the limitations of technology and the importance of ethical reflection in decision-making. They can actively engage in ethical reasoning, questioning the values and consequences associated with the prevailing technological systems. By cultivating a mindful approach and remaining attentive to the impact of technology on individuals and society, individuals can contribute to a more ethical and balanced relationship with technology within the context of Technopoly. Individual ethics are crucial in challenging the dominance of Technopoly. They serve as a moral compass that enables individuals to question the assumptions and values imposed by the system. By maintaining a strong sense of personal ethics, individuals can resist the dehumanizing effects of Technopoly and ensure that ethical considerations are not overshadowed by technological efficiency, and by cultivating ethical awareness and actively engaging in ethical reasoning, individuals can contribute to a more balanced and ethically grounded relationship with technology in the modern world.

II. Technology in *Saturday*

McEwan's *Saturday* offers a literary exploration of the effects of technological progress on modern life, particularly through the perspective of its protagonist, Henry Perowne. As a neurosurgeon, Perowne epitomizes the rational, scientific mindset that thrives in a highly developed, technologically driven society. His admiration for the city of London—its infrastructure, architecture, and seamless integration of modern conveniences—reflects a worldview deeply embedded in the culture of Technopoly, where technological achievements define the measure of progress. However, while Perowne enjoys the privileges of a system that prioritizes efficiency and modernization, his experiences throughout the novel also hint at the limitations of such a worldview, particularly in his blind trust in science and rationality.

The city construction of London manifests a great achievement in technology. At the Perownes' own corner, "a triumph of congruent proportion; the perfect square laid out by Robert Adam enclosing a perfect circle of garden— an eighteenth-century dream bathed and embraced by modernity, by street light from above, and from below by fiber-optic cables, and cool fresh water coursing downpipes, and sewage borne away in an instant of forgetting." To him, "the city is a success, a brilliant invention, a biological masterpiece" (6).[120] As Perowne drives towards the city of London, his love for London is stronger than ever. The architecture, drainage system, streets, etc. of the City of London all indicate contemporary modernization. As the elite class, Perowne enjoys the convenience brought by the highly developed contemporary city. The dynamic, revolutionary force of science has pushed human civilization to an unprecedented phase in which the whole world is enjoying the benefits it has brought. Perowne, who enjoys modern life so much, is heavily influenced by this force. In the description about his house, we can glimpse the vision of the life of the elite.

> They give straight on to the pavement, on to the street that leads into the square, and in his exhaustion they suddenly loom before him strangely with their accretions - three stout Banham locks, two black iron bolts as old as the house, two tempered steel security chains, a spyhole with a brass cover, the box of electronics that works the Entryphone system, the red panic button, the alarm pad with its softly gleaming digits. Such defences, such mundane embattlement: beware of the city's poor, the drug-addicted, the downright bad. (33)

The comfortable and luxurious houses are a testimony to the rapid development of contemporary science and technology. The accumulation of external materials such as mansions and luxury cars has become the only sign of the success of contemporary urbanites. "A silver Mercedes S500 with cream upholstery—and he's no longer embarrassed by it." In Theo's words, "It is a doctor's car, as if this were the final word in condemnation." However, he is very proud of his Mercedes with "the long nose and shining eyes at the stable door" (62). It is the sign of the elite class, in which people enjoy more about the materialism that modern technology brings them.

For Perowne, material possessions hold little appeal—he has no interest in buying clothes, fine wine, or art. However, purchasing a luxurious car seems practical and aligns with his sense of rationality, as it represents both efficiency and technological sophistication rather than mere indulgence. This pragmatic approach to consumption reflects his broader worldview, shaped by a reliance on logic and utility. Similarly, although his home is equipped with an advanced and tightly controlled security system designed to safeguard against intrusions, this very system transforms his house into a fortress. While it offers the illusion of safety, it also creates an emotional barrier, isolating him from the outside world. The advanced technology that is meant to protect him paradoxically reinforces a sense of vulnerability, suggesting that absolute security is ultimately unattainable. More importantly, this physical and psychological detachment symbolizes a broader cultural condition—one marked by indifference and alienation. Individuals like Perowne, members of the elite class, rely on high-tech systems to insulate themselves, enclosing their lives within increasingly sealed environments. In doing so, they not only keep potential threats at bay but also distance themselves from authentic human connection, reflecting the dehumanizing tendencies inherent in a Technopoly-driven society.

Modern people's strong concern about materialism is one of the pursuits of the urbanite and a sign of success. They are excluded from their capabilities of emotional expression. They have lost their basic human emotions and become a cool robot which is driven by high-tech. Science can bring advanced technology and rich materials, but not the happiness expected by human beings. In a sense, technology is an anti-natural force, and the machines created by technology are alienated forces.

In *Saturday*, Perowne is depicted as the instrumentalized person. His whole life is so smoothly planned. After graduating from high school, Perowne is admitted to a medical university. After his hard work at school, he gets a job in a hospital. He works hard day and night, and keeps participating in training, and later makes himself a famous and successful surgeon. His life is just like a screw in a machine. When people put themselves into the position, they will automatically become a link in this operating chain. In order to make the machine have a normal and standardized operation, people will be trained to be accustomed to the machine. Perowne's successful career is achieved at the cost of his freedom from other interests. "If the individual were no longer compelled to prove himself on the market, as a free economic subject, the disappearance of this kind of freedom would be one of the greatest achievements of civilization."[121]

His love for his wife

In a Technopoly-driven society, where efficiency, rationality, and control often take precedence over emotional depth, human relationships risk being shaped—or even constrained—by the same principles that govern technological systems. When individuals are molded to function like tools within a larger mechanism, their approach to love and intimacy may similarly reflect a preference for stability, predictability, and order over spontaneity or emotional vulnerability. This utilitarian perspective can reduce complex human emotions to manageable, almost mechanical routines, prioritizing comfort and security over passion and existential exploration. Within this framework, love is not seen as an unpredictable, transformative force but rather as another domain to be efficiently maintained and controlled.

In *Saturday*, Perowne's love for his wife, Rasolind, has never changed. A successful neurosurgeon with a perfect figure and gentle temper, unlike his colleagues who are passionate about affairs, seems to have no midlife crisis, a term coined by Elliot Jaques in 1965, mainly triggered by reasons like transition experienced in midlife or others.

They are the hands of a tall, sinewy man on whom recent years have added a little weight and poise. In his twenties, his tweed jacket hung on him as though on narrow poles. When he exerts himself to straighten his back, he stands at six feet two. His slight stoop gives him an apologetic look which many patients take as part of his charm. They're also put at their ease by the unassertive manner and the mild green eyes with deep smile-wrinkles at their corners. (19)

The description is about his own judgment on his appearance and also that from the patients. Even though he has reached the age that exudes the charm of a mature man, in the therapeutic industry where extramarital affairs are so popular, he has never had this kind of thought. Perowne will not be impressed by any woman other than his wife. Facing intimate attitudes from other beautiful women, he always keeps a plain and restrained smile. In his mind, his wife is his only love and he is never tired of this woman.

By contemporary standards, by any standards, it's perverse that he's never tired of making love to Rosalind, never been seriously tempted by the opportunities that have drifted his way through the generous logic of medical hierarchy. When he thinks of sex, he thinks of her. …Who else could love him so knowingly, with such warmth and teasing humour, or accumulate so rich a past with him? to find another woman with whom he can learn to be so free, whom he can please with such abandon and expertise. By some accident of character, it's familiarity that excites him more than sexual novelty. (36)

Usually, this kind of strong feeling mainly exists between lovers who are just developing a romantic relationship. The love and passion between married couples gradually fade by the torture of the trivial in daily lives, by the pressure from work, or by disharmonious relationships. To him, that is not true. His love never fades. "What a stroke of luck, that the woman he loves is also his wife." (39) Perowne's loyalty to his wife appears admirable, yet he wonders in the novel whether this steadfastness reflects a flaw, a form of cowardice, or simply a lack of desire for adventure and change. As an extreme rationalist, he implicitly questions whether having affairs with other women would hold any real value. This raises a deeper question: is his affection for his wife genuinely rooted in love, or is it merely a product of his rational, controlled approach to life?

Habit is second nature. If you love someone for a long time, you will naturally get used to everything about them, like their look, their laugh, and their frown. He has become a part of your life, and love has become an imperceptible and inseparable habit. This is the case with Perowne.

"In the near-total darkness, how small she seems in the hugeness of the bed. He listens to her breathing, which is almost inaudible on the intake, quietly emphatic on the exhalation. She makes a sound with her tongue, a wet click against the root of her mouth" (23). Simple companionship often becomes the truest form of peace of mind. When love turns into a habit, it is sustained by the passage of time. Perowne's enduring affection for his wife has been internalized over the years, transforming his love into an unconscious part of his existence—much like a screw within a machine. In the context of modern technology, individuals are fixed within the framework of an industrialized system, functioning as tools designed to maintain efficiency and achieve systemic goals. This mechanization of human roles extends to emotions, where even love can become a routine, integrated seamlessly into the machinery of everyday life.

Therefore, it is the same with their love-making. Whenever they have some time for love, they have to leave their phones connected in case of some emergency. However, strangely enough, every time they are getting started, one of the phones will ring, either for Rosalind or for Perowne. Therefore, he will get dressed quickly and run for the hospital in a hurry, usually with something left behind him, like keys or loose change. On his ten-minute walk to the hospital, his desire fades away. Their life is like a programmatic process, and they calmly accept any bug in the process. Nothing is going to change Perowne's passion for his work. His rational way of thinking ensured his professional success and glory, but love, marriage, and childbirth became chess pieces on the road to his career. All his energy is devoted to professional cultivation. His success comes at the expense of the pleasure in his personal life. The more he is used to the fixed way of his routine, the less happiness and excitement he can feel. For Perowne, work is the whole of his life, and nothing else seems to matter. He only enjoys the sense of fulfillment that his work brings him. Similarly, Rosaline is used to this lifestyle too. Their sex lives have to give way to their work. They are so accustomed to being interrupted by the phone. "Once he's ridden the lift to the third-floor operating suite and is in the scrub room, soap in hand, listening to his registrar's difficulties, the last touches of desire leave him and he doesn't even notice them go" (22).

As one ascends the career ladder, professional growth often follows a proceduralized path, reinforcing the role of the individual as a mere cog in a larger machine. Science and technology have achieved remarkable success, bringing unprecedented material abundance to human society. However, technology, as an anti-natural force, creates machines that ultimately become alienated powers. When Technopoly dominates society, this force reverses its original purpose, reducing human beings to tools. Under the influence of mechanization and Technopoly, urban individuals are increasingly diminished to mechanical components, formatted and objectified through repetitive tasks performed day after day, eroding their sense of individuality and autonomy. In cities where efficiency and function are paramount, it completely ignores the communication between people, and ignores the subtle experience of people in the same space. Since architecture has become a commodity, people in it may be regarded as standard robots. The richness and diversity of people have been completely obliterated and the intrinsic nature of man has been ignored under such spatial and architectural spheres. People are reduced to the victim of efficiency, a passive, numb machine dominated by standard space.[122]

This dominance of efficiency and standardized space not only dehumanizes individuals but also has profound implications for ethics. As technology and mechanization permeate every facet of life, they reshape moral frameworks, reducing human interactions to transactions based on utility and function. In such a society, traditional ethical values that emphasize empathy, individuality, and personal connection are increasingly marginalized. The focus shifts to outcomes, productivity, and the optimization of systems, leaving little room for moral deliberation based on human needs or values. The ethics of care, which once governed interpersonal relationships, is replaced by the ethics of efficiency, where human beings are treated as interchangeable components within a vast, impersonal machine. As a result, moral concerns are overshadowed by technological imperatives, and individuals are left navigating a world where their worth is defined not by their humanity but by their ability to fit into predefined roles and systems.

His attitude to his job

In a society dominated by Technopoly, where efficiency, precision, and productivity are prioritized above all else, individuals are often conditioned to define their worth through professional achievements and measurable success. The mechanization of human life under the influence of technology reduces personal experiences to systematic routines, leaving little room for spontaneity or emotional exploration. Within this framework, work becomes not just a means of survival but the very essence of existence, reflecting the technocratic ideal where human value is tied to output and functionality.

Perowne's life perfectly embodies this Technopoly-driven mindset, divided into two main parts: preparation for his career—medical school studies and hospital internships—and dedication to his career through relentless hard work in hospitals. His life trajectory revolves entirely around professional pursuits, with little regard for non-professional activities. The extreme excitement he experiences is derived solely from his work, where he exhibits unwavering attention and seriousness. Years of rigorous effort have refined his medical skills to a state of near perfection. For Perowne, work is everything; his extreme dedication deprives him of leisure, illustrating how the technocratic culture shapes individuals into highly specialized tools, optimized for efficiency but detached from the richness of emotional and existential experiences.

> For certain days, even weeks on end, work can shape every hour; it's the tide, the lunar cycle they set their lives by, and without it, it can seem, there's nothing, Henry and Rosalind Perowne are nothing. (21)

Without work, their lives are not normal. Like the screw in a machine, without it, the machine may not work normally. Perowne's willingness to choose to give way to his work is not surprising. His wife, Rosalind, is also a workaholic. "Rosalind's work proceeds by a series of slow crescendos and abrupt terminations as she tries to steer her newspaper away from the courts" (21). They care more about the glory the work brings them than anything else.

> Henry can't resist the urgency of his cases, or deny the egotistical joy in his own skills, or the pleasure he still takes in the relief of the relatives when he comes down from the operating room like a god, an angel with the glad tidings life, not death. Rosalind's best moments are outside court, when a powerful litigant backs down in the face of superior argument; or, rarer, when a judgment goes her way and establishes a point of principle in law. (21)

With their passion for their work, they have been completely formatted as a work machine. In modern society, it is sad that a large number of projects in this industry are done this way. Everyone receives a module and finally puts it together to achieve a function. The biggest problem with the Technopoly of doing things is treating people like tools. The couple are specialists in their respective fields, and they have strange habits unlike normal couples do. "Once a week, usually on a Sunday evening, they line up their personal organisers side by side, so that their appointments can be transferred into each other's diary along an infrared beam" (22).

The Perownes, caught by the "jaws of work," ended up using work as the only thing to rely on. To Perowne, work becomes the compulsory and primitive need for him to live on. He could not feel life without work. Perowne enjoys the sense of fulfillment and achievement that his work brings him. He does enjoy the feeling of being a "god" whose duty is to save the patients out of the call from hell.

Operating never wearies him—once busy within the enclosed world of his firm, the theatre and its ordered procedures, and absorbed by the vivid foreshortening of the operating microscope as he follows a corridor to a desired site, he experiences a superhuman capacity, more like a craving, for work. (11)

    He was like a tireless screw. Whenever he is in his position, his object is completing the task. As a surgeon, his time is taken over by one operation after another, making his every act the result of mechanical and logical speculation. Intense and busy work kidnaps people's emotions and souls, gradually eroding their capacity for reflection and emotional depth. In this state of constant productivity, individuals begin to equate their sense of purpose and identity with their professional roles. As a result, they become screws in the chains of a mechanical system, finding solace in the excitement and achievement arising from their work. Although they enjoy a comfortable material life, their spiritual life has been completely expelled by this omnipresent work at any time and in any place or in any institutional environment. People become the object of the work or the tools of technology.

    The fundamental purpose of Perowne treating his patient is to allow them to return to work. He compares human beings to "hot little biological engines" which "devise their own tracks" (13). He, as the specialized talent, considers the human body as the object. His purpose is to repair the damaged machine to return it to the track of the mechanical process. "Some fail, a handful endure with their lights a little fogged, but most thrive, and many return to work in some form; work—the ultimate badge of health" (22). In the contemporary city, if a person who has the ability to work loses his job, a serious consequence may occur—the loss of one's role in the process and being worthless. That is to say, the happiness and inner desire of contemporary people are firmly controlled by the machinery chains, and no one can afford to lose their part.

    On Saturdays when people are supposed to take a rest and enjoy their leisure time, Perowne can have some leisure time too, but he has no idea how to enjoy it. Even though he knows that he can skip shaving this day, instead he does it as usual. On Saturday's schedule, playing squash with friends is a typical weekend routine, just as making love with his wife, visiting his mother after the squash game, and preparing dinner are. "There's a momentum to the everyday, a Saturday morning game of squash with a good friend and colleague, that he doesn't have the strength of will to interrupt" (88). At his age, playing squash is a little too much for him, but just like shaving, it is just as fixed as a screw in a machine, and Perowne is hard to make any change. On his way to the racquet club, he is involved in a minor car accident which brings him into a confrontation with a small-time thug. Perowne's professional views find something profoundly wrong with this young man, Baxter, whom Perowne soon discovers is a criminal. He uses his medical knowledge to make a break for it and escapes. In the process of negotiating with Baxter, he believes that "the matter is beyond pity." He compares human brains to "an expensive car" which is "intricate" (84). Similar to his comment on the razor as "this industrial gem," the modern technology "sharpens his thought" (48). These products of industrial progress give too much fascination to him. Just as what is mentioned above, in the stage of technocracy, technology controls human beings and human cultures. Due to the expansion of the scope of social interaction, the increasingly differentiated social structure, and the increasing degree of specialization and refinement of technology, people have been excluded from other fields and gradually share no more common senses. In this regard, Simmel[123] believes how the specialization required in modern urban life leads to a fragmented sense of self. He argues that the fine division of labor in capitalist societies reduces individuals to specialized roles, diminishing the holistic meaning of their work. This results in emotional detachment, mechanical repetition, and the loss of creative passion. What is even worse is that it will be a never-ending process, and the future will be worse than it is today.

Perowne's mechanical behavioral habits can be seen from his conflicts with Baxter. Faced with such a person with Huntington's disease, Perowne uses his medical knowledge to get him out of the predicament, but does not expect to put himself and his family in another more dangerous situation. After Perowne gets away from their conflicts in the street, Baxter later breaks into his house to take revenge on Perowne's humiliation. In order to protect his family, Perowne pushes

Baxter downstairs. When Baxter is lying unconscious in a hospital bed, Perowne chooses to do the operation himself and thus saves his life. Perowne doesn't care on whom he is going to perform the operation; it is the work itself that he cares about. This is a mechanical choice of a person who is so used to the automated process; therefore, there is nothing to do with who the patient is. "Back at work and, lovemaking and Theo's song aside, he's happier than at any other point on his day off, his valuable Saturday. There must, he concludes as he stands to leave the theatre, be something wrong with him" (221).

Modern technology has changed people's interpersonal relationships. These modern organizations set up rules and regulations which strictly govern the behavior of the people working in them. People have to show formal and impersonal behavior, which causes them to be alienated from each other. In order to achieve more efficiency, people are specially trained to be an expert only in one specific area, just like Perowne and his wife, respectively a neurosurgeon and a newspaper lawyer. In the face of the big machine of society, individual personality, qualities, hobbies, values, and other elements that have nothing to do with the normal function of the machine are ignored. Society presents the attributes of machines, and man is "dehumanized" and regarded as parts of machines.

As society becomes increasingly governed by technological systems and efficiency-driven frameworks, ethical considerations are also reshaped. In such a system, individuals are often reduced to mere cogs in the larger societal machine, their identities and moral agency subordinated to the demands of the system. The focus on specialization and the impersonal nature of professional roles diminishes the capacity for empathy, moral judgment, and meaningful human connection. The ethical frameworks that once emphasized personal dignity, the importance of relationships, and the value of individual moral choice are increasingly displaced by an ethos of functionality and optimization. Human beings, now trained to excel in narrow, mechanized tasks, lose sight of the broader ethical principles that sustain social cohesion, and in doing so, become detached from the human essence of care, compassion, and responsibility. In this world dominated by technology, the individual's worth is not measured by moral virtue or personal fulfillment, but by their ability to perform their designated function within the system. Thus, the ethical consequences of living in a Technopoly are far-reaching, as human beings become more aligned with the machine, stripped of their humanity and the ethical foundations that define them.

Section Two　The Collision between Rationality and Sensibility

Around the beginning of ancient Greece, philosophers began to think about the origin and development of man and the world. Since the birth of human beings, almost every action of everyone has been more or less affected by their feelings, and sense is the quality or state of being sensible, or the capacity to feel or perceive. The way of doing things according to people's own feelings is called "sensibility." Later, some scholars tried to find answers from the phenomena of nature, so they gave birth to natural science, which is called rationality. It means that people think and do things with certain kinds of "reasons."

At the beginning of human history, instinct and sensibility prevailed. For instance, if a person encountered a wild animal in the forest, their immediate instinct would be to flee in fear. However, as human society evolved, reason became more crucial for human development and societal progress. With advancements in technology, people are no longer as vulnerable to the threats posed by nature. Rational thinking, driven by technological development, has become a key factor in advancing civilization, enabling humanity to overcome natural challenges and achieve progress in various fields.

The German philosopher Friedrich Nietzsche framed the Greek gods Apollo and Dionysus as emblems of two fundamental forces of human nature, that is, rationality and sensitivity. The two forces of nature he introduces show up everywhere. He names the two halves of this dichotomy the Apollonian and the Dionysian, after two Greek gods.

In general, Apollo represents forces related to order and logic, while Dionysus is related to chaos and irrationality. The Apollonian and Dionysian dichotomy remains a useful way to view art, psychology, and society. Apollo, the god of the sun, truth, light, and logic, is the namesake for the first, ordered half.

This is the half that covers everything that is structured. Sculpture, an art which is pure form, is the most Apollonian art. Rational thinking, which is based on logical structures, is also Apollonian. Since this drive tends to put things into their place, it also tends to individualize and distinctly separate people and ideas from one another. The kind of person who likes to impose order on every situation is Apollonian. They favor reason, logic, and precise definitions, while they despise chaos.

Likewise, we all know people who throw order to the wind, follow every impulse they have, are drawn to chaos, and hate restraints. Dionysus, the god of wine, festivals, and madness, lends his name to the later, frenzied half. Music is the pure Dionysian art form since it doesn't appeal to our rational minds but rather to our emotions. The Dionysian doesn't categorize and tends to blur the boundaries between the self and nature.

While most of us would look at these kinds of people and see nothing more than personality differences, Friedrich Nietzsche saw an enduring dichotomy inside all of us which emerges from nature itself and can be applied to art, psychology, ethics, and politics.[124]

Over the years, human beings have accumulated as much rational knowledge as possible through rigorous sciences such as mathematics, biology, and physics. We can say that modern society is established on rational logic. In some way, people who master the power of reason will help them disassemble a goal, set a reasonable path for the realization of each sub-goal, and finally promote iteration through scientific and rigorous methods to achieve the goal. Rationalism advocates a scientific spirit and encourages people to use the laws of science to reveal the laws of nature and understand the world. Scientific rationality aims to improve human life. With the help of new methods and new tools that are created to serve human progress, all inventions and discoveries have fulfilled human life. The affluence of materials doesn't help to establish a stable and harmonious world; instead, interpersonal relationships are excessively rational. Without the constraints of moral and ethical guidance, people gradually lose their empathy and emotions. Though rationally driven people show diligence, self-discipline, and rationality, they have fewer emotional fluctuations, habitually observe people and things around them, study the logic and relationships behind them, and finally make choices with a greater probability of success.

Perowne's characters have all the features we have mentioned above. He is diligent, rational and calm in the confrontation of danger. He strictly follows a rational way of thinking and behaving. However, Perowne's daughter, Daisy, is a gifted writer in her twenties, with her first collection of poetry set to be released within the next few months. Henry's eighteen-year-old son, Theo, is a passionate musician and is beginning to gain some recognition as a blues guitarist. His children are immersed in music and literature, which he believes has no practical value in life. He is successful in his career but not in his relationship with his children. There exist communication difficulties between Perowne and his children.

In 1959, the physicist and author C. P. Snow—then fifty-three years old, a former research chemist, and, more recently, a top civil servant and best-selling novelist—delivered a speech with the title "The Two Cultures and the Scientific Revolution" that referred to a gulf of mutual incomprehension and a mutual lack of sympathy and appreciation that Snow identified as having grown up between "literary intellectuals" on the one hand and "natural scientists" on the other.[125]

> The man of science is often disposed to assume an air of superiority, when he looks upon the narrow and partial views of the mere artisan. The latter in return laughs at the practical blunders of the former. The defects in the education of both classes would be remedied, by giving them a knowledge of scientific principles, preparatory to practice.[126]

This plot is set to show the contrast between rationality and sensibility. As a mature neurosurgeon, Perowne has formed the whole principles of his own philosophy. He advocates science, technology, and rationality, all of which, in his view, are the forces for human progress and development. He enjoys the development and convenience that scientific and technological progress brought about. He never truly appreciates the beauty of literature. Perowne has never read books out of the field of medical science for over fifteen years.

> Not famous to Henry Perowne, who read no poetry in adult life even after he acquired a poet father-in-law. Of course, he began as soon as he discovered he'd fathered a poet himself. But it cost him an effort of an unaccustomed sort. (165)

The emotionally enthusiastic father-in-law, who is a poet in person, shows his bias against Perowne, regarding him as "one more tradesman, an uncultured and tedious medic, a class of men and women he distrusts more as his dependency on it grows with age" (165).

In order to change his stereotype of rationalism and sensitivity, his daughter usually gives him a list of readings. In fact, the conflicts between the above two dimensions have been very popular among middle-class families in British society. Edgar Allan Poe once had a "Sonnet—To Science," in which he gave people his view on the damage science has done to the arts, particularly the art of poetry. "Sonnet—To Science" is a fourteen-line sonnet, in which the narrator uses Roman mythology to further his case against science. One of the most important themes of "Sonnet—To Science" is how science is removing the magic of myth, art, and beauty. In the speaker's eyes, this makes the world less special and less capable of inspiring him to write. Poe decided that if science was neither lovable nor entirely wise, then the duty of the poet was to take arms against it and fight for the conservation of the Elfin and their classical analogs. This is the conflict between literature and science. Science is not perfect, but without literature, the myth and beauty of the arts will disappear.

As a modern poet in classical literature, what Daisy believes is "his astounding ignorance, guiding his literary education, scolding him for poor taste and insensitivity" (7). There was always a question in Perowne's mind about Daisy's intention to cultivate his literary taste, because, as a doctor, he's seen enough death, fear, courage and suffering, which can supply materials for half a dozen literature. Still, completing a list of readings from his daughter Daisy has become a way for him to keep in touch with his daughter. It is worth noting that the list of readings mentioned in the first two chapters of the novel extensively involves the literary classics of the Victorian period and modernism, such as Henry James's *Daisy Miller*, Joseph Conrad's nautical novels, and so on. This is reminiscent of the "progressive" thinking myth that pervaded the mainstream British social discourse in the 19th century. This grand narrative, which advocated industrial civilization and instrumental rationality, was challenged from the beginning by social and cultural celebrities such as Thomas Carlyle and Matthew Arnold, who advocated the replacement of religion with literature and the renewal of traditional British culture and spirits[127]. For him, being able to deeply understand the "upbringing and civilization" of the British nation in front of Daisy[128] will be an important way to resolve aesthetic anxiety in intergenerational communication.

However, it is his rational way of thinking that ensures his professional success and glory. He devotes all his energy to his professional cultivation. Compared with his sense of love, work is everything. He will go to the hospital in minutes even in the middle of making love with his wife. His success comes at the expense of his emotions, and his extreme seriousness and dedication to the profession make him have no time to take care of his emotional affairs. Let alone the reading assignment given by his daughter.

In the novel, when Baxter and his fellows break into the house and take revenge for Perowne's humiliation that day, Perowne first uses his pathological knowledge to analyze Baxter's violence. "There's no obvious intellectual deterioration yet—the emotions go first, along with the physical coordination. Anyone with significantly more than forty CAG repeats in the middle of an obscure gene on chromosome four is obliged to share this fate in their own particular way" (179). His lack of empathy and sympathy makes it hard for him to understand that Baxer's demand is nothing but his reputation. "Perowne himself is also responsible... Baxter is here to rescue his reputation in front of a witness" (180). It never occurs to him that his abuse of professional knowledge and rational reaction to others' sufferings lead to Baxter's revenge and outrage against his family.

The tension in the house builds when Baxter asks Daisy to take her clothes off. To everybody's surprise, Daisy's "weighted curve and compact swell of her belly" show her pregnancy.

> He's pointing with his free hand across the table at Daisy's book. He could be concealing his own confusion or unease at the sight of a pregnant woman, or looking for ways to extend the humiliation. These two young men are immature, probably without much sexual experience. Daisy's condition embarrasses them. Perhaps it disgusts them. (188)

Baxter is so shocked and embarrassed; he asks Daisy to read one poem from her book to conceal his restlessness. "Read one. Read out your best poem," he said to Daisy. Daisy can't let the gangsters hear her own poems with sexual implications, so she recites Matthew Arnold's *Dover Beach* at the suggestion of her grandfather. Ironically, for Arnold, "science is the opposite of poetry, a 'knowledge not put for us into relation with our sense of conduct, our sense for beauty, and touched with emotion for being so put.'"[129] Neither Perowne nor Baxter recognizes the famous poem, classifying it as Daisy's work. While the poem touches Baxter, "his grip on the knife looks slacker, and his posture, the peculiar yielding angle of his spine, suggests a possible ebbing of intent." Baxter is now immersed in this ecstasy, and the poetry reminds him of the place where he grew up, "that a mere poem of Daisy's could precipitate a mood swing" (189)[130]. Baxter understands the beauty of the poetry and his anger has been pacified, which eases his anxiety about his revenge. He falls into a state of Dionysus, which gives him an impulse to return to his nature. The essence of the Dionysian spirit is passion, and in the burst of passion, people forget themselves, forget their troubles, and merge into the eternal will hidden behind the world. The reading of the poem arouses Baxter's passion for forgiving Perowne and his desire for the treatment of his disease, which is the turning point of the outrage. Unable to comprehend this Dionysian impulse, Perowne attributes it to pathological factors, interpreting it as "of the essence of a degenerating mind," and pushes him down the stairs.

Though at the beginning of the outrage, Perowne "can't convince himself that molecules and faulty genes alone are terrorizing his family and have broken his father-in-law's nose" (180). In his usual thinking, but for scientific and technological progress, he can save people from the torment of illness with a scalpel, not through any other abstract form. As a rational person, he has a clear understanding of reality himself. He advocates the use of reason to solve problems, which, in his perception, works well when he has conflicts with Baxter during the day. But this time, his rational logic doesn't work to convince Baxter when the whole family is under threat from Baxter and his accomplice. Because when confronted with such a person who has lost his belief and pursuit in life, his rational persuasion is meaningless. Perowne is cut off by Theo. "Stop it Dad! Stop talking. Fucking shut up or he'll do it" (185).

Literature, which, in Perowne' eyes, is the useless abstract form, does help Baxter finish a huge transformation from a brutal terrorist to an amazed admirer. In this novel, McEwan used "'Dover Beach' as the poem on which his novel's narrative turns, and drawing implicitly on Arnold's position as a critic who seeks to separate poetry and science as two distinct ways of thinking, McEwan dramatizes the differences between poetry and science he has set up in the novel," by borrowing Arnold's *Dover Beach* to affirm "Arnold's position…the slippage of a belief in the divine to a belief in poetry's redemptive power."[131]

At the same time, the beauty of the poem has also deeply touched him. This is the collision of rationality and sensibility. Rational as Perowne is, the lines of the poem surprise him.

> They are unusually meditative, mellifluous and willfully archaic. She's thrown herself back into another century. Now, in his terrified state, he misses or misconstrues much, but as her voice picks up a little and finds the beginnings of a quiet rhythm, he feels himself slipping through the words into the things they describe. He sees Daisy on a terrace overlooking a beach in summer moonlight; the sea is still and at high tide, the air scented, there's a final glow of sunset. (189)

McEwan does not quote the original poem directly but depicts the mood of the poem through Perowne's understanding and imagination of the poem. Although Perowne is not that interested in novels and poetry, he does not completely lose his sensitivity to art. He listens to Bach's piano music during surgery, and when he listens to his son Theo's blues music, he can also feel the introversion and calmness of the blues music. As he listens to Daisy's reading of the poems, Perowne immerses himself into the image of the poem, with the imagination of Daisy and his lover at the beach. However, his rationality blinds him from feeling the Dionysian spirit, which he believes "the poem's melodiousness is at odds with its pessimism." (187) Perowne may not fully understand or can't determine what role a poem can play in his own life, but it can't be denied that it does save their family's life.

    The novel raises some extremely important questions. On the one hand, it is the question of the role of art and literature in culture and society, and on the other hand, it is the question of the limitations of technology. Scientific development is indeed an important way to promote a convenient way of life and modern technology in the world, but it also causes moral problems for human beings. In the novel, the experience of Henry Perowne gives us the doubt and concern of McEwan. Perowne's rational way of thinking deprives him of the emotional response to anything happening in his life. His brain works accurately and calmly in front of any emergent or dangerous event. McEwan arguably presents "Perowne's smugness as a metonym for the material West's indifference to world affairs, as he muses, for example, on 'progress' alongside 'hunger, poverty and the rest' while listening to Schubert in his Mercedes."[132]

    Saturday is supposed to be a day to put down work and enjoy physical and mental relaxation and freedom, but under the contemporary urban values, the pursuit of human values is all directed to interests and ends, so in the end everything becomes a tool and means to achieve one's self-interest. People who are too rational and suppress their sensibility often appear very calm and indifferent. To McEwan, continuous success in the scientific and technological field may cause conflicts between the rationality and sensitivity of people. In the novel, McEwan does not deny Perowne's success, but science and technology may not solve the most essential and authentic problem of human existence. We can see that the most fundamental problem that science and technology bring is the degeneration of human nature. The inner world and spiritual realm of man can never be comforted and explored by science and technology. "McEwan studies is itself likely to develop this seam of inquiry into his work as issues such as consciousness, evolutionary psychology, madness and mental degeneration are explored in greater detail."[133] Rationality and sensibility coexist in our lives and play an important role in different situations. In fact, the resolution of this domestic violence invasion crisis has indeed brought about a reconciliation of the conflict between science and literature. Perowne's story expresses McEwan's long-standing view that in the most cutting-edge metropolis, culture, technology, civilization, and law have all died out, leaving a lifeless, gloomy society in which human thoughts and emotions have degenerated to the point of inferiority. And this inferiority is closely related to man's worldly success and to his material wealth.

In conclusion, the tension between rationality and sensibility plays a profound role in shaping ethics, especially in a world where technology and scientific progress dominate. While rationality, with its focus on efficiency and objectivity, often drives human behavior toward external success and material wealth, sensibility—rooted in emotion, empathy, and the exploration of the inner self—serves as a necessary counterbalance to prevent the dehumanization that may arise in a highly rationalized society. McEwan's narrative suggests that the erosion of both cultural and ethical values, brought about by an overemphasis on rational achievement, risks the diminishment of the very qualities that define our humanity. Ethics, in this context, becomes a delicate negotiation between the heart and the mind, with the loss of one threatening the integrity of the other.

Section Three   The Collision between Civilization and Barbarism

Civilization, as a proper noun, refers to a collective state where individuals are esteemed for upholding high standards of behavior and exhibiting a significant level of development. This notion encompasses not only societal values but also individual ethics. Civilized societies place emphasis on the cultivation of personal integrity, kindness, wisdom, and respect for the laws of nature. Within this framework, individuals are expected to adhere to ethical principles that promote the well-being and harmonious coexistence of all members of society. Ethics in a civilized society, therefore, entails a commitment to fairness, justice, and the protection of human dignity, ensuring that every individual's rights are respected and their needs considered.

Barbarism, conversely, denotes an uncivilized state characterized by a lack of adherence to ethical standards. Those associated with barbarism often display a disregard for moral principles, such as empathy, compassion, and fairness. This state of uncivilized behavior often manifests as a rudeness of manners and a general ignorance of arts, learning, and literature. Barbarians tend to prioritize their own interests over the common good, disregarding the impact of their actions on others and exhibiting a lack of personal ethical responsibility. In this framework, ethics is perceived as secondary to personal or collective power, with individuals taking advantage of others for selfish gain, irrespective of the harm they may cause.

Civilized individuals are typically well-educated and have adapted to the demands of society. They recognize the importance of personal ethics and strive to act in accordance with established societal norms while upholding their own ethical principles. These individuals prioritize integrity, compassion, fairness, and responsibility in their interactions with others and their decision-making processes. They view ethical behavior as a crucial element of a civilized society and actively seek out opportunities to assist those in need, including the less fortunate. Ethics, for them, is not merely a matter of legal compliance but a moral commitment to promoting social welfare, peace, and equality, which is integral to the fabric of civilization itself.

In contrast, barbarians, characterized by their uncivilized state, often lack a strong ethical foundation. Their actions tend to be driven by self-interest and personal gain, disregarding the ethical considerations that promote the welfare and cohesion of society. Such individuals may exhibit a disconnection from empathy and a disregard for the ethical implications of their choices, often engaging in behaviors that exploit and ridicule others, including the poor. In their view, ethics are a hindrance to their pursuit of power and wealth, leading them to manipulate and oppress others without concern for moral consequences.

Civilized people revere natural science and knowledge, and worship scientists and knowledgeable individuals for their contributions to society. They advocate the use of science and technology to create wealth in ways that promote the greater good and improve the quality of life for all people. In their ethical framework, the pursuit of knowledge and wealth is not only seen as an intellectual endeavor but also as a moral obligation to uplift society as a whole. In contrast, barbarians advocate the use of monopoly, robbery, intimidation, exploitation, and oppression of others to obtain wealth. In this way, their actions undermine the moral foundations of society, prioritizing material gain over ethical principles such as justice, equity, and respect for human dignity.

Ultimately, the ethical divide between civilization and barbarism underscores the difference between a society that values the welfare of all individuals and one that is driven by the pursuit of power at the expense of others. Civilized ethics prioritize collective well-being, while barbarism emphasizes personal gain, even when it harms others. In a truly civilized society, ethical principles form the cornerstone of all actions, ensuring that the achievements of science, technology, and progress serve the common good rather than the interests of a few at the expense of many.

In the novel, McEwan created an elite from civilized society, a glorious neurosurgeon, who has a career, money, status, a house, and a family, and is a typical successful and civilized person. He has superb medical skills which have earned him a high reputation among colleagues and patients. His wife is a lawyer; his father-in-law is a famous poet; his daughter Daisy has published her first collection of poems; and his son Theo is also an accomplished blues musician. With a successful career and a happy family, Perowne is a typical representative of the upper-middle class in modern Western society, enjoying the satisfaction and comfort brought to him by modern civilization. He owns a mansion facing the square and a very luxurious car. Perowne's life is busy and orderly, and even on Saturdays his schedule is very tight, playing squash with colleagues, visiting his mother, listening to his son's concerts, and preparing dinner with his family.

This is a life with a high level of civilization that most people would admire.

At the same time, McEwan also created a savage character, Baxter, a Huntington's disease patient with a rough and wild temperament, belonging to the lower strata of society. Perowne and Baxter have very different personalities, and are at two extremes in social status.

However, this Saturday is doomed to be an unusual one. The story is set on the day before the invasion of Iraq. On this day, a massive anti-war march broke out in London. It is only a year and a half from 9/11, and the shadow of 9/11 hangs over everyone's heart. When Perowne wakes up in the early hours of the morning and sees a crashed plane, he quickly associates it with a terrorist attack. "Airliners look different in the sky these days, predatory or doomed." (15) Behind the superficially glamorous modern civilization are violence, barbarism and the horrors of war. From the "three stout Banham locks and two black iron bolts" on the house, people are reminded of the fact that "the city's poor, the drug-addicted, the downright bad."

The large-scale demonstration in the center of London against the invasion of Iraq is violent and outrageous. The parade has nothing to do with Perowne, who is politically neutral. Sitting in his luxury car, he appreciates the prosperity of the city, and enjoys the convenience of scientific and technological progress, with the zeal of celebrating the success of this era. He is never concerned about war or terror around the world, even though people now are plagued by war, violence, and terror all the time, and there are unpredictable crises hidden in peaceful life. Even when the streets are blocked, he continues to drive forward, thinking that "he only wants to cross this road, not drive down it; or at least, he'll receive his due: a little drama of exchange between a firm but apologetic policeman and the solemnly tolerant citizen" (66). To him, it is the privilege brought to him by modern civilization. Ironically, he is immediately confronted with a violent clash with Baxter's car. The first thing that comes into his mind is that he has to report to the insurance agent, which is another convenience brought by civilization. However, the clash becomes his nightmare. In Perowne's mind, he enjoys a lot the achievements of modern civilization and he himself is also one sample of it, because he is the top neurosurgeon who brings hope to the patients. Baxter, in most readers' minds, is the embodiment of barbarism and ignorance, disease and defect, aggression and loss of control. Perowne tries to suppress Baxter with traffic rules and the police, but in the end, he is beaten by Baxter. Perowne uses his professional knowledge and rational thinking to get him away from more harm, which is a victory of civilization, but the victory with deception and humiliation finally makes him pay for it. It seems that the incident caused by the barbarian Baxter brings disastrous consequences to civilization.

The criterion to judge people civilized or not is not the class they belong to or how much money they have. It is how much they want to repay society. If they care only about themselves and make fun of the poor, in some way, they are no more than barbarians. Just as we have discussed, Perowne uses his knowledge to deceive Baxter, and he feels very pleased about this. Although Perowne escapes the threat of physical violence by doing so, the violent suppression by his professional judgment on Baxter ignites the trigger for the invasion of his home. In a sense, the Baxter invasion in the late afternoon can be seen as a "counter-violence" confrontation. In his second conflict with Baxter, he still wants to manipulate Baxter but is coldly refuted by his daughter, who in the end saves the whole family.

Is Baxter truly a barbarian? He does try to hurt Perowne's family with a knife, but his understanding of the poem shocks the readers. The poem stimulates the tenderest part of him, recalling the sweet memories long buried in his heart. Without Perowne's humiliation in the day, the barbarian part of Baxter may not be provoked, and thus there won't be revenge at night. The awakening of his conscience allows him to return to his innocence, and seeing the hope of life and the dawn of civilization, he immediately restores his rationality and stumbles into the arms of civilization.[134] However, at the moment when the barbarian Baxter opens his heart and turns to Perowne for help, the civilized man suddenly pushes Baxter down the stairs, causing him to be seriously injured. Who is actually a barbarian?

In reflecting on the dynamics between Baxter and Perowne, it becomes clear that the distinction between civilization and barbarism is not as straightforward as it initially appears. Baxter, though initially depicted as a barbarian due to his violent actions toward Perowne's family, displays moments of vulnerability and introspection that challenge this label. His emotional response to the poem, which triggers tender memories and a glimpse of his conscience, complicates the binary between civilization and barbarism. It is this awakening of his humanity that reveals the possibility of redemption, where the cruel, barbaric instincts are momentarily subdued by the stirring of a more compassionate self. Had Perowne not humiliated him earlier, Baxter's violent tendencies may have remained dormant, highlighting the significant role that external provocations play in shaping human behavior.

However, it is crucial to consider that while Baxter experiences this brief awakening, the final act of aggression from Perowne—pushing him down the stairs—questions who the true barbarian is. Perowne, despite being part of the "civilized" elite, resorts to violence to assert his dominance and maintain control. This stark contrast between Baxter's potential for redemption and Perowne's willingness to use violence suggests that barbarism is not confined to one side of the social spectrum. The true barbarism lies in the willingness to dehumanize and act violently, regardless of one's social status or supposed adherence to civilization.

The events of 9/11 compel society to reevaluate the supposed progress of technological civilization, especially when faced with the destructive power it can unleash. This catastrophic event calls into question the ethical foundations of modern civilization, revealing that material progress and technological advancement are not synonymous with moral or ethical advancement. In times of conflict and destruction, such as in war, humanity often sees a tragic erosion of ethical principles, where violence, brutality, and destruction overshadow rationality and compassion. The ethical implications of these clashes between civilization and barbarism are profound. Wars, driven by political and material motivations, often blur the lines between the so-called civilized world and the barbaric. Humanity is left to grapple with the uncomfortable truth that civilization, for all its intellectual and technological achievements, is deeply intertwined with violence and destruction. The ethical responsibility lies not in blind adherence to progress or technological advancement but in ensuring that human dignity, empathy, and peace are prioritized in all human endeavors. Ultimately, the true measure of civilization is not in the technological prowess it attains but in how it maintains and nurtures ethical conduct, compassion, and a commitment to peace amid the destructive forces that often accompany progress.

Section Four   The Urban Cultural Dilemma

In *Saturday*, McEwan meticulously explores the intricacies of contemporary urban life, using London as both a setting and a symbol of modern civilization. The city is portrayed as a space where technological advancements, material prosperity, and scientific achievements coexist with deep-rooted ethical conflicts, emotional isolation, and existential anxieties. McEwan's narrative does not merely depict the external grandeur of the urban landscape but explores the psychological and moral dilemmas faced by individuals navigating this environment.

At the novel's outset, Perowne awakens to the sight of London, marveling at its architectural beauty and the sophisticated systems that sustain it—a cityscape shaped by centuries of progress. Yet, beneath this veneer of success lies a paradox: while the city thrives materially, it simultaneously cultivates emotional detachment, moral ambiguity, and a disconnection from authentic human experiences. This juxtaposition sets the stage for McEwan's exploration of the urban cultural dilemma, where the very forces that propel civilization forward also contribute to its ethical and spiritual crises.

In the novel, in the beginning, when Perowne gets up and looks out of the window, he is amazed by the highly developed city.

> Standing here, as immune to the cold as a marble statue, gazing towards Charlotte Street, towards a foreshortened jumble of facades, scaffolding and pitched roofs, Henry thinks the city is a success, a brilliant invention, a biological masterpiece - millions teeming around the accumulated and layered achievements of the centuries, as though around a coral reef, sleeping, working, entertaining themselves, harmonious for the

most part, nearly everyone wanting it to work. (6)

    The modernized city is the most wonderful achievement of science and technology. The architecture, the street light, and the drainage system indicate that Perowne enjoys the wonderful convenience of city life. However, the architecture, the skyscrapers or infrastructures with the same style to some extent indicate the spiritual predicament that the advanced technology brings to them. The overcrowded subways and streets, the perennially congested roads, and the shadows of the clusters of high-rise buildings all cause pressure on people. When the landscape turns into the skyscrapers in the city, people lose something fundamental and original, something intuitive and compassionate. The uniformity of the modern city fragments individuals into homogeneous parts, eroding the distinct attributes that define human existence. In this meticulously planned and standardized environment, personal identity is diminished, and people become victims of the very technological progress that promises to enhance their lives. The repetitive architectural structures and monotonous urban landscapes strip individuals of their uniqueness, fostering a sense of repression and alienation.

    The rapid advancement of science and technology has thus given rise to a mechanized urban world where individuals gradually lose their subjectivity, reduced to mere cogs within the vast machinery of modern civilization. Immersed in this uniform environment, people become detached from their inner selves, finding superficial comfort in the illusion of progress and prosperity. Perowne embodies this condition—entrenched in the routines of contemporary life, he remains complacent, unaware of his own entrapment. He has surrendered his capacity for independent thought and the will to actively shape his existence, willingly dissolving into the shadows of the modern cityscape. At once a product and a perpetuator of this mechanical world, Perowne himself is disconnected from the deeper, non-material dimensions of human experience, as evidenced by his inability to appreciate his children's artistic pursuits and his indifference toward the transformative power of poetry.

    The cover of the May 2017 issue of *Landscape Society* published by

Nanjing University is a very vivid interpretation and embodiment of the urban landscape: people in the cinema wear the same 3D glasses, and everyone faces the same direction, watching the same virtual image and feeling the same emotional experience. When emotional experience becomes the object of regulation and unity of urban culture, people lose the nature of what makes people human and become part of the huge urban landscape. People assimilated and alienated by instrumentalism are attracted to the same interest throughout their lives, voluntarily guided by the virtual screen in front of them until they are swallowed up by the vast urban landscape. In the whole process, people have no response to the world they face, do not have any subjective behavior, but only passively accept, and enjoy illusory satisfaction in this process of acceptance.

Just like Perowne's life arranged as an instruction book: learning medical knowledge and performing surgeries. In the process, he has a wife and children, but the phone call can ask him to leave his family at any time for surgery; he goes to the gym, but it is arranged passively and he can't enjoy himself in the game; he cannot understand his children's feelings about poetry and music. In his world, his life is arranged by studies and surgery, a life defined by luxury cars and mansions. However, the luxurious lifestyle can't cover the absence of the soul. The sameness deprives people of their uniqueness.

This mechanized routine reflects not just Perowne's personal life but also the broader condition of urban existence, where efficiency and order dominate at the expense of individuality and emotional depth. The rigid structure of daily life, governed by schedules, responsibilities, and material pursuits, leaves little room for spontaneity, self-reflection, or genuine human connection. The uniformity extends beyond personal habits to the very fabric of the city itself, where the architectural and social environment reinforces conformity and isolation. This transition from the personal to the collective highlights how the urban landscape mirrors and perpetuates the emotional detachment experienced by individuals like Perowne, creating a cityscape where both the physical and psychological spaces are marked by uniformity and disconnection.

"A rectilinear curve sweeps him past recent office buildings of glass and steel where the lights are already on in the February early afternoon. He glimpses people as neat as architectural models, at their desks, before their screens, even on a Saturday. This is the tidy future of his childhood science fiction comics, of men and women with tight-fitting collarless jumpsuits—no pockets, trailing laces or untucked shirts—living a life beyond litter and confusion, free of clutter to fight evil" (130). City life has never been easier. It is on Saturday when Perowne looks through the window and sees people dressed in the same kind of clothes, busy in their office, just as if it isn't Saturday. In the same building, people dress in the same way and in the same compartment. The sameness obscures people's characteristics and suppresses their expression of their own identities. People inside the tall buildings work in their own compartments which separate them from mutual communication. The sameness in the urban society erases people's differences in personality, and finally makes them willingly incarnate into the same parts of a machine. When people are manipulated by high technology, they are just like robots. The tall building within which the offices are located is the symbol of modern technology, and the people in it are just like the parts of a huge machine. The scene is perceived by Perowne as the greatness of modernity other than the deprivation of people's leisure time. As an elite in science, Perowne can fully understand the role that technology plays. When he saw the roads connecting the city, "for seconds on end he thinks he grasps the vision of its creators - a purer world that favors machines rather than people" (130). The division of society creates convenience in one way, but in another way, it is a rupture of the soul of the people. The more subtle the division is, the less mutual empathy people may have. "Independence of thought, autonomy, and the right to political opposition are being deprived of their basic critical function in a society which seems increasingly capable of satisfying the needs of the Individuals through the way in which it is organized."[135]

 Although Perowne views the buildings made of "glass and steel" as symbols of technological advancement, along with the well-organized streets, drainage systems, and safety facilities that make the city appear desirable, his experiences in the heart of London reveal a contrasting reality. He encounters traffic jams, strikes, demonstrations, and car accidents—disruptions that symbolize the inherent setbacks and vulnerabilities within an advanced technological society.

These incidents expose the fragility beneath the city's polished surface, highlighting the limitations of technology in addressing deeper societal issues. Ironically, the very progress that fosters material prosperity also contributes to spiritual emptiness, mental health issues, and a growing crisis of social and personal belief. This paradox underscores Perowne's own professional success as a neurosurgeon—his expertise thrives precisely because the psychological and existential void created by modern life leads to an increased prevalence of mental disorders, making him both a beneficiary and a byproduct of the technological civilization he admires.

For the urbanites, the procession of expensive commodities is another way to show one's success. The accumulation of materials such as mansions and luxurious cars has become the only sign of the success of contemporary urbanites. Perowne owns a silver Mercedes S500 with cream upholstery. To the elites, the luxurious car is just a sensual part of his overgenerous share of the world's goods and he's no longer embarrassed by it. When he sees his car a hundred yards away, parked at an angle on the rise of the track, he can't stop loving an inanimate object, possibly and permissibly, because he can't stop loving the civilization created by technology. His car is picked out in soft light against a backdrop of birch, under the flowering heather and thunderous black sky. His Mercedes gives him "vague satisfaction" as people cast envious eyes. His mansion also embodies contemporary high-end scientific and technological achievements. He lived in a wealthy quarter of London with layers of guards on the door. The above makes Perowne proud of being one of the small number of elites who can afford to live a rich and comfortable life. Cars and houses are not used to meet the primary needs of human beings. They are the signs of being elites. His abundant material life displays the urban elite's dominance over the commodities in society. In the novel, the gap between classes is still increasing, for the ordinary people can only pursue their rights through protests, while the rich people can enjoy themselves by playing squash games, with no concerns about the protests.

Perowne's life experience is a typical example of "squeezing into the upper class" through his hard study and work. When he was young, Perowne lived in a suburb with his mother. His upward motivation urges him to step into the upper middle class. Now he can afford to buy what is labeled with the illusionary sense of achievement. Before his confrontation with Baxter, he may have no idea about the desperation of the lower class. This is the main reason for him to cause much trouble to his family soon after. In their communication, his rationality shows his condescending attitude towards Baxter.

> Baxter is one of those smokers whose pores exude a perfume, an oily essence of his habit. Garlic affects certain people the same way. Possibly the kidneys are implicated. He's a fidgety, small-faced young man with thick eyebrows and dark brown hair razored close to the skull. The mouth is set bulbously, with the smoothly shaved shadow of a strong beard adding to the effect of a muzzle. (73)

The modified words Perowne uses, like "oily, fidgety, muzzle," directly show his contempt for Baxter, who, in his eyes, is a hooligan. That is why he is so confident in using his professional knowledge to humiliate Baxter. To him, people from the lower class like Baxter don't deserve to enjoy the achievements of modern technology. He shows no empathy for the disadvantaged. This arrogant and aggressive attitude becomes the prologue of the violent event.

The accumulation of capital and profits expands the city. The entertainment space in the city where people can enjoy nature and relax now concedes to the shopping areas, which can inspire people's desire to consume more commodities. The leisure time of urbanites is passively controlled by commodities and the urbanites are reified. According to his covenant, "to deride the hopes of progress is the ultimate fatuity, the last word in poverty of spirit and meanness of mind." Perowne acknowledges that "certainly in this city, lucky gods blessed by supermarket cornucopias…warm clothes that weigh nothing…wondrous machines" (65). Obviously, in his mind, material abundance is not and is not going to be acquired by ordinary people.

In *History and Class Consciousness*, Lukács mentions that "in the capitalist society, the phenomena of reifications are pervasive in human activities."[136] The reified people who are driven by the pursuit of materialism have no empathy for others and gradually lose their emotions. McEwan once said that empathy is the core of humanity and the start of morality. With no empathy, people experience "the indifference and estrangement of interpersonal relationships, and the loss of the sense of belonging in a highly-materialized world."[137] In the city, instead of walking along the street to enjoy the view and relaxation, Perowne sees "a spot he's always liked, where the affairs of utility and pleasure condense to make color and space brighter: mirrors, flowers, soaps, newspapers, electrical plugs, house paints, key cutting urbanely interleaved with expensive restaurants, wine and tapas bars, hotels" (102). What he sees is the commercial messages, whose primary emphasis is on capital and profits. He praises the prosperity of the scene because he is living in an "age of affluence."[138] Advanced technology and material civilizations make people's faith in machinery reach the point where it is absurdly disproportionate to the purpose for which it is intended to serve.

In the postindustrial urbanized city, the pursuit of materialism often consumes the urbanites, leading to a disregard for individual ethics. Within this context, individuals who become heavily materialized and reified rely on external possessions to cultivate a sense of superiority. However, behind the abundance of material possessions lies an emptiness within one's soul. This emptiness is reflected in the protagonist, Perowne, who experiences alienation from mundane life. He struggles to establish genuine connections with his children, his communication with his wife becomes stereotypical, and his relationship with his father-in-law is hostile.

Contemporary urban life fosters an environment where people indulge in false and luxurious lifestyles, ultimately resulting in a loss of empathy. Perowne's life, similar to Andy Warhol's art (Warhol's pop art, known for its repetitive imagery of consumer goods and celebrities), is portrayed as gorgeous and cookie-cutter. Warhol's paintings express the superficial beauty that masks the underlying monotony and boredom of contemporary cities, achieved through the endless replication of different objects. This infinite repetition conveys the indifference, emptiness, and alienation experienced by contemporary urbanites. The monotony hidden beneath the polished surface of contemporary life aligns well with McEwan's exploration of urban existence, rationality, and emotional detachment in *Saturday*. Similarly, Perowne's life is characterized by endless repetition, as his constrained existence revolves around the pursuit of material possessions, such as his mansion and Mercedes. Just like Marilyn Monroe in Warhol's paintings, who symbolizes emptiness through her copied smile, Perowne mimics the empty symbols of material wealth and status that contemporary society covets. However, in doing so, he loses touch with his own soul, reduced to a mere fragment of a machine.

In the portrayal of Perowne and the critique of contemporary urban culture, individual ethics are notably absent. The pursuit of materialism and the shallow values of the urban society lead to a neglect of personal integrity, empathy, and deeper connections with others. McEwan's concerns regarding spiritual desolation and emotional dilemmas stem from the erosion of individual ethics in the face of distorted cultural values. The exploration of the balance between scientific and technological rationality and the goodness of human nature highlights the importance of maintaining a moral compass and ethical conduct within the rapidly advancing urban landscape.

As technology defines and shapes life, the contemporary city quietly transforms into a wasteland for the human soul. Success may be present, but true happiness eludes individuals within this environment. This phenomenon stems from the overwhelming influence of science, technology, and instrumental rationality. While rationality can encompass the observation of the external world, it should also involve self-exploration and self-awareness. The development of science and technology should not serve as an excuse for people to lose their sensitivity and ethical values. This is why the balance between scientific and technological rationality and the innate goodness of human nature becomes a recurring theme in McEwan's works. Through his nuanced prose, McEwan reveals the distorted cultural values embedded in contemporary urban life, exposing the spiritual desolation and emotional dilemmas that emerge from this distortion.

Chapter Seven   The Ethical Failure in *Solar*

Solar, published in 2010, is McEwan's eleventh novel. As soon as it was launched, it received widespread attention from critics at home and abroad. *Solar* is based on global warming in a macroscopic context, and the chaotic emotional and academic life of physicist Michael Beard is narrated in the third person. *The Telegraph* commented that "*Solar* can be called his first A comedy novel ... is a calm, cunning comedy novel about arrogance, infidelity and current affairs." Jeff Giles from *Entertainment Weekly* comments on this novel: "The plot of *Solar*—a jerk builds such a tower of lies that it seems certain to fall on him—is not the cleverest thing McEwan has ever dreamed up. But it's a surprising book in other ways. Decades ago, McEwan wrote about the violence we do to others. *Solar* is about the violence we do to ourselves."[139] Christopher Tayler from *The Guardian* reviewed the novel from the aspect of cause-effect point of view. "Lightness, however, comes less easily to McEwan, whose style depends on deliberateness and a certain ponderousness. The ominous lining up of causes and effects and the patient tweaking of narrative tension don't always mesh well with the aimed-for quickness and brio. ... At the same time, the overarching plot pulls off a clinching novelistic coup, using comedy to sneak grimmer matters past the reader's defences."[140] To the protagonist, Michael Beard is a fascinatingly repulsive character. "Beard could have been the richly flawed character that would carry *Solar*. However, despite the many ponderous ruminations on his own sensual and moral weaknesses, his smug lack of any humility or self-reproach gives the reader little purchase for any enduring interest. ... Forgive the pun, but Solar is purely light entertainment—no bad thing in itself but lacking the scope and tenacity that one might expect from McEwan."[141]

Solar is combined with energy development, personal and public crises. McEwan exposes the distorted ethics of contemporary social elites in the form of black humor. His judgments about his dissolute private life are quite beyond the common morals and do not align with the readers' ethical judgments.

The novel chronologically tells three important periods in Michael Beard's life and inserts some memories of his student days in Oxford. This eminent Nobel laureate physicist leads a turbulent life. Although Beard's career has developed smoothly, his personal life is quite another matter. He uses his reputation to secure huge payments for himself, puts his name on the letterhead of prestigious scientific institutions, and absentmindedly leads a government-backed initiative to combat global warming. Discovering with dismay, he finds that his best achievements were made when he was a young man. Past his career peak, it is by dint of the honor of the Nobel Prize that he is now heading a research center for wind energy sources. There is a young researcher, Tom Aldous, one of Beard's assistants, actively seeking an opportunity to discuss the potential of cheap, sustainable solar energy with Beard, and Beard begins to see a lot of new possibilities. In 2000, his fifth marriage collapses in the situation that his beloved wife Patrice has an affair with their builder, Tarpin, and the assistant, Aldous. When Aldous dies in accidentally comic circumstances that he strikes his own head on the coffee table, Beard greatly profits from the event and claims Aldous' work as his own. Beard lets another of his wife's lovers be the scapegoat for the accident, Tarpin, who is indeed arrested, convicted of Aldous's murder, and duly jailed for 18 years.

Thanks to Aldous' research on solar energy, Beard has experienced another career success by 2005, but gets fired by the government for giving improper remarks about women in a press conference, as he states that natural limitations of the female gender is the reason why the scientific community lacks women researchers. The ensuing anger over his comments triggers a media storm, leading to his past feminization experience being scrutinized by the media. Beard gets entangled in a love crisis again when he has a sexual relationship with Melissa, a younger woman who owns a string of dance supply shops. Beard does not plan to marry her but Melissa informs Beard that she has already stopped taking birth control pills and is currently pregnant. When Beard knows the matter, he flies into a rage and asks her to have an abortion.

In 2009, 62-year-old Beard is now a father and in poor physical condition, worrying about a suspicious-looking lesion on his wrist. The construction of a solar power plant in Lordsburg, New Mexico, progresses to the last stage, where he has another intimate relationship with a waitress, Darlene, although Beard gets along well with Melissa and their three-year-old daughter, Catriona. All the retribution for the discreditable affairs he has done bursts on the eve of the opening ceremony for the solar power plant. Tarpin is out of jail and turns up asking Beard for a job opportunity. Melissa comes to New Mexico hoping to break them up. A patent lawyer gets evidence to expose his pilferage of Aldous' research achievements. Confirmed by the doctor, the lesion on his hand is cancerous. His business partners abandon him, leaving him with millions of dollars in debt. Someone has destroyed the power plant by smashing the solar panels. The story ends up with an "unfamiliar, swelling sensation" in Beard's heart, which is a sort of love for his daughter or may well be the onset of a heart attack. Family indeed serves as the foundation of society, and family ethics play a significant role in shaping an individual's behavior within the social context. In *Solar*, McEwan explores the erosion of these ethical foundations through the protagonist, Michael Beard, whose dysfunctional personal relationships reflect a broader moral decay. Hegel's insights into the fundamental essence of the family concept—(a) marriage as the initial stage and immediate form of the family; (b) the family's property and estate, representing external assets and responsibilities; and (c) the education of children and the eventual dissolution of the family—are subverted in Beard's life. His multiple failed marriages, neglect of familial responsibilities, and emotional detachment illustrate the disintegration of traditional family values in the face of self-interest and hedonism. McEwan uses Beard's personal failures to mirror the ethical crises within contemporary society, where the stability of the family unit is undermined by individualistic pursuits, echoing the environmental and moral degradation central to the novel's theme.

Family ethics should be defined as the relationship between individual family members and their family. Individual family members can acquire ethical relations only in the family community, and the behavior between members has ethical values. These ethics are crucial in shaping the dynamics and functioning of the family, as well as influencing individual performance in the social context.

Individual ethics within the family are integral to maintaining a healthy and harmonious familial environment. Each family member's adherence to personal moral principles, such as honesty, kindness, and accountability, shapes the interactions and relationships within the family. Individual ethics guide behavior and promote mutual understanding, empathy, and cooperation, fostering an environment of love, trust, and support. By upholding family ethics, individuals within the family unit not only enhance their own well-being but also contribute to the larger social fabric. Strong family ethics provide a solid foundation for raising responsible, compassionate citizens who can positively impact society at large. It is through the cultivation of ethical relationships, values, and behaviors within the family that the broader ethical framework of a society can be strengthened and sustained.

Marriage, as a direct ethical relationship, first includes the natural family life. It involves the commitment between partners and the mutual respect, trust, and care they cultivate. Ethical behavior within marriage encompasses qualities such as fidelity, communication, and support for one another's growth and well-being. Since ethical relations are substantive relations, they include the whole of life, that is, the reality of their life processes. Some selfish people are less responsible for the family, indifferent to family awareness, to family affection and others, and even advocate the abnormal life of marriage. In this state, even some non-extreme contradictions and conflicts will evolve into irreconcilable extremes, and the family will inevitably face disintegration.

Furthermore, the education of children is a vital component of family ethics. This involves instilling moral values, teaching empathy, promoting integrity, and fostering the development of ethical principles in the younger generation. Parents play a significant role in modeling ethical behavior and guiding children to become responsible, compassionate individuals who contribute positively to society.

Within the context of family ethics, it is crucial to address the issue of male dominance. Historically, patriarchal systems have often resulted in a hierarchical structure where men exerted significant control and dominance over family affairs. This dominance manifested in various forms, such as decision-making authority, control of resources, and social expectations that favored men over women. Such gender-based power imbalances can have profound implications for family ethics, as they may hinder equitable relationships and impede the development of individual ethics within the family unit. Traditional gender roles often assigned men positions of authority and power within the family structure, resulting in imbalances and inequalities. However, contemporary family ethics emphasize the importance of egalitarian relationships and equal partnership between spouses. This involves challenging gender stereotypes, promoting mutual respect and shared decision-making, and recognizing and valuing the diverse strengths and contributions of each family member, regardless of gender.

In recent times, societal progress and evolving values have challenged and questioned the traditional notions of male dominance in family dynamics. There is a growing recognition of the importance of fostering egalitarian relationships within families, where decision-making, responsibilities, and emotional labor are shared equitably between partners. This shift acknowledges the need to embrace individual ethics and mutual respect within the family, creating an environment where all family members can thrive and contribute to the collective well-being.

The concept of ethical failure serves as a crucial lens through which we can examine the character of Michael Beard in *Solar*. Beard's self-centeredness and moral decay are not simply personal flaws but are deeply embedded in the traditional structures of family ethics and gender relations that shape his worldview. His inability to transcend the patriarchal values instilled within his upbringing—the belief in male dominance, entitlement, and the subjugation of others—reflects a broader ethical collapse within society. Beard's actions, driven by a desire for fame, power, and personal gratification, expose the inherent flaws in a family structure that prioritizes patriarchal authority and ego over mutual respect and responsibility. The novel critiques not only individual selfishness but also the structural forces that enable such behaviors, particularly the gendered dynamics of power and control. As Beard's narcissistic pursuit of self-interest clashes with the ethical responsibilities of family and society, McEwan challenges readers to reflect on the consequences of these failures and the need for a more equitable moral framework—one that values both personal integrity and the well-being of others in a world still deeply influenced by gendered hierarchies.

Section One   Beard's Narcissism

This historical context of gender roles and family dynamics provides a critical backdrop for understanding the character of Michael Beard in *Solar*. Despite living in a more progressive era, Beard's attitudes toward relationships and women are deeply rooted in outdated, patriarchal notions that echo the traditional male dominance of the mid-20th century. His narcissism and emotional detachment reflect an inability to adapt to evolving family ethics, as he consistently exploits and objectifies the women in his life, treating them as extensions of his own ego rather than as equal partners. This dissonance between societal progress and Beard's personal failings highlights the persistent challenges in achieving genuine gender equality within modern family structures. McEwan uses Beard's character not only to critique individual moral flaws but also to expose the lingering influence of historical gender norms on contemporary relationships.

Major legislation including the 1944 Butler Education Act and the 1946 National Insurance Act changed the lives of women in postwar Britain. The life of the average married woman in the 1950s and 60s was very different from that of today's woman. Very few women worked after getting married; they stayed at home to raise the children and keep house. A married woman took her husband's last name and was financially dependent on him. The man was considered the head of the household. For the women with no money and no career, if the marriage was unhappy or they met with violence, they had no way to get away from this marriage.

It was still unusual for women, especially working-class women, to go to university. Also, because of women's lack of education as well as men's resistance, many professions were closed to women. Once a working woman became pregnant, she had to give up her work.

In sum, women in the 1960s and 70s were still largely financially dependent on their husbands. The 1964 Married Women's Property Act allowed women to keep half of any savings they made from the allowance received by their husbands. Even though more women began to work and earn their own money, many still received an allowance from their husbands and were therefore financially dependent on them.

Feminists felt that women started life being dependent on their father and then on their husband. Then there came the Marriage Bar. The Marriage Bar required single women to resign from their jobs upon getting married and disqualified married women from applying for vacancies. Women were not allowed to apply for or work at some occupations, for example, factory work, clerical work, teaching in some local authorities and service industry jobs. Because people believed that it was not possible for a woman to be able to combine both work and domestic life well. The Marriage Bar was gradually lifted in the UK from 1944 onwards. No matter how many examples of women who had a job and could support the families there were, the conviction that women would not be able to work with their full attention prevailed. "For all these reasons many UK feminists in the 1960s and 70s were strongly opposed to conventional marriage and campaigned, through the fifth demand, for legal and financial independence for women."[142] With the emerging movements of female liberation and the sex revolution, the traditional sexual relationships encountered great challenges, which led to people's more tolerant and equal sex attitudes. With the passage of the 1969 divorce law, the family structure in Britain underwent dramatic changes, resulting in a record-high divorce rate and the prevalence of the idea of staying single among the youth.

The protagonist, Beard, born in 1947, is brought up by the faux-friendly and unfaithful parents who have experienced sexual liberation in person. His mother, Angela Beard, has a series of affairs that stretches over eleven years. Beard, who has been married five times, is extremely indiscreet about his marriages, spoiling the sacred free rights of getting married and divorced. Beard himself is a mess, grotesque and downright unlikable to boot, yet oddly irresistible to women. In his own eyes, "he belonged to that class of men—vaguely unprepossessing, often bald, short, fat, clever—who were unaccountably attractive to certain beautiful women. Or he believed he was, and thinking seemed to make it so" (11).[143] He never reviews his own mistakes in marriages. His marriages, all of which are based on carnal desire instead of love, are doomed to be aborted. His five divorces and countless affairs not only reflect his distorted moral attitude towards marriages, but also reveal the social problems in the current British society to some extent.

Solar starts narrating Beard's fifth disintegrating marriage with Patrice. In the novel, McEwan gives us Beard's family background through Beard's narration. Michael Beard grew up in a family with a defective marital relationship between his parents. In his family, they all fail to perform their ethical identity and accomplish the responsibilities. Henry Beard fails to take the responsibility as a husband or a father. His experience as a survivor in the war greatly affects his emotions and feelings about life. The cruelty of the war leaves him nothing but the longing for peace. His father is "like many men of his generation, he did not speak about his experience and relished the ordinariness of postwar life, its tranquil routines, its tidiness and rising material well-being, and above all its lack of danger" (244-245). He remains indifferent whether granted favors or subjected to humiliation. He never talks about his trauma with his family. The war has washed away his enthusiasm toward life and love. He cherishes the peaceful life that is a treasure for his generation and spends his time on things he likes. He coldly accepts his loveless marriage as the price he must pay for what he has done. His absence for his love to the family finally causes the failure in the marriage. "Early in the marriage, for reasons that remained private, she withdrew her love from him. She lived for her son..." (164). Michael Beard's mother, Angela Beard, soon loses her interest in the marriage and her husband after marriage. Under this circumstance, she gives all her love to her son and adores him so much that the way she shows her love is to feed him. "She bottle-fed him with passion, surplus to demand" (163). She spared no effort to satisfy Michael Beard's appetite. "Once he was on solids, and for the rest of her life, she cooked for him with the same commitment with which she had held the bottle, sending herself in the mid-nineteen sixties, despite her illness, on a 'cordon bleu' cookery course so that she might try new meals during his occasional visits home" (163). From the description, his mother never fully understands how to love a person. The way for his mother to love him is to feed him. This late makes "her legacy"—Beard—a fat man who relentlessly craves the attention of beautiful women, particularly those who can cook.

Because Angela shows no love to her husband, and also her husband cares less about her feelings, Angela Beard begins a series of affairs with different men that have stretched over eleven years. She jumps from one man to another in years. When Beard is seventeen, he finds that his mother comes back home, exhausted. This is the family Beard grows up in, which makes Beard emotionally dysfunctional. His father fails his duty as a father to educate him about love and life, while his mother gives him the wrong idea about love. He doesn't care about his parents' feelings. However, Beard never talks about her mother's affairs with his father. It is a topic they can't touch. Therefore, when he comes back home from school, he will read, play, build, or glue in his room, even read pornography and masturbate in the room. "His head was full of math and girlfriends, physics and drinking" (226).

In the family, the father's "non-existence" will lead to incomplete family education. The widowed-type family will force the mother to pay too much attention to the child to compensate for a lack of paternal love. This circumstance will force the child to form dependent personality characteristics and mostly aggravate the child's Oedipus complex. The relationship between husband and wife is the enlightenment of the child's future marriage. The state of the relationship between husband and wife in the family will leave a mark on the child's subconsciousness, affecting his or her future treatment of the opposite sex and his or her attitude toward marriage. The disharmonious parents with unequal relationships may affect their children in various aspects, like problems in interpersonal relationships or children's marriages. Their future emotional relationship will be in a mess, resulting in the breakdown of the relationship with their lover, and the recurrence of tragedies like their parents. Beard's marriage in the novel is just the result of the influence of his parents' marriage. Besides, the love-absent family also causes children's emotional flaws. Love not only provides material satisfaction, but also shows the care from others. In a family without love from both parents, they can't raise a child with a sound personality. Beard's narcissistic personality contributes to this kind of family.

The basic feature of narcissistic personality is the exaggeration of the sense of self-worth. Such people exaggerate their achievements and talents without any reason, believing that they should be regarded as "special talents" and believing that their ideas are unique and that only special people can understand them. Narcissistic personalities have arrogant behaviors and are very concerned about a sense of power. They lack empathy in intimate relationships with others, and meanwhile, they may exert their power over the other part.[144]

In *Solar*, Beard exhibits many traits characteristic of narcissistic personality disorder, particularly in his inflated sense of self-worth. Throughout the novel, he consistently exaggerates his own contributions to the scientific community, often attributing much of his success to his own brilliance, despite the fact that his achievements are frequently tainted by personal and professional failings. He views himself as a uniquely gifted individual, deserving of admiration and deference, and is quick to dismiss the contributions and intellect of others.

Beard's narcissism also manifests in his relationships, where he seeks out admiration and validation, particularly from women. He craves the attention of beautiful women who fulfill a specific, self-serving role in his life—either as sources of pleasure or as embodiments of his success. His disregard for genuine emotional connection in these relationships highlights his lack of empathy, a defining feature of narcissism. Beard's interactions with those around him, whether personal or professional, are often transactional, focused more on what others can provide him than on mutual understanding or respect.

Moreover, his sense of entitlement and belief in his superiority also lead him to exert control over others. This is particularly evident in his manipulation of situations and people to maintain his sense of power and to protect his ego from any form of criticism or threat. Beard's inability to recognize his flaws and his tendency to project an image of invulnerability are symptomatic of his narcissism, reinforcing the idea that, despite his failings, he believes himself to be above reproach. In the novel, Beard who is 53 with no handsome appearance and well-shaped figure believes in himself that he is very attractive to women.

He is a typical womanizer and egoist. Every time he has a marital relationship with a woman, he will be the one who betrays the marriage. His frivolous character that he inherited from his mother drives him to chase one woman after another, no matter whether she is a student or a waitress. His self-ego makes him irresistible to extramarital sex. Beard seldom dedicates himself to love and responsibility. The first divorce is really easy, which makes him unscrupulous in later marriages. "Perhaps it was the ease of their parting in the old rectory that made him so incautious about marrying again, and again" (176). He has one marriage after another, with one rolling out and the other rolling in. In each marriage, he shows no concern over his wives but flirts with other women. None of his marriages has ever lasted over six years; most of the ex-wives can't bear his endless love affairs. The good thing is that there is no child in each marriage. "It was lovers he needed, not wives." (50) In the marriages, he shows no respect to his wives, exerting his masculine power over women, doing whatever he wants to hurt his wives. In the previous marriages, what makes him proud is that he is on speaking terms with all the exes. He never feels sorry for his extramarital affairs that cause so much pain or trouble to his exes. It seems that Beard is quite proud of his divorces and his relationships with his ex-wives. His unfaithful behavior leads every one of his marriage to failure until his fifth marriage to a woman named Patrice, who becomes his nightmare. Patrice takes the revenge of Beard's adultery by having extramarital affairs with other guys. Unlike his previous wives, who have done nothing but end the marriage after suffering from his extramarital affairs, Patrice greatly destroys his egoism.

> What engines of self-persuasion had let him think for so many years that looking like this was seductive? That foolish thatch of earlobe-level hair that buttressed his baldness, the new curtain-swag of fat that hung below his armpits, the innocent stupidity of swelling in gut and rear. Once, he had been able to improve on his mirror-elf by pinning back his shoulders, standing erect, tightening his abs. Now, human blubber draped his efforts. How could he possibly keep hold of a young woman as beautiful as she was? (13)

Patrice's love affairs greatly hurt him, which in turn arouses his desire for Patrice. "What impressed him was his ability to think of nothing else. ... he was really thinking of her, or of her and Tarpin" (15). He endeavors to save this marriage and to change Patrice's mind. He even goes to Tarpin's house to confront him for hitting Patrice. However, before Beard can react, Tarpin strikes him with an open hand, landing a powerful blow on his right cheek and ear. The impact nearly knocks Beard off his feet, leaving him momentarily dazed and disoriented. Regaining just enough composure, Beard flees from Tarpin's place, humiliated and defeated. He overestimates his power over Tarpin. People with high levels of narcissism focus too much on themselves, and fantasize that they are superior to others in every way, and even believe that they have the right to enjoy special treatment. In his heart, he despises Tarpin for his low status as a handyman. That gives him the courage to confront Tarpin. However, when he does stand in front of strong Tarpin, Beard is nothing but an older man. "Even eight consecutive press-ups were beyond him. Whereas Tarpin could run up the stairs to the Beards' master bedroom holding under one arm a fifty-kilo cement sack" (13). Tarpin is depicted as an impulsive, violent, and irrational person who is the direct opposite of rational and calm Beard. Later, Beard uses his talents to deliberately frame Tarpin despite justice and puts him into prison, even though he feels revulsion at touching Tarpin's stuff, temporarily getting rid of him.

From the academic perspective, the narcissistic, short-sighted Beard feels the crisis that he might be replaced by the young generation. This fear of obsolescence not only intensifies his insecurities but also drives his desperate attempts to assert his relevance both professionally and personally. The younger Beard, who surprised all the world by the Beard-Einstein Conflation in the Solvay conference in 1972 and the appendix of the verisimilar Swedish Academy of Sciences speech, speaks highly of Beard's achievement. As a Nobel Prize winner, Beard has been known for his "Beard-Einstein Conflation, which had brought him his prize, awarded prizes and medals himself, accepted honorary degrees, and gave after-dinner speeches and eulogies for retiring or about-to-be-cremated colleagues." Seemingly, he is an absolute authority on academia, but in fact he knows that his brilliance has begun to decline since the moment of creating the "Beard-Einstein" theory, and now he is nothing more than a scientific moth with no progress. Compared with him, the postdoctoral researchers at the Centre are passionate about research, full of expectations for the future, and have a strong ability to learn, and they talk about some self-evident physical problems that confuse the Nobel laureate.

> Two decades had passed since he last sat down in silence and solitude for hours on end, pencil and pad in hand, to do some thinking, to have an original hypothesis, play with it, pursue it, tease it into life. The occasion never arose—no, that was a weak excuse. He lacked the will, the material, he lacked the spark. He had no new ideas. (26)

After the Beard-Einstein conflation, Beard becomes increasingly eager to secure his reputation as a prominent speaker, prioritizing self-promotion over genuine scientific research. Rather than dedicating his efforts to meaningful academic contributions, he focuses on selling his personal narrative to maintain public attention. This relentless pursuit of fame and recognition satisfies his narcissistic need for ego validation, allowing him to bask in the remnants of his two-decade-old acclaim.

In a society dominated by consumerism and materialism, where success is often measured by wealth, status, and public recognition, Beard's ambitions are shaped by these superficial values. His narcissism manifests not only in his exaggerated sense of self-importance but also in his relentless desire to be admired and envied. This self-obsession turns him into an opportunist, exploiting both professional and personal relationships to serve his own interests. As a result, Beard is depicted as a greedy, selfish, immoral, and hypocritical man whose achievements are less the product of genuine talent and more the result of manipulation, deceit, and an insatiable hunger for validation.

> He lent his name, his title, Professor Beard, Nobel laureate, to letterheads, to institutes, signed up to international 'initiatives', sat on a Royal Commission on science funding, spoke on the radio in layman's

terms about Einstein or photons or quantum mechanics, helped out with grant applications, was a consultant editor on three scholarly journals, wrote peer review and references, took an interest in the gossip… (20)

For many years, he has rested on his laurels. Instead of pursuing further improvement in physics, he keeps enjoying his previous glory. "Like a shipwrecked man, he had clung to this single plank, and counted himself privileged" (49). Every week, he takes "the grubby morning train from Paddington to Reading" to work on the project set up by the government. Narcissistic individuals tend to have an inflated sense of self-importance, often perceiving themselves as exceptional or superior to others. They harbor beliefs such as "I am special" or "I am better than others," which reflect their exaggerated self-esteem. When Beard arrives at the location where the project is being done, "the vibrations came to rest as he acknowledged with raised forefinger the friendly salute of the security guards—how they loved a supremo!". He enjoys the position as "the distinguished visitor, the Chief," who can "speak up for the place in the press, encourage the energy industries to take an interest, and squeeze another quarter-million from the blustering Minister" (27). He is never ashamed of having any progress in his research, but proud of deceiving the government for the funding. His selfishness and greed are vividly exposed.

The project set up by the government is meant to solve the shortage of petroleum. Actually, the scientists in the Center and even the government don't care much about it; instead, they care more about the profits. Beard's irresponsible proposal of the project with the purpose of procuring more funds at last turns into a failure, because Beard's impressive facade over a rickety interior puts him into a very awkward position. "Beard preferred to go around alone to witness guiltily the consequences of his casual proposal" (28).

In this situation, he meets Aldous, who is going to save his career, but at the same time, he puts himself into an unpardonable place later. Since Beard's academic achievement falls into stagnation, a young, idealistic postdoc, Tom Aldous, proposes to Beard several times about his idea of using photosynthesis to produce clean energy on an industrial scale, but is rebuffed by Beard. There is a strong sense of jealousy or contempt for Beard. Narcissistic individuals' distorted self-perception leads them to overestimate their abilities and achievements, while simultaneously downplaying the contributions and worth of those around them. For him, egoism will easily make him jealous of others. The defects in Beard's personality, like his greed, egoism, and his deficiency in family responsibilities, lead to his plagiarism. Once when Aldous takes Beard back home, Aldous meets Patrice with whom he has love affairs, and the affair costs him his life. Only until his death does Beard spot the significance of the proposal from the annoying Aldous. He immediately realizes the proposal can become a comeback to his career. Subconsciously, narcissists perceive external objects and individuals as extensions of themselves, valuing them only insofar as they serve their own interests. Beard exemplifies this mindset; he feels no shame for his act of plagiarism. Instead, he openly mocks it during a public conference, displaying a blatant disregard for ethical integrity. He skillfully employs deceit and manipulation to justify his misconduct, using his cunning to deflect criticism and maintain his self-image.

> All Beard asked, beyond a reasonable return, was sole attribution. For what could precedence or originality mean to the dead? And details of surnames were hardly relevant when the issue was so urgent. In the only sense that mattered, the essence of Aldous would endure. (159)

In Aldous' folder labelled with "strictly for the eyes of Professor M. Beard" (253), Beard takes this as a rightful excuse to plagiarize Aldous' achievement. He keeps exaggerating his contribution to this research in his plagiarism. He makes small modifications to Aldous' examples in the research. "There's a guy in a forest in the rain and he's dying of thirst. He has an axe and he starts cutting down the trees to drink the sap. A mouthful in each tree. All around him is a wasteland, no wildlife, and he knows that thanks to him the forest is disappearing fast" (36). In his revision version, he only adds some adjectives and changes the last sentence into "All around him is devastation, dead trees, no birdsong, and he knows the forest is vanishing." His shamelessness is beyond imagination. Instead, with the thought that he never needs to pay a price for his plagiarism, Beard has lots of optimistic judgments like the following. He uses "the day after tomorrow a new chapter would begin in the history of industrial civilization, and the earth's future would be assured" to end his speech, even though he may feel sick every time after his lies. "At a given signal, the Nobel laureate would throw a switch and the new era would commence" (293). He flaunts his previous honor, "the Nobel laureate," and optimistic prospect by mentioning "a new chapter" and "the new era". His self-conceit makes him mistakenly overstate his achievements, misreads his disclosed shame, and leads to his misconduct. "The practice of plagiarism often helps place people in positions of authority who do not deserve such positions."[145] He never believes anyone who likes to refer to "the planet" as proof of "thinking big" but blurts out that the planet is sick in a speech at the Savoy Hotel in London. He himself is "half-convinced" about climate change, but tries to convince others by listing evidence of global warming such as the IPCC report and the greenhouse effect. He dismisses Aldous's ideas as "the familiar litany", but copies his idea verbatim in the meeting. Although the self-proclaimed rational Beard claims to share Albert Einstein's belief that "physics was free of human taint," he meticulously weaves a plan to send his lover Tarpin to prison, plagiarizes the academic achievements of his subordinates to activate his life on the brink of extinction.

To the narcissist, they have a sense of omnipotence about themselves and never think they are wrong. If there is a problem, it must be someone else's problem. Beard never thinks he has done anything immoral in his marriage or his career. These people often show their contempt for others' mistakes. Their excessive arrogance and exaggerated talents make them expect to receive special attention from others. Though Aldous shows his respect for Beard and shares his proposal of plant photosynthesis for the development of solar energy with Beard, in Beard's eyes, "none of these fabled places had diluted the pure inflections of his rural accent and its innocent swerves and dips and persistent rising line, suggestive to Beard of hedgerows and hayricks"(28). He never truly respects Aldous even though he himself likes to talk about all his research and new ideas with Beard, while Beard shrinks inside his Harris tweed jacket, and shows his contempt towards Aldous as if he is an outstanding pupil, endeavoring to provide the answers he thinks he knows his teacher wants. Beard despises Aldous just because he takes himself as a forever Nobel Prize winner; he is superior to others in intelligence, even though he hasn't had any new research since then. His egoism makes him feel like God to the young scholar who is trying his best to lick his boots. He is the one who keeps alive the spirit of the young man. He even comforts himself that he should not be too hard on himself. After Aldous's death, he completely usurps Aldous' idea, and shamelessness and self-ego blind his eye. "I am the inventor and first mover of the project." "Here on the open plain, he was an eminence, almost a Legend." "The eight-year journey from the slow deciphering of the Aldous file to lab work, refinements, breakthroughs, drawings, field tests must be completed." Beard feels himself to be at the center of the world.

> How delicious it was, not only the food, but to be here, cosily ignored, in an obscure corner of the American heartland, and to know that the din, the construction, the digital media and soon, jet fighters and marching bands, this imminent industrial revolution, owed their existence at this spot among the palmillas and dried grasses to what he had once conceived eight years ago, lying on a dirty sofa in a basement flat five thousand miles away. (204)

Beard inflates himself, and he takes all the credit in a serious way. His long possession of his laurel not only fulfills his vanity, but also enlarges his desire for materialism. However, the moment when Beard thinks he has controlled everything and success is at hand, there comes Jock Braby. The wolf has a winning game when the shepherds quarrel. There are not many descriptions about Jock Braby except some implicit information like "Michael Beard was the new Centre's first head, though a senior civil servant called Jock Braby did the real work" (259). Beard directly judges Jock Braby as the sort to kick one in the face, then ask a favor. Surprisingly, Jock Braby is seemingly dispensable but important in the plot schemes, because he secretly takes advantage of Beard's achievements in the name of the British government. The answer to the secret is that Jock Braby personally makes a copy of this document despite the confidential label in 2000. He does nothing until Beard has put the theory into practice. Braby mugs and takes advantage of Beard's effort with the support of the British government and the Energy Centre.

Beard's inflated sense of self-importance blinds him to the complexities of the political and institutional forces surrounding him. While he indulges in self-glorification and materialistic pursuits, he remains oblivious to the subtle power dynamics at play. This vulnerability sets the stage for his eventual downfall, as it is not just personal ambition but also the interplay of hidden agendas and bureaucratic manipulations that shape his fate. The novel shifts from focusing solely on Beard's narcissistic tendencies to exposing how individuals like him become pawns in larger societal and governmental frameworks. This transition underscores the idea that personal flaws, when combined with external opportunism, can lead to inevitable consequences beyond one's control. In *Solar*, McEwan portrays Beard's relentless pursuit of fame, fortune, and personal desires as a reflection of the broader social environment in which modern individuals are consumed by ambition and self-interest. This ego-driven pursuit often takes precedence over ethical considerations, with individuals willing to compromise moral integrity to achieve personal gains. Through Beard's character, McEwan exposes the flaws and shortcomings that hinder meaningful contributions to humanity, particularly in the realm of scientific progress. Beard's narcissism, opportunism, and moral hypocrisy not only undermine his professional endeavors but also reflect the deeper cultural malaise of a society driven by consumerism and materialism. Individual ethics play a crucial role in understanding the cultural crisis depicted in *Solar*. The characters, driven by egoism and personal desires, often prioritize self-gratification over ethical considerations. McEwan's exploration of ethical space challenges individuals to confront their own flaws, limitations, and responsibilities in relation to both human relationships and the environment. It prompts readers to reflect on the ethical implications of their actions, including how personal desires and ambitions may impact others and the natural world.

In *Solar*, McEwan implicitly critiques Beard for his decisions driven by narcissism, opportunism, and a relentless desire for personal gratification. He exploits relationships, plagiarizes intellectual property, and disregards the environmental crisis he ostensibly seeks to address—all to bolster his own status and material comfort. McEwan uses Beard's moral failures to highlight how the absence of ethical will reduces individuals to mere agents of self-serving ambition, incapable of genuine contributions to societal or ecological well-being. The novel suggests that true progress—whether scientific, personal, or societal—requires the cultivation of ethical consciousness, a recognition of one's responsibilities not just to oneself but to others and to the planet. Without this ethical grounding, even the most brilliant intellects, like Beard's, are rendered hollow, their achievements tainted by moral bankruptcy.

Through the exploration of individual ethics, McEwan encourages readers to critically examine their own behavior and the societal values that may contribute to the cultural crisis. By highlighting the ethical dimensions of human interactions and relationships, both with others and with the environment, *Solar* serves as a reminder of the significance of individual ethics in addressing the complex challenges of the modern world.

Section Two   Beard's Phallocentrism

The concept of Phallus was proposed by Lacan with the advent of the symbolic realm (Oedipus stage), and it is first and foremost associated with the "desire of the mother." For in the Oedipus complex, the phallus plays a central role in what Freud calls the "phallic stage" of psychosexual development. In this stage, children of both sexes are predisposed with questions revolving around the possession of the phallus. Driven by the dialectic of identity, the child moves from identifying with his mother to identifying with his mother's desires, that is, by making himself the object of his mother's desires. In this stage, children firstly discover that their mother doesn't have a phallus, which causes them to raise several concerns as to their own impending or prior castration.

According to Freud, the phallus functions as the biological marker of the duality of the sexes. He equates the phallus to the actual male organ we all know as the penis, and claims that it is the actual encounter with its presence or absence that has great repercussions on the child's physical development. In his reformulation of the Oedipus complex, Lacan adopts Freud's notion of the centrality of the role of the phallus in the course of the child's development. Nevertheless, unlike Freud, Lacan does not strictly equate the phallus to the male organ, but claims that it is in fact a signifier. More specifically, Lacan argues that the phallus is the signifier of lack—something that sticks out and stands in the place of a lack in the psyche.[146] As it expands, it accentuates a part in the mother which does not directly correspond with the child's needs—a part which is not given to the child, but given to someone else. Therefore, at this stage of the Oedipus complex, the child is very much preoccupied with it, trying to retake its place as the sole object of the mother's desire. In order to be that object for the mother, the child constructs a montage of images corresponding with whatever he deems as desirable for the mother beyond itself. Lacan would call this montage, or Gestalt, the imaginary phallus. This object that satisfies the "desires of the other" will be named Phallus. Phallus is the desire of the other, and since the desire of the other dominates the desire of the subject, the Phallus is nothing more than the scepter of the authority of the other.

Besides the concept of phallocentrism, there is another concept close to it. Androcentrism, on the other hand, refers more broadly to the social theory and political movement that prioritizes male experience, perspectives, and interests, often to the exclusion or marginalization of women's voices and concerns. It can be understood as a structural and societal framework that centers men and positions male experiences as the norm against which all other experiences are measured. Androcentrism implies that the world is predominantly organized around men's lives, with institutions, language, laws, and even knowledge production shaped by male perspectives.

In addition to critiques of social relations, many proponents of androcentrism also focus on the analysis of gender inequality and the promotion of men's rights, interests, and issues. As nouns, the difference between phallocentrism and androcentrism is that phallocentrism is the privileging of masculinity in the construction of meaning; phallocentrism with a view to logocentrism, while androcentrism is an ideological focus on males and men, and issues affecting them, possibly to the detriment of non-males. Androcentric is the evaluation of individuals and cultures based on male perspectives, standards, and values. The phallus is more of a symbol in patriarchy, a symbol representing male domination and authority. Androcentrism involves behaviors, circumstances, and cultures that focus on or are dominated by a male perspective. Androcentric societies downplay the feminine perspective and minimize the importance of female contributions. If females are recognized at all, their accomplishments are minimized or even trivialized. Androcentric behavior may be intentional or accidental, overt or subtle.

The connection between these two concepts lies in their shared foundation of patriarchy and male-centered power structures. Phallocentrism often supports and feeds into androcentrism, as the symbolic elevation of male authority (via the phallus) influences social systems that center male experience and privilege male voices. Androcentrism, in turn, reinforces phallocentrism by normalizing male-centered ways of thinking and living in everyday life. Both concepts highlight how gender hierarchies shape societal structures, particularly the ways in which men's authority and experiences are placed at the center of human experience, marginalizing or disregarding women's perspectives and needs. In *Solar*, Beard's obsessive male-centric ideology is clearly reflected in his actions and attitudes, particularly in how he interacts with the women in his life. As McEwan insightfully observes, "Men's behavior," says McEwan, "is somehow invisible, we don't see ourselves as having a behavior that is identifiably male—we are just human."[147] This statement points to the ingrained nature of patriarchal thinking, where male actions are often normalized and unquestioned. Beard embodies this ideology, which operates not only in his professional world but also in his personal relationships.

In the third part of the novel, Beard recalls his pursuit of his first wife, Maisie, during their time at Oxford. This recollection offers a glimpse into the way his male-centric ideology manifests in his relationships with women. In an attempt to win her affection, Beard dedicates an entire week to preparing Maisie's favorite poems by Milton, believing that by catering to her intellectual tastes, he can secure her admiration. However, this act, which seems sincere at first glance, is fraught with self-doubt, as he later reflects on it with the thought: "His Milton week made him suspect a monstrous bluff." Despite the underlying insecurity, Beard's actions succeed, and Maisie becomes his first wife. This scene illustrates the performative nature of Beard's masculinity, driven by the need to impress and dominate in ways that are inextricably linked to his male-centric view of the world. It highlights his willingness to manipulate situations and people to fulfill his ego-driven desires.

> Going after Maisie was a relentless, highly organised pursuit, and it gave him great satisfaction, and it was a turning point in his development, for he knew that no third-year arts person, however bright, could have passed himself off, after a week's study, among the undergraduate mathematicians and physicists who were Beard's colleagues. The traffic was one-way. (169)

"One-way" means that the science boys can conquer the girls of Arts easily, and one week will be enough. On the contrary, if the boys of liberal arts want to capture the hearts of science girls, it is difficult because Science is not like Art that one can grasp within a week. This ideology corresponds to Snow's concepts of "two cultures,"[148] i.e., a gulf of mutual incomprehension and a mutual lack of sympathy and appreciation that Snow identified as having grown up between "literary intellectuals" on the one hand and "natural scientists" on the other. These two groups undeniably exist, eyeing each other across "a gulf of mutual incomprehension," feeling mutual "hostility and dislike," sharing almost no common ground. The situation is deplorable, and in Snow's view, dangerous and destructive. This expression of one-way traffic shows Beard's philosophy of regarding science as the predominance like male-dominance in society.

In *Solar*, McEwan deliberately exposes the conflict between science and literature, using this tension to critique both the limitations of scientific rationality and the neglect of the humanities in addressing deeper ethical and existential questions. Unlike McEwan's previous novels, where he skillfully blends the language of science with artistic sensibilities to create a harmonious interplay, *Solar* presents a more pronounced dichotomy. This contrast serves to highlight the protagonist Michael Beard's intellectual and moral shortcomings.

Beard, a Nobel Prize-winning physicist, epitomizes the narrowness of a mind consumed solely by scientific achievement. He fails to grasp—or even appreciate—the purpose and nobility of the arts and humanities. For Beard, literature, philosophy, and the broader ethical reflections they inspire hold little value compared to empirical data and scientific prestige. His singular competence in a narrow field of science becomes the sole foundation of his fame, yet it also underscores his intellectual superficiality. This inability to engage with the humanities reflects not just a personal flaw, but a broader societal issue: the overvaluation of scientific success at the expense of ethical reflection, cultural depth, and emotional intelligence. Through Beard's character, McEwan critiques a worldview that prioritizes scientific progress while neglecting the moral and philosophical dimensions necessary for genuine human development.

> This understanding was the mental equivalent of lifting very heavy weights—not possible at first attempt. He and his lot were at lectures and lab work nine till five every day, attempting to come to terms with some of the hardest things ever thought. The arts people fell out of bed at midday for their two tutorials a week. He suspected there was nothing they talked about there that anyone with half a brain could fail to understand. He had read four of the best essays on Milton. He knew. And yet they passed themselves off as his superiors, these lie-a-beds, and he had let them intimidate him. No longer. (170)

The difference between the Science and the Arts Students is also a prevailing bias in the society. Whether in the past or in the foreseeable future, science and engineering talents have played an indispensable and key role, which directly gives people the impression that what the science and engineering talents do is practical things, and they can get practical results which are really beneficial to society. When it comes to the liberal arts, people cannot see their contribution to society. The bias held by Beard makes his hegemonic power seen both in marriage and in profession.

In his first marriage, Maisie is "active." "She read up on social theory, attended a group run by a collective of Californian women, and started up a 'workshop' herself, a new concept at the time…" (170). She begins to find the problems in their marriage, to be specific, Beard's phallocentrism.

> He was too much of a rationalist to think of many good reasons why he should not help out around the house. He believed that it bored him more than it did her, but he did not say so. And washing a few dishes was the least of it. There were profoundly entrenched attitudes that he needed to examine and change, there were unconscious assumptions of his own 'centrality', his alienation from his own feelings, his failure to listen, to hear, really hear, what she was saying, and to understand how the system that worked in his favour in both trivial and important ways always worked against her. (174)

Within a short time, she confronts the blatant fact of patriarchy and her husband's role in a network of oppression. Beard's hegemonic power extends from the institutions to the family, which, in his defense, "that sustained him as a man." However, under the influence of the feminist movement, Maisie gradually feels the insult from Beard's behavior at home. To Maisie, what once seemed like ordinary domestic routines now reveal themselves as mechanisms of masculine domination, from his dismissive attitude toward her opinions to his insistence on maintaining control, even in the most intimate aspects of their relationship.

> There were other ways of knowing the world, women's ways, which he treated dismissively. Though he pretended not to be, he was squeamish about her menstrual blood, which was an insult to the core of her womanhood. Their lovemaking, blindly enacting postures of dominance

and submission, was an imitation of rape and was fundamentally corrupt. (175)

Maisie gradually becomes aware of how Beard's actions reinforce his patriarchal authority, including his approach to sexual relations, which reflects his sense of entitlement and disregard for mutual consent and emotional connection. This awakening exposes the deep imbalance in their marriage, where Beard's egoism and self-absorption overshadow the principles of respect, loyalty, and reciprocity that are fundamental to marital ethics. In traditional family values, a marriage is built on mutual obligations, shared responsibilities, and emotional partnership. However, Beard neglects these ethical foundations entirely. His narcissistic tendencies and rigid adherence to phallocentric ideals not only erode the integrity of their relationship but also exemplify how personal egoism perpetuates systemic gender inequality within the family structure. Beard totally neglects his responsibility as a husband. His egoism makes him strongly stick to phallocentrism. When Maisie realizes her own place in the family and society, she decides to leave Beard to pursue her identity as an independent woman both in family and society. What Beard feels is not regret nor pity, but "a compound of joy and relief, followed by a floating, expansive sensation of lightness, as if he was about to drift free of the sheets and bump against the ceiling" (175). Beard is so excited that he urges fierce impatience for her to be gone at three in the morning. He expects the "prospect of freedom" before him, does whatever he wants, and invites women home without being guilty.

From ancient times, men have enjoyed family power and women are subordinate. Due to the stubbornness of old traditions and old ideas, male-centric ideas still survive in contemporary society. Women as "the Second Sex" are not born but acquired. Whether in the East or the West, there is a historical phenomenon of male domination of society and family, and the essence of patriarchy is personal despotism, which is the cultural oppression of the natural relationship between the two sexes. The male-dominance that has been long rooted in Beard's mind makes his later four marriages still a failure. In marriage, "he was such a careless, faithless, disorganized friend, too elusive, too strongly intent on never marrying again. His frame could not withstand a sixth marriage" (110). He is obsessed with his non-commitment to a solid relationship with extramarital affairs and each divorce brings him the familiar recognition of freedom and his immorality. The divorces in turn assert Beard's hegemony in marriages, because in each marriage, he is the marriage-buster.

Phallocentrism, as an ideology that positions the phallus—or male sexual dominance—as the central organizing principle of the social world, profoundly shapes Beard's perception of relationships and his own identity. Beard's chaotic love life is a direct manifestation of this phallocentric mindset. His erotic and emotional disconnection is not merely a result of personal flaws but is deeply rooted in his belief in male superiority and entitlement. This ideological framework drives his compulsive pursuit of sexual conquests, viewing women less as equal partners and more as objects that affirm his masculinity and dominance.

Beard's five failed marriages and numerous extramarital affairs reflect a pattern of emotional detachment and an inability to cultivate genuine, reciprocal connections. Instead of fostering meaningful relationships, he reduces intimacy to a means of satisfying his ego and reinforcing his sense of male power. His relentless pursuit of new sexual relationships, despite the repeated failures in his personal life, underscores how phallocentrism distorts not only his view of women but also his capacity for emotional growth and ethical responsibility within intimate relationships. He continues to indulge himself in free sexual love to avoid the monogamous family bondage. He later has two girlfriends, Melissa and Darlene. To Beard, they are merely love partners to meet his sexual desires.

Melissa Browne is most willing to play the role of lover and mother. She is very kind to him, soft and patient. She is also so pretty that Beard thinks she is the only viable love in his life. However, as we have discussed, he is finding a perfect lover for himself. The viable love is just what he uses to deceive Melissa's love. Like many women, she thinks he is a brilliant scientist, a genius in need of rescuing. His false appearance arouses her interest and love to take care of him. Despite recognizing himself as a careless, faithless, and disorganized partner, Beard convinces himself that he will never marry again. He harbors a faint sense of guilt, acknowledging deep down that he doesn't deserve Melissa because she is too good for him. However, his overwhelming selfishness prevents him from letting her go, as his desire to possess and control outweighs any genuine consideration for her well-being. To Melissa, marriage is the final destination for a woman and a mother. Family in human society is the foundation of social life. Colleen says, "Family system theory espouses the view that the family is an emotional unit, whose members are inextricably interconnected and who function as a system."[149] In Beard's eyes, he perceives Melissa not only as "beautiful, interesting, and good," but also speculates that she may exhibit signs of the Electra complex—a psychoanalytic concept describing a young girl's unconscious sexual attachment to her father. Melissa used to live with her mother, with whom she always fights, but she loves her father. "She was in love with a bald fat man who seemed to her the essence of seriousness and high purpose, who was the father of her child as well as the father she longed to care for, the father who had not yet fallen in love with his fate, but who, she calmly knew, was bound to yield" (249). Beard may not have the healthy family ethics that can give him the correct guidance. Melissa believes that he could possibly fit the part of a good father and husband, while Beard thinks Melissa's longing is to "return him to his natural state, his truest self, the one he failed to claim to" (159), which, in the bottom of his heart, he refuses to become.

Compared to Beard's inability to love, Melissa expresses her love boldly. From the description, we can see Melissa's deep love for and appreciation of the man and her strong desire for marriage. In this relationship, Melissa devotes herself much more than her counterpart. When Beard comes back home, he wrecks Melissa's work by sitting down in the bed, shrugging off his coat, opening his briefcase and removing his shoes. In his own words, he does his best not to litter. Melissa never complains about it. She cooks for him as he visits every time and even runs him baths. She buys him shirts, silk ties, cologne, wine, scotch, underwear, and socks. When Beard is about to leave, she books his flights. However, Beard doesn't show his response to this love. He only buys Melissa expensive presents from the airport duty-free. "Long ago he had learned never to declare love to anyone. With Melissa he dreaded the question these three words of supernatural torque must raise" (166). He admits openly his inability to love, which, in turn, reveals his true feelings of avoiding any sense of responsibility. Beard is entirely self-centered, indulging blithely in his hedonistic pursuits, particularly in his sexual relationships. His phallocentric worldview reinforces this behavior, as he equates his masculinity and dominance with his sexual conquests, viewing women merely as extensions of his desires rather than as equal partners. To be highly cherished by Melissa, Beard takes it for granted that she should fulfill his emotional and physical needs without reciprocation. His sense of entitlement is rooted in a male-centric ideology where the phallus symbolizes not just biological difference but also the locus of power and control. He conveniently uses the statement that he doesn't understand and could not quite forgive this lapse of judgment as an excuse to absolve himself from guilt, thus justifying his exploitation of Melissa while maintaining his self-image as blameless. "Like many clever men who prize objectivity, he was a solipsist at heart, and in his heart was a nugget of ice, which Melissa sensed and intended to melt" (146). His views of marriage have been so distorted that he believes that he could still enjoy eroticism and refuse to take the ethical responsibilities, as long as he does not fall in love and remains unmarried.

> Beard comfortably shared all of humanity's faults, and here he was, a monster of insincerity, cradling tenderly on his arm a woman he thought he might leave one day soon, listening to her with sensitive expression in the expectation that soon he would have to do some talking himself, when all he wanted was to make love to her without preliminaries, eat the meal she had cooked, drink a bottle of wine and then sleep—without blame, without guilt. (146)

Beard's desire to maintain his relationship with Melissa is driven purely by his sexual needs, reducing their connection to a matter of physical gratification rather than genuine affection. It is his phallocentric mindset that dictates the dynamics of their relationship, where intimacy is solely a means to satisfy his own desires. Throughout his time with Melissa, his thoughts are dominated by an "incrementally erotic" fixation, objectifying her as nothing more than a vessel for his fantasies. Rather than seeing Melissa as an equal partner, he views her primarily through the lens of his sexual appetite, perpetually consumed by his self-indulgent cravings. This relentless objectification underscores Beard's inability to engage in meaningful, reciprocal relationships, as his ego and desires consistently overshadow any authentic emotional connection.

> Melissa's partner in all things, cocooned in the stock room, perhaps improving the inventory software or planning special events, with talks and demonstrations, and so placidly tracing the passing years in a swoon of sex and dullness, and one evening, obedient to Melissa's prompting—impossible tawdry dream!—persuading Lenochka to make a threesome on the wide bed in the meticulous flat on Fitzroy Street. (139)

In the face of such a nice and pretty woman, Beard doesn't stop at searching for one-night love. Darlene, the second woman, comes into Beard's love life. He meets the waitress Darlene when he engages in his project in Lordsburg. Their relationship soon deepens into sexual partners. "For Beard the affair was an unexpected sexual renaissance, with piercing sensory pleasure, much like that near-inversion of agony he remembered from his twenties" (66). He enjoys "such extremities of sensation" that he can get from a woman of fifty-one. He assumes that this might be "his last throw at such ecstasy," so he cherishes his last chance and then her. However, when he sees that "she was gazing at him with an expression he had not seen before, a look of smug maternal possession that troubled him faintly" (208), he realizes that it might be hard to acquit himself well from the relationship. His sense is correct. Darlene wants equal love in their relationships. She is a daring pursuer. Her boldness will finally make Beard pay a price for his erotic reaction. "'Michael?' she whispered. 'Honey?' … 'Did I ever tell you that I love you?' … 'I love you. And d'you know something?'" All of these show her loving care for Beard. The answer she wants to hear is the equal love to her from Beard. Disappointingly, Beard's extremely simple, either "Mm." or "Yes." The answer means that he just wants to put her off, and in his view, sex surpasses true love. In other words, he loves no one but himself. What he cares about is free sex, with no responsibilities.

However, the story doesn't develop according to Beard's wishes. Beard enjoys having casual sexual partners without any intention to further advance the relationship, while Melissa and Darlene both want to marry Beard. Darlene acts braver than Melissa. She phones Melissa to compete for Beard immediately as she realizes that he is still unmarried. Melissa chooses to wait silently and gently. "She endured his absences, the silences from abroad, because she was certain he was bound to see the matter her way in the end" (221).

Darlene's actions are more direct and impulsive; she asks Beard to marry her in the heat of the moment during sex, and he agrees, driven purely by his erotic arousal rather than any genuine emotional commitment. Predictably, once his passion subsides and rationality returns, Beard denies the promise without hesitation, revealing the superficiality of his consent. The contrasting approaches of Darlene and Melissa in their pursuit of love and marriage highlight their longing for emotional security, social recognition, and the ethical identity tied to traditional roles as wives and mothers. Their desires are grounded in the hope of establishing meaningful, reciprocal relationships, rooted in mutual respect and responsibility.

Darlene phones Melissa to declare her victory. Beard's passive and negative evasion finally irritates the two women. Beard's phallocentrism renders him incapable of fulfilling such expectations. His worldview, dominated by male-centric ideologies, reduces relationships to transactional, pleasure-driven encounters devoid of emotional depth or ethical accountability. He perceives commitment, family, and responsibility as constraints on his autonomy and masculine dominance. This inability to form ethical bonds reflects a deeper moral failure, where personal gratification consistently overrides any sense of duty toward others.

The two women's battle breaks out at the end of the novel. The two women's joint appearance in the scene. He watches from afar the two "stormy, furious and rumpled" (384) women coming to him. The instability of Beard's marriage lies in the high degree of inconsistency between love and sex and his unwilling effort in keeping the marriage. Melissa, the cohabiting girlfriend who pursues a unified marriage of spirit and flesh, tolerates Beard's infidelity unconditionally and gives birth to a daughter. However, all of these don't evoke a response from Beard. "With Melissa he dreaded the question these three words of supernatural torque must raise. Would he commit to her for the rest of his life and father her child?" (105). He rejoiced that he "never really loved." Here the only sexual desire is needed and no love is needed.

Beard's defiance of marriage and family probably results from his exclusive egoism and his unconsciousness of male-dominance. Beard's narcissism and phallocentric mindset not only sabotage his relationships but also expose the ethical void at the core of his character—a man driven by desire, yet incapable of genuine connection or accountability. "He had never cared much about what others thought" (74), and besides having sex to satisfy his own needs, he never likes to be part of a group, whose implication is not to take the responsibilities. At the end of the novel, when everything collapses around him, Beard still can't express his affection for his daughter who comes to hug him. Beard, the notorious man, carries the author's deepest compassion. "He felt in his heart an unfamiliar, swelling sensation, but he doubted as he opened his arms to her that anyone would ever believe him now if he tried to pass it off as love." (63)

Besides his chaotic love life, Beard automatically shows male superiority and hegemonism and attacks females in other circumstances. Beard is co-opted onto a physics committee which involves many old male physics professors and one female, Nancy Temple, who is proud of being a professional woman.

"It was true, women were under-represented in physics and always had been. The problem had often been discussed, and (he was mindful of Professor Temple as he said it) certainly his committee would be looking at it again to see if there were new ways of encouraging more girls into the subject. He believed there were no longer any institutional barriers or prejudices. There were other branches of science where women were well represented, and some where they predominated" (183-184).

In Beard's response to a journalist's question about the under-representation of women in physics, "he was mindful of Professor Temple as he said it" (115) helps to reveal Beard's male chauvinism and superiority. Neglecting the acquired factors like the traditional social division of labor and the historical prejudice against women's intelligence, Beard believes that the gender imbalance in physics is boiled down to innate reasons: "widely observed innate differences in cognitive ability" (184) of males and females.

It is the aggressive response of Professor Temple to Beard's arguments that ignites the ensuing furious debate and upgrades the severity of the topic, which also reflects that the audience is accustomed to women's discriminated and oppressed status in patriarchal society. "Before I go outside to be sick, and I mean violently sick because of what I've just heard, I wish to announce my resignation from Professor Beard's committee" (185-186). Nancy's resistance is the embodiment of her struggle for women's voice and female status. Beard, who could be invincible by virtue of superior intelligence, eventually rebels. It is a complete failure. Nancy Temple's direct response is a fight for women's position and rights. Professional women are in the weak position since they have lots of queries and oppositions to break the traditionally male-dominated patterns. Men have the right to speak in the science field. Female scientists are not absent, and their research output is not less than that of men, but they do not enjoy the same attention that society gives to male scientists. In the scientific community, they are also vulnerable, and their voices are not heard by many people. Their research results have often been delayed in history or even usurped by males. Since the female revolution, the suppressed female consciousness has been awakening. Women need to spare more effort and endure the moral and public query and critics to get equal status as men beyond the family.

Beard and Nancy's discord results in a press conference where Beard debates with a cognitive psychologist called Susan Appelbaum. This is also a paraphrase of the debate in 2005 between Stephen Pinker and Elizabeth Spelke who have totally different opinions on gender determinism.[150]

"As a woman she was a poor hegemon, and being unconfident, poorer still (Beard thought he was getting the hang of this term)" (119). The long-rooted discrimination in Beard's mind reveals his attitudes towards women. Appelbaum is deprived of speaking directly and her words and the audience's response are reported, interpreted, and evaluated unreliably by Beard. Facing accusation, Beard is still unaware of his male chauvinism and responds maliciously to the female's righteous request of being treated equally.

Beard's interactions with professional women, such as Appelbaum, expose his deeply ingrained male chauvinism and patriarchal biases. His dismissive attitude and condescending evaluations reflect a mindset that undermines women's authority and intellectual competence. By controlling the narrative—reporting, interpreting, and evaluating women's words through his subjective, unreliable lens—Beard reinforces a gendered power dynamic where women's voices are marginalized and distorted. His inability to recognize or address his own discriminatory behavior highlights not only his personal ethical failure but also the broader systemic issue of gender inequality in professional spaces. Beard's conflicts with competent women are not merely interpersonal disputes; they serve as critical commentaries on how patriarchal ideologies persist within male-dominated institutions, where women's legitimacy and authority are constantly questioned, and their professional identities are often overshadowed by male-centric perspectives. Through Beard's character, McEwan critiques the subtle yet pervasive forms of sexism that continue to shape gender relations in modern society.

McEwan's sarcasm towards Beard's complaint about the easiness of humanities and the complexity of physical science reflects the author's own ability to deftly write a scientifically grounded novel like *Solar* with complex physical jargon, despite being a novelist. McEwan's satire and critique of Beard's androcentrism align with the eco-feminist perspective he advocates. Beard, as a representative of the elite class, exemplifies extreme egoism and is depicted as hypocritical and despicable. These individuals pursue utilitarianism, attempting to exploit their social status to gain maximum benefits, but ultimately their vain reputation leads them to a ridiculous and tragic end.

Through his exploration of Beard's character, McEwan explores the dark side of society and exposes the weaknesses of human nature. He skillfully uncovers the secrets to solving moral dilemmas within the intricacies of daily life and the actions of human will. Beard's image serves as McEwan's critique of the mental disorders caused by extreme individualism and the proliferation of liberalism in contemporary society.

Ethics permeate the narrative as McEwan examines the ethical dimensions of Beard's character and the social dynamics he represents. The author challenges the egoistic and hypocritical behavior of the elite class, highlighting the ethical implications of their actions and the consequences of their disregard for others. McEwan's exploration of the dark side of human nature prompts readers to reflect on their own ethical values and the moral implications of their choices.

Furthermore, McEwan's critique extends to broader ethical concerns, particularly the pervasive influence of patriarchal power structures, the marginalization of women in both personal and professional spheres, and the erosion of moral responsibility in the pursuit of self-interest. Through Beard's narcissism, phallocentrism, and ethical failures, McEwan exposes how individual egoism and gender-based dominance are deeply intertwined with societal norms that prioritize power, success, and material gain over genuine human connection and ethical integrity. Beard's disregard for family ethics, his exploitative relationships, and his manipulation of professional dynamics serve as a microcosm of larger societal issues, where ethical considerations are often subordinated to personal ambition.

In conclusion, McEwan's portrayal of Beard and his exploration of the character's ethical shortcomings reflect a broader critique of patriarchal dominance, moral decay, and the ethical void created by unchecked individualism. By dissecting Beard's flawed character, McEwan invites readers to confront the ethical crises embedded in modern society, particularly those related to gender inequality and the loss of moral accountability. Through this narrative, McEwan challenges readers to reconsider their own ethical frameworks, question ingrained societal norms, and advocate for a more just, empathetic, and ethically conscious world.

Chapter Eight   The Ethical Imbalance in *Sweet Tooth*

Sweet Tooth is Ian McEwan's 15th book of fiction. It is a "Tootsie Roll Pop of a literary confection—hard-boiled candy enrobing a chewy surprise at its core."[151] The novel, whose political background is set 40 years ago, is about a secret mission by Britain's MI5 intelligence service to sponsor writers to write fiction as they require. Its title is from a spy plan named Sweet Tooth during the Cold War. Instead, it focuses on "the softest, sweetest part of the Cold War, the only truly interesting part, the war of ideas." (Norah Piehl). "Sweet Tooth is playful, comic, preposterous even. But it's impossible to ignore that its protagonist is a young and fairly gauche English person—female this time—failing miserably (though perhaps not so dangerously) in her job as a spy... There are stories within stories, ideas within ideas, even images within images ... Because this isn't really a novel about MI5 or the Cold War or even—despite the rather obviously ladled-on research about Heath and Wilson and miners' strikes and the IRA—the 70s. This is a novel about writers and writing, about love and trust. But more than that—and perhaps most incisively of all—it's a novel about reading and readers." (The Guardian)

Sweet Tooth by Ian McEwan is the story of Serena Frome and her brief tenure with Britain's famous MI5—Military Intelligence, Section 5. The story begins in the present day as Serena tells the reader about her experience some forty years before when she is a young woman. She reflects on her life, beginning with her childhood in an upscale community in Camden. Her father is an Anglican Bishop and her mother, the perfect Bishop's wife. Serena displays an aptitude for math at a young age. However, her real interests lie in literature. Therefore, when she is going to apply for college, she is going to study English. However, her mother—a feminist in her time—insists on her studying math; otherwise, she will not forgive her for the rest of her life. She doesn't want Serena to abandon her natural gifts in math just because she is a girl. Then, Serena majors in math at Cambridge.

At college, Serena has a boyfriend named Jeremy, but their relationship is not normal. The truth will be disclosed later in the novel that he is into men. Jeremy introduces Serena to his history professor, Tony Canning. Serena then falls in love with the older man. Tony, who is married, completely dominates his relationship with Serena because he is old enough to be her father. She totally accepts the relationship with Tony. Tony prepares Serena for the interview of MI5 and trains her to be a spy. In the end, he gets rid of her by blaming her for breaking up his marriage. Serena is devastated, but she still successfully passes the interview with MI5 and gets the job. Later, she gets the truth of Tony's leaving because he has cancer.

In the job, Serena is offered the position of junior desk officer and reluctantly accepts it. She is hoping to have something happen with Max, her superior, but it ends when he announces that he is engaged to a girl from an upper-class family. Serena is then given a cover operation, whose task is to convince a young writer, Tom, to use fiction as a weapon to do propaganda. Serena and Tom eventually become involved and fall in love. Max discloses Serena's position to Tom out of jealousy. At the end of the novel, Serena is forgiven by Tom.

Throughout Serena's life in the novel, four characters greatly influence Serena and even change her life path. Beginning with her growth in the family, the first figure that appears is her mother, who is eager to transform Serena's fate by sending her to study Math at Cambridge, but the result turned out to be the wrong subject. Who comes next is the history tutor Tony Canning whom Serena meets in Cambridge, and she drifts into a love affair with him, during which Serena has the opportunity to take a position at MI5 but is abandoned by him later. At MI5, Serena has a superior, Max, and she starts flirting with him. However, she is looked down upon, actually. After engaging in the secret project Sweet Tooth, Serena conceals her spy identity and becomes the lover of writer Tom Haley. Their love is under lies until the project is revealed.

Ethics is a discipline that discusses moral values, and ethics aims to define concepts such as good and evil, right and wrong, virtue and vice, justice and crime to solve moral problems. Defined from the perspective of interpersonal relations, ethics is the moral code that should be observed when dealing with the interrelationship between people, people and families, people and society, and people and the state. It is the moral code that individuals must abide by when living in a group society.

The Second Sex, published in 1949 by Simone de Beauvoir, challenged political and existential theory, but its most enduring impact is on how women understand themselves, their relationships, their place in society, and the construction of gender. Beauvoir examines women's issues from the perspective of cultural criticism and existentialism, and discusses the real situation, status, and rights of women in the historical evolution from primitive society to modern society, from philosophy, literature, history, biology, psychology, ancient mythology, customs and culture, revealing that patriarchal society is the cultural root of inequality between the sexes. The concept of women as the "second sex" raises important considerations regarding gender equality, social justice, and ethical treatment of individuals. The academic term "otherness" is a philosophical basis for Beauvoir's feminist thought. In order to elevate the theory of women's liberation from idealism to the theoretical height of cultural analysis, Beauvoir used the "other" as a tool for cultural analysis to give a basic description of the situation of women. "For the male it is always another male who is the fellow being, the other who is also the same, with whom reciprocal relations are established."[152] For women, they are always under the guardianship of males: "a subject to the authority of her father or of her older brother...that of her husband. She is only the intermediary of authority..."[153]

Women define themselves according to the definition of men rather than women themselves. There exists a relationship between subordinate and dominant, secondary and primary, object and subject, other and self between women and men. Women have historically been subordinated to men, and their status as the other seems absolute. It seems that their status is a natural phenomenon with no possibility to change. Thus, in a patriarchal society, women are always the other. Beauvoir pointed out that women are the other and that this situation is not chosen by women themselves, but by men, or more precisely by the entire patriarchal culture, because in the course of human civilization, the way of thinking is also established by men under their ideology.

In the book, Beauvoir explores why women become the other: first, a woman's control over the world is limited by her biological attributes. Their oppression limits their ability to act. Moreover, compared with men, women's physical identity and psychological identity in the process of growing up are more tortuous and complex. Second, the phallus culture represented by men in patriarchal societies disciplined women and confined them to the family. Women became the property of men and were enslaved by men in the same way that slaves were enslaved by their masters. Third, the myth of women created by men forms an ideology at the cultural level, subtly shaping the subservience of women. In the history of human civilization, evolution forced her to become a passive "other": "But to be a 'true woman' she must accept herself as the Other ... whereas a woman's independent successes are in contradiction with her femininity, since the 'true woman' is required to make herself object, to be the other."[154] Beauvoir pointed out that if we want to awaken women's sense of self, restore women's subjective status, and gradually realize women's emancipation, we should recognize that the other is mutual, and recognize that women are also the self and the subject.

The Second Sex sheds light on the subordinate position of women in society and the ethical implications of such inequality. By labeling women as the "other" and positioning them in relation to men, a power dynamic of subordination and dominance emerges. Women are often defined and valued based on societal norms established by men, rather than by their own intrinsic worth. This hierarchical relationship perpetuates a system where women are treated as secondary, objectified, and marginalized.

The relationship between people is, of course, very complicated. However, to sum up, there are no more than five kinds of relationships: superiors and subordinates, parents and children, husbands and wives, brothers and sisters, and acquaintances and strangers. Mencius further proposed: fathers and sons have relatives, kings and subjects have righteousness, husbands and wives are different, elders and children are orderly, and friends have faith. Combining ethics and interpersonal relationships is to add ethics to interpersonal relationships. The most important thing between parents and children is to show affection to each other. Between superiors and subordinates, there has to be respect for each other. Between husband and wife, there must be a reasonable division of labor relationship. Between brothers and sisters, the order must be respected. Among friends, we must attach importance to sincerity and faithfulness. In the novel, the interpersonal ethics have fallen into a kind of dislocated one. All four characters are intimate with Serena, and all of them are trusted by Serena. With the development of the story, their relationship with Serena has experienced huge variations due to misunderstanding, lies and betrayal. No matter what the relationship is, Serena is in the inferior position, which confirms the Second Sex theory.

Section One Power Imbalance in the Parent-Child Relationship

Serena is the daughter of an Anglican bishop and grows up in the cathedral precinct. In her early years, Serena's mother exerts a profound influence on her. As a vicar's wife, her mother is well-behaved. She has "a formidable memory for parishioners' names and faces and gripes, a way of sailing down a street in her Hermès Scarf, a kindly but unbending manner with daily and the gardener" (3).[155] Serena's mother gets along well with others in the neighborhood. She is also very virtuous in supporting and looking after her husband without complaint. She "combined with utter devotion and subordination to my father's cause" (3). She cares about her husband's daily life and respects and supports him. She does everything for her husband, promoting him, serving him, and easing his way at every turn. She prepares boxed socks and irons the surplice hanging in the wardrobe, cleans his study dustless, and dares to make any noise on Saturday in the house when he writes sermons. She is such a wonderful wife who does everything perfectly. She fully accepts her position as the secondary, a subject to her husband. That is why Serena "hadn't understood about my mother was that buried deep beneath this conventional exterior was the hardy little seed of a feminist" (4).

Just because of the seed, her mother hopes that Serena can become an independent woman instead of being a mediocre housewife all her life, just like herself. However, Serena wants to go to a "provincial university" to acquire a lazy English degree, but the idea is precluded by her mother. As a result, she insists on sending Serena to study Math at Cambridge, which turns out to be the wrong major for Serena. Her mother tells Serena that she would never forgive her, and she would never forgive herself if Serena were to read English and "became no more than a slightly better educated housewife than she was." "She said it was my duty as a woman to go to Cambridge to study math. As a woman? In those days, in our milieu, no one ever spoke like that. No woman did anything 'as a woman.'" (4)

From what her mother tells her, although Serena's mother isn't satisfied to be a housewife, she sacrifices her dream of being an independent woman. Even though she does everything perfectly, being a housewife is not her pursuit. To be the bishop's wife, she endeavors to keep the parish stable and harmonious. To herself, she is the Other, who counts on her husband for the finances, but the seed of feminism inside her makes her aware of the power of knowledge and the importance of being independent. That makes her strong in her character. In the very few interactions between Serena and her mother, most of the words are said by the mother to Serena. We can see her mother shows her strong control over Serena, even though her mother loves her a lot. They don't have many body contacts, from which we can see their relationship isn't that close, like a normal family. In the mother's words, going to Cambridge to study math is an irrefragable decision. "I didn't follow the logic of this, but I said nothing" (4). Her mother's strong sense of cultivating Serena into an independent woman causes the imbalanced power between them. Their parent-child relationship is not based on mutual affection but on her mother's overwhelming power over her. This parent-child relationship operates less on emotional support and more on the imposition of authority, reflecting the societal tendency to define women's paths through prescriptive roles.

Serena's mother expects her to "have a proper career in science or engineering or economics" (4), fields that symbolize rationality and male-dominated authority, contrasting with English, which she dismisses as a route to becoming merely a "better educated housewife." This expectation reveals not only a fear of Serena slipping into traditional female roles but also an internalized bias that equates value with male-coded domains of knowledge. On the one hand, her mother's determination to prevent Serena from becoming the stereotypical "Other," as described in Simone de Beauvoir's theory, stems from her anxiety over Serena's potential conformity to domesticity. Although Serena neither comprehends nor challenges her mother's ambitions, her passive compliance underscores how deeply entrenched patriarchal expectations can suppress a woman's agency. "I knew the answers to questions before I even knew how I had gotten to them. While my friends struggled and calculated, I reached a solution by a set of floating steps that were partly visual, partly just a feeling for what was right" (2). This reflection symbolizes not just Serena's intuitive intellectual ability but also her unconscious adaptation to external pressures—a coping mechanism shaped by her mother's controlling influence. Thus, Serena's life trajectory becomes a microcosm of the broader social mechanism that conditions women to internalize secondary roles, even under the guise of independence.

On the other hand, Serena's mother's latent feminism manifests in her relentless push for Serena to confront challenges independently. This underlying ideology grants her mother a subtle yet pervasive power to manipulate and guide not only Serena but also those around her, shaping their choices under the guise of empowerment and resilience. "Within a week my mother had spoken to my headmaster. Certain subject teachers were deployed and used all my parents' arguments as well as some of their own, and of course I had to give way" (11). Even though there is a great disparity between them, Serena is inferior to her mother in terms of power relations, without the right to speak and express her thoughts to her mother, but to obey her mother's guidance.

Her mother's strong will and Serena's trust in her mother cause Serena an unhappy life at university. Entering Cambridge, she begins to realize how mediocre she is in mathematics. She behaves poorly, is teased by her professor and fellow classmates, and lives an unhappy life. "So I abandoned my ambition to read English at Durham or Aberystwyth, where I am sure I would have been happy, and went instead to Newnham College, Cambridge, to learn at my first tutorial, which took place at Trinity, what a mediocrity I was in mathematics. My Michaelmas term depressed me and I almost left" (11), which completely changes her life orbit and destiny.

This disillusionment not only leads to Serena's academic dissatisfaction but also deepens the emotional chasm between her and her mother. Serena's internal struggle reflects the conflict between personal desire and imposed expectations, a hallmark of the oppressive dynamics experienced by women as the "second sex." Her mother's authoritative influence, masked as guidance, deprives Serena of the autonomy to shape her own identity. Thus, Serena's academic failure is not merely an individual shortcoming but a manifestation of the broader patriarchal structures where even maternal figures, shaped by societal norms, perpetuate cycles of control and suppression under the guise of empowerment.

In addition to her mother, the relationship between Serena and her father is also very distant. She addresses her father as "the bishop." From the address, we can see Serena has to show her full respect to her father, which puts her into a submissive position. Just because of her father's dominant status in the family, her mother asks "the bishop" to persuade Serena to study math at Cambridge, because she wants more pressure from the family to influence Serena.

"I sulkily lolled in his clubbish leather armchair while he presided at his desk, shuffling papers, humming to himself as he ordered his thoughts" (4). Clearly, the two people are, without any body contact, not in such an intimate relationship as is widely found between any other normal father and daughter. Though her father doesn't treat Serena as her mother does, he still tries to use his "surprising and practical line" to list some questions to illustrate that "If, however, I applied to do English there (never my intention; the Bishop was always poor on detail) I would have a far harder time" (5). The funny thing is that being an authority in the family, her father makes a mistake about the task given by his wife, from which we can see he cares little about the family members.

Serena shows more respect towards her father than her mother. Compared with her competent mother, Serena tends to seek attention and caring from her father. She has deep feelings towards her father partly because of the feeling from the Electra complex and partly due to the contrast between her mother and her father. "The castration complex and the Electra complex reinforce each other. Her (the daughter's) regret strengthens her love, for she is able to compensate for her inferiority through the affection she inspires in her father."[156] In the patriarchal family, the father is the authority and women are in the subordinate position. They may fight for the attention and love of authority.

"He didn't know that sometimes Lucy and I fought over him in our teens. We longed to have him for ourselves, if only for ten minutes in his study, and we each suspected the other was the more favoured. Her tangle with drugs, pregnancy and the law had permitted her many such privileged minutes. When I'd heard about them on the phone, despite all my concern for her, I felt a twinge of the old jealousy" (196).

From Serena's relationship with her parents, their family is one of the traditional patriarchal ones with the father as the dominator and the mother as the appendage. Brought up in this family, the girls' attachment to men is cultivated from an early age. This is the main cause of Serena's subordinate relationship with other men in her life. In the family, there also seems to be an unbridgeable gap between her parents and her. In her own description, there is no harmonious state between children and parents in a general family. Instead, she is always being controlled and has no communication with their parents. The superior position of her mother in the family makes her ignore Serena's opinions on her own choice. Because of these, Serena is not only estranged from her mother, but may also grumble and misunderstand her mother. The strong bonding between parents and children is greatly influenced by their unequal power in their relationship, which in turn causes an unhealthy ethical relationship.

This dynamic reveals the paradox of Serena's upbringing: although her mother appears to exercise authority within the household, this authority is itself a product of patriarchal structures that position her as both an enforcer and a victim of gendered expectations. Serena's mother internalizes the values of a male-dominated society, channeling them into rigid expectations for her daughter under the guise of maternal guidance. As a result, Serena's identity is shaped by conflicting forces—on one hand, the demand for independence and success, and on the other, the implicit lesson of submission to patriarchal norms. This internalized contradiction fosters Serena's emotional dependency on male validation while simultaneously alienating her from authentic self-realization. The ethical failure within this family structure lies in its inability to foster mutual respect and autonomy, instead perpetuating cycles of control, repression, and emotional detachment across generations.

The influence of parents' dominance on children's ethics is a significant aspect of ethical development. The relationship between parents and children forms the foundation for moral understanding and behavior. Parents, as primary caregivers and role models, have a profound impact on shaping their children's ethical framework. Parents' power and authority can manifest in various ways, such as decision-making authority, setting rules and expectations, and exercising control over their children's lives. The manner in which parents exercise their dominance can significantly influence children's ethical development. Parents who consistently display ethical behavior and reinforce moral principles create an environment that nurtures the development of their children's ethics. However, if parents abuse their dominance or engage in unethical behavior, it can have negative consequences on their children's ethical development. Children are highly receptive to their parents' actions and attitudes, and they may mimic unethical behavior or adopt questionable ethical values if they witness their parents engaging in such conduct. Serena's mother's example of being submissive in the family role affects Serena's approach to handling relationships with men.

Section Two   Unequal Position in the Relationship between Serena and Tony

During her study at Cambridge, Serena meets Tony Canning through her boyfriend, Jeremy Mott. Tony, a professor almost as old as her father, turns out to be "an old MI5 hand himself," the British spy agency. After Serena meets

Tony, the trajectory of her life changes a lot. Serena meets Tony in her twenties, who plays the role of a teacher, and a relatively minor role as a lover. Tony's patriarchal desire to control Serena perpetuates the whole time of their engagement. In their relationship, Tony masters the absolute discourse right. In order to achieve his hegemonic dominance, he disciplines, controls, and instrumentalizes Serena. Serena is actually the trainee of the thoughts and words of others. In her own words, "I was a girl with untutored tastes. I was an empty mind, ripe for a takeover" (8), reflecting how Tony successfully imposed his influence, shaping her thoughts and identity to align with his own patriarchal control. As we have discussed above, Serena's father may be one of the reasons that she has established an intimate relationship with Tony. She seeks the fatherly love and care she lacks from her own father, and through Tony, she experiences a form of patriarchal affection that fills this emotional void. In their relationship, Tony is the absolute. His authority traps Serena into the subordinate position with no complaint. "I was touched. He was the first man in my life to buy me an article of clothing. A sugar daddy. (I don't think the Bishop had ever been in a shop.)" (33) As Serena's boyfriend, he takes really good care of her. He buys her gifts and clothes. To her, "he was also a worldly, a gentlemanly lover. His style was courtly" (29). As her mentor, he teaches Serena about history and current affairs in order to pass the test of MI5. Serena follows the instructions of Tony just as she does with her mother. When Tony finds Serena has little knowledge about British history, he gives Serena a reading list and even examines Serena regularly. "When exams were over, Tony said he was taking charge of my reading. Enough novels! He was appalled by my ignorance of what he called 'our island story.' He was right to be." At first, she is not that interested. "Despite my history lessons, I felt I had no stake in the nation's fate." She does all this due to Tony's arrangement. According to Beauvoir, women cannot determine and design their role in the world, and can only confirm their existence through men, and the basis of the existence of women is to play the role as men want and become the target of men's desire. In the end, she is a subordinate, a secondary person opposed to the primary. He is the subject, the absolute, and she is the other. Serena is on her way to becoming the woman Tony wants and fulfilling Tony's aim.

Tony's lecture about history and political knowledge laid a good foundation for Serena's excellent performance in the MI5 interview. Serena has no idea about what will confront her. Her future life is totally changed without her own awareness. "He would change my life and behave with selfless cruelty as he prepared to set out on a journey with no hope of return" (19). Under Tony's instruction, Serena has made big progress. "Those weekends were an extended tutorial in how to live, how and what to eat and drink, how to read newspapers and hold up my end of an argument and how to 'gut' a book" (19). However, in her mind, it is just an obligation, a job interview, and a few weeks away, she will be free. With the father-like love from Tony, Serena doesn't even question all the arrangements. She does whatever Tony may think is good for her. "So what was I doing, applying to the Security Service to help maintain this ailing state, this sick man of Europe? Nothing, I was doing nothing. I didn't know. A chance had come my way and I was taking it. Tony wanted it so I wanted it and I had little else going on. So why not?" (27) From this, we can see Serena doesn't fight against Tony's autocracy but obeys it mildly, taking it as "what Tony wants, I want it." The inequality of identity confirms the asymmetry of males and females. Men set positive standards and references, while women are negated and marginalized. They are the property of men and can be discarded as objects at any time.

Their relationship ends abruptly a few days before the interview. When Tony knows that he is seriously ill and can't be cured, he abandons Serena cruelly in the middle of the street. Tony has several options but he chooses the cruelest one, which hurts Serena badly. "He said it gently, lovingly, like a caring father, one I was about to lose." At this heartbreaking moment, what is in Serena's mind is still Tony's fatherly image. "But I stood there like a tragic fool and I watched him go. I saw his brake lights come on as he slowed to join the traffic. Then he was gone, and it was over" (38). This moment starkly illustrates Serena's internalized subjugation within patriarchal structures. Despite Tony's betrayal, she remains emotionally tethered to the paternal image he represents, revealing how deeply ingrained patriarchal conditioning shapes her identity and emotional responses. The fact that she passively accepts the breakup—standing immobile, describing herself as a "tragic fool"—demonstrates her learned helplessness and emotional dependency on male authority figures.

Beauvoir's assertion that "to be a woman means to be an object, the Other"[157] resonates powerfully here. Serena is positioned as an object within Tony's narrative, devoid of agency or voice in decisions that profoundly affect her life. Her emotional attachment to Tony is not merely romantic but rooted in her longing for paternal validation, which reflects the broader societal conditioning that equates male approval with self-worth for women. Serena's biological and emotional vulnerability, socially constructed rather than innate, reinforces her role as the "Other," subjected to the whims of male authority without recourse or autonomy. This dynamic underscores the enduring impact of patriarchal ideology on women's personal relationships and self-perception. Women's biological disadvantages inevitably disturb the imbalance in productivity between the sexes, and thus make them into the Others. Serena has no choice and no say about the breakup, but accepts it obediently.

Since Serena has grown immensely dependent on Tony for so long, she is so used to his fatherly education and manipulation of her. In the patriarchal society represented through Tony, Serena's future is coldly planned. First, she has a bishop father, which "no one ever needed to spell it out, but background remained important, and having the Bishop in mine was no disadvantage" (18). Second, Serena is not only beautiful but also intelligent, qualities that Tony leverages as he trains her to become a capable spy. Abandoning Serena and contributing her to the MI5, Tony has his selfish consideration. On the one hand, Tony has once betrayed his nation. Tony is deeply ashamed of his own betrayal and tries to make up for it. That is one of the reasons why he trains and recruits Serena, who has a good family and educational background. Tony wants this to be his compensation for his betrayal. On the other hand, Tony's abandonment of Serena is part of his interdisciplinary training program. As an accomplished spy, Serena must abandon her individual emotions at the service of her work. If Serena can let go of the emotional entanglement between her and Tony, then she will achieve a certain success in her career.[158]

The unequal position in a relationship, particularly for girls, can have a profound impact on their ethical development. When a girl finds herself in a position of subordination or power imbalance within a relationship, it can shape her understanding of her self-perception and her ability to exercise autonomy.

In a relationship characterized by inequality, a girl may be subjected to various forms of mistreatment, discrimination, or disregard for her opinions and rights. This can lead to the internalization of negative beliefs about her own worth, limited agency, and diminished self-confidence. As a result, her ethical decision-making may be influenced by the unequal power dynamics at play. Just like Serena, she is so submissive to Tony's orders without a second thought.

It is crucial to recognize and challenge the unequal positions that girls may find themselves in within relationships. Promoting gender equality, empowering girls to assert their rights and autonomy, and fostering environments that value their voices and contributions are vital steps towards nurturing their ethical development.

Furthermore, when girls experience unequal power dynamics, they may be more susceptible to societal pressures and expectations that undermine their ethical autonomy. Cultural norms, gender stereotypes, and social conditioning can reinforce ideas that limit a girl's agency, self-expression, and ability to assert her own ethical values. This can result in conformity to societal expectations rather than independent ethical judgment, which can be seen from her work at MI5.

Section Three   Discriminated Relationship between Serena and Max

Maximilian is Serena's colleague in MI5. He comes from a family of academics, and he has been transferred across from MI6 and is already on desk officer status. Their relationship begins with an assignment named "Sweet Tooth" which is also the title of the book. Sweet Tooth is the name of a secret mission launched by MI5 to sponsor potential young writers to publish literary works which will support the British government in the press and media.

After entering the agency, although Serena says their relationship starts from friendship, she soon becomes obsessed with Max and begins to flirt with him. While Max, another hegemonic and manipulative character, has always looked down on Serena and other women. He believes that women are incapable of keeping their professional and private lives apart.

> You have all these colleagues, they're pleasant, charming, good backgrounds and all that. Unless you do operations together you don't know what they're up to, what their work is and whether they're any good at it. You don't know whether they're beaming idiots or friendly geniuses. Suddenly they're promoted or sacked and you've no idea why. That's how it is. (108)

"Women were of a lower caste," which breaks Serena's dream that she could do her bit for her country. Though from the 1820s, the social position of women has improved. Women started to have a career and have gained the right to vote politically. However, the long-rooted discrimination against women can't be erased overnight. Max, as a typical phallocrat, likes to take the leading position in both workplace and personal relationships. He probes into all aspects of Serena's life while ignoring Serena's real needs and desires. He doesn't care about Serena's feelings and pries into Tony's details. In the end, he behaves like a father comforting a little girl: "'That's it for now,' he said, touching the tip of my nose with his forefinger, acting like the firm parent talking down to a demanding child" (71).

Although Max is Serena's superior, Serena has always regarded Max as a friend or even a lover. As a matter of fact, though Max is attracted by Serena's beauty, he has never thought of a serious relationship with her. In Max's mind, however, the relationship between them is not equal: "…in this small part of the adult world, and unlike in the rest of the Civil Service, women were of a lower caste" (61). His contempt toward women shows that he does not have any admiration or caring for Serena. Instead, he just does not take this relationship seriously, and easily abandons Serena to choose a better partner.

Later, he chooses a fiancée who has higher social status than Serena and easily breaks off the affair with Serena. After knowing about Max's engagement,

Serena feels a sense of loss and inferiority. She thinks that she is once again abandoned by Max, after Tony. "He was leaning forward on his fingertips which were splayed against the desk and he seemed to be indicating the door behind me by faintly inclining his head. Throwing me out with minimal effort" (113). Because Max comes from a good family and is her superior, Serena is in a low position in the relationship with Max. She tries to hide her emotions and is very eager to get Max's attention and recognition. In the eyes of Max, whose male hegemony controls him, Serena has nothing that can benefit him. Serena has no say in their relationship, only to be abandoned with no mercy. "It was shallow stuff. I couldn't quite admit to myself how upset I was by the news of his engagement. His self-control irritated me. I wanted to provoke and punish him and here it was, I had my wish, he was on his feet, fairly quivering" (114). During the argument, Max is trying not only to express his thoughts, but also continues to instill his ideas in Serena, and also refutes the ideas of Serena. Max arrogantly thinks his idea is right, and he not only controls Serena in reality, but also wants to control Serena's thoughts. "If you pretend to know more than you do, if you pretend to knowledge that hardly tallies with a few months in the Registry, you'll give the wrong impression." Max is warning Serena, exhorting Serena to keep a low profile and not to show off. "So stop acting as though you know more than you do." "Best to go now. Just do your own work. Keep things simple" (115). It seems that Max is helping Serena. However, there seems to be a sense of mockery and disdain in his words.

In the eyes of a person with male hegemony in his mind, Max does not think that Serena has control power and mature thoughts; instead, he feels that Serena's behavior is a bit ridiculous. He even thinks that he deserves such a right. His patriarchal mind, which places the male group in a dominant position, not only oppresses women, but also objectifies women and regards women as their prey. Serena is his prey, and he can let it go or capture it at his own will. To be such a person who is fickle in love, before long, Max again leaves his fiancée and comes back to find Serena, hoping to start again. His phallus thought makes him believe that Serena is still in love with him, while Serena has already fallen in love with Tom.

Max's attempt to control Serena's thoughts and behavior shows his need for authority and dominance, particularly in a space where he feels entitled to dictate the terms of interaction. His advice to "stop acting as though you know more than you do" and "keep things simple" is presented as a well-meaning suggestion, but it has the underlying effect of keeping Serena in her place, limiting her intellectual autonomy. Serena's internal conflict, marked by her desire for Max's attention and validation, speaks to the larger theme of women being conditioned to seek approval from men, which further perpetuates their subjugation. Despite her apparent resistance in moments like this argument, Serena ultimately conforms to Max's will, revealing how ingrained these power dynamics are in shaping her sense of self and worth. The subordinate position of women in the workplace can have a significant influence on their ethics. When women find themselves in a position of subordination or power imbalance within a professional setting, it can shape their ethical decision-making, their perceptions of fairness, and their overall professional experiences.

In many workplaces, women face challenges such as gender bias, discrimination, unequal opportunities for advancement, etc. These systemic barriers can create an environment where women's voices are marginalized, their contributions undervalued, and their ethical perspectives overlooked. Women may face a dilemma between maintaining their job security by conforming to unethical practices, or taking a stand against such practices despite potential negative consequences. This distorted ethical framework can cause individuals to compromise their integrity in order to appease their superiors. Serena's affection for Max can be regarded as this.

In essence, this interaction highlights the subtle yet pervasive nature of male hegemony, where men not only dominate women physically or socially but also attempt to control their thoughts, emotions, and aspirations. Max's actions reinforce the broader societal structures that limit Serena's freedom, leaving her to struggle in a relationship where she is never fully able to express or assert her true self.

Section Four   Untrustworthy Relationship between Serena and Tom

After joining the project of Sweet Tooth, Serena's task is to approach a writer named Tom Hailey. To complete the mission, Serena reads Tom's fictions and gets in touch with Tom as the identity of an agent in Freedom International to provide a stipend for him. Serena first falls in love with Tom's works. She then falls in love with Tom soon after she meets him. Although she knows that she is on a mission, she disregards her superiors' command and supports her lover to publish the work which finally annoys the government.

At the beginning of the project, Serena visits Tom on purpose to start her mission, and she is supposed to be in the predominant position with Tom. Before their meeting, Serena reads about Tom's main life experience, his life tracks and finances through the secret files of MI5. Tom has nothing comparable to Serena. She can go through Tom's materials and background as she pleases. In the asymmetry of information, Serena is supposed to control the meeting and even Tom absolutely, since she has read Tom's works and has an intuitive understanding of Tom's ideology. Tom is like millions of other common "faces" who have nothing special. "He was girlishly slender, with narrow wrists and his hand when I shook it seemed smaller and softer than mine. Skin very pale, eyes dark green, hair dark brown and long, and cut in a style that was almost a bob" (165). His mediocre family background and know-nothing-about-Serena situation are assumed to put Tom in a disadvantaged position, but Serena doesn't behave like a professional. "And it was true, in my nervousness I had taken on a distant, official tone. I needed to relax, be less pompous, I needed to call him Tom. I realised I wasn't much good at any of this." However, "he was self-consciously playing the part of the friendly don, coaxing a nervous applicant through her entrance interview" (120). Despite Tom's relatively unremarkable background and lack of knowledge about Serena, the imbalance between them stems from Serena's self-perception and behavior. Her nervousness and self-consciousness during the interview reflect a broader issue of self-doubt, where she consciously and unconsciously adopts a tone that places her in a subordinate role. She recognizes this, as indicated by her realization that she needs to relax and "be less pompous," yet her instinctive response is to adopt a position of deference and insecurity. From the beginning of their relationship, Serena has put herself in a subordinate position. The reason is obvious. Till the end of the novel, Serena is so used to accepting the manipulation and control by Tom.

Tom, on the other hand, is aware of his role as the one in control, though he adopts a friendly and approachable demeanor. His role as a "friendly don" masks his subtle manipulation, as he guides Serena through the interview process in a manner that reinforces his power while presenting it as a form of benevolent guidance. This dynamic reveals how Serena's self-worth and sense of agency have been shaped by the dominant forces in her life, including societal expectations and gendered power structures. Her habitual subordination to men, fostered by her upbringing and relationships with other male figures, makes it difficult for her to challenge or resist Tom's manipulation.

Her incompetence and lack of confidence are aroused by her childhood experience with the absence of her father's love and her submission to the patriarchal society. The girls are "taught that to please she must try to please, she must make herself object; she should therefore renounce her autonomy."[159] In her relationship with men, Serena is the one to please. Her understanding about the relationship is distorted. Perhaps because of the lack of paternal love in childhood, girls will unconsciously look for a "paternal" boyfriend when they grow up. They are easily and involuntarily falling in love with a man who is much older than her or who can tolerate her, because she does not get the love, care and respect from her father. The parents are distant to the point of barely believable indifference: much later in the novel, Serena thinks, "Would the Bishop even notice I'd been away?" As a result, besides Tony, Tom's tolerance of her greatly attracts her. Her desire for the father's love, unconditional protection and coddling for a man is the typical symptom of the Oedipal complex.

Her submission to the patriarchal world can also be seen in her empathy for her mother. "I think I must have absorbed the general spirit of camaraderie and cheerful devotion to duty among the women. I was becoming like my mother. She had the Bishop, I had the Service. Like her I had my own strong-minded inclination to obey" (93). In *The Second Sex,* the complex relationship of mother and daughter is that mothers will saddle their children with her own destiny. Under their care, "women apply themselves to changing her into a woman like themselves."[160] There is no maternal instinct. The little girls learn all of these from their mothers. "She is so taught; stories heard, books read, all her little experiences confirm the idea."[161] The social ideology has already set the fate for women.

In the agency, women are the lower class. They are only given paperwork to do and, at the same time, face the risk of being fired for no reason. Their position in the patriarchal world is like a housewife in the family. They devote their whole life to the family, but they still face the chance of getting divorced. Just like Serena's mother, "all she demanded in return—my guess, of course—was that he love her or, at least, never leave her" (10).

Though Serena is aware of the paternal manipulations around her, she plainly accepts it. "These clever, amoral, inventive, destructive men, single-minded, selfish, emotionally cool, coolly attractive. I think I preferred them to the love of Jesus. They were so necessary, and not only to me. Without them we would still be living in mud huts, waiting to invent the wheel" (90). She accepts the manipulation from these men, the symbols of a hegemonic patriarchal society. Tom, like Tony, is one of them.

"I stood in front of him humbly, as I used to in front of my father in his study" (84). "Again, I had that feeling I sometimes used to have when the Bishop called me into his study for a talk about my teenage progress. The feeling of being naughty and small" (283). In her relationship with Tom, she is so obsessed with the feelings that she doesn't say no to her submissive position. Her nature of dependence is more prominent in their relationship.

Even though Serena sacrifices a lot in this relationship, there exists the untrustworthy and unequal situation in it. She, who is supposed to play the main role in the relationship because she is the spy, subdues Tom's talents in literature. It is Tom's talent in literature that greatly attracts Serena and makes her willing to give in. The relationship that she has been familiar with in her previous relationships puts Serena in the position of paternal patronizing. From the very beginning, we can feel that Serena is actually satisfied with the gender roles. After reading Tom's novels, Serena feels the urge to meet the novelist. She is deeply attracted by Tom's construction of the plot and character. She even tries to fit herself into the characters in the novel, to feel what they feel in order to understand the novelist well. "And I suppose I was, in my mindless way, looking for a something, version of myself, a heroine I could slip inside as one might a pair of favourite old shoes. Or a wild silk blouse" (58). Her whole-hearted devotion to the young writer makes her willingly give all her love to him. In a relationship, the partner with a low value in love is generally more likely to suffer from gains and losses passively. Serena is the weak one.

For such a sensitive and sensible woman, Serena is too easily controlled. Tom's novels in some way play a role of mental manipulation to Serena. Tom is constantly using his dominance in the creation to satisfy his own gender charm and creative desires. The manipulation of Serena through his creations allows Tom to reinforce his power, not just in their personal relationship, but in his own sense of self-affirmation and gendered superiority. Tom always thinks he is in total control over Serena, which is the strong hatred from when he knows that Serena is deceiving him. "How accomplished you were at appearing to be no more than you seemed to be, no more than yourself. Bitterly, sardonically, I wished meteoric promotion on you." The hatred is so hard that he even wants to kill Serena. "I should tell you that in that hour, if your lovely pale throat had appeared upturned on my lap and a knife had been pushed into my hand, I would have done the job without thinking" (252).

His hatred is not rooted in a deep emotional betrayal or personal devastation but in the perceived insult to his masculinity. His desire to maintain absolute control over Serena, both in their professional and personal spheres, is threatened by her autonomy, leading him to view her as an affront to his male dignity. This reaction underlines a significant critique of traditional masculinity, where a man's sense of self-worth is often linked to his power over women. Love will make him forgive Serena's involuntary mistake. However, his description gives us the feeling that his hatred is caused by her insult to his male dignity. "This wasn't, or wasn't only, a calamitous betrayal and personal disaster. I'd been too busy being insulted by it to see it for what it was…" (254) This moment of extreme hatred shows the extent to which Tom's identity and sense of power are wrapped up in the subjugation of women. His inability to see Serena's actions as anything other than an affront to his masculine pride exposes the deeply entrenched patriarchal structures that govern their relationship. Ultimately, Tom's violent thoughts—though momentary—demonstrate the destructive consequences of such unchecked patriarchal entitlement and the ways in which women are often reduced to symbols of male control, not fully recognized as individuals with their own desires and subjectivity.

In their contact, Serena has made many attempts to confess her identity to Tom, but out of fear of consequences, she has to hold back her words to the point of her mouth. She uses the metaphor of "like a woman who slips over the edge of a cliff and makes a lunge for a tuft of grass that will never hold her weight" to express her situation. On the one hand, she could not let the MI5 she serves know about this matter, because it violates her work discipline; on the other hand, she can't confess to Tom that she knows that telling Tom her true identity means that she would lose him and make him hate her. In the midst of a dilemma, the only "life-saving straw" that Serena could grasp in order to maintain a temporary balance is to conceal the truth and lie to MI5 and Tom in an attempt to use lies and deception to protect her love. However, the cat will come out, so does the truth. The cruel reality breaks the balance between the two sides.

However, the ending of the novel isn't very upsetting. Serena fears that she has lost Tom's love forever. Now he knows she has deceived him. Tom, however, had known about the program for months, and instead of ending the affair, has decided to turn the story into a novel. The reader now discovers that the author of *Sweet Tooth* is in fact Tom, despite its being written from Serena's first-person perspective. As the novel ends, Tom asks Serena in a letter to marry him.

By the end of the novel, Serena's consistent submission to Tom signifies how deeply ingrained this hierarchical power dynamic is. Her inability to assert herself, even in an academic or professional context, reflects her broader struggle with autonomy and self-definition. Serena has internalized her role as the subordinate "Other" to such an extent that it becomes second nature to her, further illustrating the pervasive impact of patriarchal control on her life.

Serena's character embodies the struggle of women who strive for an independent identity while still grappling with the constraints imposed by a patriarchal society. The ethics delves into issues of autonomy, agency, and the oppressive nature of gender norms. While Serena may challenge traditional stereotypes and exhibit resistance against male chauvinism, she remains a product of the male-dominated construction and discipline prevalent in society. The influence from her family and the way she is brought up make her feel compelled to conform to societal expectations or traditional gender norms, even if it goes against her personal desires or beliefs.

Sweet Tooth shows more than just human emotions. Moreover, it also projects the difficult choice between human emotions and ethics, bringing us a lot of ethical examination and enlightenment about the nature of human beings. In the patriarchal ideology, Serena has not escaped the control of a patriarchal society just because she is a pretty woman, the marker of gender identity. Through this, McEwan critiques not only individual relationships but also the societal structures that perpetuate the oppression of women, making it all the more difficult for them to break free from these patterns. In McEwan's works, the portrayal of female characters who exhibit a submissive nature to men raises important ethical considerations. The ethics surrounding women who are submissive to men require a careful examination of power dynamics, gender roles, and the impact on individual autonomy. By exploring the ethical dimensions of Serena's character, we gain insight into the moral challenges faced by women striving for independence within a patriarchal society. It emphasizes the importance of ongoing efforts to promote gender equality, dismantle oppressive structures, and create inclusive spaces that allow individuals to live and express their identities freely.

Conclusion

As a mature writer with a sense of social responsibility, the style of his later work is very different from the earlier novels. However, it is worth noting that McEwan has consistently maintained a focus on ethical dilemmas throughout all stages of his creative career, exploring them across his entire body of work.[162] McEwan presents various ethical issues to the reader, trying to create a special moral tension to educate people through the chaos of ethics and the fragmentation of ethical values.

Post-war Britain, particularly in the mid-to-late 20th century, was marked by social turmoil, economic crises, and a decline in traditional values and religious beliefs. This period saw an unprecedented moral crisis that lowered ethical standards across society. A good writer must not only have the ability to observe life in detail, but more importantly, be able to express the observations through the works, which are often what we have experienced. Ethics is based on people's obedience to ethical taboos, which forms the basis and guarantee of human ethical order. While in McEwan's novels, there always exist ethical issues like social, political and moral corruption, family and marriage relations, the interpersonal ethical dilemma, etc.; McEwan employs modern and post-modern narrative techniques to disclose the ethical dislocation and distortion in society and reproduces the sexually violent and abnormal social and family life. His depiction of the complex social life and the ethical situation in society, and his exploration of the essence of human nature and the meaning of life make him an eminent and essential figure of British literature.

McEwan's early works, such as *The Cement Garden* and *The Child in Time*, particularly emphasize the dynamics of family relationships, often centering around teenage protagonists. He has acknowledged that childhood remains a pervasive theme in his fiction, as he believes individuals carry their childhood experiences throughout their lives. He recognizes the significance of acknowledging and embracing this aspect of our identity, as denying it can have perilous consequences. As his own range of experiences and emotional depth expanded over time, it naturally impacted his writing. For example, in novels like *The Cement Garden*, the teenage protagonists, such as Jack and his siblings, find themselves thrust into parental roles when they are not yet fully developed, both physically and psychologically. The lack of parental guidance requires the children to take on familial responsibilities and roles, which can result in confusion about their identities. Ultimately, this confusion results in unforgivable mistakes. Through such narratives, McEwan examines the fragility of human ethics, demonstrating how distorted family relationships contribute to moral dilemmas. In *The Child in Time*, although the actual child is absent, rebellious and vulnerable adults yearn for and retreat into the woods, seeking to recapture the essence of their lost childhood. However, this unhealthy pursuit of their past typically does not yield positive outcomes. Through these narratives, McEwan aims to use the power of literature to examine and reconstruct human ethics and morality, shedding light on the distorted and chaotic ethical dilemmas present in contemporary society.

Beyond childhood and adolescence, McEwan also scrutinizes marital relationships and the parent-child bond. Dysfunctional family structures in his novels often serve as catalysts for ethical crises. The integrity and health of the family structure play crucial roles in determining the ethical fabric of the family. When this structure is lacking or compromised, ethical problems are likely to arise. Throughout many of his novels, an unhealthy family structure pushes its members to the brink of dissolution or strains their relationships. In *Saturday*, for instance, Perowne finds himself with an insurmountable barrier between him and his artistically and literarily talented children. In *Solar*, extramarital affairs destabilize Beard's marriage, ultimately leading to tragedy. By exploring the intricacies of family dynamics, McEwan highlights how the absence of a sound family structure can have profound ethical implications. The fragility and breakdown of these relationships can create a ripple effect, influencing the choices and actions of individuals within the family unit. These portrayals serve as a reflection of the ethical challenges faced by individuals in contemporary society.

McEwan's evolving writing style reflects a growing concern for gender dynamics and patriarchal oppression. As his writing style matured, he began to exhibit more pro-feminist tendencies in his depictions of gender relations, as seen in novels like *Sweet Tooth* and *Solar*. The deep-rooted patriarchal ideology not only exacerbates family conflicts and distorts marriages but also assigns default roles to women, perpetuating inequality and injustice. In *Sweet Tooth,* Serena serves as a victim of the patriarchal society, navigating its constraints and limitations. *Solar* offers a clear depiction of a female scientist's fight against Beard, highlighting the struggles and obstacles women often face in male-dominated fields. McEwan openly supports gender equality and challenges traditional gender roles. Through his writing, he aims to expose the injustices that women experience and advocate for equal rights and opportunities. "McEwan himself … expected that women's writing would provide some of the most exciting departures in English fiction."[163]

As his career progressed, McEwan shifted his focus towards depicting the lives of the elite, providing insightful critiques of the British social hierarchy. By uncovering the hypocritical nature of the upper echelons of society, he reveals the underlying roots of social problems. The elites often emphasize the importance of maintaining independence and privacy within their personal spaces, effectively creating a separation between themselves and those in lower social classes. Characters like Perowne, who uses his professional knowledge to humiliate the hooligan Baxter, exemplify this disconnect. Similarly, Beard in *Solar* distances himself from the young post-docs, yet ultimately resorts to plagiarism to further his own goals. McEwan's portrayal exposes the corruption and moral failings of politicians, as depicted in works such as *The Child in Time, Saturday,* and *Solar*.

McEwan's ethical explorations extend beyond family and social hierarchy to broader moral dilemmas such as indifference to familial bonds, false self-identification, and interpersonal ethical conflicts. His earlier works often explore disturbing themes, including violence, incest, murder, and sadism, while his later works shift toward more conventional ethical dilemmas. Despite this shift, his fundamental goal remains the same: to reveal social realities and contemplate the meaning of human existence.

McEwan's novels are intricately woven into the fabric of contemporary society, capturing readers' attention with their realistic portrayal of social life. Through his storytelling prowess, he exposes the darkness and complexities that exist within interpersonal relationships and sheds light on the aspirations and desires of ordinary individuals navigating these circumstances. Furthermore, McEwan explores the relationship between humanity and nature, revealing the disregard for environmental ethics that strains this connection. He implicates both the government and men's anthropocentric perspectives, highlighting how instrumental rationality can disrupt the harmony between humans and the natural world. This rationality often leads to indifference and alienation, causing further damage to both individuals and the environment. McEwan's focus on ethics and morality extends beyond the narrative structure of his stories. He subtly presents his own ethical standpoint through the process of storytelling, establishing his own ethical standards and guiding the reader's ethical judgment. He conscientiously selects social issues that resonate with the zeitgeist as the themes and content of his narratives. This enables readers to perceive and comprehend the ethical dilemmas prevalent in society, ultimately prompting introspection and self-reflection.

The exploration of ethical dilemmas in McEwan's novels serves as a catalyst for readers to consider their own ethical values and beliefs. By presenting complex and morally challenging situations, he invites readers to reflect on their own actions, decisions, and the broader ethical implications of their lives. Through this engagement, readers gain a deeper understanding of the ethical quandaries that exist within society and are encouraged to evaluate their own roles and responsibilities in shaping a more ethical and just world.

Moreover, McEwan's narratives extend beyond mere entertainment or storytelling; they serve as a medium for raising important social and ethical issues. McEwan utilizes his storytelling prowess to depict the distorted and chaotic ethical dilemmas prevalent in our current societal landscape. His keen observation and examination of the ethical dimensions of human experiences elicit emotional and intellectual responses from readers. This interaction sparks critical thinking and fosters a sense of empathy, as readers become more attuned to the ethical complexities and dilemmas faced by individuals within society.

McEwan's storytelling exhibits unparalleled honesty and sincerity, compelling readers to delve deeply into the complexities of human minds and emotions. Through his exploration of people's innermost thoughts and emotional states, he emphasizes the significance of establishing healthy and meaningful ethical relationships. McEwan's narratives depict the ongoing struggle of individuals, both men and women, as they strive to form relationships that can sustain, nourish, and strengthen them within the tumultuous world of contemporary society. The novels intertwine with the realities of contemporary society, delving into the intricacies of interpersonal relationships and exposing the moral dilemmas faced by ordinary individuals. By shifting his focus to the elite and uncovering their hypocrisy, he shines a light on the roots of social problems. Through his storytelling, he invites readers to critically examine power structures, reflect on their own ethical choices, and strive for a more just and compassionate society. McEwan's narratives serve as a reminder of the ongoing struggle individuals face in navigating the complexities of contemporary society while striving for meaningful connections and a more sustainable world.

By digging into the complexities of family relationships and exposing the darkness and flaws within interpersonal relationships and societal systems, he encourages readers to critically examine the role of family structures and their impact on ethical behavior. Through his narratives, McEwan prompts us to reflect on the importance of fostering healthy family dynamics, recognizing the interplay between personal ethics and the relationships we forge within our own families.

Besides, McEwan's work extends beyond the examination of patriarchal societies and the plight of women. He examines the relationship between humanity and nature, advocating for environmental ethics and highlighting the destructive consequences of instrumental rationality. Through his writing, he urges readers to reflect on the establishment of healthy ethical relationships and offers a culmination of his major themes and concerns.

McEwan's works go beyond entertainment, using literature as a tool to interrogate social and ethical issues. His narratives expose the ethical chaos of contemporary society, provoking intellectual and emotional responses from readers. By shedding light on the moral challenges of family life, gender inequality, social hierarchy, and environmental concerns, he encourages critical thinking and empathy.

Ultimately, McEwan's novels serve as both mirrors and critiques of modern ethical dilemmas, compelling readers to reflect on their personal and societal responsibilities. His ability to interweave social critique with profound human insight ensures his place as one of Britain's most significant literary figures.

Reference

Chapter One

[1] MCEWAN I. The great listener[EB/OL]. (2000-11-29)[2025-08-04]. https://www.theguardian.com/books/2000/nov/29/fiction.highereducation1.

[2] ROBERTS R. Conversations with Ian McEwan[G]. Jackson: University Press of Mississippi, 2010: x.

[3] HEAD D. Ian McEwan[M]. Manchester: Manchester University Press, 2007: 49.

[4] GROES S. Ian McEwan: contemporary critical perspectives[G]. 2nd ed. New York and London: Bloomsbury Academic, 2013: 6.

[5] 马凌. 床笫之间是荒原[M]//伊恩·麦克尤恩. 床笫之间. 周丽华, 译. 上海：上海译文出版社，2010：167.

[6] 余华. 麦克尤恩后遗症[M]//伊恩·麦克尤恩. 最初的爱情, 最后的仪式. 潘帕, 译. 南京：南京大学出版社，2008：ii.

[7] First love, last rites[EB/OL]. [2025-08-04]. https://www.penguin.co.uk/books/354914/first-love-last-rites-by-ian-mcewan/9781784703608.

[8] Books written by Ian McEwan[EB/OL]. [2025-08-04]. http://ianmcewan.com/books/index.html.

[9] In between the sheets[EB/OL]. [2025-08-04]. https://www.kirkusreviews.com/book-reviews/ian-mcewan/in-between-the-sheets.

[10] Books written by Ian McEwan[EB/OL]. [2025-08-04]. http://ianmcewan.com/books/index.html.

[11] ROBERTS R. Conversations with Ian McEwan[G]. Jackson: University Press of Mississippi, 2010: 31.

[12] ABBASIYANNEJAD M. A reflection of Ian McEwan's life in his

fiction. English language and literature studies[J], 2012, 2(2): 57.

[13] ROBERTS R. Conversations with Ian McEwan[G]. Jackson: University Press of Mississippi, 2010: 35.

[14] ibid. 2010: 108.

[15] MCEWAN I. Mother tongue: a memoir[M]//LEADER Z. On modern British fiction. Oxford: Oxford University Press, 2002: 34-44.

[16] GROES S. Ian McEwan: contemporary critical perspectives[G]. 2nd ed. New York and London: Bloomsbury Academic, 2013: 12.

[17] SLAY J. Ian McEwan[M]. New York: Twayne Publishers, 1996: x.

[18] MCEWAN I. Mother tongue[EB/OL]. (2001-10-13)[2025-08-04]. http://ianmcewan.com/resources/articles/mother-tongue.html.

[19] SMITH Z. Zadie Smith talks with Ian McEwan[G]//ROBERTS R. Conversations with Ian McEwan. Jackson: University Press of Mississippi, 2010: 117.

[20] HEAD D. Ian McEwan[M]. Manchester: Manchester University Press, 2007: 47.

[21] YARDLEY J. Pathological lovers from Ian McEwan, a triangle with a twist[EB/OL]. (1998-01-27)[2025-08-04]. https://www.washingtonpost.com/archive/lifestyle/1998/01/28/pathological-lovers/87db1705-b86d-4952-bf03-e336a2f2af47.

[22] WOOD M. When the balloon goes up: *Enduring Love* by Ian McEWAN[J/OL]. London review of books, 1997, 19(17). [2025-08-04]. https://www.lrb.co.uk/the-paper/v19/n17/michael-wood/when-the-balloon-goes-up.

[23] HELLER Z. "Saturday": one day in the life[EB/OL]. (2005-03-20)[2025-08-05]. https://www.nytimes.com/2005/03/20/books/review/saturday-one-day-in-the-life.html.

[24] ARMSTRONG A E. Ian McEwan: an inventory of his papers at the Harry Ransom Center[EB/OL]. [2025-08-01]. https://norman.hrc.utexas.edu/fasearch/findingAid.cfm?Eadid=01073.

[25] LEAVIS F R. The Great Tradition: George Eliot, Henry James, Joseph Conrad[M]. New York: George W. Stewart, Publisher Inc.1950.

[26] MALCOLM D. Understanding Ian McEwan[M]. Columbia:

University of South Carolina Press, 2002: 15.

[27] ibid. 2002: 73.

[28] KELLAWAY K. At home with his worries[EB/OL]. (2001-09-15) [2025-08-01]. http://www.guardian.co.uk/books/2001/sep/16/fiction.ianmcewan.

[29] SEDAGHAT M. The relationship between history and ethics in Ian McEwan's Black Dogs[J]. Advances in language and literary studies, 2014, 5(3): 43.

[30] ibid.

[31] https://verhaar.weebly.com/critical-perspective.html.

[32] KIRN W. Human orbits[EB/OL]. (2010-04-16)[2025-08-04]. https://www.nytimes.com/2010/04/18/books/review/Kirn-t.html?pagewanted=all&mcubz=0.

[33] YARDLEY J. "Sweet Tooth" by Ian McEwan[EB/OL]. (2012-11-09)[2025-08-04]. https://www.washingtonpost.com/opinions/sweet-tooth-by-ian-mcewan/2012/11/09/ce53a8fe-2352-11e2-ba29-238a6ac36a08_story.html.

[34] COOKE R. Memories with a dash of thrill[EB/OL]. (2018-09-15)[2025-08-04]. https://gulfnews.com/general/memories-with-a-dash-of-thrill-1.1064485.

[35] HEAD D. The Cambridge companion to Ian McEwan[M]. Cambridge, Eng.: Cambridge University Press, 2019: 75-90.

[36] PETR C. Playfulness as apologia for a strong story in Ian McEwan's *Sweet Tooth*[J]. Brno studies in English, 2015, 41(1): 101-115.

[37] Nutshell[EB/OL]. [2025-08-04]. http://ianmcewan.com/books/nutshell.html.

[38] MCALPIN H. In McEwan's latest, the "machine" is too like you[EB/OL]. (2019-04-23)[2025-08-04]. https://www.npr.org/2019/04/23/714887136/in-mcewans-latest-the-machine-is-too-much-like-you.

Chapter Two

[39] AUDI R. The Cambridge dictionary of philosophy[M]. Cambridge: Cambridge University Press, 2015.

[40] STERLING S R. Culture, ethics, and the environment: towards the new synthesis[J]. Environmentalist, 1985, 5(3): 197-206.

[41] NIE Z Z. Introduction to Ethical Literary Criticism[M]. Beijing: Peking University Press, 2014: 13.

[42] 张玉能. "人是符号的动物": 符号诗学与西方美学传统[J]. 学术月刊, 2008（10）: 114-120.

[43] ibid.

[44] 聂珍钊. 序言: 文学伦理学批评[G]//聂珍钊, 邹建军. 文学伦理学批评: 文学研究方法新探讨, 2006: 3.

[45] 李定清. 文学伦理学批评与人文精神建构[J]. 外国文学研究, 2006（01）: 44-52.

[46] 聂珍钊. 文学伦理学批评: 人性概念的阐释与考辨[J]. 外国文学研究, 2005（06）: 9-19.

[47] 聂珍钊. 文学伦理学批评: 基本理论与术语[J]. 外国文学研究, 2010（01）: 12-22.

[48] 敏泽, 党圣元. 文学价值论[M]. 北京: 社会科学文献出版社, 1999, 30.

[49] 高楠. 中国古代艺术的文化学阐释[M]. 沈阳: 辽宁人民出版社, 1998.

[50] 聂珍钊. 文学伦理学批评: 文学批评方法新探索[J]. 外国文学研究, 2004（05）: 19.

[51] 苏晖. 学术影响力与国际话语权建构: 文学伦理学批评十五年发展历程回顾[J]. 外国文学研究, 2019, 41（05）: 34-51.

[52] 聂珍钊. 文学伦理学批评: 文学批评方法新探索[J]. 外国文学研究, 2004（05）: 16-24+169.

[53] 刘建军. 文学伦理批评的当下现状[J]. 外国文学研究, 2005（01）: 21-23.

[54] 乔国强. "文学伦理学批评"之管见[J]. 外国文学研究, 2005（01）: 24-27.

[55] 王宁. 文学的环境伦理学: 生态批评的意义[J]. 外国文学研究, 2005（01）: 18-20.

[56] 李定清. 文学伦理学批评与人文精神建构[J]. 外国文学研究, 2006（01）: 44-52.

[57] YANG J C. Realms of ethical literary criticism in China: a review of

Nie Zhenzhao's scholarship[J]. Foreign literature studies, 2016, 38(05): 33-40.

[58] SHANG B W. The rise of a critical theory: reading introduction to ethical literary criticism[J]. Foreign literature studies, 2014, 36(05): 26-36.

[59] 苏晖. 学术影响力与国际话语权建构：文学伦理学批评十五年发展历程回顾[J]. 外国文学研究，2019，41（05）：34-51.

[60] 车凤成. 文学伦理学批评视野中的"文学观"追问[J]. 浙江工商大学学报，2008（05）：35-42.

[61] BOOTH W C. The Rhetoric of Fiction[M]. 2nd ed. Chicago: The University of Chicago Press, 1983: 23-60.

[62] LOCKRIDGE L S. The ethics of romanticism[M]. Cambridge, Eng.: Cambridge University Press, 1989.

[63] 李定清. 文学伦理学批评与人文精神建构[J]. 外国文学研究，2006（01）：44-52.

[64] 强昌文. 个体主义伦理观与权利[J]. 安徽大学学报，2006（06）：67-72.

[65] 朱赫今. 伊迪丝·华顿小说创作中的伦理取向[D]. 吉林大学，2014：10.

Chapter Three

[66] CHILDS P. Contemporary novelists: British fiction since 1970[M]. Hampshire: Palgrave Macmillan, 2005: 167.

[67] WELLS L. Ian McEwan[M]. New York: Bloomsbury Publishing, 2009: 34.

[68] SHANG B W. The unbearable lightness of growth: ethical consciousness and ethical selection in McEwan's *The Cement Garden*[J]. Foreign language education, 2014 (04): 71.

[69] SLAY J. A prevailing ordinariness: society and interpersonal relationships in the fiction of Ian McEwan[D]. The University of Tennessee, 1991: 38.

[70] SISTANI R R, HASHIM R S, HAMDAN S I. Psychoanalytical tensions and conflicts of characters' interactions in Ian McEwan's *The Cement*

Garden[J]. Social and behavioral sciences, 2014 (118): 450-456.

[71] DHALL T C. Family environment and school performance[M]. Delhi: Kalpaz Publications. 2004: 18-19.

[72] Merriam-Webster.com Dictionary. Family values[EB/OL]. (2025-07-13)[2025-08-04]. https://www.merriam-webster.com/dictionary/family%20values.

[73] FAIRBAIRN W R D. A revised psychopathology of the psychoses and psychoneuroses[M]//FAIRBAIRN W R D, Scharff D E, BIRTLES E F. Psychoanalytic studies of the personality. London and New York: Routledge Publishing, 1952: 39.

[74] MCEWAN I. The cement garden[M]. London: Vintage Books, 2006: 9.

[75] ibid., 9; 40.

[76] KLEIN M. Love, guilt and reparation[M]//KLEIN M, MONEY-KYRLE R E. Love, guilt and reparation & other works 1921-1945. New York: Delacorte Press/S. Lawrence, 1975: 307.

[77] MCEWAN I. The cement garden[M]. London: Vintage Books, 2006: 40.

[78] BAUMRIND D. The influence of parenting style on adolescent competence and substance use[J]. The journal of early adolescence, 1991, 11(1): 59.

[79] BRETT C. Understanding life: an introduction to the psychology of Alfred Adler[M]. Oxford: Oneworld Publications, 1997: 184.

[80] MCEWAN I. The cement garden[M]. London: Vintage Books, 2006: 27.

[81] CHILDS P, TREDELL N. The fiction of Ian McEwan[M]. Basingstoke: Palgrave Macmillan, 2006: 35.

[82] NOIVILLE F. The contemporary British novel: a French perspective[J]. European journal of English studies, 2006, 10(3): 298.

[83] SLAY J. A prevailing ordinariness: society and interpersonal relationships in the fiction of Ian McEwan[D]. The University of Tennessee, 1991: 139-140.

[84] ANSBACHER H, ANSBACHER R. The individual psychology of

Alfred Adler: a systematic presentation in selections from his writings[G]. New York: Basic Books, 1956, 126.

[85] 齐美尔. 桥与门[M]. 涯鸿, 宇声, 译. 上海：三联书店，1991：111.

[86] CHILDS P. Contemporary novelists: British fiction since 1970[M]. Hampshire: Palgrave Macmillan, 2005: 175.

Chapter Four

[87] WEICH D. Ian McEwan: reinventing himself still[EB/OL]. (2004-04-01)[2025-08-05]. https://www.powells.com/post/interviews/ian-mcewan-reinventing-himself-still.

[88] The child in time[EB/OL]. [2025-08-05]. https://www.kirkusreviews.com/book-reviews/ian-mcewan/child-in-time.

[89] SLAY J. Ian McEwan[M]. New York: Twayne Publishers, 1996: 7.

[90] CHILDS P, TREDELL N. The fiction of Ian McEwan[M]. Basingstoke: Palgrave Macmillan, 2006: 59.

[91] MALCOLM D. Understanding Ian McEwan[M]. Columbia: University of South Carolina Press, 2002: 5.

[92] HUGO V. Cromwell[M]. Paris: Garnier-Flammarion, 1968.

[93] POWERS J. Natural bonds[J]. The nation, 1987, 245(14): 491.

[94] RYAN K. Ian McEwan[M]. Plymouth: Northcote, 1994: 19.

[95] ROBERTA S. The theft of a child and the gift of time[EB/OL]. (1987-09-20)[2025-08-01]. https://www.latimes.com/archives/la-xpm-1987-09-20-bk-8876-story.html.

[96] MCEWAN I. The child in time[M]. London: Vintage, 1992: 36.

[97] 程心. "时间中的孩子"和想象中的童年：兼谈伊恩·麦克尤恩的转型[J]. 当代外国文学，2008（2）：88.

[98] MCEWAN I. The child in time[M]. London: Vintage, 1992: 23.

[99] ibid., 9.

[100] GARRARD G. Ian McEwan's next novel and the future of ecocriticism[J]. Contemporary literature, 2009, 50(4), 695-720.

[101] 舒奇志. 主体的欲望与迷思：解读伊恩·麦克尤恩的《时间中的

孩子》[J]. 当代外国文学，2008（3）：83-90.

[102] MCEWAN I. The child in time[M]. London: Vintage, 1992: 186.

[103] SLAY J. Vandalizing time: Ian McEwan's *The Child in Time*[J]. Critique: studies in contemporary fiction, 1994, 35(4): 205-218.

[104] BYRNES B C. The work of Ian McEwan: a psychodynamic approach[M]. London: Paupers' Press, 2002: 181.

[105] SLAY J. Vandalizing time: Ian McEwan's *The Child in Time*[J]. Critique: studies in contemporary fiction, 1994，35(4): 205-218.

[106] MCEWAN I. The child in time[M]. London: Vintage, 1992: 21.

[107] 余华. 在细雨中呼喊[M]. 北京：作家出版社，2012：4.

[108] MCEWAN I. The child in time[M]. London: Vintage, 1992: 52.

[109] RYAN K. Ian McEwan[M]. Plymouth: Northcote House, 1994: 17.

[110] 陈丽. 重复·并置·讽喻：麦克尤恩《时间中的孩子》的空间叙事[J]. 浙江外国语学院学报，2016（5）：60-65.

Chapter Five

[111] Atonement[EB/OL]. [2025-08-05]. https://www.penguinrandomhouse.com/books/111380/atonement-by-ian-mcewan-introduction-by-claire-messud.

[112] MCEWAN I. Atonement[M]. New York: Anchor Books, 2003: 96.

[113] 聂珍钊. 伦理选择概念的两种涵义辨析[J]. 外国文学研究，2022，44（06）：15-25.

Chapter Six

[114] THRAILKILL J. Ian McEwan's neurological novel[J]. Poetics today, 2011, 32(1): 175.

[115] GROES S. Ian McEwan: contemporary critical perspectives[G]. 2nd ed. New York and London: Bloomsbury Academic, 2013: 1.

[116] UKEssays. The character of Henry Perowne in Saturday English literature essay[EB/OL]. (2015-01-01)[2025-08-05]. https://www.ukessays.com/essays/english-literature/the-character-of-henry-perowne-in-saturday-english-

literature-essay.php.

[117] HUGHES T A T. *Saturday* by Ian McEwan[J]. Practical Neurology, 2018, (0): 1. https://doi.org/10.1136/practneurol-2018-001946.

[118] POSTMAN N. Technopoly[M]. New York: Knopf Doubleday Publishing Group, 2011: 24.

[119] ibid. 2011: 23.

[120] MCEWAN I. Saturday[M]. London: Jonathan Cape London, 2005: 6.

[121] MARCUSE H. One-dimensional man: studies in the ideology of advanced industrial society[M]. Boston: Beacon Press, 1991: 62.

[122] LANDOW G P, EVERETT G. Auguste Comte, positivism, and the religion of humanity[EB/OL]. (2024-07-27)[2025-08-01]. https://victorianweb.org/victorian/philosophy/comte.html?utm_source.

[123] 汪民安. 身体、空间与后现代性[M]. 南京：江苏人民出版社，2005：128.

[124] HENDRICKS S. What Nietzsche really meant: the Apollonian and Dionysian[EB/OL]. (2022-02-15)[2025-08-05]. https://bigthink.com/personal-growth/what-nietzsche-really-meant-the-apollonian-and-dionysian.

[125] SNOW C. The two cultures and the scientific revolution[M]. Cambridge, Eng.: Cambridge University Press.1959.

[126] Reports on the course of instruction in Yale College[M]//POTTS D B. Liberal education for a land of colleges: Yale's *Reports* of 1828. New York: Palgrave Macmillan, 2010: 85-140.

[127] 陈丽，陈兵. 自由与焦虑：麦克尤恩《星期六》中的异化书写[J]. 解放军外国语学院学报，2020（3）：128-134.

[128] RAYMOND W. Keywords: a vocabulary of culture and society[M]. Oxford: Oxford University Press,1983: 59.

[129] REES-JONES D. Fact and artefact: poetry, science, and a few thoughts on Ian McEwan's *Saturday*[J]. Interdisciplinary science reviews, 2005, 30(4): 336.

[130] MCEWAN I. Saturday[M]. London: Jonathan Cape London, 2005: 189.

[131] EES-JONES D. Fact and artefact: poetry, science, and a few thoughts

on Ian McEwan's *Saturday*[J]. Interdisciplinary science reviews, 2005, 30(4): 336.

[132] CHILDS P, TREDELL N. The fiction of Ian McEwan[M]. Basingstoke: Palgrave Macmillan, 2006: 146.

[133] ibid., 151.

[134] WANG S L. Reflections upon the predicament of human existence: on Ian McEwan's paradoxical writing of *Saturday*[J]. Journal of Shenyang University, 2022, 24(3): 316-322.

[135] MARCUSE H. One-dimensional man: studies in the ideology of advanced industrial society[M]. Boston: Beacon Press, 1991: 8.

[136] GEORGE L. History and class consciousness: studies in Marxist dialectics[M]. LIVINGSTONE R, trans. Massachusetts: The M.I.T. Press, 1972: 10.

[137] 侯维瑞. 现代英语小说史[M]. 上海：上海教育出版社，1985：19.

[138] BAUDRILLARD J. The consumer society: myths and structures[M]. London: Sage Publications Ltd, 1998: 1.

Chapter Seven

[139] GILES J. Solar[EB/OL]. (2010-03-24)[2025-08-01]. https://ew.com/article/2010/03/24/solar.

[140] TAYLER C. Solar by Ian McEwan: Ian McEwan approaches the climate crisis in comic mode[EB/OL]. (2010-03-12)[2025-08-05]. https://www.theguardian.com/books/2010/mar/13/solar-ian-mcewan.

[141] URQUHART J. Independent on Sunday[EB/OL]. (2010-03-14)[2025-08-01]. https://complete-review.com/reviews/mcewani/solar.htm.

[142] https://www.bl.uk/sisterhood/articles/marriage-and-civil-partnership.

[143] MCEWAN I. Solar[M]. London: Jonathan Cape, 2010: 11.

[144] PINCUS A L, LUKOWITSKY M R. Pathological narcissism and narcissistic personality disorder[J]. Annual review of clinical psychology, 2010 (6): 421-446.

[145] HEXHAM I. Items of academic interests: the plague of

plagiarism[EB/OL]. [2025-08-05]. http://c.web.umkc.edu/cowande/plague.htm.

[146] The significance of the phallus[EB/OL]. (2018-01-21)[2025-08-05]. https://leonbrenner.com/2018/01/21/the-significance-of-the-phallus.

[147] JAMES D. A boy stepped out: migrancy, visuality, and the mapping of masculinities in later fiction of Ian McEwan[J]. Textual practice, 2003, 17(1): 81.

[148] SNOW C P. The two cultures[M]. Cambridge, Eng.: Cambridge University Press, 2012.

[149] HENNESSEY C M. A sacred site: family in the novels of Ian McEwan[D]. Drew University ProQuest Dissertations Publishing, 2004: 1.

[150] GARRARD G. "Solar": apocalypse not[G]//GROES S. Ian McEwan: contemporary critical perspectives. 2nd ed. New York and London: Bloomsbury Academic, 2013: 131.

Chapter eight

[151] MCALPIN H. Delicious deceit abounds in McEwan's "Sweet Tooth"[EB/OL]. (2012-11-13) [2025-08-01]. https://www.npr.org/2012/11/13/164954966/delicious-deceit-abounds-in-mcewans-sweet-tooth.

[152] DE BEAUVOIR S. The second sex[M]. 1st ed. New York: Vintage, 1997: 96.

[153] ibid. 1997: 97.

[154] ibid. 1997: 268.

[155] MCEWAN I. Sweet tooth[M]. Toronto: Vintage Canada, 2013: 3.

[156] DE BEAUVOIR S. The second sex[M]. 1st ed. New York: Vintage, 1997: 67.

[157] ibid. 1997: 77.

[158] 尚必武."那些年，谍影重重的故事"：评伊恩·麦克尤恩的长篇新作《甜牙》[J].外国文学动态，2013（02）：19-21.

[159] DE BEAUVOIR S. The second sex[M]. 1st ed. New York: Vintage, 1997: 283.

[160] ibid. 1997: 286.

[161] ibid. 1997: 287.

Conclusion

[162] 沈晓红. 伊恩·麦克尤恩主要小说中的伦理困境[D].上海外国语大学，2010.
[163] MCEWAN I. The state of fiction: a symposium[J]. The new review, 1978, 5(1): 50.